Dark Sacrifice

Dark Sacrifice

ANGIE SANDRO

FOREVER
YOURS

New York   Boston

Copyright © 2014 by Angie Sandro
Excerpt from *Dark Paradise* copyright © 2014 by Angie Sandro
Cover design by FaceOut
Cover copyright © 2014 by Hachette Book Group, Inc.

Forever Yours
Hachette Book Group
237 Park Avenue
New York, NY 10017
hachettebookgroup.com
twitter.com/foreverromance

First ebook edition: August 2014

Forever Yours is an imprint of Grand Central Publishing.
The Forever Yours name and logo are trademarks of Hachette Book Group, Inc.

The Hachette Speakers Bureau provides a wide range of authors for speaking events. To find out more, go to www.hachettespeakersbureau.com or call (866) 376-6591. The publisher is not responsible for websites (or their content) that are not owned by the publisher.

ISBN 978-1-4555-5485-0 (ebook)

ISBN 978-1-4555-5486-7 (print on demand)

For Nate, Kierstan, and Maxwell. I love you.

Dark Sacrifice

CHAPTER 1

LANDRY

Jailhouse Blues

Jail sucks.

Prison's got to be worse. I don't even want to imagine how much, and since I haven't been hauled before the judge and sentenced yet, I don't have to. So while it's not all sunshine and daisies in my 10 x 5 steel-barred world, I count my blessings and pray for an out that doesn't involve me getting shanked.

I walk in front of the guard, making sure I don't stray too close to the bars of the other cells, and keep my gaze trained on the far door, ignoring the shouts of the prisoners. My shoulder blades twitch. Tingles run up my spine. The crinkling of the orange jumpsuit, the clank of the shackles attached to my wrists and ankles, and the *shush* of my shuffling feet on concrete adds to the humiliation of being accused of attempted murder.

I'm innocent of that allegation, but I kinda think I deserve to fry for all the things I did that led me here.

I feel like the lowest piece of shit.

The temptation to ask the guard who my visitor is builds with each step, but I keep my question behind clenched teeth. I've been locked down in Cellblock A for weeks now, classified as a high-risk violent offender and housed with all of the other rapists and murderers. If I want to survive, I've got to follow the rules—the spoken and the unspoken.

Rule One: *Keep your mouth shut.*

Rule Two: *Watch your back.*

Since my case is a high-profile crime, I take it a step further and also watch who's in front, side…*fuck*…I need another eye. Although exhausted 'cause I'm so on guard, I can't get a good night's sleep, which doesn't help keep me alert when I need to be. It's a catch-22 situation.

"Who's here for me?" I blurt out. *Damn.*

"No talking, Prisoner 245." The guard sounds bored. He probably says the same line every time he takes someone out of their cell. Only the prisoner I.D. number changes.

I must look pathetic. I broke Rule One within minutes of hearing about my visitor. It's just driving me crazy not knowing who's here. I'll know soon enough, but the anticipation gnaws at my insides. 'Cause I hope it's her. Pray it's her. That she's finally forgiven me.

Hell, who else could it be? My so-called friends on the *outs* think I'm dirt. Nobody came to the hospital while I recovered from my injury. After I got arrested, not even the nurses spoke to me unless it was about my eye. *Keep the socket clean. Take your antibiotics. Let us know if you're feverish. Are you in pain? Here are some meds. Oh, it's not about your eye. Your chest hurts. Why?*

'Cause Mala LaCroix hates me.

How do you know?

'Cause she said so. Rather, screamed it. "I hate you, Landry. It's your fault Mama's dead." Not a lot of room for doubt…or hope to hold on to when the girl you're in love with accuses you of murdering her mother.

The guard unlocks the door from my cellblock. The shouts of the prisoners fade as the heavy metal door clinks shut. The narrow, gray hallway stretches before me. At the end will be the visiting room.

God, please let it be her.

This is the longest walk of my life.

The chain catches my ankle, and the stumble takes me to a knee. The guard yanks on my arm, and I stand quickly. "Keep moving."

With a grunt, I shuffle forward.

The spirit of my dead sister, Lainey, possessed Mala and used her body to expose who murdered her. A win for my big sis. Not so much for the girl whose body she inhabited. Mala's pretty non-violent, but her eyes burned with hatred after she remembered my part in her mom's death. If the doctor hadn't sedated her before she could reach me, she gladly would've plucked out my other eye.

My hand lifts, but the handcuffs are connected to a chain looped around my waist, and they keep me from rubbing the ache in my chest.

The hallway ends at a door. The guard pulls out a key and opens it to reveal a small room divided in half by a glass window. A telephone hangs on the wall. I duck my head and shuffle forward, afraid to meet the eyes of the girl on the other side of the glass.

"Sit down. You have five minutes," the guard says.

I slide onto the metal stool bolted to the floor. "Thanks," I say, staring at the roach crawling across the cement. I lift a foot and squish it. The guard grunts and leaves the room, locking the door behind him. A banging on the glass brings my head up.

Dena Acker scowls and waves the phone at me. I read as her lips move. "Pick it up, idiot."

My mouth twitches.

The phone's dirty, but the short cord won't reach my jumpsuit so I can't wipe it off. I put it to my ear with a grimace. "Hey."

"Hey? Is that all you've got to say?" Dena scrunches up her nose, reminding me of her cousin, and the pain in my chest flares again. It's amazing how much alike she and Mala are. It's hard to look at her.

"Dude, you're totally blowing the best five minutes of your short life."

My gaze flicks up to meet hers. Worry flickers in the green. "Are you serious?"

"Have you gotten a better offer lately?" Springy red curls, only a little darker than the color filling her cheeks, fall across Dena's face as she shakes her head. She brushes them back with a huff. "Gosh, that sounded dirty. Didn't mean it to be, you know?"

"I know." I lean forward. "Thanks for coming."

"Sure."

"No. I mean it. You're my first visitor."

"Well, technically, I'm here for someone else so it doesn't really count. Not that I wouldn't visit you on my own, but I'm not."

"You're not making any sense."

"I know. Sorry. I'm here because I'm worried about Mala."

I suck in a breath, gripping the phone. "What do you mean?"

"Did you know she's still stuck in the psych unit?" She leans forward, gripping the phone so hard her knuckles whiten. "I tried to visit, but they said she can't have visitors unless it's immediate

family. I guess distant cousin doesn't count. But she's being released in a few days. I thought maybe you'd like for me to give her
a message."

I stare at the fingerprints smearing the glass. *What do I say?*
"She thinks I killed her mother. She won't want to hear anything
I've got to say, Dee."

"But you didn't…"

I did. "Doesn't matter. Let it go."

"Landry, we both know it's not true." Her voice chokes. "I was
there too. I saw what happened."

Panic rushes through me. "Shut up!" Sweat runs down to sting
my good eye and soaks the patch over my dead one. Dena wraps
her arms around herself, shivering. I'm hot; she's cold. We're both
terrified because we're so fucked.

All of us. Mala too. Only she doesn't know it yet.

Air fills my lungs. It smells—a putrid body funk oozing from
the walls. I take another deep breath anyway, trying to slow my
racing heart. I glance at the sealed door, then the phone. If this
conversation's being taped, then Dena just buried herself. "God,
are you crazy, Dee? Keep your mouth shut," I whisper. "It's not
safe. You're on the outs. At least with Mala and me locked up,
we're safe. Rathbone, my dad, your dad … they're still out there."

Her voice wobbles. "I'm not scared of them."

"You should be." We both witnessed what they're capable of.

I scratch around the healing scar partially covered by the eye
patch. The stitches itch.

Dena stares at me for a long moment. Her eyes flicker with
whatever she's considering, then her jaw firms. "Doesn't matter
what they try. I can get you out of here. If I tell the DA what I
saw, he'll let you go. This isn't fair. It's not fair for Mala to think
you had anything to do with Ms. Jasmine's murder. And it's not

fair that I'm doing nothing to help." Her lips pinch, and her gaze moves over my shoulder. The sound of the opening door makes her sit back. "I can't let it go, Landry. I *won't*."

The pain in my chest intensifies as my lungs constrict. My breathing grows harsh. I know the signs of a panic attack. I've had a few in the last couple of weeks. It takes a few seconds to slow my racing thoughts.

"Give me a few more weeks, Dee. The DA doesn't have the evidence to take my case to trial. He'll have to drop the charges, and you won't have to get involved. I'm fine. This place sucks, but I get three meals a day. I'm learning to make license plates…"

Dena's harsh laugh at my joke trails off into a sob. "I don't have a few more weeks. Dad disappeared. H-he hasn't even tried to contact us. The money's running out. I can't support the kids on my paycheck from Munchies. I don't know what to do, Landry. I want my best friends back."

"Mala doesn't know about *us*, does she?"

"No, I never told her. I promised you I wouldn't, but this secret makes me feel like I'm the worst cousin in the world!" Her wail cuts off with a choked hiccup, and she runs the back of her hand beneath her nose, then looks at her hand in disgust. "Eww…"

"Yeah, not the brightest move."

She gives a soggy laugh. "Shut up."

A shadow falls over the table, and I whip around. The guard walked up on my blind side. I'm still not used to people being able to sneak up on me so easily. It makes me jittery.

The guard takes a quick step back, balanced on the balls of his feet in case I've lost my mind enough to attack him. It must happen more often than I think—crazed prisoners flipping out in the visiting area.

When he sees I'm okay, his raised hands drop. "Two minutes."

I nod and turn back to Dena.

Her wide eyes flicker. Rather than showing her that I can handle myself in here, she just witnessed how much at a disadvantage I am because of my injury. Not good. Dena's impulsive, and she doesn't have a clear sense of self-preservation when it comes to helping her friends. I'm scared for her.

"I've got to go." I lay my palm against the sticky glass. "Don't come back here…and be careful, okay?"

Dena presses her hand adjacent to mine, and for a brief second, I imagine her warmth through the thick glass, then she hangs up the phone. Her shoulders slump as she walks to the locked door and waits to be buzzed out.

* * *

I stare up through the wire springs at the saggy, stained mattress above my head. Thank God my cellmate isn't a bed-wetter. A murderer, yes. I think waking up with a mouthful of piss every morning is ten times worse than worrying about whether I'll wake up at all. He tried to assert his dominance over me my first night, but a quick elbow to the face kept him from going hands-on in the shower. If I'd been thirty pounds lighter and three inches shorter, I'd have CALEB'S BITCH tattooed on my ass.

We've kept an uneasy truce for the last five days. I sleep with my only eye open. Okay, that's a slight exaggeration. But I'm definitely on edge, all the time. Going out into the rec yard is like rolling the dice. Who's gonna try to increase their rep by stepping up to me today? Will I make it back to my cell? So far, double sevens say it's my lucky day.

A snore comes from above, and I squint, wishing I had X-ray vision to see if Caleb's faking it. The tension between us has been building over the last day. A snitch, wanting to get on my good side, told me someone offered a lot of cash—more than most convicts see in their lifetime—to take me out. Money like that is hard to say no to. It's maybe even worth the risk of frying in the electric chair if it lets you take care of your family.

Caleb's looking at twenty years, less if he gets parole. Only an idiot would try to take me out while we're stuck sharing a cell with no one else around to shift the blame onto. Paranoia has me searching for threats where there may be none. It's more likely I'll get hit by another prisoner when the guards aren't around. I make sure to stay in groups when out of my cell. I need to find a protector, but so far I haven't been willing to do what it takes to earn a spot. I'm screwed. I'm just not desperate enough to *be* screwed.

God, I've got to get out of here.

Dena said that Mala's being released. What's gonna happen to her? Where is she gonna go? What if I'm not the only one with a death threat on me? I can't protect her from in here.

Hell. I couldn't protect her before.

My brain itches—a tickling at the base of my brain. A rush of anticipation floods through my body. I squeeze my eye shut as warmth spreads from my toes upward until I'm blanketed in it. The scent of orchids overpowers the stench of Caleb, and I draw in a deep breath. My muscles relax, and the ache behind my eye drains like water trickling down a drain.

She's here.

A whisper of a caress traces across my cheek. I want to press my face against the hand, but I don't move. Too afraid I'll scare her away. Her emotions ripple across my bare skin...that's the only way I can think to describe the sensation. Only I can't tell what she's feeling: anger, fear, disgust…hate? No. That's what I'd feel toward me in her situation. A tiny piece of me hopes the reason Mala comes to me every night isn't to plot her revenge but 'cause she still cares.

CHAPTER 2

MALA

Cuckoo's Nest

White walls and a white ceiling lit by over-bright, flickering fluorescent bulbs combine with the sharp scent of bleach, sending shards of pain stabbing into my head. The multicolored robes and pajamas of the ghosts popping in and out of the tiny hospital room remind me of a kaleidoscope—one of those toys stuffed with spinning, shifting, colored patterns. It's hard enough for me to concentrate during the best of times. Tonight my blazing headache makes it nearly impossible.

"Thirty-six, thirty-seven..." I whisper, separating the routine counting of the ceiling tiles from outlining the details of my plan. I'm running out of time. In forty-eight hours, I'll be released from the psychiatric unit I was committed to for evaluation after that psychotic ghost, Lainey Prince, shoved me out of my body and used me to expose the truth about how her mother and Dr.

James Rathbone refused to get her medical treatment after she delivered her baby.

So much evil has happened in my life. Enough for me to think I've gone crazy in truth, but I refuse to give up like Mama did. I won't let my "breakdown" destroy my dream of living a normal life. I will have a husband, children, and my dream job. I'm not stupid or ignorant of the challenges facing me. No police department will risk hiring an unstable officer. I can't even take credit for solving Lainey's murder, even though I figured out pretty much everything...a little late, but I did.

What hurts most is losing my clerical position at the Sheriff's Office. Too much of a liability, they told my mentor, Detective Bessie Caine. But giving up on becoming a cop without a fight—not an option.

Rage and grief surge, and I slam my fist into the mattress. The action releases some of the building tension. I inhale deeply and sigh, letting the air trickle out across my lips, then repeat the process. With each breath, my rapid heartbeats slow, clearing the anger fogging my thoughts.

My mind sharpens, and I focus again on the ceiling tiles. "One, two, three..."

I've spent the last twenty-nine days thinking up a plan to redeem myself. So what if it involves a little bit of personal retribution? Landry's father, Reverend Prince, and Dr. James Rathbone, the Bertrand Parish Coroner, murdered my mother and escaped into the swamp. I'm going to hunt them down like rabid dogs and bring them to justice. Dead or alive.

And I'll use the reverend's son to do it.

If I can survive two more sleepless nights without losing it. As long as I stay focused on counting the tiles, I'll be fine. I won't give in to the whispered pleading of the ghosts who flock to my room for help.

Like Ms. Anne. The semitransparent old woman standing at the end of my bed, wearing nothing but the flannel nightgown she died in, kind of draws the eyes. Even sick and tired ones like mine. Ms. Anne was a patient in the mental ward. She passed away three days ago, but she hasn't passed on to wherever good little spirits go when their journey on earth ends. Heaven or hell? Somewhere in between? I don't really give a damn. No pun intended. I was an inch away from finding out the answer after one of the men who killed Mama shot me. I almost bled to death. Nope. I'd like to avoid firsthand knowledge of the afterlife until I die of old age.

Ms. Anne folds her hands in front of her as if in prayer. "Do you plan on ignoring me all night?"

I shiver from the cold spot she brings and roll to face the wall. Sick of seeing her. Tired of the guilt. Helping ghosts got me into this mess in the first place. I'm working on becoming more selfish.

"Please, Malaise. You were always nice to me. I want to rest, but I can't. Not without you."

This is her second night holding vigil in my room, stealing my sleep. I resent her and the other spirits lurking out of sight, waiting for me to cave to her pressure. When I first got locked up, I couldn't help talking to the dead. They looked alive. And I've never liked hurting someone's feelings by being disrespectful, especially my elders.

But once word spread around the hospital that I saw them, ghosts flocked to my room like a murder of crows, squawking and psychically shitting all over my mind until I thought I really would go crazy. It felt like I walked around with a bubble of static electricity hovering over my skin—repeatedly shocked, my nerves jangling with a tingly, mind-numbing feeling. The more spirits who came around, the sicker I felt.

That's when I started taking psych meds. The pills fogged up my brain pretty fierce until I adjusted to them, but they helped me manage the spirits' connections to a degree. Now I can tune them out if I concentrate hard enough.

Ms. Anne paces in front of my bed. "Mala, please. Tell my daughter I left my grandmother's wedding ring for her. It dropped behind my bed. She missed it when she cleaned out my room. Please. I want her to have it."

I close my eyes and count backward from a thousand. By the time I reach seven hundred and eighty-five, my body has grown heavy and my thoughts drift. A smile lifts the corners of my lips as I let go. Thank God for meds.

Since being kicked out of my body, I'm no longer tied to it. I shift out of my skin and will myself to glide past Ms. Anne. Maybe my ability to astral project is a dream, but I think it's real. Why else would I find myself in the parish jail standing over a sleeping Landry Prince? *Again.*

He lies on the bottom bunk in a dinky cell with his back to the wall. Even in sleep he seems alert, like he can't fully let down his guard. A black curl hides the eye I blinded. Guilt always sours my stomach when I look at his eye. I stabbed him when he'd only been trying to save my life. To be fair, I thought he planned on killing me. If he'd taken the time to explain that night…maybe things would've worked out differently. Maybe we would've thought up a plan to rescue Mama before she was murdered.

Or maybe I'd be dead.

I heave a heavy sigh, thankful I don't have a sense of smell as a spirit 'cause it probably stinks of feet and butt in the room. His cellmate doesn't look to have the best hygiene. It creeps me out the way he watches Landry while he sleeps. Hell, we're watching him together, but my stalking doesn't have a serial killer vibe to it.

The shadowed hulk on the top bunk rolls. The faint light bounces off the shiny object in his hand as he jumps lightly to the ground. He lands in a squat and pivots on the balls of his feet to face Landry. I can't make out the guy's features clearly, just an oversized, jutting forehead, smooth-shaven head, and lips twisted in a grimace. He quivers, and his clenched fist rises.

Between one breath and the next, he lunges.

I throw myself toward the guy, screaming "Landry!"

Landry's eye pops open, and he sits up, looking around wildly.

His cellmate dives through my body. He doesn't even shudder inside the cold spot and lands on top of Landry. He stabs downward.

Landry raises his arm, blocking the shank aimed for his heart. The razor-sharp tip slides into Landry's stomach at an odd angle. The block causes the guy to lose his grip on the shank, and the sharpened toothbrush remains stuck in Landry's abdomen. The guy punches Landry in the face, once, then again.

I crouch beside the bed, watching them thrash around, unable to help him. With a shout, Landry grabs the guy by his forearms. They roll off the bed, still fighting. Landry lands on his back, and the guy pins his arms to the ground with his knees. I see a flash of white a second before the guy slams the pillow over Landry's face and leans his upper body on top of it.

I run to the bars. The guard runs toward the cell. It looks like he trudges through mud. Each step takes an hour—sixty minutes longer for Landry to suffocate. The boy has enough issues.

He doesn't need brain damage from oxygen deprivation on top of them.

Landry grabs my shoulder and spins me away from the bars. "Mala, what's going on?"

"I came," I babble like an idiot. "Like every night. Only I caught him…Why is he's trying to kill you?"

"Who's trying to kill me?" He punctuates each word with a shake. "Why can I see you?"

Half of my brain figures out what's happening, but it takes the other half a few seconds to catch up, and only because Landry's cellmate still crouches over his physical body, holding the pillow over his face. *Oh, saints, Landry can see me.*

"No!" I cry. "Don't die. Go back, Landry. Please."

"What do you mean die? Mala—" His gaze follows mine. "Shit! That's me. Caleb's killing me…"

I shove him toward his body. He has to get back inside before it's too late.

A spinning black hole forms in the air, hovering a foot off the ground. Inky tentacles snake out of the mouth of the vortex and twine around Landry's waist. He shouts and grabs for my hands, straining to hold on to me as his legs lift in the air. More tendrils shoot out of the mouth and wrap around his ankles, spooling up his body until he's cocooned in darkness. I jerk on him with all my strength, but I can't break the suction. He's dragged from my arms—sucked toward the freaking darkness trying to eat him.

I awake in my bed, screaming.

My skin itches like a thousand baby spiders are skittering across my skin. I slap and brush off my arms, rolling off the bed. The bed sheets tangle around my legs, and I fling them off with a shriek. I crawl to the door and kick and pound on the metal surface, yelling for the orderly on duty.

Kevin rushes into the room. "Mala?"

"Help me!" I grab for his arm.

With a deft twist of his body, he locks my arm up behind my back and presses my face against the wall in two seconds flat. "Calm down."

I squeeze my eyes closed against the pain in my shoulder and try to relax against the wall. I can't stop trembling. "He's dying. Help me."

The huge man releases my arm but blocks the door so I can't shove past him. He studies my face for a long moment. His shoulders relax in response to whatever my body language broadcasts. His lips flicker in the tiniest of smiles, and I want to smack him. His eyebrow rises as if he reads my violent thought. "You chilled enough to explain what's going on now?"

I release the breath I'm holding and drawl, "Yeah, like a Popsicle."

"So, who's dying?"

I fold my hands in front of me, looking a lot like Ms. Anne when she begged for my help. Karma, what a bitch. "Now, this is gonna sound crazy, but I need to call the police." I talk faster and faster in my attempt to convince him to help me. "It may not be too late. I just need to know if he's still alive. He has to be, right? He can't really be dead."

"Girl, you right. You really done lost your mind if you think I'm taking you to use the phone. Why don't you calm down before I have to medicate you."

My eyes widen at his tone. He'll do it. Shoot me up with a knock-out drug and I'll be dead to the world for my last day, or worse, he'll blab to Dr. Rhys about my "breakdown," and I'll be committed indefinitely.

I draw in a hiccupping breath. "I'm okay, Kevin."

"You sure? Don't sound okay to me."

"I had a horrible nightmare. One of those dreams where someone you know dies, and it feels so realistic that it totally freaks you out and you can't rest until you hear that person's voice and know for sure they're okay." I give him my best impersonation of a sad puppy. "Please, help me out on this. It'll take five minutes. Otherwise, I'll be worried. It might mess up my release. I don't want Dr. Rhys to have any reason to keep me locked up."

Kevin shakes his head and laughs. "Don't give me that hangdog look. I'll take you, but I'm only doing this 'cause you remind me of my little sis."

"Thanks. I'd hug you if I knew you wouldn't smash my face into the wall again. I owe you big, and I'll pay you back someday. I swear."

"Just don't make me regret this," Kevin says, and leads me out of the room.

My heart thunders as I stretch my legs to keep up with his longer stride. I focus on Kevin's back, praying Landry's ghost won't appear. If he had to die, I'd rather he didn't haunt me for eternity. The memory of that inkblot of a black hole sends a shiver down my spine. The last sight I had before I vanished had been of the darkness settling over Landry's body like a cloak. It soaked into his skin, burning him. Burning my palms. They still feel raw where I tried to hold on to him. He'd thrown his head back in a scream of agony so piercing I couldn't help but echo it. I've never seen or heard anything like what happened to him.

Not that I know squat about the supernatural, but the darkness doesn't seem like a good sign. I've always read when a person dies, they see a tunnel of white light. That their loved ones wait for them at the end. Landry should've seen Lainey and her baby waiting for him. Has he done so much wrong in his life that his ending won't be harps and winged cherubs?

Maybe Landry's destined for a hotter afterlife.

I squeeze my hands together, praying it isn't so. I believe that, as long as a person lives, they have a chance at redemption. I just have to find Landry and keep him alive long enough for him to atone for his sins. That is my task, right? Why I witnessed such horror in the first place.

"Use my cellphone," Kevin says.

I jump at the sound of his voice. We've arrived at the personnel office. "Got it," I say with a thumb up and a watery smile. "And Kevin…thanks. I owe you big."

"You got five minutes." Kevin leaves to finish his rounds. The cramped office contains dusty file cabinets and stacked boxes. I sit behind the desk, debating who to call. Someone with the authority to check on Landry. Someone who will believe me without question, and frankly, being able to explain my fear will stretch most people's imagination. Bessie's the best choice since she has the power to get information from the jail quickly, but I don't want to disturb her in the middle of the night. That leaves only one other person I can trust, but I'm not sure George will be willing to do Landry any favors. Not even to prove his professed love for me.

With a deep breath, I punch in the numbers before I chicken out. The rings echo in my ear. I twist a strand of hair around my finger, nervously rehearsing what I'll say when he answers.

"Hello?" The woman's sleep-husky voice throws me off. My mind speeds into triple overtime, and a million questions pop up so fast that I can't form the words to keep up. I open my mouth, but only a squeak comes out.

"Anyone there?"

"Who is it, Izzy?" George's muffled voice asks.

The image of the two of them in bed flashes before my eyes, and I gag on the vomit creeping up my throat. With a choked scream, I end the call with a shaking finger. "Damn you, George Dubois."

Why didn't I say that when he could hear me? Why did I hang up? Why did I let him kiss me? Izzy…who the fuck…Oh. My. God. That nurse—the smug one who smiled whenever she stuck a needle into me. George hooked up with that skank? How could he sleep with another woman after declaring his love for me?

I pace across the room, squeezing my hands together so I don't punch something. *Breathe, Mala. Breathe.*

What did I expect? We're not together. He can date or fuck whoever he wants. We're not in a committed relationship. Oh, God. What if I'm wrong about when they got together? She didn't seem to like me while I was in the hospital. He never told me about dating Lainey. What if he and Izzy have been keeping their relationship secret?

I'm the cheater. I kissed a guy with a girlfriend. How did I sink so low? I jerk hard on the end of my braid. Sharp pain radiates through my scalp, bringing tears to my eyes and clearing the fog of rage swirling in my thoughts. *I've really gone insane.*

I'm freaking out about the state of my love life while Landry may be dying? I'm *such* an idiot.

The phone rings, and I answer it. "Hello?"

"Hello…Mala, is that you?" George asks.

I drop the phone and jump away from it like it turned into a striking snake. "Oh, saints!"

What do I do? I don't want to talk to him. I stare at the phone, wishing it would vanish, then pick it up. I clutch it like a potato fresh out of the microwave—with only the tips of my fingers—ready to drop it if the conversation gets too hot.

"Mala, I recognized your voice, and I can hear you breathing."

"G-George, yes?"

"What's wrong? Are you hurt?"

Hurt, yes. You squished my heart, you jerk! I shake my head. "No, no, I'm fine, but Landry...ah, Landry needs your help."

"What are you talking about?"

"He was stabbed by his cellmate tonight. Could you find out"—my voice chokes on the words—"if he's alive? Please."

A long silence falls between us, followed by a heavy sigh. "Who told you?"

My knees unhinge, and I hit the floor hard. "Then it's true? He's dead?"

"The call came from the station right after you hung up. Tell me how you found out before I did. And why did you hang up?"

"Because I didn't want to talk to your *girlfriend*," I yell, and hurl the phone at the wall. It hits with an audible *thunk* and falls to the floor. I bury my face against my knees, shivering. My eyes burn, and I squeeze them closed against the tears that I refuse to let fall.

"Damn, girl." Kevin blocks the doorway with his ginormous bulk.

"I'm sorry," I whisper. "I think I broke your phone."

"You *think*?"

"I'll buy you a new one once I get out of here."

"Don't worry about it. I'm two years past-due for an upgrade anyway." He bends to pick up the mangled mess on the floor. "You didn't take a piece to slash your wrists with later?"

"Slashed wrists aren't my style, Kev," I say, dipping into the deep well of sadness I felt upon finding Lainey Prince with her body drained of blood in the bayou. I never want anyone to find me dead like that.

"Bad news?"

I press my palms against burning eyes. "The worst if you consider it verifies the fact that not only do I see ghosts, but I'm also psychic. That dream I had about my friend…"

"Whoa, dead?"

Tears trickle down my cheeks, and I scrub them away, nodding.

CHAPTER 3

LANDRY

Hotter Afterlife

I watch myself die.

Feel the *snick* as my soul severs from whatever connects it to my body. I can't stop it from happening. Like Humpty Dumpty, I can't put myself together again. No matter how much I want to stay or how tightly Mala holds on to my hands, I'm jerked away.

The last flash of fear in her eyes before she disappears fills me with regret.

I never got to apologize.

I'm really dead.

This is how it feels to be a spirit. *It hurts. So bad!*

My mouth opens in a silent scream. Pain eats the edges of my thoughts. Each bite gets bigger and bigger. Soon there won't be anything left of me. *Landry…I'm Landry Prince.*

Shadow soaks into my skin. My flesh burns as if alcohol's being splashed over thousands of paper cuts all over my body.

The pain will consume me if I don't control it. *Breathe.*

My lungs ache when I inhale. I cough on the sulfuric stench of the dry, hot air, then draw in another breath, letting my chest expand to its fullest. Beating thuds fill my ears, echoing in the black void surrounding me.

I hate the dark.

My fear increased after I lost half of my sight. Now I'm trapped in total darkness, unable to see what waits for me. And something does. I sense it. My skin feels clammy. Why I still have physical sensations when I don't have a body, I don't know.

I don't want to be here.

I want out!

God, help me. This isn't how I imagined death while sitting in church every Sunday, at least not for me. Where are the angels, the fluffy, white clouds, and the all-you-can-eat cheeseburgers?

How long do I stand in this spot? For eternity?

My foot slides across the ground in a hesitant step. I thrust my hands out, wishing for light. *Where's the door? The white tunnel? Lainey?*

A rustling comes from the ground.

I freeze, afraid to take a step, listening. I know this sound…it's the slithering of scales across stone. I force myself to take another step. The sound mirrors mine, gliding closer in the dark. My inner ear tingles as I listen to it glide closer. My mind creates a picture…a vision I don't want in my head. The snake sounds big. Like an anaconda-eating-a-grown-man big.

This must really be hell.

Death's chock full of my worst nightmares—darkness, snakes, and never-ending pain. I'm being tormented for my sins.

You're totally screwed. It's too late to repent.

I squeeze my eye shut, but being blind already, this doesn't help to block the image. It only grows larger and more menacing. I shudder, wrapping my arms around myself. How long before I feel the bite of fangs? Will it strike fast? What will hurt more, the sharp, needlelike jabs into my skin or the venom shooting into my body?

Cold sweat breaks out on my skin and evaporates immediately in the heat. My nonexistent heart races like I'm tweaking. If I wasn't already dead, I'd be afraid of having a heart attack. I can't hear over the sound of my rough breaths. I can't tell where the snake is. It could be beneath my feet or across the room. *Please be across the room.*

My mouth is dry.

I shuffle forward a few steps, unable to stay still while I'm being stalked. A smooth, rounded body brushes against my foot, and I spin around. My arms pinwheel to keep my balance as the snake coils around my ankles. I kick out. The snake retaliates by tightening its grip, winding around my body by constricting its muscles. My arms and legs are pinned to my sides.

I yell, trying to frighten it. Okay, lie.

I panic.

The sharp scent of musk fills my nose, and I gag on the rank smell. The head slides beneath my chin, the flick of its tongue vibrates across my lips. I don't close my mouth fast enough. The taste of rotten meat fills my mouth as the snake's head slides onto my tongue. My jaw stretches and bone cracks as the whole head thrusts itself down my throat.

My nails cut into my skin as I claw at the bulge in my neck. Light-headed from lack of air, I fall to my knees. The snake glides down my throat, coiling inside my gut. My stomach undulates. Pressure bulges the muscles. My internal organs shift to make room for the parasite.

No! I'm dead. I don't have organs.

This isn't real.

The building internal pressure pulses outward. My nerves fill with fire. It's a hundred times worse than the tingle from hitting my elbow. It rushes up my spine, then expands to fill my brain with an alien awareness.

The creature opens its eyes and evaluates my worthiness to exist.

I can't fight this thing. It blasts my resistance to smithereens, crushing my will like an ant. If I want to survive, I'd better huddle in a terrified ball in the corner of my own mind and hope it forgets I'm here. It's in control, and I'm nothing but a passenger along for the ride.

White light flashes, like from a door opening.

The creature shrinks from the brightness, squealing as if burned. It lifts my arms to cover my face. I use its distraction to leap from my hiding spot and wrest control of my soul from the creature. It's only for a second. Too little, but also just enough.

I fall into the light.

And my sister, Lainey, catches me at the bottom.

CHAPTER 4

MALA

Evil Pocahontas

*D*on't cry. Not here. Not now.

If I do, I won't stop. The pressure of holding in my emotions builds and makes my eyes leak anyway, and I brush an escaped tear from my cheek before it can be seen by any of the women gathered in the circle.

"Guess this is my last group session." *Hold it together, girl.* I aim a smile in my psychiatrist's direction. "Dr. Rhys has decreed that I'm no longer a danger to myself or others so I'm flying the coop tomorrow morning."

Dr. Rhys shifts in his metal chair like his butt's sore. Poor guy doesn't get much exercise. He's spends the majority of his day sitting down, counseling crazy women. "We'll miss you, Mala," he says, smiling at the other women in encouragement. "You've become an integral part of our family."

I throw up a little in my mouth at the doc's chipper attitude.

God love him. I doubt "family" accurately describes the other mental patients. The cognizant ladies in our group therapy session nod and give a tiny round of applause. The others stare into space and drool.

Well, everyone except for the coffee-eyed woman who gives me the shivers. She stares, not into space, but directly at me, with a gaze so sharply focused that it feels like she's carving through layers of my skin and muscle to peer into my soul.

I don't give her the satisfaction of acknowledging her presence. Staring is plain rude, and I don't care if she's insane. Rudeness via insanity doesn't hold much weight with me these days. If she has a problem, then she needs speak like a big girl and tell me what it is. That's what group therapy is for—to work on our issues.

Dr. Rhys taps his pen on his notepad, an unconscious broadcast that he has a touchy question to ask. The cringe-worthy kind is his specialty. Did Kevin tell the doc about Landry dying? He promised to keep my secret. It's hard enough pretending everything's okay—that my life hasn't broken into tiny, sharp pieces that no amount of superglue can stick back together—without being called on it in front of everyone.

My chest tightens.

Stop thinking about him.

I glare at the rude girl seated in the chair across the circle from me. Her eyes look like raisins mashed into the dark hollows of her sunken sockets. Flesh stretches over her high cheekbones and angular nose, while black hair tangles about her shoulders. She could act as a double for the Disney Pocahontas, if the cartoon girl smoked crack cocaine. I despise everything about her from her dirty, bare feet to her black, holey jeans and stained T-shirt.

Sharp pain throbs in my eyes, like the girl poked an invisible needle into my tear ducts with the power of her glare. If I blink, she'll win the staring contest. Or worse. The tears in my eyes will overflow, and the whole group will see the pain I'm doing my best to hide. They'll ask questions. Make me relive Landry's death. I won't be able to hold it together.

The woman next to me jabs an elbow into my side. "Are you okay, Mala?"

How long has Dr. Rhys been waiting for me to answer his question? Did I zone out longer than socially appropriate? Did I drool? "I'm sorry, Doc. Did you ask me something?" I run the tips of my fingers across my lips. My hand trembles. Can he see it from where he's sitting?

Dr. Rhys waves his pen in my direction. "Do you want to share with the group what your plans are after your release?"

I blink at him, then glance around the circle. "I'm staying with Bessie Caine. She'll pick me up tomorrow morning."

"Is she okay with helping you get to your counseling appointments? I want to make sure you continue with your progress on an outpatient basis."

She'd drag me to them by my hair if I refused. "She's very conscientious—"

"Bitch!" Creepy Poca lunges forward. Her chair flies backward and crashes to the floor. I stiffen. She looms closer in my peripheral vision. Each step pounds with menace, as if she holds herself at a steady pace only through sheer willpower. Tension vibrates her body as she screams, "Don't believe a word she says. She's a lying bitch."

I glance at Dr. Rhys. He stares at me with a tiny frown, and I send a silent plea to him. *Call one of the orderlies to escort this girl out!* What's his problem? Is he waiting to see whether I'll beat her ass for disrespecting me?

I inhale and exhale through my mouth. "Bessie will get me to my appointments."

The girl lunges forward and grips my shoulders with both hands, burning my skin despite the layer of clothing between us. Breath like rotting fish curls my nose, and my stomach clenches. I let out a high-pitch squeak and lean back in the chair, trying to put space between myself and what I now recognize as the spirit of a very pissed-off dead girl.

Uncle Gaston, Mama, where are you? Help me.

I grit my teeth so I won't cry out. Poca the Poltergeist is deliberately trying to scare me. I won't let her win.

"I won't be ignored, Mala. I'll suffocate you while you sleep. I'll haunt your every moment until you beg for mercy if you don't acknowledge me," she whispers, squeezing my shoulders.

A crackle of energy makes the hairs on the back of my neck rise. The spirit of Ms. Anne shoves forward, passing through my body from behind. She plants her hands on the girl's chest and knocks her off me.

I squeeze my eyes shut, shivering from the residual chill. Their energy sucks at mine. My thoughts go foggy…

Focus…ten, nine, eight…

A warm hand touches my bare arm, and I open my eyes. Dr. Rhys squats down in front of me, and I meet his concerned gaze. "It will be okay, Mala. Hang in there. I promise it'll get better."

I try to swallow, but my mouth is dry. I nod, infusing fake confidence into the movement, but at the same time, my gaze darts around the room. Ms. Ann and Poca are gone.

Why would the stupid poltergeist deliberately scare the snot out of me, then vanish without telling me what she wants? Unless Ms. Anne's tougher than she looks and she scared her away. I shrug and swipe the tears from my cheeks. My heart and breathing slow. I wish I believed Dr. Rhys' words. I keep waiting to get better. To be able to tell the difference between spirits and real live people, but even with medication, the ghosts keep popping into my life. This one is stronger than most of the recent spirits haunting me. Her strength to manipulate physical objects rivals Lainey's. I sure as hell don't want to go down that rabbit hole again. The last time I almost didn't survive.

My shoulders ache. If I show Dr. Rhys the burns on my skin, will he believe me? No. More likely he'll think I injured myself. The only people who ever believed me about seeing ghosts are now ghosts themselves.

I blink, my eyes focusing on the creases around his down-turned mouth. *Poor guy.* "Don't worry. I'm okay, Doc. Just overcome with how thankful I am to everyone for getting me through this time of mourning. I really appreciate everyone's love and support."

The Bullshit-O-Meter detects rising levels.

Dr. Rhys pulls on an invisible pair of knee-high boots, obviously not up to wading through my newest crisis so close to going off shift for the night. He releases my hands and rises. "Okay, ladies, you're dismissed."

With a heavy sigh, I refer to the checklist I keep in my head. My last scheduled requirement—group. Done—check.

* * *

I'm curled up on the plastic sofa in the dayroom watching the five o'clock news when Kevin, followed by George, walks through the door. A rush of déjà vu hits. George looks the same as the last time he visited. Right down to the LSU T-shirt and jeans. I shoot a glare in Kevin's direction, and he shrugs. *The traitor!* Why did he let George in? I spilled my guts to the orderly last night. He knows I don't want anything to do with George "Cheating Ass-hole" Dubois.

I clench my lips together, damning them for the residual tingle stirred by the memory of George's kiss. He'd totally blown away my defenses. A couple of days ago, I thought I'd give the relation-ship a chance. That my life would be better with someone who wouldn't betray me like Landry did.

Boy, am I the worst judge of character.

The hurt and confusion makes my heart ache. Worse, I want to do him bodily harm. Which would get me locked up in here for another month since I was committed for beating him up in the first place.

After the first glance, I don't look back in George's direction. Maybe he'll get the hint and get out of my face. He hovers over me for a long moment then flops down next to me on the sofa. I scoot to the far end, jabbing the volume button on the remote as fast as I can to drown out his voice.

A large, white-smocked body inserts itself between me and the television. Kevin holds out his hand, and I drop the remote onto his meaty palm. Within seconds, the sound has been lowered, and I have to listen to George breathing—may he choke on his own spit!

"How long do you plan on pretending like I don't exist?" George asks.

"Until you take the hint and go poof." I flick my fingers out in his direction as if shaking off a smooshed bug. "I don't want to talk to you." I uncross my legs and crawl off the sofa. He grabs my arm and pulls me down onto his lap. My arms instinctively wrap around his neck— to catch my balance and *not* for any other rea-son.

I attempt to stand again. His grip around my waist tightens. He places his fingertips beneath my chin and lifts my head, but I refuse to make eye contact. No way will I lose myself in the shifting shades of his moss-green gaze. "Let go, George."

"You're not storming off in a huff without listening to my side."

"Side? You've got a side? 'Cause last night it sounded like *Izzy* pretty much owned you."

He flinches. "There you go jumping to conclusions without hearing the truth."

"How is stating the truth jumping to conclusions? It was obvious you were in bed. What's she doing at your place if not exactly what I think you were doing?"

"*Our* apartment. Isabel and I live together."

I lunge forward. He follows.

I push his hands from my arm. "Stop touching me or I'll ask Kevin to kick you out."

He holds his hands in the air. "I swear we're not together anymore."

"How long?" My nostrils flare.

"We moved in together four months ago." He runs his fingers through his red-gold hair until it stands up in spikes. It makes him look like a lost little boy.

Don't soften, Mala. He did wrong.

I shake my arm free. "Months…" I whisper, staring at the ground. "You've had a live-in girlfriend for months? She's the nurse from the hospital, isn't she? Oh, God. I'm such an idiot. No wonder she got such a kick out of keeping me drugged out of my mind."

"Mala—"

"Stop, no more lies."

"I'm telling you the truth. I've never lied to you."

"No, you just avoid telling the whole truth."

"What do you want me to say, Mala?" He stares at the ground. "I told Isabel I have feelings for you, and she broke up with me. We're not together, but I can't kick her out of her own apartment. I owe it to her to stick around until she finds a new roommate."

He didn't break up with her. *She* dumped *him*. Huge difference. God, my head hurts. It's too much. First, Landry dies right in front of me…now this. I can barely process it, but I have to. I have to make some sense of it all or I'll go crazy.

"Why didn't you mention all of this before?" I meet his gaze and hold it. No avoidance. "I was fine with us just being friends, but you kissed me first. You're the one who said you wanted to explore us having a relationship. God, George. I trusted you. When I asked for time to work out my feelings for you and Landry, you should've told me about Isabel. Instead, I find out like this." I brush a tear from my eye.

"Mala, please. Don't cry."

Traitorous tear ducts. "Don't mistake my tears for weakness. I'm not crying over you. I'm crying for me." I shake my head. "I can't do this right now. I'm too confused."

"I told you the truth. Why can't you just believe in me?"

I stare at George's open face as every thought and emotion flickers in his rapidly changing expression. I've known him forever. I can read each crease, frown, and grimace without him having to speak. His sincerity is so potent that I actually feel guilty for doubting him. He's always been there for me—my very own superhero. But what if he's lying to himself about how deep his feelings are for me? What if he only feels protective because he found me after I got shot? Seeing me half-dead from blood loss might've messed with his head.

I'm a stinking hypocrite—worse than he is. What right do I have to chastise him when, even though I should hate Landry, I can't? I try…and try. I remember Mama's screams as she burned. How he wouldn't let me go to her. But I hurt so much knowing he's dead, and I feel like an idiot because I'm waiting for him to come back to me.

I'm waiting for a ghost.

Still, the thought of kissing George again feels like a betrayal of Landry's memory.

Ugh. This is so confusing. I need to make some rules!

Rule one: No kissing…'cause that just scrambles my brain to mush.

Tension drains out of my shoulders with my decision. I blow out a heavy sigh. "I believe you, Georgie."

His smile makes my breath catch. He pulls me into his arms and leans in. I turn my face away at the last minute so he kisses my cheek. He pulls back with a low groan. "Now what?"

"I believe you, but I shouldn't have kissed you. I'm not ready to be in a relationship—even one with no offer of exclusivity and only PG-13 benefits." The words are like a punch in my gut. Landry said almost the very same thing to me. *No. Stop thinking about him.* He's dead, and George is alive. My feelings for Landry shouldn't factor into my future happiness. Except how do I ignore a Landry-size hole in my heart that won't ever be filled? Not by George or anyone else.

Hating Landry was so much easier when he was alive.

George studies my face with a frown. Does he read my confusion? "So what does that mean for us?"

"I'm not sure. We'll take it slow. Friends first, right?"

He studies my face for a long moment. Maybe it shows my grief. They say eyes reflect the soul, and every piece of me aches.

Rather than argue, he pulls me down onto the sofa. I resist, trying not to touch him at first, but soon I curl up into the warmth of his side, glad I'm not alone. *Jeopardy!* distracts us. By the time we're halfway into the show, it feels like old times.

I solve the final question and get a tight squeeze as a reward from George right as Marcheline Dubois sweeps into the room with her typical flare for dramatic entrances. Her silver hair is worn upswept into a high bun and emphasizes her narrow features. Dark brown eyes boil with emotions too hot to contain within her small frame. "Mala, darling, I'm here," she cries, throwing her arms open wide.

She sees George hugging me, and her arms drop. "George Jr.?"

"Aunt March, what are you doing here?" George asks as he bounds to his feet.

Her penciled-in eyebrows arch, and she taps her lips with the tips of her fingers. "Shouldn't I be asking you the same question?"

I resettle on the sofa in a more prim and genteel position. She's his aunt and my boss. I don't want her to think poorly of me for hanging on him like a floozy. Course, I'd feel better about the situation if George didn't look as shocked as his aunt.

Hmm, I'm feeling like a dirty little secret. *Again.*

CHAPTER 5

MALA

Dirty Secret

My stomach curdles at the pitying expression that crosses Kevin's face when he looks from Ms. March to me, and I slap my hand across my mouth to cover the sour, nervous hiccup. Hopefully Georgie won't smell the chili I ate for lunch, but he's focused on his aunt.

Kevin avoids my questioning gaze, moving to a corner of the room. This whole situation seems odd. He should be cracking up over this confrontation. His sense of humor is as warped as mine. Then there's the fact that Ms. March is here at all. We're not allowed to have visitors other than family. George counts as law enforcement—he apparently gets a special pass—but not Ms. March.

The crow's feet around her dark eyes deepen, and the skin flap beneath her narrow chin vibrates as she squares her shoulders. "I'm waiting for an explanation, George Jr."

"What's the big deal, Aunt March? Mala and I are friends."

"Friends don't mistake each other's laps for chairs, darling."

He blushes. "It's not like that, I swear."

My eyebrows lift. Ten minutes ago, "friend" was the most hated word in existence. Now he's throwing it out like birdseed at a wedding. "He's telling the truth, Ms. March. We're keeping our relationship casual. No kissing…or anything else. So don't worry. I don't have plans on becoming your new niece-in-law."

"Ironically, that's the reason why I'm here," Ms. March says, striding across the room with sharp clicks of her high heels. She lowers herself into the plastic chair across from us and crosses her legs at her ankles. Her hands fold on her lap, clenching so tightly her knuckles turn white.

George sits so stiffly he appears to have a stick rammed up his ass. He glances at me with wide eyes. "What's going on, Aunt March?"

"Yeah, you burst into the room like your tail caught fire." I wipe my sweaty palms on my jeans. "And what's with the cryptic comments? Is everything okay?"

She drums her fingers on the edge of the chair. "Well, I didn't expect George Jr. to be here, but I guess it's for the best. This news will undoubtedly affect him too." She squeezes her hands into tiny fists. "I've gathered my courage and decided to defy your father."

"Defy my father?" George scowls down at the floor. "Is that wise?"

"Well, of course not," Ms. March huffs, rocking back in her chair. "But I'm doing it anyway, so don't scold me. I feel bad enough it has taken twenty-one years to gather my courage to say this. Since I've already damned myself, I might as well toss my wings into the lake of fire." She closes her eyes and says, "I've come to see your sister."

George glances at me, and I shrug back. How does he expect me to have the answer? I'm psychic, not a mind reader.

"What sister?" I ask for both of us.

Ms. March waves an all-encompassing wrinkled hand in my general direction, since her eyes are still squeezed shut. When we don't answer, she cracks open a single eyelid to study our expressions. "Mala," she says with emphasis on the M and a birdlike tick of her chin toward me.

I pull on a fake scowl, trying not to laugh. "Merciful heavens, Georgie, shouldn't you have told me you're my brother before we kissed?"

"I'm not your brother," George practically growls. "My aunt is confused."

Ms. March stiffens her spine. "I'm neither senile nor deranged, George Jr. That girl is your father's blood kin, which makes her genetically more your adoptive father's daughter than you."

"Whoa, Ms. March. What's going on?" Panic makes me choke on the words. "This isn't funny."

George takes my hand. "Don't listen to her. She's playing some sick game, and I don't know why. She's never liked me."

Ms. March's eyes water. "It breaks my heart to hear you say that, Georgie. I love you as much as I love Mala. It's my brother's fault we've never been on good terms. I've always resented the fact G.D. claimed another man's son as his own—legally adopted you and gave you his name—but abandoned his own flesh-and-blood daughter to be raised in poverty."

George stares from me to her.

"Shut your mouth, boy, before you swallow a fly," Ms. March says.

"Mala…she's…you're saying…"

"That's right. Malaise is a Dubois. If you look close, you'll see her resemblance to your father, and to me."

"Holy shit!" George drops onto the sofa like all the air *whoosh*ed out of him. "So that means Dad had an affair with Malaise's mom?"

"To be fair, your parents had hit a rough patch at the time. Your mama's happiness, and yours, was the main reason he never claimed Malaise."

"And Mama's inheritance," George says bitterly. "All the money my real father left her after he disappeared. It must've been a dream come true for old G.D. Mama never would've agreed to stay married to him if she knew he had a bastard."

I wave my hand to get their attention. "Uh, the bastard child's right here."

Marceline's face blanches. "Oh my dear, this isn't how I wanted you to hear all this. Your father should be the one to tell you about himself, but he keeps putting it off. After we found out about Jasmine passing, I went to him again. He's too damn scared of ruining his marriage, his business, and his reputation to claim you, but he's an idiot." She reaches out to take my hand. "You're not alone, Mala. You have family…you have *me*."

"I should be screaming right now." I glance at George. "Am I seriously not bothered by this news?" *Damn those antianxiety pills.*

"Maybe you're not upset, but I'm pissed that my dad cheated on my mother." George pushes to his feet. "I'm going home."

Marceline approaches George and lays a hand on his arm. "I know you need to speak to your father, but your mom doesn't know any of this. Why don't you take a few minutes and think how this will hurt her?"

"Of course it'll hurt her. Do you seriously think I can keep this a secret? Isn't it about time she learned the truth?" He jerks his arm free. "This should've been out a long time ago. If it had, maybe Mala wouldn't be locked in the mental ward and her mama wouldn't be dead."

The panic finally hits when I realize he plans to leave. "Wait, George. Don't go."

His cheeks redden. "I can't stay. Not now."

"But why? Let's talk this over. Figure out what to do."

Marceline comes over to the sofa. "Mala, darling, I'll be here."

I pace to George's side, but he refuses to meet my eyes. "I don't understand why you'd lay this on us. Why now?" I spin back to Ms. March…or should I call her Aunt March? "Why didn't you wait until I was alone or left it until after I got released from the hospital? You knew how much this would hurt Georgie."

"If I waited, I never would've been able to tell you. I've put this conversation off for years. Now Jasmine's dead. I couldn't leave you thinking you have no family. I've always watched out for you, and you need me now, more than ever."

George snorts. "Be grateful she's being honest for once. At least she cares about your feelings. She never has about mine. I guess it's because we're not *blood*. Isn't that right?"

I reach out, wanting to comfort and be comforted by him, but he brushes my hand aside. "Georgie, don't go, please."

He backs away from me like I've got herpes. "I'm sorry."

Reality crashes down as he walks to the door. He doesn't look back. Marceline's arms circle me, and I jump. Damn she's stealthy for an older lady. Didn't even hear her coming, and now I'm stuck.

"What a jerk," I say, turning into her embrace.

Ms. March presses my face against her shoulder. A large, wet stain imprints on the bosom of her silk shirt before I notice my tears. It takes a long time to pull myself together. She hands me a lilac-scented tissue from her giant purse. "It'll be all right, my darling girl. Let it all out."

I sniff. "Well, this stinks. He's not coming back, is he?"

"Maybe not for a bit. He's in shock."

He's not the only one.

Ms. March stares at me like she expects me to be excited that she decided to acknowledge my existence. I find the situation hypocritical, and I'm pissed.

"So," I say slowly, "you're my father's sister?"

"That's right." She brushes my hair back from my face with a trembling hand. I force myself to remain still, even though I want to move away. She catches my unease because she pulls back with a sigh. "I'm sure this is very difficult for you to understand."

"Not really," I say with a shrug, but it's a lie. I'm confused as hell.

"This is bound to cause a stir in our community." She picks at a loose thread on her sleeve. "Life will be even more difficult for you, I'm sorry to say."

"Difficult for you and my"—bitterness coats my tongue with a sour taste as I say —"father." I glance up to meet her gaze, and I give a half smile. "I'm used to being the object of scandal. Everyone knew about Mama being a prostitute. I bet a few of her regular clients' wives will be thrilled to hear the news of George Sr.'s paternity." I ignore her attempt to speak. "What I don't understand is why you never told me, Ms. March. I've worked for you for years." I meet her gaze and glance away. "Are you ashamed of being related to me?"

Ms. March gasps. "No, not you, darling. You're perfect. None of this is your fault." She grabs on to me again. I don't fight to get free of the hug. It feels too good to be in her arms as I listen to words I've always dreamed of hearing.

"I've loved you from the moment I held you in the hospital. You were the most beautiful baby in the nursery, and I swore I'd take care of you. No, the problem was that I promised to keep our relationship secret. I tried to talk your father into claiming you when you were born. I said, 'G.D., that's your kin. Be proud she's healthy and beautiful.' But, back then, he didn't have a pot to piss in, and he had ambitions. He wanted a proper wife and family. Your mama wouldn't have been able to help him get those things, not with the way she carried on and all those pesky rumors about her and her family."

Everything fucked up in my life always stems from Mama's reputation. She never cared how her choices affected me. It's not fair but I don't know why I'm so upset. I should be used to it by now. I just wish my own father would've seen me as a person and not an extension of her.

I shake my head, opening my stinging eyes wide. I don't want to cry again.

Ms. March releases her grip and leans back to study my face. Whatever she sees makes her frown. "Mala, I know this is a lot to take in. But I love you. I want you to come home with me."

Shock makes me step back from her. "Oh. Well, that's…uh."

"Is this a problem?" She edges closer.

We move around the room like we're zydeco dancing. "Yeah, I love you too."

"But you don't want to live with me?"

A huge part of me wants to say "yes." I've basically raised myself, and it would be nice to have someone take care of me for a change. This woman has been a huge part of my life. She's never failed me in the love department. By living with Aunt March, I can avoid facing the pain of going back to the home Mama died in. But the longer I wait, the harder it'll be.

"I appreciate the offer, but it's a little late." I pick at a hangnail. A quick glance up shows her dejected expression. "I'm twenty, Aunt March, not twelve. It's time for me to grow up, don't you think?"

She sighs. "I guess I understand. Still, the offer is open."

I grin and pat her shoulder. "At least, if I had to finally find my father's family, it's someone I can stand to be around. I've always liked you."

"And you've always held a special place in my heart." Aunt March smiles back. "Well, it's getting late. You have a big day tomorrow. Call me if you change your mind."

With a heavy heart, I watch her walk out the door. I almost call her back, regretting my decision, but it's for the best. Staying with her would be a supremely easy out. Plus I bet her old plantation house is full of restless spirits. They'd drive me insane with all of their demands.

When Ms. Anne saved me from Spooky Pocahontas, I realized that, no matter how hard I try to block out the spirits, it doesn't work. It just pisses them off. Or makes them sad. If ignoring them doesn't make them go away, then isn't it time to try something different? I have a debt to pay to Ms. Anne. If I help her with her problem, maybe she won't follow me home.

I tell Kevin all about Mama and Lainey and my new ability to "see" ghosts, and he agrees to become my ghost-busting partner in crime. He even consents to let me search Ms. Anne's old room. He says he's helping because he believes me, but I think he believes it'll be therapeutic if I confront the truth that I'm delusional. Part of me agrees with his unspoken stance on confronting the crazy. I still don't quite believe what

I'm seeing is real. I need the tangible proof of a ring for my own peace of mind.

Kevin's bulky presence infuses me with courage. With a deep breath, I step into the old woman's bedroom. At first it appears empty, then a surge of energy crackles across my prickling skin. A blurry, flickering image catches my peripheral vision, but I concentrate on Ms. Anne. She paces in front of me, and with each step, she solidifies. Her clouded eyes focus in my direction, and she hisses. Her braided, salt-and-pepper hair bounces on her shoulders with each step. Moans rumble up from deep in her gut and echo against the walls, soaking her sorrow and pain into the paint. The sound ripples in waves over my skin, raising goose bumps. It's the kind of intense emotion people sometimes feel when entering a house where someone has died, a residual resonance of the haunting spirit's emotions.

My heart races. This afternoon, the woman seemed sane. Now, not so much.

"Ms. Anne?" I whisper.

She spins with a low growl, and I lurch back into Kevin. His heavy hands grip my shoulders, which keeps me from bolting from the room. "Mala?"

I twist to look up at him. "It's Anne, Kev. She's kind of turned do-whack-a-do."

He raises an eyebrow. "More than me, who's listening to you about seeing her spirit?"

"I don't know what's wrong with her. This afternoon she seemed normal. Sane. Which I know is strange. Wasn't she suffering from dementia when she died?"

"Yeah."

"Well, she's out of it again. I'm not sure if she even knows who I am."

Kevin folds his massive arms, then shrugs. "Maybe her spirit is losing energy. You know. Like a battery draining."

Wow, score one for Kev. That actually makes sense. If she didn't have the energy to maintain her presence, then her spirit would start to degrade. Lainey didn't, but Uncle Gaston said she sustained her rage by siphoning my energy.

I take another step, raising my hands. Ms. Anne's gaze follows me as I cross the room to kneel by her bed. I don't want to look away from her because I'm afraid she'll attack, but her eyes brighten as I fumble beneath the mattress.

"It's in the back corner," she whispers. "I wasn't strong enough to move the bed."

A quick tug on the metal frame assures me I need help to move it too. "The ring's in the far corner. Can I borrow your muscles?"

"What, and make you stronger? Nope. I'll keep them and help you move the bed instead." Kevin flexes an arm.

"Ah ha, show-off. Think you're so funny."

"I need charm to balance out my good looks."

Together we pull the bed from the wall. The wedding ring winks at us from the corner—a shining beacon on the dust-covered floor. "Do you see it?" I glance at Kevin. He reaches down and picks it up with his thick fingers.

He sets the ring on my palm. It feels like it weighs a ton once the full meaning of its existence falls on me. I close my eyes. My lungs squeeze so tight with emotion that my chest aches. I can't breathe. Tears force themselves from between my sealed eyelids, and I let out a choked sob. "I can't believe it's real."

"Believe it. You're not as crazy as everyone thinks." He rubs my head. "Sorry for thinking you'd stab me in the eye."

"I thought the guy deserved it at the time. Everything else that happened wasn't me. It was Lainey," I whisper, staring at the ring. I glance at Ms. Anne. "Kevin will get this to your daughter."

At the man's nod, the woman smiles and fades.

CHAPTER 6

MALA

Cursed

I huddle beneath my blanket and stare at the ceiling tiles above my bed for the last night. Tomorrow, I go home. Whatever that means now that Mama's dead.

Three hundred and forty... three hundred and thirty-nine...

My body grows heavy as if weights are attached to my arm and legs, and I sink into my mattress. The heaviness settles on my chest, pressing my lungs flat. I let out the last puff of air. My spirit mingles with the carbon dioxide; the poisonous gas sighs over my parted lips before it leaves my physical body.

I float over the bed, lost. Where do I go with Landry gone? Do I try to find his spirit?

Between one thought and the next, I'm standing in his empty jail cell. His pictures, clothing, and the bloodstain on the floor... they're all gone. Nothing of Landry remains here. Where could his spirit be? Did the black vortex suck him someplace I can't follow?

I'm back at the hospital.

Dizziness drops me to my knees. The instantaneous transitions from one location to the other come without my conscious direction. I don't have time to prepare myself, say "To the blankety-blank—away," then magically appear at my intended location without a hair out of place and makeup refreshed. Not that I wear makeup anyway.

Hell. Focus, Mala. Why am I back at the hospital? Is Landry's spirit here? Is he trying to find me too?

I twist to stare down the hallway. Fluorescent lights hum and flicker overhead. Inaudible whispers, a shushing of sound filters from open doors. I breathe out a cloud of frost that glitters like twinkling stars in the air and feel the icy tingle of cold concrete beneath my palms. The stench of antiseptic burns my nose.

I pinch my arm and wince. "Where am I?"

Plaster flakes off the walls. Grime covers the cracked linoleum. This isn't the hospital I'm used to seeing, with its pristine cleanliness and order. This is a darker dimension, like I somehow slipped between the cracks in the fabric of reality.

I watch way too many sci-fi shows.

"Hello?" I yell. "Anyone here?" My words echo down the hall. *Good going, Mala. Alert every monster in this place to your location.*

A rattling *clank* . . .

It takes me a second to process the sound of a motor turning on—an air conditioning unit or boiler? So stupid. I'm overreacting. Nothing can hurt me; I'm here only in spirit. My physical body is safe in my hospital bed.

I want out of this place. If I'm here for a reason, I need to find it. Or at least find a quick way back into my body. I'm in a cross section of the hallway. It stretches in four directions. In front and behind me, the walls shine from reflected light. White sheets cover abandoned hospital equipment. Trash litters the floor. Doors, painted red, stand out from the grimy, grayish white paint of the walls. The last door to the right at the end of the hallway stands open.

Welcoming.

The hallways stretching to my right and left are the complete opposite. Pitch black, thicker than road tar—the complete absence of light—forms a visible barrier I don't want to step across. It reminds me of the black hole that swallowed Landry.

A sound from the darkness freezes me. I stretch out my senses, listening.

Heavy breathing…

…turns into malevolent laughter, like one of those creepy clowns. High-pitched giggles that make the hairs stand up on the back of my neck.

"Mala," the voice cracks, hoarse with age. I recognize her, but don't.

Don't want to.

Can't.

A raspy sound. A shush. A single flame lights the darkness, then twin glowing orange circles. The pungent scent of tobacco burns my nostrils. Footsteps move in my direction. I back up. If she touches me, I'll burn.

No. It's a sensory memory. This isn't real. None of it.

Sizzling agony pierces the wound in my shoulder as a forked tongue thrusts inside me, sucking out my blood. My soul. Drinking me down. Binding me to her.

I press my hand against my shoulder. Warm, sticky liquid covers my palm. "Aunt Magnolia," I whisper, "don't."

"You swore at the crossroads, where all bonds are formed. Come to me."

It's obvious which direction I should go in. Even though I'm scared.

I take a step.

Darkness wraps me tight, smothering my senses. No sight, sound, taste. I float...at peace.

* * *

Bessie's late. I've been sitting in the dayroom, plucking at piano keys for half an hour, having already finished with the checkout procedure. The duffel bag with my psych medication and personal belongings sits at my feet. All I need is her. When Bessie finally enters the room, all the air rushes from my body. Part of me didn't believe I'd really get to leave. I thought for sure something had gone wrong.

I sprint to throw myself into her muscular arms and bury my face in her shoulder.

She pats me on the back for a long minute then pushes me away. "Are you this happy to see me, or is something else wrong?"

I sniff. "I'm so happy I can't stop crying tears of joy."

"And this has nothing to do with Landry getting hurt?"

Hurt? Not dead? I grip her arm. "What do you mean? Landry got hurt?"

Bessie ducks her head. "George said he told you about Landry getting attacked. I'm not springing this news on you, am I?" She rubs my arm.

"No, his roommate shanked him and then smothered him with a pillow—"

"George told you that?" she blurts out.

No, I saw it with my own eyes. Oh God, my head's gonna explode. I rub my temple hard, trying to stop the veiny knot from throbbing. "Bessie, he's dead."

She shakes her head. "Who?"

"Landry's dead. George said he died."

"Oh, yes, he did…die…"

I want to pull out my hair. "Bessie!"

"The guard knew CPR. The shank got caught on a rib so it didn't hit any vital organs. He'll be sore and laid up here in the hospital for a few days before they ship him back to the jail. Matter of fact, I've got to go check—"

My legs give out on me halfway through her explanation, but she doesn't notice until I'm sitting on the floor. She grabs my hands and pulls me to my feet.

"Can I visit him, please?" I rock from foot to foot. "I've got to see him. The last thing I said to him…" I groan. *He thinks I hate him.* "We can stop off at his room, right?"

Bessie's been shaking her head the whole time. When I finally shut up, she says, "I'm sorry, but he's still in protective custody. Plus, you're not family."

"Please, Bessie." I take her hand. "I thought he was dead. I haven't slept. Won't be able to…"

"*Cher*, you're not a cute little girl who can wrap me around her finger anymore."

"Fine, let me suffer not knowing if he's really okay."

"We'll walk past his room on the way out of the hospital. Maybe you'll be able to peek inside the room to verify I'm telling the truth since you don't believe me."

Whoa, guess two can play the guilt game.

We're buzzed through the locked doors leading out of the

psych wing, and I follow Bessie onto the elevator. My heart races faster when the doors open on the second floor, and she strides down the hallway. "Are you sure about this?" she asks. "It's not too late to change your mind. Landry will never know you were here."

"I have to see him." My hands shake, and I lift the duffel bag onto my shoulder. Sweat stings my eyes. I can't get the image of his death out of my head. I have to see Landry, to know for sure he really lives, or I'll be a scattered mess.

"What about your mama?" Bessie turns to face me, blocking my path.

I stop rather than running over her like I'm tempted to do. Why do we have to talk about this now? Landry almost died. No, he *died*. Something came out of the vortex and grabbed him. Darkness covered him—tried to eat him. I tried to save him, like he saved me, but I failed. Or maybe I didn't. Ugh, I'm so confused.

Focus on what you know for sure.

"Bessie, he didn't kill Mama. His daddy and his friends did that."

"He's incarcerated for attacking you."

"Because I was whacked out of my head and couldn't remember what really happened that night, but I do now. Landry saved my life. If he hadn't taken me away, I would've watched Mama die and probably would've been killed myself. I couldn't have come back from seeing that. I'll never testify against him."

"You mean that, don't you?"

I spin at the familiar voice. Assistant District Attorney Mitchell Cready stands in the last doorway to the right at the end of the hallway. During my early ghost-walking days, I spied on this guy while he interviewed Landry about Mama's murder.

Cready seems like a good person, if overly determined to the point of not paying attention to the evidence right in front of his flat face. I get that he wants to use Mama's death to further his career, but I won't let him do it at the expense of justice.

Cready walks over to me—or rather struts. "Bessie said you were being released today." He gives his impersonation of charming. In reality, he looks like a yawning gator—all teeth and no personality. "I thought I'd meet you in person and check on Landry's status. Kill two birds with one stone, so to speak."

I snort and cross my arms. "Not sure how you can justify keeping him in custody with no evidence. Now he's been assaulted. What do you think the press will say once the news leaks?"

Cready holds up his hands, palms forward. "Hold on, don't attack me."

"If you're this defensive over a simple question, how are you ever going to placate the press? They'll be all over you like flies on cow pies," I say, trying to sound mature by not cussing him out. With arms crossed, I stalk toward him until we're nose to nose. "What are you doing to keep Landry safe? Why did his cellmate stab him in the first place? It's a bold move—murder—a potential death sentence. He has to have more of a motive than Landry snores in his sleep."

Cready doesn't back down. "What do you know that I don't?"

My eyes widen, and I stumble back. Crap! I almost spilled too much. I'd seen how Carl watched him before the attack, like he was waiting to receive the order to take him out. Don't ask me why I know this, but I believe it with all of my heart. Maybe part of my gifts also leads to mind reading, except I bet reading that guy's mind would be like gazing into a Port-A-Potty.

Cready glares at Bessie. "What did you tell her about the attack?"

"I didn't have to say anything. Mala's sharp. She's the one who figured out Mrs. Prince and Doc Rathbone killed Lainey. Everyone forgot about the girl's murder after what happened to Jasmine, but I haven't."

My head swells. I didn't think anyone realized I had solved the case, given I'd been possessed and on a rampage at the time. A huge grin stretches my lips.

Bessie's jaw flexes. "Speaking of girls getting murdered, Cready. We need to talk."

He nods, then tips his head at me. "I'll arrange for Landry's release. I'd already been thinking about dismissing the charges."

"Huh?" I glance at Bessie. "Seriously, just like that?"

Maybe I should consider law school if I can't clear my reputation enough to get a job in law enforcement. But that's a worry I put on hold because Cready's still talking and what he's saying gives me hope.

"Bessie's right. You solved Lainey's murder. You're smart enough to know whether Landry participated in your attack. If you're not willing to testify against him, then I'm wasting taxpayer dollars keeping him in custody."

I release the breath I've been holding. "So he's free."

"Why don't you go give him the good news while I speak with Bessie."

I glance at her. Sparks are about to fly out of her ears. What pissed her off? She can't be this upset over Landry being released.

I edge around Cready, nod to the officer standing guard at the door, and enter the room. I don't breathe for several seconds. I can't. Landry is lying on the bed. The blanket tucked around his waist reveals his abdomen and the bandage wrapped around his wound. His face is a swollen, bruised mess. My stomach tightens in sympathy. Despite the damage, he appears peaceful—body fully relaxed without the tension that filled him while in jail. Angelic. *Yeah, right.*

"I know, I know. I'm pretty. You can't help but stare," he slurs his words. His good eye cracks, but the lid is swollen. I'm not sure if he can see me.

I swallow around the lump in my throat. "I've never thought of you as pretty, Frog Prince."

His frown turns into a wince. "Oh, Mala."

"Who did you think you were flirting with?" I hate the jealousy in my voice.

"If I'd known you'd be stopping by, I would've made myself presentable. Combed my hair or put on deodorant. I thought I was talking the nurse into an extra Jell-O cup." His hand inches across the bed, palm upward. I cross the room and thread my fingers through his.

His hand trembles slightly in mine. He's weak. But warm and alive. My chest tightens with the emotions threatening to erupt from within me, but I hold them back, afraid I'll freak him out. "How are you feeling? Are you in a lot of pain?"

He shakes his head.

"Did you hear Cready? He's dropping your charges."

"So I can go home. Not that I have a family to go back to anymore." He pauses. "Guess you don't either. I'm being…insensitive."

The words sting with bitterness. Is he thinking about what happened to Mama? Or his parents? I sit on the edge of the bed and lay our clasped hands on my lap. "Yeah, you are a little. At least your parents are still alive."

"True…" The distance widens between us. He's lying right next to me, but our emotional connection has been severed, like he's built a wall blocking me from getting too close. I don't like it. I won't let him cut me off.

I squeeze his hand. "Actually, this once-upon-a-time orphan has gotten more offers than she can use."

Curiosity reestablishes our connection. "What does that mean?"

I lower my voice so it doesn't carry into the hallway. "I'll tell you the whole story later, but mostly it means I'm gonna be selfish. I had about enough of being ordered around while in the mental ward. Mama never paid too much attention to me, and I'm used to taking care of myself. I don't need a babysitter."

"Then you're going home?" His hand tightens.

"Yeah." I ignore the obvious question. How will I handle living in the house where Mama was murdered? Well, seeing as how the spirits of Mama and Uncle Gaston are waiting for me to return, I'll do just fine. My family's untraditional but still intact. "I'll stay with Bessie for a day or two. I need to go to the college to talk about my financial aid. Oh, no. With your parents out of the picture, how will you pay for school?"

"I think I'll skip out on this semester. I won't be welcomed on campus after what happened. People will blame me like they did in jail. Besides, my football scholarship's gone with my depth perception."

My stomach clenches as my gaze immediately goes to his damaged eye. I've avoided looking at it, but without the eye patch, the damage is clearly visible. I stomp hard on the guilt. Sympathy won't do him any good. "Poor baby, welcome to Mala's world. I've dealt with people spreading rumors about me my whole life. I'm sure there will be even more now. I've survived. So will you."

"I a-a-almost didn't. I would've died if not for you." He squeezes my hand.

Is he talking about— "Oh, my God. You remember?"

"Yeah, getting stabbed and smothered leaves a lasting impression." Sweat breaks out across his forehead, and a moan rips through him. His grip tightens. "I'll never forget dying and seeing you screaming for me to come back. The burning cloud. The pain…" His body convulses. The hand holding mine jerks upward, and I fall across his chest.

"Landry? Landry, what's wrong?" I lay my palm across his forehead. "You're burning with fever."

"I'm cold." His teeth chatter. The spasm turns into a full-body shiver.

"Hang on. I'll call the nurse to come give you some meds." I push up, but he won't let me go. He's panting, unable to slow his breathing. A blood circle encases the dilated pupil of his swollen eye. "Let me go, Landry." I press my hand against his chest. The flesh beneath my palm ripples like millions of worms are wiggling beneath his skin.

"It won't stop."

"What won't stop, Landry?"

"The snake in the darkness crawled inside me. It's burrowing deeper." The handcuff around his right wrist keeps him bound despite his struggle to break free. "Get it out of me, Mala. Please."

"Calm down. You're gonna hurt yourself." He's totally lost it. Nothing I say stops him from trying to get out of bed. Blood runs down his wrist from where the metal cuts into his skin.

I run to the door and throw it open. "Help!"

A nurse collides with me in the doorway, and I drag her by the arm into the room. "Help him, please. He's in pain."

The lights overhead flicker like strobe lights, blinding flashes that force my eyes half shut. Between the slits of my vision, I see flashes of grimy, peeling plastered walls. A rotting fish smell makes my nose wrinkle.

Landry's screams echo within the room.

"What's happening?" I yell.

Slime covers my palm. I glance at the hand still on the nurse's arm. Her skin rots, sloughing off to reveal shiny white bone. I try to pull my hand free, but sticky ooze stretches from my hand to hers, and it won't shake off. Maggots wriggle in the slime…on my fingers. A scream bubbles in my throat, threatening to break free, but I clench my teeth. I won't let it out. I won't let her win.

Evil Poca's found another way to come at me. She's playing dress-up. Well, I won't join her game even though it's *ever* so much fun to be scared witless. I drag my gaze from the ghost as I back toward the bed.

"I warned you," the nurse yells. "Stop ignoring me."

"Mala!" Landry wraps his free arm around my waist and drags me onto the bed. His moan rips from deep within his chest. He's not reacting to pain anymore. He's staring at Evil Poca. "Oh, God…she's rotting."

Shit! He sees ghosts. How much of this is illusion, not delusion?

I cup Landry's cheeks with both hands and turn his head until he faces me. "Stop screaming, Landry. She's not real. None of this is real. It's all in our heads." His gray eye glitters, wild with a primal fear so deep I'm afraid he's seconds from a complete mental breakdown. I press my forehead against his. "Close your eye."

He tries to turn back to the ghost, but I won't let him. "Don't look, Landry. She'll go away if you ignore her."

I clamp my eyelids shut so hard my ears hum. An orange glow rises in the dark. My eyeballs ache, but it's good. The pain helps me to concentrate. I begin to count out loud. On ten, I open my eyes and pull back. The room has returned to normal. No more freaky alternate dimension. Unfortunately, Landry and I aren't the only ones in the room. Bessie stands in the doorway, staring at us as if we've lost our ever-lovin' minds. To her we probably have, since we're both screaming and carrying on as if someone has died.

"Mala Jean, what's going on?"

I swallow hard. Not much to say. "We had an emotional re-union."

"I can see that." She walks toward us.

I glance at Landry. He's still breathing heavily. His eye looks a little wild, and his hair stands on end. Seeing ghosts really fucks with your mind, especially when you don't realize it's all in your head. They look so real…so corporeal.

My only source for supernatural answers is Auntie Magnolia. I've been apprenticed to a hoodoo queen—a black arts practitioner, according to Mama, which is even worse to my way of thinking. But maybe she's the person I need to speak with since whatever happened to Landry when he died seems to be of the evil persuasion. Magnolia would be real good friends with it.

I lean over to whisper in Landry's ear. "We'll talk later."

"Why do most of our conversations end this way?"

CHAPTER 7

LANDRY

Crawling Out of the Darkness

The vision in my right eye turns glassy at the edges, like I'm peering through the narrow lens of a prism. My chest feels tight. Each breath wheezes with an unnerving gurgle as air struggles to pass through my constricted lungs. A tremor hits my handcuffed arm, and pain flares when the metal cuts into my bleeding wrist again. Why can't I control myself? It's like my body's in revolt, determined to give me a painful reminder of how lost I am.

The blond nurse who enters the room with Bessie restrains my free arm and shouts for the jail guard standing duty outside. Her words filter into my brain, a rush of sounds but no meaning. Only her agitated tone cuts through the fear that consumes my mind and body—a pressing weight that smothers me with each step Mala takes toward the door. She's the only thing holding me together, and she's leaving.

My throat closes. *I'm suffocating.*

Nobody acknowledges me.

Mala, I'm dying. If I don't say it louder, she'll leave. Meaningless, guttural mewls pass my lips. I've forgotten how to speak. *How pathetic…* I jerk my arm again. *Can't she hear me screaming?*

Bessie pulls on Mala's arm when she half turns back in my direction. I grip the sheet, trying to sit up. The nurse slaps a hand to my shoulder and shoves me back onto the bed. A curse flies to the tip of my tongue but falls back down my clogged throat.

Bessie whispers in Mala's ear.

What is she saying?

Disgust darkens the detective's eyes when she glances over Mala's shoulder. She knows exactly what she's doing—separating us one slow step, one hateful word at a time. She wraps her arm around Mala's back and steers her out of range of my peripheral vision. I turn my head to compensate for my blind left eye, and Mala reappears like a magical creature—as beautiful and fragile as one of the porcelain statues decorating the shelves in her living room, yet strong enough that she hasn't broken no matter how many times I've dropped her.

Whenever I see Mala, my heart tries to cut its way out of my chest. *Such an idiot. I deserve to die.*

Failure burns. I couldn't protect her when she needed me the most. I did nothing when she got shot but fall to the ground and cry until Dad carried me away. The whole time, Mala fought alone to survive. She never would've been in danger if I hadn't been a selfish prick and begged her to help find Lainey's murderer.

Don't call for her to come back. Be a man, not a pussy. I bite down on the inside of my cheek to keep from breaking my own promise. Blood trickles down my throat, and nausea causes my stomach to buck. The vision in my right eye dims then blacks out, mimicking my left. Panic forces me upright with a gasp. The light turns on again. I pant for air. Hands press on my shoulders, forcing me back into the bed. I rock my head from side to side. The guard appears, standing on my left, and the nurse on my right side.

"What's the matter with me?" I beg for an answer.

Do they hear this time?

I reach for the nurse's hand but misjudge the distance.

The nurse takes my wrist instead and checks the IV line inserted into a vein. "He's having a panic attack," she says.

The prison guard's garlic-tainted breath blows in my face. "Maybe we should leave the handcuff on until the meds take effect."

"You gave me drugs?" *But I just woke up.* I try to focus on the woman's blurry face. She bobs in and out of my line of sight like I'm standing on the deck of a ship. Dizziness makes me want to beg her to stand still. My stomach clenches again, a reminder that I haven't eaten solid food in two days. Acid burns my throat, and I cough.

The nurse pops into view again. At least at first I think it's the same woman, and then details sharpen. Her features have changed. Long, tangled black hair curls across her dirt-stained, blue scrubs. She would be beautiful if the vision didn't show the decay eating the flesh off of her frame. Her icy fingers trace the angled planes of my cheekbone. The skin burns, then turns numb. I breathe out a cloud of frosted air and blink rapidly, trying to focus on her wavering form. Shadows coil around the edge of her body—an aura of darkness, weaving patterns over her skin.

I close my eye, breathing deeply.

When it reopens, I whimper. "Mala said you're not real."

Her smile sends prickles across my bare skin.

"Don't fight us. We're trying to help," the guard's voice comes from my left side, and I jump. I stop myself from turning away from the ghost in front of me. She can't hurt me if I don't take my eye off of her.

No. That's not right. Mala said ignore her.

A heavy weight hits the underside of the mattress and lifts it an inch into the air. I grab on to the metal rail. High-pitched, *chitter*ing and *snicki*ng noises come from beneath the bed, then the sound of ripping. Vibrations from inside the mattress shake me.

I lunge forward. "It's coming!"

Don't they hear it? Feel it?

The guard holds me down like a lamb for sacrificial slaughter. My blood's going to stain these sheets. They'll regret not listening. "Stop," I beg the nurse, who holds padded restraints in her hands. "Don't…don't tie me up, please. Help me."

Sharp claws dig through the padding. The monster struggles to reach me. I told Mala about it, but I didn't have time to fully explain what's happening to me. If I had, would she have left me alone with it? Or would she have stayed to fight with me?

Unless none of this is real. What if this is all in my head?

Additional restraints tie me to the bed. They wrap around my legs and arms. Heavy, padded straps I can't break. The heaviness in my chest changes, and my muscles relax. The drug the nurse injected into the IV drags me down.

CHAPTER 8

MALA

Into the Wild

Bessie hustles me out of the room.

"Call me when you get out," I say over my shoulder. Landry watches me leave in silence. His expression shows he's terrified but trying to be strong. Guilt wiggles inside, but I can't stay. The real nurse and prison guard enter the room. They have a better chance of calming him down than I do. Still, each step drags. I'm abandoning him. What if the ghost attacks again? He can't protect himself. He doesn't know how to block the spirit's entry. I've had months to practice building mental shields, and I'm still fooled.

What I don't get is how he can see ghosts in the first place. He's always been sensitive to the spirit world, but I thought it was only because of his connection to Lainey. Did this happen because he died? Or is it that snake he said buried itself inside of him?

Bessie tugs on my arm, and I follow her through the hospital without making a fuss. As we exit the sliding glass doors, I throw one last look over my shoulder and shudder. I hated hospitals before. Now I'd have to be unconscious and dying to come back. I lift my chin to the sky and let the warm, cleansing rain wash over my face. The air smells of earth, pure and crisp. No more bleach or blood. I'm free.

Bessie covers her head with her hands. "Let's go!"

The impatience in her voice snaps me forward, and I hit almost every puddle during my dash through the rain to her car. Bessie has the door open by the time I catch up. I toss my duffel bag onto the floorboard, then slide onto the front seat next to her. I study her from the corner of my eye. The darkness in her expression sends a ripple of unease through me.

I wipe my wet palms across damp jeans and ask, "Want to talk about why you're upset?"

"What did Landry do to make you scream like that?" Fury makes her voice vibrate. She slaps on the windshield wipers.

Why does everything have to be a fight? "Nothing."

"So you said."

"Because it's true. You and George are always so determined to see the worst in him."

"George? What does he have to do with this?"

"You're both always quick to blame Landry."

"And you're always quick to defend him." She glares out the window. Tension keeps her shoulders bunched. Drops splash against the windshield so hard it's like peering through a sprinkler.

I twist in my seat so I face her. "I love how much you care about me. That you always see the best in me. Even going so far as to praising me to Cready, but…" My gut clenches, and I breathe out the words. "I'm not worth it."

Her eyes widen.

I hold up a hand. "I'm the one to blame for all of the horrible things that have happened to Landry. Losing his eye. Being locked up in jail. His attack."

"That's bull—"

"No, it's the truth! You saw his face. He got the shit beat out of him. How could he do anything to me in his condition?" Bessie's expression tightens. There's no point in continuing the argument. She's too protective. *God, thank you for this woman.*

With a grin, I poke her shoulder. "You know, this isn't even about me and Landry. You were pissed before you entered his room. What did you talk to Cready about?"

She doesn't crack. "Work."

"A murder?"

She turns a slow scowl in my direction.

"It is, isn't it? A murdered woman."

"What makes you think so?" Maybe because the ghost's pissed off and keeps appearing before me. Man, it would make my life easier if I could trust Bessie with the truth. "You told Cready you needed to speak with him after talking about Lainey's murder."

"You are too sharp for your own good."

"So who was she? How did she die?"

Bessie spears me with her gaze. "How about if you don't refer to the woman in the past tense since we don't know for sure she's dead? Right now she's listed as a missing person."

My palm itches from the gooey feel of rotting flesh still coating my hand. Will it ever wash off? "Is she a nurse?"

"Yes. Gloria Pearson disappeared four weeks ago—the night Reverend Prince escaped from the hospital. I'm sure he had help since he was in no condition to drive. Gloria's car still hasn't been located."

"Ah, he kidnapped her to help with his escape. Then killed her."

"Mala," Bessie snaps. "Missing person."

Given the fact that Gloria haunts the hospital, she probably died there. Whether her body remains hidden on the hospital grounds or has been disposed of in another location is the question I need to answer.

I get her being angry. Being murdered would piss anyone off, but why does she despise Bessie, if the *bitch* comment refers to her and not me? Does she feel like Bessie should've found her body? Does she want me to find her? Crap! I really don't want to get involved, but if Reverend Prince kidnapped her, I already am.

I'm gonna find that psycho before he hurts anyone else. And I've got the biggest lure of all time—the soon-to-be-released son of the devil himself. Landry Prince is going home, and Daddy will be waiting.

I can't wait to join in the happy family reunion.

* * *

Bessie's daughter, Maggie, had fried up some okra and buttermilk-soaked chicken. The meal waits on the buffet table when I walk into their house. The smell sets my mouth to watering, and I barely spare time to give her a hug before I rush to the table. I have a plate of food in one hand and a mouthful of chicken by the time I turn to the dining table and see who else makes up my welcome home party.

Georgie sits at the end of the table. Far enough away that if he drowns in his own gravy, I won't have to give him CPR. Why in the world would he invite himself over? He's the last person I want to have a conversation with.

The jerk leans back in his chair and gives me a lazy grin. My heartbeat kicks up a notch. Damn his infernal soul! Does he have to be so hot? Lately, every time I see him, I think the same thing.

I flop down in my chair, fanning myself with one hand. "George," I say with a haughty nod.

Maggie's boyfriend, Tommy, leans around George and waves. "Welcome home."

"Yeah, welcome home," George says.

My stomach sours. My first home-cooked meal in over a month, and he's *ruining* it. So unfair. Maybe if I concentrate hard enough, I can pretend he doesn't exist. It works on ghosts.

One hundred, ninety-nine, ninety-eight... ooh, deviled eggs.

I snatch four off the platter. Maggie sets by my elbow.

Bessie sits on my other side so I'm squished between her and her daughter. Maggie and her boyfriend, Tommy, give each other long, penetrating looks throughout dinner. They monopolize the conversation, which suits me fine since I don't have to come up with small talk. George sends a raised eyebrow in my direction during a particularly uncomfortable silence, and I shrug.

"Okay, what's going on?" I ask, unable to take the suspense. "If I'm making you all uncomfortable, let me know."

"What?" Maggie's voice hits squawk decibels. She shifts in her chair and melts me with sad eyes. "Oh, no. I'm sorry. We're the ones making you uncomfortable, aren't we?"

"Told you this was a bad idea," Tommy says around a mouthful of food.

"It's the only time we'll all be together. Mala's going to stay with her aunt soon."

I frown at Maggie. I hadn't told her or Bessie about my aunt problems. Either of them. Did George blab the news about

Marcheline to Bessie? Who I decide to stay with is nobody's business but my own.

Maggie stands up, and Tommy puts down his fork, a rarity, which means whatever she's about to say is important. "'Kay, I might as well get this over with before I make the situation worse and this dinner gets out of control." She turns to her mother. "Everyone else already knows this. Tommy asked me to marry him, and…well, I said yes."

I sit back in my chair, wishing I could dive beneath the table to avoid the explosion. This is why Maggie used me as a buffer between herself and Bessie. I shake my head at Maggie in sympathy. Poor girl picked the worst day to spring this news on her mother. If she'd bothered to run it by me first, I would've warned her about Bessie's sour mood.

My breath catches when Bessie calmly wipes her mouth, folds the napkin, lays it on the table, and rises. "Conference in my office," she tells Maggie. "This means you too, Tommy."

The air puffs out, and I suck in a deep breath, light-headed.

Whew! Thank God I'm only an honorary member of the family.

They trail Bessie out of the room, like scolded puppies with their tails between their legs. I bite into a crispy chicken thigh. The juice fills my mouth, and I moan. *So good.*

"Well, that was awkward," George says.

A startled laugh erupts out of me, and I almost spit out my chicken. I'd forgotten about George. *Awkward? Very.* I chew up the mouthful. What sort of response does he expect? "Uh, yeah."

"This is probably something they should've told Bessie about without guests present."

"Maybe they needed us to provide moral support. Did you see Bessie? She didn't even lose her cool. Everything will be fine."

"You might be right."

"Do you approve of the marriage?"

He quirks an eyebrow. "Do you want me to answer that question here?"

I glance toward the closed office door and shake my head. I haven't had time to wrap my mind around the idea of a Tommy and Maggie wedding. She told me about it, and I didn't take her seriously. After that, Mama died. I didn't think of much else at that point. Even with Bessie's outward appearance of calm, I still listen for the screams. The odds are fifty-fifty that I'll be attending Maggie and Tommy's funerals instead of a wedding, but I won't say no to a slice of wedding cake.

Tension tightens my shoulders, and my head aches from my racing thoughts. The last three days I've been bombarded with nonstop drama. I can't even process…it's too much to deal with. I lean back in my chair and close my eyes. "I just want to go home," I whisper. *Is that too much to ask for?*

George clears his throat, and I grimace. *Now what?*

"I can drive you, if you want."

My eyes pop open. *Do I?*

"Let's go." I stamp down the guilt as I write Bessie a quick note about "wanting to give them privacy to discuss the wedding" and "thanking Maggie for the brunch." I practically run from the house, afraid they'll come out of the office and catch me. George leans against his forest green Land Rover. I totally missed seeing it in the driveway when Bessie and I pulled in. Where the hell was my mind?

"Thanks for the ride." I gift him with a smile. He kind of deserves it with this latest rescue attempt.

"We need to talk."

Famous last words. I stifle another groan and don't run off.

George acts like the perfect gentleman. He's tricky like that.

He opens my car door, takes my duffel and throws it in the back-seat, then waits for me to climb in before closing the door for me. He even keeps silent during the drive. My anxiety reaches higher levels once we leave town and turn onto the gravel road winding through the bayou. It's been over a month since Mama died. I'm scared to see what the place will look like. Will there be signs…bloodstains? Will the air still be tainted with the scent of smoke and burnt flesh?

A shiver forces my trembling hands under my arms. I rock forward, trying to catch my quickening breaths before I go into full panic mode.

George stares at the road and asks, "Sure you want to do this?"

"Can't avoid it or *you* forever." I meet his gaze and nod. "I see confusion in your eyes. You have feelings. Glad I'm not hitching a ride with a complete sociopath."

I turn to stare out the window.

"That's not fair, Malaise. I was shocked by Aunt March's news."

"Shocked? Oh, I totally get being shocked." I grip the armrest with a shaking hand. "I almost passed out when Bessie told me that Landry's alive. That he didn't die like you said." My voice rises, "How could you keep *that* from me, George?"

A muscle in his jaw ticks.

"The whole time you were visiting me…he was in the hospital. You said nothing."

"So what!" His face is cold when he glances at me. "After what that asshole and his father did, why do you care?"

"Landry saved my life! You know how I feel—"

"That's why I didn't tell you!" he yells. "I'm sick of you defending that asshole. After everything that's happened…don't be stupid enough to trust him again. I warned you about him."

The condescension in his tone makes my blood boil. *How dare he*—

"This is why you offered to bring me home. So you could say 'I told you so?'"

"If you had listened—"

"Fuck you," I choke out, so pissed I can barely speak. "Since you're a psychic, maybe you should've warned me that a mob would come to my house and execute my mother for being a witch."

"That's not fair!"

I suck in a hiss. "Let me out."

"No."

"Stop this car right now, or I swear I'll jump."

George swerves to the side of the road, does a hard U-turn, and brakes so hard my head thumps the back of the headrest. I throw open the door, and he grabs my arm. "You gonna walk all the way home just to spite me?"

Pain makes my temples throb. "Damn right, George. I'll take getting eaten by a gator over spending another minute with you." I snatch my arm free and climb out. The rev of his engine makes me stumble back. His tires kick up a backwash of muddy water to drench my clothing. He accelerates without pause, and I watch until his taillights disappear around the corner.

"Damn you, George," I yell, shaking my fist dramatically at the heavens. Lightning doesn't strike his car, nor does it make me feel better. I blink at the wet leaves and gray sky overhead and drag in a deep breath. The scent of the bayou fills my nostrils, and my shoulders relax. I'm home. Finally home.

I never should've left Bessie's with only a vague note. She's probably worried about me. But I don't feel bad about being home, only the way I got here. I turn in a slow circle with a frown.

Up ahead, the stop signs signaling the crossroad shine in the haze. I break into a slow jog until I reach the path by the bus stop that leads to my house. I set my hands on my knees and lean forward to keep my balance while climbing the slippery hill into the woods. This is always so much harder when I'm carrying my backpack.

Crap! I left my bag in George's car. I wonder if he'll give it to Bessie. If he does, he'll also tell her about the fight, and it'll be another thing for her to give me hell over when she shows up at the house to give me hell for leaving. I shove aside the leaves blocking the path after a month of disuse. Mud and overgrown plants force me to watch my step. I slow even more when passing the stretch of bayou where I found Lainey Prince's body. Memories flood through me.

My problems started on the day I dragged that girl's body from the swamp. If I'd left her for gator bait, Mama would still be alive. I wouldn't see ghosts. My life would've gone on in the same direction as it had before.

No Georgie or Landry to break my heart.

One stupid decision and the course of my life changed forever.

The humidity sends trickles of perspiration down my back, soaking into my T-shirt. Flyaway strands of hair frizz in tight curls around my face, and the ends, dipped in sweat, stick to my cheeks. The woods look beautiful this time of year. The sky peeps between dark green leaves and the lighter gray-green Spanish moss. Bluish lichen spots some of the tall trunks and thick vines. Toadstools pop up from rich brown soil.

How do people not see the beauty in the decay? The new life growing within the rot proves death is not the end but the beginning of a new plane of existence. The spirits still lingering on this side of the veil are stuck. They can't go back. And they can't go forward until whatever keeps them here is concluded. I helped Lainey and Ms. Anne find peace. Now I don't have to worry about them haunting me anymore. Maybe helping the ghosts is the only way to keep me from going insane. Ignoring them sure didn't help Mama cope with her ability.

A broken limb has fallen across the path, and I stop to pull it free. The dirt beneath the leaves is still wet, which makes the fresh boot prints stand out. They point in the direction of my house. Adrenaline zings through me, and stomach acid burns the base of my throat. The last time I found prints in the mud, Landry had been debating the merits of taking me out assassin style. He ended up changing his mind. Whoever happens to be on my property might not have the same tenderhearted nature.

My nearest neighbors live five miles away. One and a half if I take the trail past the pond. The other side of my property borders Forest Service land. Sometimes hunters get lost and end up wandering around, but it's not hunting season.

My heartbeat quickens as I glance around. The density of the undergrowth keeps me from seeing too deep. There are a lot of places for someone to hide—like behind the fallen log to my left or behind the bushes up ahead.

I quickly strip the broken branch of stems and leaves. It forms a solid weight in my hand, and I give it a test swing. If anyone comes after me, it'll make the perfect club.

A twig snaps.

I spin.

Leaves rustle in the tree next to me. A crow sits on the branch. It cocks its head to the side and studies me with a beady eye. Its wings spread, and feathers ripple as it stretches. I draw in a deep breath. *Calm down.* I can't see or hear anything when on high alert.

I focus my senses outward. I think I'm alone. At least, no other human seems to be near, but I can't discount the prints. I'm stuck out in the boondocks, too far away to try to get back to town on foot.

I follow the prints until they dry up. Unless the guy takes an unexpected detour, my house is the final destination.

At the border of woods and yard, I pause, afraid to rush out. I scan the yard. The only movement comes from the chickens, and they don't seem startled. The lights are off inside the house. Only Mama's truck is parked in my driveway. How long should I wait?

My grip tightens on the branch. With a deep breath, I crouch down and cross the yard—dodging from tree to tree like a total idiot. My heart pounds, and by the time I reach the stairs, I can barely catch my breath. Clumps of mud in the shape of footprints dirty the steps. They might be the same size as the boot prints I found in the woods. I climb the stairs. The creaks from the rotten wood sound like a train whistle, and I freeze. I'm one hop away from dashing back to the safety of the forest.

I drop to my knees. If anyone looks out the front window, I'll be invisible. I crawl up the last stair and roll onto the porch. The squeaky spots are easier to avoid as I slither snakelike on my belly to get to the new front door. Seeing it, shiny blue and unbroken, makes my stomach clench at the memory of the cracking sound the old door made when the rev and his men kicked it down and burst inside to drag Mama out.

I squeeze my eyes shut, choking back the memory.

The doorknob turns in my trembling hand, and my jaw clenches. Bessie said the door would be locked when she gave me the new key as we left the hospital. This whole scenario feels wrong on so many levels. I blow out a slow breath. The door swings open—silent, with only a draft of humid air preceding my entry. Muddy footprints track across the linoleum and end in the doorway leading into the living room. The mud is dry, unlike the ones in the woods. When were they made? They could be from the workers who installed the door. That's the most likely explanation.

I don't hear anyone moving around, but they could be hiding, waiting for me to get overconfident so they can sneak up on me from behind. I enter the living room with the branch raised, ready to swing. The only eyes staring back are Black Velvet Elvis Presley's. Wish he could talk. Tell me if the rest of the house is clear.

I check the kitchen then cross back through the living room to go down the hall to check the bathroom, leaving the last room…Mama's bedroom.

I pause in front of her closed door. I press my ear against the wood. Muted voices leak from beneath the door. My hand shakes as I reach for the doorknob, then with a scream to wake the dead, I throw open the door and run inside.

CHAPTER 9

LANDRY

Xena, Warrior Princess

A shadow blocks the morning sunlight streaming through the blinds. I crack open my swollen eyelid to see DA—short for Dumb Ass—Cready, the man who's trying to fry me for murder, standing over the bed with a Cheshire Cat grin on his face. A shiver of fear runs down my spine. *This can't be good.*

I tense, hands gripping the blanket. Time for the bomb to drop. The nurse said my injuries are healing. Is he sending me back to jail? Or did he really tell Mala he would drop the charges yesterday? My sketchy memories from the day before have more of the hazy shadows of a nightmare than reality, but I swear I couldn't have made up this one on my own.

Cready drops his briefcase on the end of the bed. He runs a long-fingered hand down the front of his gray, double-breasted, high-dollar suit, looking more like a loan shark than a prosecuting attorney. "I see you intend on playing the innocent victim role to the end," he says, flicking an imaginary piece of lint off his shoulder. His gaze rakes over me. "I admit it. You've won."

Ah, straight to the attack. The guy doesn't waste time.

I'm not exactly sure what he's implying, but I'm pretty sure I'm on trial. Better to plead the Fifth than fall into whatever trap he's laying for me. I pinch my lips together. Several minutes pass in silence. The tension builds. My jaw aches from clenching my teeth together. I'm seconds away from jumping out of my skin when he chuckles.

The sound raises the hairs on my neck. The crack in my will rebounds off the walls as I break first. "Get to the point," I snap.

"Surely Malaise LaCroix gave you the good news."

Yes! It wasn't a dream. "The news?"

"You're going to make me say it? Fine. I've spoken with the judge. The charges against you have been dropped. You're a free man."

"Are you serious?"

"Yes. As much as I hate to admit it." Cready takes a step back with a snort. "God, you disgust me! You, your father, the others involved in Jasmine LaCroix's murder. How can you even look her daughter in the eye, knowing what your father did? What you helped him do. You may have escaped justice for now, but I swear, I won't stop until I find the evidence to lock you away for the rest of your life."

Weariness fills me. "So, you still don't believe I'm innocent?"

"Why should I?"

"I told you what happened. I saved her. Doesn't that matter to anyone? I lost an eye. I almost got murdered in jail." I thrust upward, but the handcuff bites into my wrist. "Stop looking to me as your scapegoat and catch the ones involved. Rathbone, Acker, my dad—"

"Your dad? Oh, I'm very interested in finding Reverend Prince." He pauses to study me with narrowed eyes, then shakes his head. "Maybe you really are as stupid as you portray. Let me ask you a question, and I dare you to give me an honest answer."

I let out a heavy sigh. My head feels too heavy to hold up. I sag back onto the pillow and shut my eye. "Go ahead."

Thick, minty breath blows across my face. "Are you not curious about how dear old pa managed to escape?" Cready presses a heavy hand down on my shoulder when I try to rear up. His lips twist as he says "Don't you think the timing was impeccable? How *did* a man in a coma escape from the hospital without anyone seeing him?"

"I don't know," I whisper.

The hand on my shoulder tightens, and I wince.

"Come on, Landry. You know your father better than anyone else. What do you think happened?"

I lick my dry lips. My voice cracks as I say "Someone helped him."

Cready snaps his fingers. "Bingo. Give the man a prize." He steps away from the bed, tugging down his sleeves. "That would be my supposition too."

"It wasn't me," I say quickly. "I was already in custody."

"But you knew his plan. The reverend would never leave his only son to take the fall for him. No, he would have a contingency plan. He couldn't break you out of jail, but the hospital…He's done it before."

The silence between us stretches until I work out what Cready's implying. My breath catches then releases in a rush. "You think my dad set up my attack to get me out of jail?" I press against the pillow. On some level it makes sense, but…"You're wrong. Caleb didn't go for a minor injury just to get me admitted to the hospital. He tried to stab me through the heart. If I hadn't woken up and fought him off, I'd be dead."

"Now I can't seem to believe that."

"Ask my doctor…" *Calm down. Don't freak out now.* "Hell, ask the guard who used CPR. Maybe you can fake a coma, but you can't fake death. Whether you believe me or not, it's the truth."

Cready gives an elegant shrug. "Fine, I'll take you at your word. Your father had nothing to do with your attack. The truth is he killed Jasmine LaCroix. Do you think Mala's safe? She's out there right now. A target. Once your father and Rathbone get rid of her, who is left to testify against them in court? Mala's the only credible witness I've got."

"I'll testify. I was there."

"You? Nobody will believe a coward trying to save his own skin. I don't. But, son, you're missing the point of this conversation."

I shake my head, frustrated by the wordplay. "Say it so an idiot like me can understand."

"I'm saying Mala won't survive the week."

My insides implode in a burst of air. My chest heaves up and down. Shiny dots float in front of my eyes. I fumble for the nurse call button. Cready takes the cable from my trembling fingers and punches it for me.

Cold sweat runs down my back. I wrap my free arm across my chest, shivering. "Why are you telling me this?"

"Because maybe I'm wrong, and you're as innocent and naïve as you claim to be." Cready opens his briefcase and pulls out documents, a handcuff key, and a large plastic bag with my property from the jail. He tosses them onto the bed. "Landry, if you really do care for Mala, then prove it. Keep her safe until I can find the men involved."

* * *

The tricky bastard played me. The only way for me to prove I'm innocent of hurting Mala, whether I'm guilty or not, is by protecting her. Crazy, but slick.

Should I call her now?

No, first I need to get out of here before Cready changes his mind.

It hurts to move, but I crawl out of bed. I'm winded by the time I cross the room to the dresser. I lean against the wall, rest my forehead on my folded arms, and breathe through the pain in my chest. My dead eye throbs, and I'm tempted to gouge the good one out with a spoon because it hurts worse than the other. A milky film covers my vision, and I blink a few times. The mucus clears enough for me to search the drawers. The only clothing I find is the jail jumpsuit I was admitted in. I can't wander around downtown like an escaped convict.

"What are you doing out of bed?" a voice asks.

I turn, falling back against the wall. My hand presses against my chest. "Ouch…" Damn rubber hospital shoes are perfect for a stealth attack. Nurse Oliver wraps her arm around my shoulders. I don't protest as she helps me walk over to sit on the edge of the bed.

"Is there a reason why you're wandering around in your condition?" she asks.

I tip my chin toward the door. "The guard's not on the door anymore, is he?"

The woman's eyebrows flicker, but that's the only sign of unease she gives.

"The district attorney let me go," I say. "I'm getting out of here before he changes his mind."

Her heart-shaped lips tighten. "There's no need for that. Besides, the doctor won't release you until he's sure your wound won't get infected."

"I'm leaving…" I breathe through a sudden spurt of pain. "Yeah, I know it's not the smartest move, but I'm ready to go home. Just give me whatever papers I need to sign. I promise not to sue if I die."

Laughter like the tinkle of bells fill the air. "As long as you promise not to blame me." A wisp of blond hair falls from her bun to curl between the V-shaped mounds of her breasts as she shakes her head. "For the record, this is stupid."

Heat fills my cheeks as I tear my gaze away from her chest. "Yeah, I know. But I've got things to do. A girl I need to see."

"Ah, so now the real reason comes out." She walks toward the door, saying over her shoulder "Guess there's no point in arguing with a man in love."

In love…I scowl but can't refute the truth. I'm whipped. Still, my feelings for Mala don't matter. What's important is that I protect her this time, even if she hates me for not saving her mom.

Nurse Oliver returns about ten minutes later with a pair of jeans and a black T-shirt from their lost and found. I refuse her offer to help me shower, unable to hide the blush. Nancy Oliver isn't hard on the eyes. She's like the sexy *Playboy* bunny version of a nurse, minus the dowdy scrubs, and I've been locked up for too long for the fantasy version of my shower not to start running through my thoughts.

I need to get out of here.

I sign what needs to be signed, while pretending not to be in pain so the doctor doesn't give me grief about being released, wave good-bye to the people who saved my life, grab my pain medication and antibiotics from the pharmacy, and finally blow the joint. It's only the longest two hours of my life. The whole time I try to come up with a plan. I worry about being too late…too weak…too naive to save the girl who means more than my life.

How can Cready trust someone like me? Why doesn't he assign real police officers to guard her?

"We're bait on the hook," I whisper.

I stand outside the automatic doors and breathe in the warm air. I'm free. Only now that I'm outside, I'm frozen with indecision. Mala said she's staying at Bessie's house. At least I know she's safe for now. Bessie would bury someone under the jail if they tried to hurt her, including me.

My first priority is finding a phone and calling for a ride. The hospital is about two miles from my apartment, and I feel like shit. But who should I ask for help? I've got to keep Dena out of it. Cready doesn't suspect her or he would've brought her in already. None of my other friends visited me in jail. There's only one person other than Mala who I think cares enough, but I haven't talked to her in months. I have enough loose change for the phone booth.

Clarice answers after several rings. "Hello?"

"Clarice, it's Landry."

"Wh-who? Landry…" The pause stretches.

"I can hear you breathing."

She sighs. "Why are you calling me?"

"I need a ride."

"Oh, I…A ride? From jail?"

"No, I've been released from the hospital. I was injured then the district attorney dropped the charges"—I pause for a moment to swallow the lump in my throat—"isn't that great?"

Her voice quivers with false gaiety. "Sure. That's awesome. Fantastic. I'm so happy for you."

"Are you? Really? 'Cause you're my best friend and not once did you visit me in jail."

"I'm sorry, I've…my brother…he…"

"Hey, don't worry about it. I forgive you. I mean, what else could you think? The evidence looked pretty good. Solid enough to keep me locked up without bail. But I'm innocent, Clarice. I swear."

"Sure, Landry. I believe you. Where do you want me to—" A muffled voice in the distance comes over the line, then gets louder. "Red, wait. It's Landry."

"Asshole. Thought you were in jail—" Redford Delahoussaye barks into the phone.

I stiffen at the sound of his voice. "Thought you wouldn't still be a jerk after I kicked your ass."

He snorts. "I went easy on you 'cause Lainey died. Why are you calling my house?"

"I didn't have anyone else to call."

"Do you think I'd let my sister go anywhere near you?" His breathing roughens.

"Look, Red, we've had our differences, but I'm innocent. Even the district attorney dropped the charges against me. I can go home, but I don't have a ride. Clarice…"

The silence on the other end is deafening. I'm not sure when he hung up. I drop the phone in the cradle, not bothering to try to reach any of my other friends. I grew up with Clarice and Redford Delahoussaye. Our parents were best friends. If they don't believe me, nobody will.

It takes hours for me to walk from downtown to my apartment, only to find out from my landlord that it has been rented out to someone else. My asshole roommate kept the deposit and sold my stuff. My truck was impounded as evidence by the Sheriff's Office. No telling how long it'll take to get back. By the time I hike clear across town to the suburban neighborhood where my parents live, the sun has set. Across the street, the lights in Dad's church shine through the stained glass windows. It's Bible study night. Despite the warmth the church gives off, I bypass it and go straight home.

The key for the front door used to be hidden beneath a potted iris on the front porch, but both the iris and the key are missing. Not to worry, though. Dad's office window poses no problem to jimmy open. I don't bother with turning on the lights. I don't want anyone to know I'm here. After a quick shower, I'll figure out how to contact Mala. She said she's staying with Bessie. The detective doesn't like me, but I'll brave her wrath if I have to.

The house feels different. I'm not sure why. I navigate through the rooms in total darkness, reminded of all the times I sneaked out in high school. Only now nobody's here to catch me. I count the steps to the staircase, then each stair. At the top of the staircase, I turn toward my bedroom. I trail my fingertips across the wall. Another ten steps gets me to the door, and I push it open.

I reel back upon entering. The overpowering stench of fresh paint stings my nose. I flip on the light. Pale pink walls with white daisies decorate my once-blue walls. There's a white crib and changing table where my bed used to be. A huge stuffed tiger snarls at me from the center of the room.

"Where the hell am I?" I back out of the room.

A blood-freezing scream from the other end of the hallway causes me to turn around.

I see the bulky flash of a dark shadow behind me. Instinctively I twist sideways, and the punch he aimed at my face smashes into the wall. I'm trapped against the corner, unable to swing my arms back. My attacker aims a flurry of punches at my head that I somehow manage to block with my upraised forearm, then I lunge forward. My palms connect with his chest, and I shove him backward.

Finally I have enough space to counterattack, but the fucking coward dashes toward the staircase. I hear the heavy *thump* of footsteps going down. "Stop!" I yell, sprinting after him. The outline of the body looks familiar. I've seen him before…if I can just see his face…but the front door slams shut before I reach the staircase.

The *whoosh* of an object moving through the air is punctuated by a high-pitched shriek from the doorway of the bathroom, and I jerk my head back. A toilet plunger misses my face with only inches to spare. The stink of toilet water fills my nose. My arm rises to protect my good eye as a naked pregnant woman brings back her arm and swings at me again with an eardrum-piercing battle cry.

CHAPTER 10

MALA

Murderous Cur

I burst into the bedroom swinging the branch. A woman standing by the bed leaps back. I try to stop the swing, but it's too late. The end of the branch passes from the left side of her skull to exit out of the right.

The force of the swing spins me around, and I stumble. My elbow smacks against the wall, and my arm goes numb. "Ow!" I cradle my elbow.

"Malaise Jean LaCroix, you tried to brain me!"

"Damn it, Mama." My knees get wobbly, and I stagger over to flop on the edge of the bed. "You scared me half to death. Are you okay?"

"Course I'm not okay. I'm dead!" She shifts her glare from me to the flickering television screen.

"What are you doing here?"

"It's my house."

"But you were at the hospital. How did you get here?"

"Hush up, I'm tryin' to get caught up on the worldly happenin's." She scowls at the news anchor, and my attention shifts from her to the news report.

A picture of Gloria Pearson with the words MISSING fill the tiny screen, and I suck in a breath. "Hey, Mama, that's Spooky Poca, the ghost nurse that keeps haunting me."

Mama glances in my direction. "Ah, I thought she looked familiar."

I blink, and when my eyes open, Mama's gone. "Wait. Come back."

Double damn and blast. She's as squirrely now as when she was alive. Keeping her in one place would take an act of Congress. I stretch out across the bed and lay my aching arm across my stomach. I wanted to ask her about Gloria. Mama spent the last month making friends with the more coherent ghosts in the hospital. Since she's an ancestor spirit, like Uncle Gaston, she's not as stone crazy as some of the other ghosts.

The walls pulse, and I sit up with a shriek.

"Calm yourself," Gaston says, appearing in the middle of the room.

I squeeze my eyes shut and drag in a deep breath. God, I'm freaked. I run shaky fingers across my eyelids, then look at my uncle. I've gotten used to his burned features. Now he's beautiful to me. If I could throw myself in his arms, I would. I'm that happy to see him. "Uncle Gaston, you sure know how to make a dramatic entrance. I didn't know you were here too."

"We're tied to you, *cher*," Mama says, walking into the room through the outside wall. "We go where you go."

"So, if I go to the Piggly Wiggly, so do you?"

"I prefer to only come when you need real assistance. Not help you decide what snack cakes to buy," Gaston says.

Okay, I guess that makes sense. I glance at the TV again, but the weatherman's moved on to forecasting another storm blowing in tonight. "Well, I'm glad you're both here. I wanted to ask you about a spirit who's haunting me, Gloria Pearson. She vanished the same night Reverend Prince disappeared from the hospital. Do either of you know anything about that?"

Gaston squats down. He cradles his rifle across his lap. "We were all a little busy that night."

Oh, yeah, I forgot. Reverend Prince escaped the same night Lainey possessed me and got her mother to confess to her murder. If not for Gaston, I might never have gotten my body back. He's a powerful...ugh, warlock? "How *did* you keep her from stealing my body for good?"

"We can discuss that some other time. For now, let's focus on this ghost. You say she's haunting you?"

"She came to me a couple of times at the hospital. She's strong and sorta mean." I toss my braid over my shoulder with a huff. "She went all vengeful on me. If she'd asked nicely, I probably would've helped her out like I did Ms. Anne. Instead she showed me some wickedly frightening images."

Mama shrugs. "Don't worry about it. Me and Uncle Gaston won't let her come after you no more."

Gaston has vanished. He's a man of few words.

Mama stares pensively at the television screen. "If you're done watchin' the news, I'd like to see somethin' more entertainin'."

I stretch back out on the bed and wave my hand. "Go ahead. I'm beat." My eyes flutter closed.

"You'll have to work the remote for me."

I frown at Mama. "Why can't you turn channels yourself?"

Mama waves a hand through the television screen.

I roll back over to the nightstand for the remote and flip through the channels. "How about *My Swamp Wedding*?"

"If I wanted to watch a bunch of hicks gettin' married, I'd haunt the church. Look, a *Sex in the City* marathon. Hold it here, please."

Carrie's legs fill the screen, and I close my eyes again. My mind drifts. I'm tempted to pop over to the hospital and check on Landry, but knowing he can see me now when I'm incorporeal kind of puts a damper on my astral stalking. My cheeks heat. Honestly I spent way too much time at the jail. I blame it on boredom while locked in the mental ward, but part of me acknowledges the truth. I worried about him.

Guilt makes my stomach burn.

Why didn't I ever pop in on George? He was supposed to be my boyfriend, but not once did I go to his apartment. If I had, I would've known Isabel lives with him. And I wouldn't feel like my heart has been shredded in a meat grinder.

"Mala, I can't handle these silly women. Turn channels for me again."

I grab the pillow and stuff my head under it with a deep groan. Ghost Mama's going to drive me stark raving mad if I have to become her obedient servant and "Yes, Mama" every little thing now that she's dead.

Time to make some rules.

I punch the pillow and sit up. "This is the last time. I'm going to sleep so make sure the channel is on something you want to watch for a good eight hours."

Her smile erases the building anger. As annoyed as I sometimes feel about seeing ghosts, I can't deny how lucky I am not to have lost Mama. Having proof of an afterlife makes me less afraid of my own death.

The remote lands on the bed, and I lie back down. "Hey, Mama." I roll onto my side to face her. "Something just dawned on me."

"Well, spit it out. I'm not getting' any younger."

"Not getting older either," I mutter, rubbing my eyes, then glare at the remote. "If you can't even work the remote…how did you turn on the TV?"

* * *

I run through the house, locking all of the doors and windows. Mama said the television was already on when she popped inside. How long it had been on, I can't speculate. Maybe Maggie or Tommy forgot to turn it off the last time they came to take care of the chickens. Or I got lucky. The Goldilocks who has been living in my house, sleeping in my bed, and eating my food left before I arrived.

I'm up at the crack of dawn, exhausted and cranky from tossing and turning most of the night. When I finally fell asleep, I dreamed about Reverend Prince breaking down my new blue door. I don't know if the dream was a premonition of danger, but I'm heeding its warning and carrying my gutting knife as I do my chores. If anyone messes with me, I'll treat them like I do catfish.

My friends did a good job of caring for my place while I was gone. I can't blame them for the massacre I find in the coop. Dead birds and bloodstained feathers litter the ground. I'd forgotten to padlock the door before crashing last night, and the smart old tom took advantage. That raccoon and I have battled for years. And he's outwitted me again at my chickens' expense.

I spend most of the morning cleaning up the mess and plucking feathers. The afternoon is spent cooking a huge pot of chicken gumbo. Half of the soup goes into the refrigerator. The rest goes in the deep freezer with the other two chickens.

The ringing phone catches me while I'm getting ready to curl up on the sofa and watch TV before bed. "Why didn't you call to tell me you got home safely?" Bessie demands the moment I say hello.

My hand tightens around the phone. "Didn't George say I made it home?"

"He did. He also said he did a walkthrough of the house. That's the only reason I didn't come out to check on you."

Thank God for my stepbrother's sudden aversion to honesty. Just thinking about him makes me furious, and I take it out on Bessie. "Well, I'm fine. Thank you for asking."

"Are you getting smart with me?"

"No, ma'am. I spent the day dealing with a bunch of dead chickens because I forgot to padlock the coop, so I'm just not in the mood for a lecture."

The line goes quiet but for the sound of breathing. "Are you still there?" I ask.

"I'm here."

"I'm sorry I didn't call."

"You really think you should be staying out there alone?"

I glance around the room. "I've lived here my whole life. I'm not moving, and you've done a great job of cleaning up the damage from…" *Mama's murder.* I squeeze my eyes shut and blow out a huge breath. *Don't think about it. Mama's still with you. It's okay.* "I know you wanted me to stay with you, Bessie, but I can't deal with a bunch of drama right now. And Maggie and Tommy's wedding is chaos in the making."

"Maybe I can move in with you." Her voice takes on a plaintive tone, and I laugh.

"Is Maggie driving you crazy already?"

"She wants to get married before school starts. One month, Mala. How am I supposed to arrange a church wedding in such a short amount of time?"

We talk wedding plans for another hour. At the end of our conversation, she's calmer, less likely to take her anger out on the general public while on duty. I put the phone down, but two seconds later it rings. I don't recognize the number. It had better not be a telemarketer or I'll jump through the phone and choke them out.

"What?" I snap.

"I need you."

My thumb hovers above the off button when I recognize the voice. Heat enters my cheeks. "I'm not sure how I should feel about those words, Landry."

"Take them in the spirit in which they are offered. I need you to pick me up."

"Oh, damn. I thought they were meant in a completely different way, but I guess I can go with this." I pull my tennis shoes out from beneath the coffee table and put them on. "You're being released from the hospital today?" The line goes quiet, and I panic. "Landry?"

His voice sounds weary as he says, "No, I got out this morning. I'm at my parents' place. Or what used to be their house. Turns out Dad's church owns the house. And they moved the new preacher and his family in."

"What about your stuff?"

"The preacher's wife, Molly, boxed it up and stored it in the leaky-ass shed. What didn't get trashed by animals or destroyed by the weather, I'll be using as a makeshift bed tonight."

A rush of anger flows through me. What kind of preacher

lets another person's property be destroyed? The least they could've done was put it somewhere safe. I pinch the bridge of my nose, trying to calm down. Anger won't help Landry feel better.

"Is that why you're calling me?" I tease. "You're trying to make me feel sympathetic so I'll offer you a place to stay?"

"No! No, I'd never ask...not with you thinking I murdered your mother and all."

I sigh. "Now you're feeling ridiculously sorry for yourself. I know you didn't kill Mama."

"Yeah, well, Molly doesn't feel the same. She threatened to have me arrested for trespassing if I didn't get off of her property. Course, part of her anger might have to do with me seeing her naked."

"Naked! What the hell, Landry?"

"Yeah, I'll tell you the story later. It's pretty messed up, but if anyone can find the humor in it, you can."

I bite back a curse. "Where are you?"

"I brought the boxes to the church's parking lot." His voice lowers. "There's a lot of people here, Mala. They're all standing around watching me."

My heart stutters. A sudden burst of fear for his safety rushes through me. "I'll be there soon." I clutch the phone and search for the keys to Mama's truck. "Stay safe, Landry."

* * *

Of all nights for Landry to camp out in the church parking lot, Bible Study Wednesday has got to be the worst. Parishioners cluster around their cars, gawking at Landry, who sits on a pile of boxes. His head hangs, and his shoulders hunch forward. Long bangs in dire need of a trim fall over his eyes. My breath catches at how incredibly sexy he looks…and sad.

That man's in serious need of a hug.

I park as close as possible to where he sits on the lawn. I still have to force my way through the crowd to reach him. Part of me fears they'll turn their insults on me, and I force my shoulders back and my chin up. *Don't show weakness, Mala.*

Displays of fear only empower bullies, and I won't give anyone the satisfaction. Landry has a lot to learn about being a pariah in this town. Hopefully he won't have to learn the hard way. People begin to shout condolences as I pass by.

A hand pats my shoulder, and I flinch. "Sorry about your mom," an unrecognizable voice says.

What's going on?

"Glad to see you, Mala dear," Mable Grant calls with a grin, showing a toothless mouth while waving a lace handkerchief in my direction, and I almost pass out. My old elementary school teacher used to swat my bottom whenever I got answers wrong. She hated me.

Now I'm being welcomed to church. Did I slip into bizarro dimension again?

A clean-cut man in a steel gray suit thrusts himself in my path. He must be the new reverend. He has that shiny, wholesome look of a young clergyman who is now responsible for the souls of a traumatized congregation.

His eyes seem kind of wild. "Child, have you come to join us today?"

I give my most feral grin and point to Landry. "Nope, I'm here for that murderous cur sitting over there."

The reverend takes a jerky step backward. "Surely you're not here to exact retribution?"

Retribution. Nice word. I'd like to do some good, old-fashioned smiting on this lot of hypocrites. "Retribution is needed for the evil deed he committed when he *saved my life.*" I wave to Landry. "Come. Let us go live in sin."

Landry flashes me a lecherous grin. He does those so well that my tummy flutters. I'm mightily impressed. "Thanks," he says.

The reverend blinks. I guess my over-the-top derision finally penetrates his fear of an all-out brawl between me and Landry on the church lawn. He frowns and shakes his head. "Are you sure you want him to go with you?"

Several folks in the crowd echo his question. I turn to the circle of people and take in their hostile expressions. I've been holding on to my anger pretty well, I think, but the judgment and condemnation in their eyes does me in.

Not like I've ever excelled at holding my tongue anyway. "What's wrong with you people? Most of you have known Landry his whole life. You sat in service with him, supported him at football games, and had him visit in your houses. I know you must feel betrayed by the actions of his parents"—I turn my gaze from face to face in the group, and eyes drop one by one—"but Landry saved my life. He ran into my burning house to rescue me and lost an eye in the process. He went to jail for a crime he didn't commit. Please don't hold the actions of his parents against him."

The Borg Collective pauses for a moment, and I hold my breath. Will they listen? Or will the mob mentality escalate this into something far worse? I subtly check for an escape route. In five big steps, I can reach Landry, and then we'll sprint for the truck.

"She's right," the reverend says, and everyone's eyes land on him. They're listening to him with an intensity they didn't have when I spoke. They respect him despite his youthful appearance. He turns to face Landry, and I relax my stance. "Landry, I'm ashamed of my behavior. I shouldn't have let my emotions get the better of me. Will you accept my apology?"

"Thank you," Landry says simply, but his voice chokes with emotion. That in itself influences the rest of the crowd. Sympathy and guilt fill their expressions. A few others shout apologies as the group disperses, heading into the sanctuary.

The reverend stays. "They're good people," he says. "We were all thrown after what happened. It's hard to believe a man of the cloth..." He shakes his head. "I'll help load the boxes into your truck. Let me know if anything's missing."

Guess he's not planning on inviting Landry to stay in his home.

He turns to me and holds out his hand. "I'm Reverend Shane Williams."

"Mala LaCroix," I say, shaking his hand.

Landry comes to stand so close our shoulders brush, and a shiver runs down my spine. I want to reach out for his hand, but I'm too embarrassed. I'm kind of afraid of this quieter, more sober Landry. "Tell Molly I'm sorry for intruding," he says to Reverend Shane. "I didn't mean to startle her. I didn't know you'd moved..."

Shane claps a hand on Landry's shoulder. "No, you have no reason to apologize. Molly should've handled it better. The pregnancy has her a little high strung."

I stiffen. "Pregnancy hormones don't make women irrational. You should be proud of how your wife handled herself."

Landry's arm wraps around my shoulder. "Yeah, Mala would've done the same thing. At least Molly stopped attacking me once she figured out why I was there."

Shane frowns. "Still—"

I pull Landry's arm down. "I'll start loading the truck. It was nice to meet you, Reverend Shane."

After loading one of the cardboard boxes into the back of the truck, I slide onto the driver's seat and wait for the men to finish. I watch through the mirror as Landry shakes hands with Shane. He slides into the passenger seat with a huge sigh.

A comfortable silence settles between us as I pull onto the road, instinctively heading home, then I glance at Landry. "So where do you want me to drop you off?"

He shrugs. "The park…"

"You're messing with me now, right?"

"I wish, Mala. I don't have any money. I don't have a house. My relatives are either dead, in jail, or on the run from the law. What do you think I should do? I almost wish I was still in jail. At least there I had a cot and three meals a day."

"And some freak who shanked you."

He shrugs again. "Rumors about a hit had been floating around for weeks. I just didn't think Caleb would be the one to take the bait. I thought we got along fine."

"You're crazy. Didn't you see the way he watched you while you showered?" I gulp, patting my lips with my fingertips. I glance at him from the corner of my eye. Did he catch the shower part?

He's grinning. "*So*," he draws out the word, "you were watching me in the shower?"

Crap!

"Whoa. Why would I want to see you naked?" I wave my hand in front of my burning cheeks.

"Oh, so you don't know where my mole…"

My gaze drops to his butt, then back to the road. The heat in my face intensifies. I flip the vent in my direction. Cold air slaps me across the face. "No comment."

He chuckles.

"Back to the original topic of where to drop you off, I take it you meant Paradise Park?" I glance at him with a sly grin. "I bet crazy Junebug will let you move into her cardboard-box apartment."

He tips his head back onto the headrest and closes his eye. Huh? Does he think I won't drop him off there? Is he that confident that I'll take care of him?

A day's growth of beard covers his cheeks. Even in the dimming light, the knife scar that bisects his left eyebrow looks red and inflamed, not having had time to fade. I study the eye patch. "Can you see anything out of your eye?"

His mouth hangs open slightly. Snores fill the cabin.

"I'm sorry for hurting you," I whisper. "Will you forgive me? If it wasn't for me you wouldn't have been in jail. You wouldn't have died."

The truck hits a rut. I grip the wheel with both hands and pay more attention to the road leading out of town. I'm glad I'm not going back home alone. I swear someone was living there. I've had a lot of time to sift through the clues I didn't notice last night—the unfamiliar, musky scent in the air, the rumpled bedding, and the food in the refrigerator. Why would Bessie restock the fridge if I was staying with her?

I had a squatter. I don't know how long the person had been staying there or if he or she had moved on, but having Landry around will make me feel a lot safer.

I park in front of my darkened house. I forgot to turn on the porch light when I left. I open the door to light up the cab. "We're here. Wake up."

Landry twists with a full-body stretch. Muscles flex and ripple, and my mouth dries. When he sees me, he smiles just long enough for my heart rate to speed as heat rushes into my face, then the brightness in his silver gaze darkens.

He opens the passenger door and climbs out, then sticks his head back into the cab. "Why did you bring me home? Won't you feel uncomfortable?"

I lick my lips. "You can either sleep on the new sofa or on the back porch in the hammock." *Or in my bed.*

"I don't know—"

"I'm afraid of living here alone. Okay?" I climb from the truck and slam the door before he can respond. I'm suddenly terrified. What if he can't handle staying here?

I stride to the back of the truck and drop the tailgate. "If you've got a problem staying with me, just say so."

"Did I say anything?"

"No."

Landry squints in my direction. He places one hand on the rim of the truck bed as he walks. "It's just…how can you even stay in this house after what happened?" He edges me aside and stretches for one of the cardboard boxes holding his belongings. "Aren't you worried about this place being haunted after what happened?"

"So far I haven't found a place that *isn't* haunted. This is my ancestral home. The only spirits here are my family, since only LaCroixes have lived and died on this land since the 1850s." I shake my head, eyeing the woman sitting in the rocking chair on the porch. "'Sides, Mama will kill me if I sell this place and move to town."

Landry follows my gaze and drops the box.

"Are you okay?"

He squeezes his eye shut. "I'm fine."

"What's he doing here?" Mama stomps down the stairs. "Thought you and Georgie Porgie got a thin' goin'. What with all the kissy face at the hospital, he's not gonna be happy."

"Kissing? George…" Landry turns in my direction.

I shove him toward the house. "Uh, why don't you go inside?"

Mama's open mouth closes with a snap. "Does he see me?"

I pick the box up off the ground and push it into his arms. "Go on."

Mama walks around me and waves her hand in front of his eye. "He can see me?"

Landry swats her hand out of his face. His arm passes right through her, and he groans. "I'm insane."

"Holy crap! How did this happen, Mala Jean? He got a batch of LaCroix blood in him I don't know about?"

I shake my head. "Plenty of people who aren't LaCroixes see spirits, Mama. I think it happened because he died."

Landry stumbles up the steps and falls into a rocking chair. "I don't feel too good. My head hurts."

Mama sits in the chair next to him. "My head's a little wobbly too, but I got an excuse seein' as how I'm dead. Damn, I could use a drink right about now." She leans forward, and Landry shivers. "Do you really see me? Hear me?"

Landry spares me a quick glance, then nods. "Ever since I woke up in the hospital."

"Yeah, he died. And there was this black whirlpool thingy that tried to suck Landry inside. This black stuff oozed onto his skin, burning into him. What do you think it could be?"

Mama smoothes her nightgown down over her lap. "How would I know?"

Oh, she infuriates me! "You've been dead for over a month now,

Mama. Haven't you learned anything about how the other side works?"

Landry reaches toward her, then stops. "Anything you can find out will help, ma'am. Please."

"Well, you know I'm not much for studyin'." Her dark eyes flick up to meet Landry's, and she shrugs. "Maybe Mala's Uncle Gaston knows."

"Is he here?" He reaches out again. This time his hand passes through her arm, and he shudders. The hairs in his goose bumps stand at attention.

Mama shrugs. "He's around."

"What do you think the black stuff could be?" I ask.

"Maybe he soaked up some evil from the other side and got a demon ridin' around inside him. Best sleep with one eye open."

"I only have one eye," Landry says.

"I was talkin' to my daughter."

CHAPTER 11

LANDRY

Goldilocks and Gumbo

Aftuer adjusting to the shock of Ms. Jasmine being not alive but still kicking, Mala and I head to the truck to finish unloading my stuff. I drag a box labeled CLOTHES from the truck and drop it on the ground. No crunching noises come from inside from anything breakable. My head tips to the side, and my gaze slides back to the woman sitting in the rocker next to Mala.

I see dead people.

I used to love that line. It's not so hilarious now that it applies to me. I've seen two ghosts. The first scared the shit out of me. Ms. Jasmine creeps me out. She looks so alive that she crackles with energy. Like I could touch her if I want, but whenever I try, a biting cold settles in my bones. My finger joints still ache as if a thunderstorm heads in my direction.

"I'm certifiable," I mumble, shaking the cobwebs out of my head and setting off rockets instead. Pain explodes behind my damaged eye and radiates outward through the back of my skull. My vision swims, and I lean forward with a groan. It hurts less with my good eye closed. For the moment, I welcome the darkness.

I hold on to the edge of the tailgate with both hands. The metal bites into my palms. It's the only thing keeping me from falling over. I breathe in through my nose and exhale. After doing this a few times, the ache dulls enough for me to open my eye.

Mala stands hunched over, peering into my face. The tip of her nose brushes the tip of mine. I rear back, tripping over the box I'd set on the ground. She grabs my arm, steadying me before I fall flat on my ass.

"Are you okay?" She wiggles her eyebrows in that funny way she has of trying to make me smile. I'm not sure if she knows she's doing it or if she does it on purpose. Either way, it works 'cause I want to make her smile in return.

"I'm fine," I lie with an easy grin.

"Are you sure?" Her fingers tighten around my bicep.

I place my hand on top of hers. "Is this an excuse to feel me up? I know you like my muscles."

Her face turns pink. *Got her!*

She jerks her hand free and shoves it into the pocket of her ratty jeans. Her nose crinkles. "You wish." She waves her hand toward the boxes. "How about if you get what you need for tonight and bring the rest inside in the morning?"

Her dark eyes meet mine again. "What?" she asks.

"I didn't say anything."

"I know. That's what's making me nervous." Her lips purse. "You know you're sleeping in my bedroom, right?" She clears her throat and rocks back on her heels. "I mean my *old* bedroom. Alone. I'll sleep in Mama's room. Although my bed sucks, literally. It's got a giant hole in the middle of the mattress."

I grin and tip my chin toward the house. "I'll sleep on the sofa. Your mama would kill me if I slept in your bed, even without you in it. She's already giving me the stink-eye."

"That's just how she looks when she's craving a drink." Mala shrugs. "At least now I don't have to worry about her stumbling home drunk."

The sadness underlying her tone makes me wince, but Mala doesn't notice. I've got to be careful she doesn't. I don't want to give her another thing to feel guilty about. I pretended to be asleep during the drive. Her apology almost broke me. I owe her more than I can ever repay in this lifetime, and the only way to do that is if I stay by her side.

I slam the tailgate closed.

Mala shuffles impatiently at my side. When she catches me watching, she says, "Hurry, I have to pee."

"Charming."

She laughs, tickled by my response. The girl's got no shame, at least when dealing with me.

That's it, Landry. Keep it light. Fun.

I can't afford to scare her off.

Truth, though, I'm not sure how long I can keep it together. I've been teetering on the edge of a complete breakdown since I woke up in the hospital. I thought the pain in my damaged eye had been intense. It's nothing compared to the constant burning beneath the surface of my skin that I've felt since I "died." Ms. Jasmine's idea about a demon hitching a riding makes me nervous as hell 'cause it feels like the truth.

I follow Mala into the house, carrying the box containing my clothing. I drop it in the middle of the new, blue sofa. The first time I ever saw this room had been the night Ms. Jasmine got dragged out. She fought so hard, kicking and scratching. I thought for sure there'd be damage to the place. *I should've helped her.* "Other than the sofa, it doesn't look different."

Mala pauses.

"I didn't mean to say that." I run my fingers through my sweaty hair, shoving it back.

Her gaze focuses on the eye patch, then darts away. "It's okay. I thought the same thing when I came home. Bessie, Maggie, and Tommy cleaned the place for me. Had the curtains and undamaged throw pillows cleaned to get out the smoky smell."

Self-conscious, I shake my head. Black bangs fall to brush the tip of my nose. I tilt my head sideways so the hair only covers the left side of my face. My chest tightens again. *Remember to breathe.*

I pace the tiny room, studying the porcelain statues on the shelves. The velvet Elvis's blue-eyed stare follows me censoriously around the room, and I feel the sudden urge to apologize to the man of the house.

I grunt. "Has Elvis ever talked to you?"

"Are you asking if I'm crazy?" Mala hustles into the kitchen.

I follow after I get over the shock, focusing on the switch in her perky little ass. Damn, she looks hot in those tight jeans. My mouth opens to comment on just how good she looks, but I catch myself before I insert fat-shoe-in-mouth and clamp my lips shut. *Don't scare her or she'll kick your ass out.*

I trip over a peeled-up strip of sea green linoleum and grab for the edge of the counter. Losing an eye screwed up my depth perception. I misjudge the distance and end up going down on one knee. I bite back the curse and push upright, breathing hard.

Mala turns with a frown. "What are you doing?"

"Uh, nothing…"

"Then stop hovering behind me and sit down." She waves toward the table. "You're making me nervous."

"Sorry," I mumble, taking a seat. I try not to watch as she pulls a Tupperware bowl from the refrigerator and pops it in the microwave, but I can't stop. She hits the buttons with quick jabs. Her hips rock back and forth as if she dances to a song I can't hear—hypnotic sways, graceful and efficient.

My mouth goes dry, and I lick my lips.

"You like gumbo, don't you?" She turns her back to the counter and crosses her arms over her breasts. I drag my gaze up to meet hers. She's scowling…so busted.

"Huh." I blink at her.

She points at the bowl and says, like she's speaking to a toddler, "Gum-*bo*, you like?"

"Yeah, me like." My lips quirk, and she grins back. Crisis averted for the moment. How long of a reprieve I get depends on whether I can get my raging hormones under control. A month in lockup messed with my self-discipline. More likely, it's just being close enough to touch Mala that's got me horny.

"Cool, 'cause there's a lot." The microwave beeps. She pulls out the bowl and sets it on the counter. Her head tilts as she studies it with a frown. "A raccoon got in my chicken coop this morning."

"Do you think it's a good idea to eat chicken killed by a raccoon? What about rabies?"

Her nose scrunches up again. She pops the lid on the heated soup and steam rises into the air. My mouth waters, and my stomach punches me. I get the message—shut up.

She gives it a test sniff. "Smells fine to me. Plus I ate some for lunch so I'm already infected."

"Boiling it probably killed any virus." I hold out my hands.

She sets the bowl on the table. "Careful, it's hot."

"Thanks." I take a bite. *Good God, the girl can cook!*

She stands over me for a long minute. "Well?"

"Delish, no poisony aftertaste." I make the OK sign with my index finger and thumb, then shoo her off.

"I hate you." She stomps back into the living room.

The spoon slips from my fingers, splattering hot soup onto the table. I'm stunned by how much those words hurt. It takes a long moment for my heart to slow enough to consider them in the context in which they were given. Why they bothered me in the first place doesn't make a lick of sense. Not like she hasn't said those words in the same grumpy tone before. I know they're not true. That she's teasing me.

Maybe the difference is that this time they should be true.

* * *

Mala fixed up the sofa with sheets and blankets while I ate. She has me change into a pair of sweats, then practically forces me beneath the covers. She settles on the end by my feet, wrapping her legs up beneath her until she forms a tiny ball.

She rubs her hands together. "They show *Star Trek Next Gen.* episodes every night. I'm on season three."

"Ah, the Borg."

"Uh-huh." She grins. "Wish we had popcorn."

"Then it'd be a real date."

Her cheeks pink, but she rolls her eyes. "You're in no condition to handle a date with me. Maybe after you've healed up so I won't break you."

"Mala Jean..." Ms. Jasmine hisses, popping into the room like a vengeful sprite, and I lean back into the sofa. "Watch your language."

Mala looks like she wants to disappear. She glances at me then curls even more into herself. Guilt makes her eyes dart around the room. It reminds me of my promise to keep my distance. It's so easy to fall back into old patterns.

Ms. Jasmine filled me with a healthy dose of caution before she died, but her ghost downright terrifies me. I'd be a fool not to heed her warning. "Sorry, Ms. Jasmine," I say.

She scowls at me and shakes her head. "Not sure I like you stayin' here, but long as you do, you'd better behave. I'll be keepin' my eyes on you."

Mala gasps. "Mama, he didn't do anything wrong. Neither did I."

Ms. Jasmine gives an unladylike snort and vanishes. A flash of her white nightgown passes the front window as she takes up position in the rocking chair on the porch. I take the remote and turn up the sound, deterring any further conversation.

We end up watching a couple of episodes. My injuries ache now that I've stopped moving. Locutus of Borg shows up prepared to assimilate when I fade, unable to fight off exhaustion. A shadow settles over my face, and I crack my lid enough to find Mala's boobs in my line of sight. Her scent fills my nose, and I stifle a groan so she doesn't hear. My hands clench into fists to keep from pulling her on top of me. I want to bury my face in her chest and inhale. If I could sleep like that every night, I'd die happy.

I squeeze my eye shut. She pulls the blanket up around my neck. I expect her to leave, but she doesn't. I peek up at her. She's staring at me with an expression—not sure I'm reading it right, but warmth spreads out from my center. She's never looked so...

Soft. Her head lowers, and she brushes her lips across my forehead.

I sink into the cushions, totally relaxed for the first time in months. After getting a kiss like the one she just gave, I don't have to worry about Mala shanking me. I'm finally safe.

Voices drone in the background.

Then silence.

The house settles. It breathes.

It screams—"Wake up!"

I'm off the couch and halfway across the living room before full awareness hits. The sense of invasion makes my body tingle. A noise comes from the kitchen, the clank of bottles scraping across shelves in the refrigerator and liquid sloshing. My first instinct says to yell, but I don't want to scare Mala if she's getting a late-night snack.

But why would she roam around with the lights off? And why would I feel such a heavy sense of dread? Moonlight shines into the dark room, casting crazy, puppet shadows on the walls. I turn fully around, checking the room to be sure nobody's sneaking up on my blind side, then I pull a fat stick out of the umbrella stand. The wooden floor creaks with each step. I wait for the intruder to be alerted to my presence, but the sounds continue.

At the entrance to the kitchen, I pause. I form a mental map in my mind. The table and four chairs are on the left side. Immediately to the right is a counter and the refrigerator. I take a deep breath and swing around the corner, stick raised. The light from the fridge makes me squint, so the full bowl of gumbo thrown in my face doesn't soak my eye, but a good portion of the soup washes in. I fall back, screaming. My back hits the wall, and I slide down it.

My eye burns so badly, I want to throw up. It hurts like my left eye did when I got stabbed.

Oh, God. What if I'm blind?

I need to wash it out, but don't know where I've fallen in relation to the sink. Is it on my left or right? I feel up the cabinet and grip the ledge.

A heavy hand settles on my shoulder, pushing me back down.

"Mala, my eye." I try to stand again. "I can't see."

"Calm yourself." The gruff voice freezes me. "You're not blind, boy. Got a bit of cayenne pepper in your eye, is all. Wash it out, and you'll be fine."

"No! You can't be here." I grab for the hand, but it moves.

"I owe a debt. Don't go interfering while I pay it."

A chill races through me. I blink repeatedly. Tears stream down my cheek, washing my eye enough for me to see my father's blurry face above me. My hands shoot out, grabbing him by the throat as I launch forward. He falls onto his back, and I crawl up to straddle him. His fist connects with my cheek. My head snaps back.

He shoves his forearm beneath my chin and pushes me off.

I grab for his pant legs. My nails grip the seam on his jeans, but he jerks his leg free. Footsteps clump across the floor, then the back door slams against the wall. I run after him. It's dark on the screened-in porch. The steps loom in front of me, and I stagger, unable to catch myself as I topple forward. The air whooshes out of my lungs when I smash into the ground. Pain flares through every part of my body, and everything goes dark.

CHAPTER 12

MALA

Dropped the Bomb

I prop my elbows on the edge of the sofa and stare down at the side of Landry's sleeping face. He's lying on his stomach with one leg and arm trailing on the floor. The blanket's twisted around his hips. I don't know how he managed to tangle himself up. My fingers twitch with the temptation to straighten it and get him all tucked in again, but I might wake him. My daring last night still shocks me. He looked so peaceful that I couldn't stop myself from kissing him.

My lips tingled for most of the night. I tossed and turned for hours before finally crashing. I didn't wake up once, and usually I do a couple of times in the night, especially since Mama…anyway, I slept like a log.

If I hurry, I can get breakfast ready before he wakes up.

I enter the kitchen, and the smile flickering on my lips fades. The pot I used for the gumbo is sitting upside down in my drying rack. There had been half a pot left when I went to bed. I know guys eat a lot, but damn. I need to hit the store and stock up on supplies pretty soon or we'll starve to death. Which leads to another problem—where am I gonna get money? I have a few thousand in savings at the bank, but the money won't last long without Mama's income to help with the bills. I've already lost my clerical position at Bertrand Parish Sheriff's Office, but I should be good at Munchies Diner & Ice Cream Parlor. My new aunt wouldn't fire me, I hope. I'm screwed if she does.

I feed the remaining chickens and gather eggs, then go inside to cook breakfast. I don't know what Landry likes, but I figure I can't go wrong with bacon and scrambled eggs. I was surprised to find the package of bacon in the fridge yesterday. It isn't something I buy for myself, or any of the other weird items stocked in the pantry, since they're so expensive. I guess this kind of food is what I get when Tommy and Maggie go shopping for me: bacon, baloney, processed cheese, and Tater Tots.

Good grief, who eats Tater Tots outside of school cafeterias?

Landry stumbles into the kitchen as I set his plate on the table. His face has a puffy, unhealthy cast to it. The bruise on his cheek looks darker today than it did yesterday, and he hobbles like an arthritic old man. He crumples into the seat and rests his head in his hands.

"How are you feeling today, Frog Prince?" I fight the welling sympathy urging me to kiss him again and plunk a glass of orange juice on the table. He grunts.

"That good, huh?" I dish up my own plate and sit down across from him. The first bite of bacon rolls my eyes up in the back of my head. *So good.*

"I've got something to tell you," Landry says, looking up. "Last night I—"

"Ate all my gumbo, I know. Saints, boy. Do you know how many hours it took to make that? You'll have to find a job if you want to stay here. I can't afford to support you if you're gonna be eating me out of hearth and home."

"Huh? No. That's not—"

"It's what I'm talking about," I interrupt, giving him the stink-eye. "M-O-N-E-Y. Don't think you get to live off me like I'm some sugar daddy."

"You're a girl, no daddy plumbing involved."

"Eww, don't make me throw up my bacon." I stuff the last strip in my mouth and lick my greasy lips.

His eye focuses on my mouth, and my breath catches. *Crap, I'm thinking about kissing him again.* If he leans across the table…*No, no, Mala Jean. It's too soon.* It's just that I missed him. And I can't believe he's within touching distance, and still staring…*Oh God!* I stick a strip of bacon in his open mouth. "Eat up, you need to regain your strength."

He pulls it out with a scowl and drops it onto the plate. "Don't you feel any sympathy for my bruised brain? Stop distracting me."

I'm distracting him? Laughter erupts from deep within me. It takes a bit to regain control because he wears such a disgruntled expression. *Poor guy.* "You're the one who keeps interrupting. This is why I'm glad you're living here. Really. I didn't know how stressed out I was until you came. I slept great last night, knowing you were in the other room. I didn't tell you yesterday, but someone squatted in my house while I was in the hospital. Goldilocks took off after I came home, but part of me worried he'd come back. I'm not anymore."

"Why not?"

"I'm just not." *Duh, why do you think? I trust you to keep me safe.* I smile, but he continues to stare at me. He seems so different from before the fire. The vibe he gives off is like he carries a deep grief inside him and the results have turned him colder and more reserved. I noticed it last night. He joked and laughed, teased me as we watched TV, but the smile didn't touch his eye.

And in some ways, the distance seems even greater today.

"What are you thinking?" I ask.

"I'm trying to figure out how I'll protect you."

I laugh his declaration off. "Protect me from what? Rogue raccoons? Don't worry. The guy's long gone."

"Maybe." He frowns. "Maybe not."

If I'd known he'd be so worried, I never would've mentioned the squatter. The doorbell rings and I get up, but Landry rushes past me. He practically runs to the front door, and I scramble to stay just a few steps behind. When I try to pass him to open the door, he pushes me behind him and holds his finger to his lips.

"Who is it?" he asks.

"Who the hell…" George sounds pissed.

I gulp and hip-bump Landry aside to open the door.

Sunlight hits the top of George's red-gold hair, making him sparkle. Not like a glittery vampire, more like a fallen angel. The uniform lends him an air of authority, and I try not to cringe beneath his glare. His hand rests on the butt of his gun, and his star winks at me on his chest. My hands get sweaty, and I wipe my palms on my jeans.

Landry stands directly behind me, breathing down the back of my neck, and I wish I could wave a magic wand and vanish. "What do you want?" I ask, not even trying to be polite.

"I came to check on you." He glances at Landry, who hovers over my shoulder. "What's he doing here?"

I stiffen my back, reminded I don't answer to George. Not like we're together. He dumped me in the middle of the road and drove off without sparing me a backward glance. What if my squatter hadn't moved on? I could've been killed. Plus, he's a liar. *No guilt.*

I tip up my chin. "Landry's my roommate."

"He's what?"

"My roommate. Paying rent." I shrug. "I didn't want to stay out here alone."

George gives Landry a heated glance. "*You're* paying rent."

"Yeah," Landry says, and I cringe at the angry burr in his tone. He goes over to flop down on the sofa like he owns the place and picks up the remote. "I'm watching TV. If you're gonna talk, take it outside."

I grimace in Landry's direction but step out onto the porch. I don't close the door. I don't trust myself with George. I'm pissed, and he has a way of making me lose my head. Besides, I'm not ready to forgive him for being such a jerk. "I'm fine. Now go away."

"Bullshit. You're crazy to let Landry stay here. Did you quit taking your psych meds?"

Low blow. Jackass. I swallow the curse. "Did you talk to your dad?"

George scowls. "*Your* father, remember. He's your bio father and my adoptive."

"Whatever."

"Not whatever, Mala. It means there's no blood relationship between us."

"So? If that mattered, you wouldn't have freaked out. The only reason I can figure for you being so mean is that you've obviously got a problem with this whole sharing-a-daddy situation."

"I have a problem with him cheating on my mother with the town whore."

The word drips off his tongue with ease. He doesn't notice me stiffen. Or my hands balling into fists at my sides. Sure he's angry, but the *whore* is my dead mama he's talking shit about.

The rocking chair tips backward, and I gulp back my startled scream. Mama materializes and gives me a devilish grin. "Oh, girl. You and Georgie Porgie found out about Senior being your daddy?"

"Yes," I hiss, not caring that George's eyes widen in surprise. "Yes, George. Mama, the town prostitute, had an affair with your stepfather and got pregnant with me."

"Hey, I wasn't whorin' around when I got pregnant with you. Senior and Georgie's mama were separated. He only married her for her money. Not like they loved each other. She was still hung up on her other husband, but he ran off and left her alone and pregnant."

I ignore her. "What if your father loved my mama? Would that make you feel better about the situation?"

Mama laughs. "He wasn't in love with me any more than I was in love with him. We had a one-night stand, and the condom broke. Gosh, you're so naive."

"Doesn't matter if he loved her or not, Mala," George says. "Wrong is wrong. I can't understand why you aren't angry about this."

"She *is* angry," Landry says, coming outside. "Sorry for eavesdropping, but you're not keeping your voices down, and I can't hear my show over the yelling."

George steps forward. "Mind your own business, Landry."

Landry shrugs. "It's just sad. You're throwing away your chance with Mala 'cause you're butt-hurt about her father having a one-night stand twenty-one years ago while your parents were separated."

George turns to me. "How does he know about this?"

Before I get a chance to respond, Landry jumps in feet first.

"How many times do I gotta tell you that Mala and I are friends? Let's get off this topic and move to something more important. Why Caleb King tried to murder me."

George rocks back onto his heels. "We'll finish our conversation later, Mala. In private."

Not if I can avoid being alone with him.

I think he reads the answer in my eyes because his lips tighten. He turns his attention to Landry. "We interrogated King, but he's not talking without a lawyer present. My guess is you pissed him off. You have a way of getting under a person's skin."

"My theory is someone hired him," I say. "Check his bank records, Georgie. I bet he's come into a fat inheritance in the last week."

Landry runs a finger over the edge of his eye patch. "I agree with Mala. One of the prisoners warned me that someone had been asking for takers. That a hit had been put out on me."

"Did he say why?" I ask.

"Dad and Rathbone are on the run. I wish I believed Dad wouldn't have me killed so I won't testify against him, but I don't know anything anymore. Mom let Lainey die…"

Silence falls over the three of us. The quiet emphasizes the noises around us: the squawk of chickens, the hoot of an owl, the shifting of feet from something large hiding in the yard. I glance in the direction the sound comes from, but I don't see anyone.

Landry takes my hand, squeezing my fingers.

George's green eyes flicker with jealousy, but he doesn't Hulk out. "Who do you think it is?"

"I think there's a fourth guy," Landry says.

My mouth goes dry. "Wh-ut?"

Landry squeezes my hand. "The night your mama died, I wasn't in any condition to drive. It was the night after Lainey's funeral..." He clears his throat. "I caught a ride with a friend who dropped me off at the end of the driveway so I walked in. I remember seeing three men dressed in black. One chased after Mala when she ran off. The other two carried me. I don't know how long it took before my dad's truck pulled up the driveway. I-it was confusing, but that means four. Dad, Mr. Acker, Doc Rathbone, and someone else."

George steps forward. "Who?"

"If I knew, I would've told you." Landry looks at me. "I never saw the other guy. After I was injured, Dad put me in his truck. Rathbone and the mystery guy drove off after taking care of your mom."

By taking care of, he meant making sure they disposed of her burned remains. It would've been the perfect murder if they'd gotten both of us too. Instead, they have two potential witnesses in me and Landry. Only as far as I can remember, I never saw the guy.

George rocks back on his heels. "So, this fourth doesn't know you can't identify him. He puts out a hit on you to be sure you don't tell. It's obvious it must be someone who was close to your father."

"What about Acker? Did you ever find him?" Landry asks.

I want to wave Landry into silence. The memory of Mr. Acker's death painfully comes to mind. I never told. At first I didn't remember. Now I don't know how to admit I let him die. What would Dena say? How would she feel knowing her father murdered Mama, and then I let him die? Our relationship would be ruined. I'd never be able to look her in the eyes again.

"Oh, hell no!" Mama yells, shoving her chair back. "Speak of the devil and he arrives."

Landry and I jump a second before the rocking chair crashes to the floor. George steps back from both of us, hand going to his gun again. His instincts are too honed for him not to figure out something weird is going on. He can probably sense the angry spirit crossing the yard. Mama tries to move between Acker and me, but the spirit is strong. He runs past her, reaches the steps, and bounces off an invisible barrier.

The salt I'd sprinkled around the house to keep Lainey out. Even with all the rain, it provided protection. Mr. Acker howls in fury. A mini-tornado of sticks and rocks launch through the air. I scream and cover my head. Landry grabs me and turns his back to the yard.

Georgie watches us like we've lost our minds, then ducks with a shout when debris pelts his back. A rock hits the side of his head, and he drops to his knees. Blood runs down his face. He searches the yard but doesn't see the ghost, only the dust devil Acker's presence causes to the visible world around him.

It hits me. How can I be in a relationship with a guy who'll think I'm insane if I explain that a ghost attacked him?

"Get Georgie in the house," I yell.

Landry wraps his arm around George's waist and drags him through the front door. I huddle by the front railing with my hands covering my head.

"Mala, come on!" Landry waves at me from the doorway.

The ground explodes, and I scream. Chunks of dirt and rocks rain down on the porch stairs, but the debris doesn't come close to hitting me. I stand with a *whoop*, shaking my fist at Mr. Acker. "Take that, asshole!"

Landry crawls over to me. "What are you doing?"

"Uncle Gaston rigged the yard with spiritual land mines." I grin at him. "He died in Vietnam. He's a weapons expert."

"How much of this is real?"

Another explosion makes the porch buckle and surge. I launch myself into Landry's arms and bury my face against his chest. "Those rocks Acker's throwing around feel plenty real." I take a calming breath and sit back, but I don't let go of him. "As a vengeful spirit, he's got mad mojo. But I also think part of this is all in our heads. Visions created within the spirit world, and we're tapped into them. It's real because we think it's real. Can it hurt or kill us? I don't know. Do people die in real life if they die in their dreams?"

The explosions cease.

Mr. Acker lies on the ground, moaning.

"What does he want?" Landry asks.

My heart swells. Landry's taking this better than I thought he would. At least he hasn't asked the one question I've been avoiding: how Mr. Acker ended up a ghost in the first place.

"We should interrogate him," I say. "Bet he knows who the fourth guy is."

Mr. Acker rolls over. "I ain't tellin' you nothin'. Not until you get my body buried."

I lurch toward him, but Landry pulls me back.

"You tried to kill me, Acker," I yell. "You don't get to make demands."

He blurs and disappears.

CHAPTER 13

LANDRY

The Exorcist

When you gonna learn how to set traps for these spirits, Mala?"

The voice comes from behind me and I turn, grabbing Mala and pulling her to my side. Burns and weeping fluids cover the man's face and body. I choke back my yell. He gives me a level look, fingering the trigger of his rifle, which focuses my attention on his Vietnam-era uniform.

Mala places her hand on my arm. "It's okay. Meet my uncle, Gaston. He's an ancestor guardian like Mama, sworn to protect me."

The tension in my shoulders relaxes. "Oh, he's not real." Of course he isn't. A live person wouldn't be able to function with as much physical damage as he has to his body. I'm afraid to ask why he doesn't appear normal like Ms. Jasmine does. Maybe he just likes to scare the crap out of people.

"I'm real enough to save your asses," Gaston says. Teeth show through an open hole in his cheek when he speaks, and my stomach lurches. He focuses on Mala. "Your brother's bleeding all over your new sofa."

Mala's instinctive glare upon hearing "brother" vanishes when the rest of Gaston's words sink in. She lets out a tiny *eep* and scoots around me to run for the door. Her high-pitched wails echo from inside. "Oh no, Georgie."

My jaw clenches, and I step forward. I can already picture the scene. Mala with George's head cradled on her lap as she presses kisses to heal his boo-boo. And if George is smart, he'll milk the sympathy for all he's worth.

Gaston steps in front of me, and I stumble back so I don't walk through him. Walking through spirits makes my bones ache for hours. Plus it's rude. Mala respects her uncle. The only way to get in good with her is to make a good impression on her family. The look he's giving me says he's not altogether pleased with my performance.

I cross my arms, prepared to schmooze him for a higher approval rating. "Thanks for your help with Acker. We would've been sunk without you."

My fabled charm works about as well on Gaston as it does on his niece. What's up with these LaCroixes and their ability to withstand my well-known charisma? Have I deluded myself all these years? Ninety-nine percent of high school girls can't be off that much. Course, Mala falls into the one percent who never noticed I existed before Lainey died and started haunting her.

Gaston's single, singed eyebrow rises. God, I hope his abilities don't include mind reading. Or if he can, that he'll be able to catch the dry inflection of sarcasm in my thoughts. Otherwise he might think I'm really this egotistical.

"You and Mala got lucky. Acker hasn't figured out how to manipulate the elements yet. If he'd been a more mature spirit, he would've turned that teensy-weensy dust devil into a full-on tornado and taken you out before I could manifest," he says, striding down the porch stairs. I pause for a long second then follow, careful to hold on to the railing so I don't fall. He points to the ground. "Mala laid salt around the house when Lainey was attacking her. It's been over a month since it's been reapplied, and with the rainfall, there are holes in the shielding."

I squint at the ground, but don't see anything. *Salt?*

"The man's got a powerful rage—a vengeful, unnatural hatred for Mala. He'll be back. How do you plan on protecting her?"

There he goes reading my mind again. I'm ashamed to admit how lost I feel. How helpless I am when dealing with this supernatural stuff.

Gaston stares toward the bayou. "You're feeling guilty."

The words slam home. Spoken out loud, they hurt more than the shank driven into my gut. I breathe out harshly, chest heaving. "Everything that's happened is my fault."

"Yes." He squats and uses his knife to dig a hole in the ground, then gently lays what looks like a land mine into the hole. Where in the world it came from, I couldn't say. Maybe he pulled it out of his ass.

The bitterness festering inside me escapes in a biting laugh. "Good to know I'm not wrong."

"You handled last night's incursion well."

I glance toward the door, afraid our voices will carry and Mala will overhear, but we're far enough away. Besides, she has George to occupy her attention. "You know about my father breaking into the house?"

"Who do you think woke you? Your father's human. My traps won't do a damn thing against him. I'll handle guarding the spiritual realm. It's up to you to keep her safe in the physical." He moves a few paces and seeds another land mine. He must be replacing the ones Acker blew up. "Do you plan on telling Mala about him?" he asks.

"I thought you would."

Gaston gives me a blank stare that makes my shoulders hunch. "Not my place. He's your father."

"I planned on telling her at breakfast, but then George showed up."

"You'd already decided to keep your mouth shut before he arrived."

I swallow hard. "Yeah, she'll only worry if she knows the truth. And honestly, I don't know what to do. He's been skulking about for weeks. She spent her first night out of the hospital here alone. Why didn't he get her then if he wanted to hurt her? He said last night that he has a debt to pay, but I don't know what that means."

"Figure it out quick."

I look up, but I'm alone in the yard.

Gaston's right. I need to figure it out, and I need to talk to the source of my confusion himself 'cause trying to decode my father's motivations will drive me crazy. Questions pop into my mind. Like why did he carry me inside the house and lay me on the sofa after I fell down the stairs? He could've left me on the ground. And when he came in, I was unconscious. I couldn't stop him from going after Mala. Instead he cleaned up the spilled gumbo and washed the pot. *Why, why, why?*

Pain doubles me over as I start up the staircase. It flares outward through my rib cage, and I gasp, trying not to choke 'cause it will only make it hurt worse. I grip the railing and pull myself up the last step, then pause on the landing as I catch my breath. Being hurt sucks.

Mala's voice floats through the open doorway. It flutters like a hummingbird, vibrating with concern and admiration, the total opposite of how she speaks to me. She must really like the dude. I'll never get what she sees in him. He's so goody-goody he makes my teeth ache, but in her eyes, he's the perfect guy, her Superman, while I'm the Frog Prince.

George sits on the sofa. His eyes have a glazed, unfocused cast. Drying blood stains his cheek and uniform. Mala sits beside him with a first aid kit on her lap. The smell of alcohol hits my nose. She dabs a cotton ball on the cut.

"Does it hurt?" she asks.

"Nah, I'm fine," George says, and I snort. What guy would say "yes"? Still, he does a good job of looking pathetic, and Mala eats it up like red velvet cake.

"I'm going to take a shower," I say, disgusted.

They're so busy gazing soulfully into each other's eyes, like lovesick cows, that they don't bother to look in my direction. I grab my box of clothing and storm to the bathroom. My fist clenches. I want to punch George, but Mala would get pissed. I'd get kicked out for sure.

Gaston's words come back.

How am I going to protect Mala? The perfect way would be to march out there and tell George about Dad hanging around. He'd call in the cavalry—SWAT team, search dogs. They'd easily track him down. Not like Dad has a lot of *Survivorman*-type skills, although he watched the television series religiously and bought Les Stroud's book. The closest he's come to surviving off the land is his annual hunting trip. Half the time he didn't come back with game. I think he only went 'cause his friends expected him to.

Which also makes his part in killing Ms. Jasmine so shocking to me, and everyone else, I'm sure. He preached about turning the other cheek. He lectured me about standing up to bullies and protecting the weak. His words taught me to fight for others and gave me the strength to protect Mala.

How could he have completely lost sight of his values and ideals? And if it happened to someone as strong as him, could it happen to me too? It scares me to even think of the possibility. To wonder what sort of violence I'm capable of committing. The same blood flows through our veins, and it terrifies me.

I'm standing in the middle of the bathroom, staring into the toilet bowl as if it's a Magic 8 Ball and one good flush will reveal the answers to my questions. The murmur of voices flows beneath the bathroom door, and I'm again reminded of how much Mala and George's relationship has changed in the last month. George finally manned up. When Ms. Jasmine said they'd been kissing, a lead ball settled in my stomach. It crushed the little bit of hope I had left of her choosing me.

I pry up the bottom of my T-shirt. It sticks to my stomach, and I grimace. Not a broken heart after all. I peel off the bandage, glad they shaved my chest before sticking it to me, and study the wound in the mirror. I tore a couple of stitches. The first aid kit's in the living room, but I'm not going back into the Love Shack to ask for it. A little blood loss won't kill me. I stick some toilet paper on my wound and sit on the toilet lid with my eye closed. Exhaustion from fighting against the pain feels heavy within me. Or is it sadness? Maybe I'm depressed.

To hell with this!

I'm not here to play house with Mala. I made a promise, and

I aim to keep it. I have to keep her safe, and the first thing I have to do is find my father. I drop the bloody toilet paper in the trash can. A search of the cabinet comes up with a heavy gauze pad and Ms. Jasmine's half-empty bottle of whisky. A quick patch-up and a few shots later, and I'm ready.

I stare at my pale face in the mirror.

I look like shit.

A dark aura hovers an inch above my skin. I squint, staring hard. It ripples and churns as if the air passing through agitates it. I hold my hand over my arm and wiggle my fingers. Heat and static electricity make my fingertips tingle.

"What is this?" I lean closer. "Are you a demon?"

The response brings me to my knees. My nerve endings catch on fire. Pain arcs through my body. My chin hits the edge of the sink, and I flop back on the ground. My limbs convulse, and I bite into my swollen tongue. The scream sticks in my throat. I can't unclench my jaw to free it.

I black out.

I wake on the floor, curled into a ball. It takes another five minutes before I gather the energy to prop myself up against the tub. Silence, broken by my harsh breaths, fills my ears. I can't stop shaking. I want to call for Mala…or Gaston or Ms. Jasmine. I'll even settle for George seeing me with my pants drenched with my own piss if they can explain what happened to me and make sure it never happens again.

Instead I reach for the faucet and get the shower running.

* * *

George and Mala have moved to the porch by the time I exit the bathroom. I avoid them by going outside through the kitchen, only stopping to throw my soiled jeans in the washing machine. It rained this morning, and I search the ground for footprints. I find them by the toolshed. A quick peek inside shows it's empty, but I find a rolled-up tarp and sleeping bag hidden behind the riding lawn mower. The footprints head toward the trail leading to the pond.

Jittery, muscular tics make my steps clumsy. I have to stop every couple hundred feet to rest and catch my breath. My memory trips back to the last time I walked this path with Mala. She'd worn baggy overalls with the pant legs rolled up to her knees, and a battered straw hat sat on her head. Her hair hung to her hips in pigtails. Just being with her that day eased my grief for Lainey.

A grin stretches my lips so much my cheeks ache.

A rustle in the bushes warns me that I'm not alone. I turn, fists raised. Dad steps out from behind a tree. I'm shocked by his appearance. Leaves and ground-in dirt coat his clothes and face. A ragged beard covers his cheeks. His eyes look wild and sunken. He's lost thirty pounds, at least.

"Put your hands down. I won't attack my own son."

"You did last night." My hands drop to my sides.

"You came after me first."

"You broke into Mala's house, threw a pot of gumbo in my eye, murdered a woman in cold blood, and kidnapped another one."

"I admit to breaking into the house. Throwing the gumbo was a reflex move. You snuck up on me. Killing, I never did. If you think back, you'll recall that I arrived to drive you to the hospital after you were injured."

I remember the sound of a truck driving in and his voice calling my name. Was that before or after Ms. Jasmine burned?

"I told you Acker went after Mala. Why didn't you help her?"

"Look, son, I was in shock over what happened. I thought

you were involved." He shakes his head. "I can't pretend to be innocent. I knew Rathbone and Acker were planning something, but I didn't care enough to stop it. Lainey getting murdered…it messed with my mind and made me susceptible to being tampered with by the devil."

"By the devil you mean Rathbone?"

"He's the author of the troubles, son. If not for him, your sister would still be alive. Your mama would still be crazy, but she wouldn't be in the psych ward. And Jasmine LaCroix would still be a heathen destined for hell, but she'd be a live heathen."

My chest clenches. "And I'd still have my eye, a football scholarship, and plans for the future." I cry out, my voice rising, "I wouldn't have a demon living inside of me."

Dad shuffles toward me but stops out of reach. "What are you talking about?"

The words trip off my tongue. "In jail, I got attacked. I died. I woke up on the other side, but it wasn't the heaven you preached about. A black hole appeared and tried to suck me inside. Lainey kept me from going to hell."

"What are you babbling about?"

He's my dad—a preacher with a straight line to God. If anyone can get the 4-1-1 from heaven on how to fix me, he can. Otherwise, I'm doomed. "Didn't you hear me?" I grab his arm. "I said I was being sucked into hell 'cause of the evil I've done. But they resuscitated me and something from the other side hitched a ride inside of me. A demon."

I see spirits.

"Dad, I need you to perform an exorcism."

CHAPTER 14

MALA

Bloodhound

I'm pretty sure George has a concussion.

Otherwise, he wouldn't be staring at me with crossed eyes. I feel horrible about him getting hurt. I should've told him about my seeing ghosts. No matter how ridiculous it sounds, at least he would've been ready for Acker's psychic attack.

Well, maybe nobody can be fully prepared for something invisible throwing rocks at their head.

What should I do? Tell him or not?

I bite my lip. The pros and cons run through my mind. Worst-case scenario is he arrests me for being mentally deranged and locks me back in the psych ward. Best case …he believes me.

Then what?

George leans back on the couch with a groan. He presses the ice pack against the lump on his head. Why isn't he saying anything? He's totally freaking me out. I should call for an ambulance.

I reach for the telephone. "I'm calling Dixie."

George's hand falls on top of mine. "I'm fine. A little dizzy, but I'll be okay in a few. I'm off-duty right now."

"Oh, the uniform confused me."

He grunts.

I fall onto the sofa. He winces when his head bounces off the back of the seat cushion. "Sorry. I mean it. I'm really, really, sorry you got hurt. This is all my fault. If Acker..."

George sits up, dropping the ice pack. "What do you mean? Acker what? Was that him in the yard? Was he throwing rocks at us?"

"Uh, no."

He grabs my arm. "Are you sure? We haven't found him yet. Dena says he hasn't been home since the night of the attack."

"No, I swear. It wasn't him." *Liar. Tell the truth.*

Acker's dead. I killed him. The words burn on the tip of my tongue. If I say them, I'll have to tell him the whole truth. Every sordid detail of how Lainey shoved Acker into the quicksand and how I didn't pull him out even though he begged for my help.

I squeeze my eyes shut. Does he hear my heart pounding? It feels like it's about to erupt out of my chest. Can he see the guilt written across my burning cheeks? I blow out a heavy breath and look toward the bathroom. The door's still shut, and I can hear the shower running. My body vibrates with the intensity of my need for Landry's support. I want him beside me. I need to be rescued before I blab the truth and damn myself.

I try to stand, but George shifts until he's lying with his copper head snuggled on my lap. The tips of his spiky hair brush the bare skin between the gap in my jeans shorts and T-shirt. "God, Mala.

I've got the worst headache. You sure it wasn't Acker?"

Admitting I killed someone is even scarier than the moment when I realized I made my choice to save Acker too late. I feel shitty enough. I don't want to see the condemnation in George's eyes, or for Dena to find out. If that makes me a coward, then I'm a wussy chicken.

"Yeah. It was a dust devil kicking up debris. You happened to get in the way, that's all." I place the ice pack back on his knot and lie like the black-tongued devil I've become. "Acker's not a fool. He's long gone. I bet he never, ever comes back."

He tips his chin. Concern sparks the gold in his green eyes. "What about his kids?"

"Dena raised them after her mom ran off." I brush a damp strand of hair off his forehead. "She'll keep on caring for them now that her daddy has too. She's tough."

The water in the bathroom shuts off.

George sits up and grabs my hand, dragging me off the sofa. "I need to talk to you, and I don't want Landry overhearing."

I follow him to the door, pausing to make sure Acker isn't in sight before leading him to a rocking chair. "What?"

"Landry said you're pissed about Dad. Is he right?"

A tight band wraps around my chest. I blow out a puff of air at the stupid question. Of course I'm angry. Why wouldn't I be? Mama with Daddy Dubois—hell, even Ms. March kept it secret from me for twenty years.

"Pissed barely covers it."

He reaches for my hand, but I move it to my lap. A frown drags down the corners of his eyes. "Tell me."

"I feel like a piece of shit scraped off the bottom of his shoes." I blink away the blurriness covering my vision. I won't cry for him. *My father. What a joke.*

I stare out across the rippling grass to the trees bordering the woods. I drink in the rich, earthy smell, letting it cleanse the foulness of my thoughts. "I feel hurt…betrayed. And disgusted"—I stab him with my eyes—"by you, George."

His eyes widen. "What?"

"You said for me to tell you how I really feel, so listen closely. I don't care about my sperm donor. He means nothing to me. You, I trusted. And now I can't even imagine a world where we're a couple."

"You don't mean that."

I lean forward. "Oh, come on. Stop lying. You totally suck at it. Do you really see us dating? Going to family dinners together? What about getting married, huh? Think our parents will approve?" I drop my hand onto his hard thigh and squeeze.

The color drains from his cheeks. He grabs my hand and moves it back onto my lap. "Don't…"

"It's okay, George. I feel the same way."

"Don't tell me how I feel."

"Admit it. The kiss, the whole idea about us being together, none of it ever felt totally right to me or for you either, I bet. I was an emotional mess. I needed someone to help ease my grief for Mama," *and Landry*, "and I love you." I flick a rock off the table and watch it roll across the deck. "We love each other, but as friends. Now I guess our feeling will morph into a brother and sisterly kind of warm-fuzzy. I'm cool with that."

George slams his hands down and pushes up out of the chair. "Well, on that note, I'll be heading out."

"Wait! What?" I scramble up. "Are you sure you're okay to drive?"

"The conversation cleared the fog from my brain." He stares at me for a long moment, and I wish I could read his thoughts. I did all of the talking. He didn't disagree, but he hasn't agreed either.

I watch from the porch steps as he walks to his Land Rover. He moves too fast for me to keep up even if I wanted to. The tension tightening my shoulders drains off as I slough off the guilt I feel about having used George. I never should've kissed him. Worse, I never should've tried to force myself into a relationship with him when, the whole time, I couldn't stop thinking about Landry.

"It's done," I whisper, waving good-bye.

Once the Land Rover vanishes down the windy driveway, I go inside, yelling "Landry, it's safe to come out now." I flop down on the sofa and start flipping through television stations. "Don't sulk. I'll let you pick the movie. Or we can play a game. Landry?"

Silence.

"Hello?" My heartbeat quickens as I get up and walk across the room. The bathroom door remains half closed but opens with a slight push. I squint, ready to slam my eyelids shut if he's naked. An oppressive weight presses around my body, like the air thickens, syrupy and muggy. The open shower curtain shows the empty tub. A steady drip forces me to tighten the faucet. A coppery taint mixed with the sharp pungency of urine makes my nose crinkle. My vision blurs as a crimson squiggly line wavers in the air, like in a comic strip. The cartoon equivalent of stink hovers above my trash can.

I breathe in. The squiggle rushes into my nose. Fills my lungs. *Blood.*

I stumble, overcome by the pure power in the blood. I inhale again and again. With each breath, the tingle grows inside of me until my skin and hair crackle. My hand trembles when I pull a bloody wad of toilet paper out of the trash can. I hold it up to my nose and inhale the sweet scent of Landry's blood. Heat rushes through my body, pulsing between my thighs. The surge of lust shakes me to my core. *Whoa, holy pheromone rush.*

I've gone all kinds of crazy.

"Landry!" The search of the bedroom and kitchen doesn't take but a minute. With each frantic step, panic fills me. The *ding* of the washing machine has me sprinting to the side porch. It's also empty. So is the side yard.

"Landry," I scream, spinning in a circle.

Crap! He left me.

I shouldn't have spent so much time with George. I know how jealous Landry gets. Why didn't I think about that? What do I do? Go after him?

No. No, he'll be back. All of his stuff is inside.

I breathe in again.

Landry's faint scent comes from the woods to my left. I scan the ground for footprints because I can't really have turned into a bloodhound. It's not really possible for me to be able to smell Landry.

Oh God, I'm a total mutant freak.

I hold my breath until my lungs strain and my vision gets spotty. My gasp brings in a rush of aromas: the sweet hint of clover, the rotten-egg stench of stagnant water, and the nose-curling sharpness of chicken poop. No blood.

At the shed, I find two sets of footprints. One I assume belongs to Landry. The other looks exactly like the boots I followed through the woods. My Goldilocks. Landry must've seen them and tracked whoever made the prints into the woods. If there really was a fourth guy at the house the night Mama died, Landry could be walking into a trap. Landry's tough. He can handle a lone guy in a hand-to-hand fight, but not if there's a gun involved.

I should call the Sheriff's Office and have Dixie send George back out. No, he's not on duty. Plus his head wound. Andy and his K-9, Rex, would be better.

What about the plan? My eyes go to the footprints, and I pause. My stomach twists. I want to throw up. This is my best chance to get revenge. I can't throw it away, even for Landry. I spent countless sleepless nights in the psych ward contemplating how I would avenge Mama. How I would be the one to bring those men to justice and prove I could be a cop. I even planned how I could use Landry against them. Now I'm more worried about his safety than my reputation...my future.

His dying made me forget my anger toward him. I won't let anyone hurt him.

Part of me wants to rush in to rescue him. It takes all of my strength to hold myself to a steady walk. My eyes scan the ground, following the tracks. Landry's scent fades. God, I hope that was my imagination working overtime and not another crazy symptom of my family's magic. My preconceptions have been turned upside down. Magic, ghosts, death visions, and freaking time rifts...Speculative fiction's supposed to be escapism, re-served for TV or books. It shouldn't intrude on the natural order of the world.

The spongy ground muffles my footsteps. A hush, broken only by the rustling leaves overhead, brings the sound of Landry's voice. I crouch down, sliding through the underbrush, planting each foot with care not to step on a branch.

Landry's voice rises...begging for help. My stomach clenches. I brush aside the leaves blocking my view with a trembling hand and freeze. Betrayal surges through me, sharp and ugly. It eats into me, stripping through the layers I've built up over the last month to dampen my hate, leaving me raw and open.

Landry stands in the clearing, holding on to a man I prayed

I'd see but didn't really believe I'd ever get a chance at. Still might not. Landry looks like he's about to take out his father all by himself, and I can't let him. Reverend Prince killed my mother, and he stands only a few feet away. He's mine.

My fingers tingle with the buildup of power, ready to shoot a blast of energy across the clearing and blow Reverend Prince apart, just like I destroyed the door when I tried to rescue Mama. It takes every bit of control to remain still. Landry's standing too close to him, and I might hurt him by mistake. If I plan the moment just right, the rev won't see me coming, and Landry won't be able to stop me.

CHAPTER 15

LANDRY

Luscious Lips

Dad stares at me for a long minute, then laughs. His whole body shakes. He glances up at me with tears streaming down his cheeks before going into another fit of giggles. *Not cool.*

"You're joking…" He chokes. "After what happened…me believing Jimmy Rathbone about Jasmine performing a hoodoo ritual on Lainey…" He wipes his eyes with the dirty cuff of his shirt. "You're testing me."

"Dad—" I release him and collapse against the trunk of a nearby tree.

He places a hand on my shoulder and squeezes. "I promise, son, I'm of sound mind. What happened to Jasmine…to the nurse you spoke of earlier…I'm of sound mind, and I have a debt to pay."

His words get me mobile again. "What does that mean? Do you plan to hurt Mala?"

"That's what I'm trying to explain, son. My inaction let harm come to that girl. I won't rest easy until I perform penance for the wrongs done to her and her mother."

"Swear to it."

A branch cracks. I turn around, searching the brush. A shadow darts into my blind spot too fast to see what made it.

Dad grabs my arm, squeezing hard. "I promise I'll give my life to keep that girl safe."

All the pent-up tension rushes out, and I sag, nodding. I believe him. My dad. "You said something happened to the nurse? Do you mean the one all over the news? Gloria Pearson?"

"Sit down." He waves to a downed log. I make my way over to it and collapse. Dad sits beside me, crossing his legs. Dirt cakes his bare ankles. I wonder if he has any clean clothes.

He tips his dark head and stares at the sky. "Rathbone and Gloria were dating. Maybe the whole time Lainey carried his baby. Of course, none of us knew about her, and I'm not sure if Lainey knew about Gloria."

"So Gloria helped you escape 'cause Rathbone asked her?"

"Rathbone didn't want me getting arrested for Jasmine's murder. He knew about George testing the knife for DNA and did the blood analysis himself. It was only a matter of time before they had proof of my being there. He and Gloria drugged me, then they sneaked me out of the hospital." His blue eyes flicker. "I didn't know about the part he played in your sister's death at the time. Poor Gloria told me when she found out about Rathbone murdering Lainey and the baby."

"Her betrayal must've pissed him off."

Dad's jaw flexes. "Jimmy probably thought he could sweet-talk me into believing he was innocent of killing my daughter. Gloria ruined that."

"So he killed her."

"He was too much of a coward to dirty his own hands. He brought someone to do the deed for him. An accomplice."

My breath catches, and I let it out slowly. "Who?" I ask, trying not to put too much emphasis on how important the answer is to me.

"Wish I knew. He didn't speak in front of me, and he wore a mask that night. I was more concerned about you. I didn't bother trying to see his face. Gloria drugged me before leaving the hospital. I faded in and out during the drive. We ended up at Acker's lodge. They kept me in a drugged fog in one of the back rooms. Guess they were waiting for his friend to arrive to take care of putting me out of my misery."

"What about Acker's kids? Did they see you?"

Dad shakes his head. "I didn't see Acker. My guess is the guy killed him too. I doubt the kids ever knew we were there."

I nod. Acker's barn is set off about half a mile from the main house. The land had a tendency to flood, which left few safe areas above the water line for farming. And Acker couldn't afford to care for large livestock. He'd come up with the idea of turning it into a hunting lodge, and with church contributions and monetary help from friends, they converted his barn. It now boasts three bedrooms with bunk beds, three baths, an area for cleaning game, and a large living room.

I've only seen the inside once. Private and secluded, it's the perfect hunting lodge since it's so close to Forest Service land. Grown men could congregate there without their nosy wives' interference. They didn't even have to worry about Acker's wife, since she ran off with another man.

I blink, realizing I've lost track of the conversation.

"I was pretty out of it," Dad says. "I overheard Gloria and

Rathbone arguing about killing me. She balked at murder. Then a car came. There was more arguing, but I couldn't make out the identity of the other man by his voice. It sounded familiar, but my head was all jumbled from the drugs. I blacked out again. When I came to, I was alone but for the bodies. I'm not sure how they died. I didn't get close enough."

"Why didn't he kill you too?"

Dad shrugs. "My guess? The guy killed Rathbone and Gloria before they had a chance to tell him about me. That or he figured I was so out of it he could take me out of the equation later. I didn't stick around for him to come back."

My stomach sours at how close he came to getting killed. "What about the bodies?"

"I went to Jasmine's house. The police had already come and gone. I figured it for the perfect place to hide out. Who would think to look for me at the scene of my crime, right?" He shakes his head. "The bodies had been moved by the time I finally gained the courage to go back. I don't know where he disposed of them. Can't feel too hurt over Rathbone's death after what he did to your sister, but Gloria…"

"How do I find this guy?"

"You don't have to worry about finding him, son. That's what I'm trying to explain. He's cleaning up Rathbone's mess, one person at a time. He's gonna come after you and Mala. No loose ends. He'll be coming here next, and I'll be waiting. I won't let anything happen to you or to Mala."

* * *

Dad and I come up with a plan. I'll hide his lurking about the property from Mala, while he does his best to protect us. The relief at not being alone in this almost has me skipping through the woods as I return to the house. Okay, maybe skip-limping—sklimping—'cause those damn broken stitches sting like the devil. My one regret is keeping Dad a secret from Mala. I swore after the whole "accusing her of murder" issue that I would be up front with her, but…hell, I can't risk her flipping out.

If Dad gets arrested, I'm screwed. There's no way I can protect her solo. How am I supposed to stop a murderer whose face I've never seen? The dude hides in the shadows. I'm bait. Pure and simple. Mala and I both are. We need someone to reel this guy in while we dangle on the hook, and I sure as shit don't trust DA Cready to pull off a save.

Mala is sitting on the front porch when I return. The sun makes her brown hair shimmer with auburn highlights. It tangles in wet curls around her waist. She catches me staring and grimaces. "I had dirt and sticks in it from Acker's attack. It's so thick, I have to let it dry out some before I braid it."

She's so pretty.

I edge up the stairs, trying to keep her on my blind side. If I can't see her, I won't feel guilty.

She bounds into view, and I jump. "Where have you been?"

I scowl. "Like you care."

"If I didn't, I wouldn't ask." She steps closer and lays the tips of her fingers against my chest, and I suck in a breath. "Your stitches tore."

"How did you know?" Can she feel my heart race beneath her palms? If she knew how little control I have when it comes to her, would she keep touching me like this? I edge aside, and her fingers drop. I draw in a slow breath.

Eyes as black as a raven's wing stare up at me. A tiny frown creases her brow, as if she's trying to read what I'm struggling to keep hidden. I look away.

"You're horrible at keeping secrets, but I'll forgive you this time."

I gulp. "Huh?"

"You should've flushed the bandage and bloody tissue down the toilet. Although my septic tank thanks you for not clogging it up." She slides her arm through mine. My gut tightens as I hold back a groan. "The first aid kit is still out from when I patched up Georgie. You're next, buddy."

Ugh, George…why throw him in my face? I pluck her fingers from my arm. "I'm fine."

"You're mad at me?" Her bottom lip pokes out in an unconscious pout.

She's killing me. "Why would I be mad?"

The darkness hovering over her returns, and she frowns.

I go inside, and she follows a few steps behind. When I try to go into the kitchen, she swivels around me and blocks the way with wide-stretched arms. "Uh-uh, not until I bandage you up."

"I'm okay…"

She shoves me toward the sofa. I fall onto it with a grunt. "Take off your shirt." Her voice trembles on the words, and her eyes stay locked on my chest as I slowly lift the T-shirt. The tip of her tongue flicks out to wet her lips. Heat fills her eyes. I close mine and lift the shirt over my head while trying to slow my heavy breathing so she doesn't notice. I drop the shirt onto the floor.

Mala drops to her knees between my legs. Her hand trembles. My stomach muscles contract when her fingertips brush across my skin. Her gaze flits up to meet mine while she removes my makeshift bandage. "Are you trying to get an infection?"

"Do I hear worry in your voice? Better watch out or I might think you care about me."

"Don't be an idiot." She takes a cotton ball from the first aid kit, pours antiseptic on it, and dabs it on my wound. I let out a low hiss. My manly quotient for the day is seriously depleted. I'm too damn tired to hide my pain. At least my dick's not embarrassing me by acting up with Mala within touching distance.

Until she leans forward and blows the sting from my wound. *I think I'm gonna die.*

I stare at a crack in the ceiling and try to think distracting thoughts. Nothing's coming to mind. My body's too hyperaware of her—the floral scent of her hair, the touch of her right breast brushing across my knee, the shine to her lips. I want to drag her across my lap and...*Shut up, brain. Just shut up.*

"You're not upset about George, are you?" Mala asks, pressing on a bandage. She gets up and flops into the chair across from me, draping one leg over the arm. Her foot rocks back and forth as she picks at a loose string on her cut-offs. She epitomizes casual, as if she doesn't care about my answer. Well, fine. Two can play that game.

I lift my feet onto the coffee table. I try to look relaxed, but tension keeps me stiff even when I fake slouch. "What does your relationship with George have to do with me?"

Her skin reddens until her cheeks look like caramel apples. "We're not in a relationship."

Ha! Liar. "Are you sure? 'Cause you both act like you are. '*Are you okay, Georgie Porgie?*'" I coo, imitating her icky-sweet voice.

Her jaw flexes. "I do not sound like that."

"Wanna bet? I had to get out of here before I threw up my breakfast."

"Take it back." Her hands ball up into fists.

"No takebacks, Mala. Admit it."

"Aah!" She launches out of the chair.

I have a second head start. I scramble over the back of the sofa, placing it between us. "*Oh, Georgie. Did my itty-witty baby get an owie?*"

"Stop talking in that annoying voice!"

Her cheeks glow even brighter, and her frizzy hair looks like she stuck her finger in a light socket. Her chest heaves with each breath, stretching her T-shirt. She takes advantage of my distraction. She lunges forward, and her breasts slam against my chest. My arm wraps around her waist as the impact of our collision sends us flying onto the sofa.

Air *whoosh*es out of my lungs.

Mala's eyes widen, and she freezes. She stares at my mouth. *Mesmerized by my luscious lips...* only it turns out to actually be the case. Her eyes go dreamy as her head tilts downward, and her lips purse. I close my eye and roll sideways.

She hits the ground with a muffled curse.

CHAPTER 16

MALA

Humpty Dumpty

Landry freakin' Prince!

I slap a piece of toast onto his plate. "Breakfast."

His nose crinkles as he pokes the toast with his finger. "Do you have butter or jelly?"

"I'm not your maid." I rub my bottom and glare at him. He pretends not to notice. Or maybe he really doesn't. Why did I try to kiss him last night, especially after he hid the fact that he met with his father? I mean, after listening to the rev's story, even I felt a twinge of sympathy for him. Maybe I even believe him about not being there when Mama died. I never actually saw anyone's face, other than Acker's. The fact he's living out in the boonies just to protect his son makes me willing to give him a chance to make good on his promise to catch the fourth guy.

Hell, I'm not totally delusional. Anger made me crazy enough to think I could go all Wonder Woman and take down the rev with my own two hands. Reality set in real quick when he talked about finding Rathbone's and Gloria's bodies. I can't fight a gun. Not even if I learn how to use my super-ninja magic to bore a hole in the bad guy's gut.

Course that power fizzled on me when I tried to use it on the rev yesterday. He didn't even fart from the pressure I put on his gut. Damn fickle magic.

I sit across from Landry and scoop up a forkful of scrambled eggs. "Mm-mm, so good…"

Landry slides back from the table with a sigh. He catches me staring as he walks to the refrigerator, and I glance away. He's limping. Did I hurt him when I fell on top of him? I'm not a thick girl, but I won't blow away in a strong wind either. I try to squash my concern, but it's so hard. Maybe I should say something about spying on him and his father. Relieve some of his guilt.

The throb of pain shooting through my butt when I shift in the chair makes my decision. Nah, he deserves to suffer.

"I'm going to town for supplies. Be ready to go in an hour," I say.

"I don't feel like going."

I fix him with a level stare.

He slams the refrigerator door. "Fine, but I need more energy to deal with a road trip. Toast isn't gonna cut it." He grabs my plate and transfers half of my bacon and eggs onto his. I don't bother to argue. What's the point?

We eat without further conversation, and the silence between us at breakfast continues during the drive into town. I cast sideways glances in his direction. What's going on in his head? The distance he's creating between us feels like a wall I can't climb.

He catches my glance and gives me a long, penetrating look but doesn't say anything.

I shift uncomfortably in my seat and sigh. I miss the way he used to tease me. I didn't know how much until last night. The sexual tension blazed so hot that I thought my body would spontaneously combust. Before Mama died, he would've kissed me until I lost my breath. Maybe he thinks he's being a gentleman. Does he want me to make the first move?

I shake my head so hard the road blurs, and I almost drive into a ditch. *Dummy, you jumped him, and he dumped you flat on your ass.* My hands grip the steering wheel as the memory of Landry's words comes back. Saying I cooed at George like an insipid nitwit. Well, he didn't say that exactly. Those are my words but I couldn't deny it. Not after seeing George bleeding from a head wound. He looked like an injured puppy, but the thing is, I never once felt like "kissing his owie." The only injury I want to kiss is Landry's. If he hadn't run off into the woods and instead spied on the rest of our conversation, he would know George and I just confused platonic love for romantic love. Which I hope will eventually morph into the love of a sister for her stepbrother.

Gah! I kissed my brother.

The more I think about it, the queasier I get. Sure, there's no blood relation, but a foul taste lingers in my mouth. I rake my fingernails across my tongue, almost choking myself in the process.

"What the hell are you doing?"

My eyes widen. *Crap! Landry.*

"A bug flew into my mouth, *blech*." I spit out the window. Saliva hits the glass and drips down the pane. "Oh, uh, can you grab a tissue from the glove box, please?"

He does so without further comment. Not that he needs to speak. His body language shouts louder than words: *I'm locked in the truck with a crazy person.* Hopefully his sense of self-preservation won't force him to leap out a moving vehicle to get away from me. He scrunches his large frame against the door, almost choking himself with the seat belt.

"Ha, ha," I say. "Very funny."

The tiniest of smiles flickers across his lips then disappears. He shifts back over and sinks back into brooding.

"Seriously, Landry, why are you so nervous? You'll get to see your friends." I wait for a passing semi truck, then swerve around a slow-moving tractor. Woodland thins and turns into orderly rows of sugarcane fields.

"What friends?" His shoulders hunch as he crosses his arms. "Do you know how many of my so-called friends visited me while I was in jail? One."

Jerks. "Well, that's cool. Maybe you'll get to see that person."

"I'm looking at her right now." He turns his glare out the window, and I lean back in the seat. No wonder he doesn't want to go. I've been on the bad end of being bullied. Someone stuck a rotting possum in my locker at work. I hope nobody does anything like that to him. He's been hurt enough.

I let him sulk in silence. He needs to get the angst out of his system before it festers into a seeping wound not even an antibiotic can cure.

On Saturdays, the local farmers set up a market in Paradise Park. I plan to do my veggie shopping there since I didn't get my garden planted this year. The streets bordering the park are packed. I'm lucky to find a spot in the parking lot of First National Bank kitty-corner from the Vietnam Memorial Rose Garden. Colorful tents are lined up in orderly rows in the square. Each section is separated, with the organic foods in one row and regular folk who want to sell extra produce in the other. Local shops also set up booths selling everything from pastries, coffee and tea, handmade clothing and soaps, fresh eggs, and organic meat, to toys and games. A freaktastic clown stands on the street corner with a tank of helium, and a gaggle of kids around him. I'm tempted to buy Landry a balloon to cheer him up.

The passenger door slams shut as soon as I shut off the engine. Landry wastes no time coming around to open my door and lift me to the ground before I can squawk in protest. He strides off while I grab my cloth shopping bag, leaving me to stare after his retreating back in shock. When he's halfway across the street, he pauses and turns around.

"This is your idea. Hurry," he yells.

"I'm coming." I shut the door and run to catch up. When I reach him, he moves around me until I'm on his blind side. He starts forward again, but slows his steps so they match mine. If I didn't know him so well, I'd think he didn't have a care in the world, but I do. He walks like he did in jail—shoulders back and tight, chest slightly raised. He scans the area, alert for a threat.

I take his hand, squeezing when he tries to pull away.

We blend into the crowd, strolling up and down the rows. It's a mix of people of all ages. A few people say hi. Most don't. A large percentage of them stare. I feel like I'm at the mercy of paparazzi.

"Smile and wave," I mutter from the corner of my mouth, jabbing Landry in the side with my elbow.

"Huh?"

"You're acting like you've done something wrong, but you haven't. Don't let these fools see you sweat. Weakness breeds violence. Like a silverback gorilla in the jungle, you need to beat your chest and fling your poop at someone."

His snort-laugh doubles him over, and I pat him on the back. "That's perfect," I say. "No worries."

He turns and lifts me into a breath-stealing hug. "Thanks," he whispers in my ear and presses a brotherly kiss to my forehead. Wish he'd move his lips a little lower. Would a few inches kill him?

My voice comes a little thick and raspy too, and I cough to clear my throat. "No problem."

How long has he been standing here holding me? We have an even larger audience than before. Now we really are the object of paparazzi-like behavior as people snap pictures of our embrace with their phones. I wrap my arms around his neck and press my cheek against his. "Cheese," I say, grinning for the cameras.

A couple of high school kids start to laugh.

One yells, "Give her another kiss, Landry."

"Yeah, Landry. Give me a kiss." I bat my eyelashes, whispering in his ear, "I swear, if you drop me on my ass in public—"

I don't have to finish the threat.

His mouth steals across mine.

I lean into him, head tilting. My arms tighten around his neck. His lips are soft and juicy, like peaches. Yum. My thoughts scatter and swirl, leaving only the sensation of his mouth on mine.

He breaks free first and lowers me to my feet. He avoids my gaze. "Did it work?" he asks, running his fingers through his black hair so it falls forward to shield his eye again. He shifts from his forward foot to his back, which somehow puts distance between us without him having to move.

I laugh, playing off the hurt. "Yeah, we gave our fans a titillating bit of new gossip to take the place of the old. Rumors about our relationship will be flying through town before lunch." I glance around to be sure. The crowd drifts away, realizing there's nothing more to see. Even better, nobody hurls insults or throws dead animals at our heads. "Let's go."

I don't wait for him to follow, but I'm conscious of his presence at my side.

There's a line in front of the shop selling fresh-baked goods. I listen to my craving for homemade muffins and fall in behind a woman with a toddler in a jogging stroller. The little boy has blue-colored honey smeared across his face from the plastic straw he's sucking on. The kid looks over my shoulder and cracks up laughing.

I catch Landry making funny faces at the kid. He finally remembers how to smile, or he does until the woman sees us standing behind her. She pushes out of the line, practically running, like we're baby snatchers or something.

Landry folds his arms and glares at the ground. Time for a distraction.

"So have you ever been to the market before?" I ask. He shakes his head, and I hold in my sigh. "Well, you're in luck. Carmela makes the best blueberry muffins you'll ever taste. They literally melt in your mouth. Actually all of her muffins are good. I also need more bread. Hell, with you eating everything in sight, I need to restock my whole pantry. The trick is to check what the other vendors are selling because, while the prices are the same, the quality of the items varies." I point to the tent beside us. "See those carrots? They're tiny compared to the ones across the way."

Landry nods.

"Don't worry. If everything goes okay, I'll treat you to an ice cream cone at Munchies for being such a good boy." I reach up and pinch his cheek. He doesn't pull away, just stares at me, and I release him.

Dying stole Landry's sense of humor.

"Boring…you're so boring now," I tease, hoping for a smile.

He sighs. "I'm trying not to piss you off."

"Well, you're doing exactly the opposite. Do I need to introduce you to my psychiatrist? He put me on some good drugs. They made me drool like a bulldog, but I'm amazingly carefree given the circumstances." I bite my lip. "Hmm, maybe that isn't such a bad idea. If you're depressed, you should see a doctor."

"I'll be fine."

"What happened to you was very traumatic."

"I'll get through it, Mala." He tips his chin. "Look, isn't that Dena?" The red-headed girl standing in line to pay for bags of veggies could be a female clone of her father—only way cuter, like a Raggedy Ann doll, and without the murderous disposition.

"Hey, cuz," I yell, waving to my way, way, distant cousin. Not that we care how far back the relationship stretches. Family is family. Too bad Mr. Acker never felt the same. Alive or dead, the man's still a jerk.

Dena's skin pales, making her freckles pop. "Mala, hello."

Her body language shouts her reluctance at coming over to us. Is it because of me or Landry? Since she gives him a tight smile but avoids eye contact with me, I'm guessing I'm the one making her uncomfortable.

Landry looks between us. "I'll hold our place in line."

I walk over to Dena and wait until she finishes paying for her groceries. She tips her head, and we head toward a relatively crowd-free spot behind one of the tents.

"What's wrong, Waydene?" I ask. "You're acting squirmier than usual."

Her fiery bangs fall in her face. "Don't call me that, *Malaise*," she hisses, poking my arm. She flushes again. "Oh, I'm so sorry. Did I hurt you?"

She scans my face as if searching for injury. I roll my eyes. "I'm fine."

Tears brighten her eyes. "Are you sure? I know you got shot. I'm sorry I didn't come see you in the hospital," she finishes in a rush.

So far, it appears nobody knows about the psych ward. My friends all think it took me a month to recover from getting shot. Which it did, but not physically. Seeing Dena brings the guilt I feel about killing her dad bubbling up.

"Don't worry about it," I say. "I'm kind of glad you didn't see me like that. I wasn't at my best after what happened."

She leans closer and glances around. "So, Landry, huh?"

My cheeks heat up. "Yeah, he's staying at my place. He doesn't have anywhere to go."

"Oh my gosh, you're living in sin with Sir Hotness?" She practically shouts the question, and I look around to make sure we weren't overheard. I pull her over to a secluded area, upwind of the Port-A-Potty, and drag her down onto an empty park bench.

"*Shh*, damn it. We're friends, Dee. Not fornicating like rabbits in my empty house beneath the nose of my mother's ghost." And certainly not with the rev lurking about. Shudders.

Dena's face blanches again, and she groans. "Oh, gosh, I put my foot in my mouth again. How can you stand to be around me?"

"I swear, if you weren't family—"

"Very funny, but I'm serious. I can't believe he's living with you. Everyone thinks he helped his dad try to kill you."

"But you know better, right?"

She swallows and meets my gaze. "Guess he told you that I drove him to your house that night."

I let out a strangled "What?"

Dena practically curls inside herself. "Oh. He didn't tell you."

"No, he didn't," I say crisply. "Spill it."

"Don't be mad at him. Promise?"

"You know I don't make promises I can't keep."

Her guilt dries up faster than a puddle on a summer's day. Once ignited, my cousin's temper flames hotter than a brush fire. She pokes my arm again, only this time she doesn't apologize. "Dad and I went to his house after the funeral. Landry said he wanted to see you, but he wasn't in any condition to drive."

"I knew your dads were friends, but not that you and Landry hung out or anything."

"Yeah, our dads played poker every week at the hunting cabin. Landry occasionally came with him. We'd watch movies, or I'd take him over to spy on you…" Her voice trails off into a guilty whisper. "Oops, I wasn't supposed to tell you that."

"Did you say *spy* on me?"

"Uh, yeah." She glances over my shoulder, and I turn. Landry has reached the front counter. My eyes narrow on his back. He must feel my glare because he glances over at me and winces.

"What exactly do you mean? Spy?"

"He came over a couple of times a month and snuck over to your house so he could watch you. I swear it's not as stalker-y as it sounds. I would've told you if he got superobsessive."

My legs go weak. "For how long?"

"What do you mean?" She blinks her sea green eyes at me innocently, but I know her. She's not as ditzy as she seems. If she's telling me this now, it's for a reason.

"How long did he watch me?"

"Oh. Since our senior year."

I squeeze my eyes shut. I meant how long did he stay at my house watching me. Thank God I never pranced around the yard buck naked. "I'm gonna kill you."

"Why? It's cute. He's had a mega-crush on you for years, but you never noticed. Shoot, I'm jealous. I've hung out with him since grade school, and he never once looked at me the way he watches you. Like now." She tips her head in his direction. As soon as he sees me staring, he turns away.

"He doesn't have a crush on me." If he did, he wouldn't keep rejecting me.

"Whatever. Continue living life like an ostrich with its head in the sand if it makes you feel better. It doesn't change the truth, only makes the situation more tragic. He's put himself out there. It's one thing to break his heart out of ignorance. It's another to deliberately stomp on his affections while knowing the truth but ignoring it."

God, I hate her logic. I prefer flighty Dena to wizened sage. I want to wipe the smug expression off of her face. Her honesty today doesn't make up for keeping Landry's obsession a secret for two years. "You've distracted me long enough. You said you brought Landry over the night Mama died?"

"Yeah, he wanted to give you a book, or diary, or something, so I agreed. We didn't know our dads were there."

Her playful tone drops, and she takes a deep, shaky breath. "I saw the fire so I got out of the truck and walked up. Oh my God, I was so scared."

"You saw Landry grab me?"

She shakes her head. "I saw my father shoot you. He chased you into the woods." She twists her fingers together. "Dad never came home. I waited, afraid he'd know I went there, and I'd get beat, but he never came back. Did something bad happen to him?"

I don't want to say. "He chased me into the Black Hole."

She doubles over, clutching her stomach. "So, he's dead?"

I nod.

She wipes a tear from the corner of her eye. "Wish I could say good riddance to bad trash, but he's…he was my father. He wasn't always bad—just crazy when it came to Reverend Prince. He thought the man walked on water. When Lainey died, I think Dad really believed your mama sacrificed her in a satanic ritual."

"Landry said a fourth guy was at the house. Do you know who he is?"

"No, the men wore masks. I knew Dad by his voice. The curses he screamed at you…"

I wrap my arms around her. "I'm so sorry you had to go through that."

"It's not your fault."

"Still…"

She sniffs and wipes her eyes on her sleeve. "Still, nothing. You almost died. Don't ever apologize for surviving. Ever! What my dad and those men did was evil."

"It still boggles my mind that four men would be so willing to conspire and commit murder. It takes a special brand of crazy to think of the idea and carry it out."

Dena shrugs. "Your mama's crazy, Dad's crazy. Reverend Prince is his own special blend of coo-coo-kachu. Gawd, I hope the psycho gene skips a generation so we'll be safe. I'll call the Sheriff's Office and ask if Andy can bring Rex out to sniff around."

"I'm not sure the scent—"

"You said he's in the Black Hole. That only means one thing."

"Quicksand," we say in unison.

I glance at my hands. "I'm so sorry. I should've told you sooner. I didn't remember what happened to him at first. I had amnesia."

"Maggie told me."

"Oh. Well, my memories came back slowly. Then I didn't

know how to tell you. I wanted to tell you in person, not by phone. But the words…I couldn't figure out how to say—"

"How to say my father tried to murder you? I get it." Dena wipes her leaking eyes again. "Do you remember where he died?"

"It was dark, so I'm not positive. I remember thorns and hiding behind a tree. The only place that comes to mind is by the blackberry patch and lightning-struck oak. If you come over this afternoon, I'll walk you to the spot. One of the bullets struck the tree…"

She lets out a low groan but nods. "I'll do my best to come after work, but…Mala, I'm not sure if I can handle this."

"You won't have to deal with this alone. I promise." I give her a hug, then watch her walk off, terrified for her. Did this news just destroy her family? Her mama ran off eight years ago. Now her dad's dead, leaving her with four younger brothers. Her part-time job at Munchies won't cover their care. At least she's old enough to apply for guardianship, but I'm afraid the kids will be farmed out to different foster homes.

She's had a month to consider what she'll do if her dad doesn't come home. She knows better than I do whether she can feed and clothe her family on her own. Hell, who knows whether she even wants to take on such a life-altering responsibility. This could be her only chance at freedom.

I spend five minutes in line to pay for my collard greens. By the time I'm done, I can't find Landry. He must've headed for the truck. I walk out of the square, inhaling. The warm air carries the fragrance of roses planted along the wall bordering the Vietnam Memorial Garden. Sweat stains the pits of my v-neck T-shirt. I'm sure I smell less than fresh, unlike the girl who walks around the corner.

Clarice Delahoussaye wears a shimmery scarf over her long

chestnut hair. She looks like a bohemian princess. Real pretty, and I'm kind of jealous since the scarf's my favorite color—periwinkle, shot through with threads of silver. It totally matches her flowing skirt, peasant blouse, and silver earrings.

When she sees me, she lays a hand flat on her head. Her fingers tremble.

"Clarice," I say in greeting, preparing for her scorn.

Instead she smiles, a sickly twisting of her lips. "Mala, you're back."

"Pretty scarf. Where did you get?"

She turns an unhealthy color green. "Don't, please."

"What are you talking about?"

"Please, I'll be good. I promise."

I back away from her. Here comes another brand of crazy.

She grabs my arm. "Please, take off the curse. I'll do anything you ask. I swear."

I wrench my arm from her grasp. Her nails dig grooves in my skin. Blood wells up and trickles down my arm. "Damn it, that hurt."

Tears fill her eyes. "I'm sorry." She drops to her knees. I leap back, afraid she's going to hit me, but she folds up her hands as if in prayer instead. "Take back the curse. I swear I won't bother you ever again. I don't even like Landry anymore. He's the son of murderers. He helped his father kill your mom. I don't want anything to do with him."

She's got such a tight grip on my pant leg that I can't rip free. I squat down and pry her fingers free of my jeans. "Clarice, firstly, I can't fix a curse. It's not in my skill set. I'm not a real witch, just a bitch. Secondly, damn it, there's no such thing as curses. Whatever you think is wrong with you is only a delusion. Something your screwed-on-backward head tells you is real but isn't."

Listen to your own words, Malaise.

"A delusion?" Clarice stands and rips off the scarf. Bald, scaly patches decorate her scalp like red polka dots, and I gasp. "If you didn't fix a curse, then what the hell's the matter with me? You said my hair would fall out. You bragged you'd get Landry if you wanted him, but I didn't listen." She folds her hands. "I'm listening now. Please, I'll do whatever you tell me to do."

If I'm not careful, I'll be overcome with sympathy for this girl. Clarice made it her mission in life to make me miserable. Unfortunately, even though I can't stand her raggedy ass, I can't leave her like this either. Her condition will only get worse. Her belief is too strong.

"Be at my house at two p.m. By then I'll have figured out a spell to help you."

She nods.

"And bring fifty bucks," I yell at her retreating back.

Landry swings around the corner and watches her jerky stride.

"How long were you listening?" I ask.

"Parent murderers, delusion, balding."

"So the whole thing?"

"Why ask questions you already know the answers to? Let's go home."

I wave at Reverend Shane, and the pregnant woman I assume is his wife, Molly, on the way out. Landry travels in his own world. He doesn't look up to acknowledge them. When did he get this intense?

CHAPTER 17

LANDRY

Hoodoo on the Internet

The house smells funny.

"Is that baloney?" Mala asks, sniffing the air like a blood-hound.

I raise an eyebrow. "What kind of baloney are you asking about?"

"There's more than one kind?"

She doesn't get the innuendo, and I'm kind of glad. When am I going to learn to keep my distance? I gave in once already today with the mind-blowing kiss. I can't afford to do it again. I can't scare her off. I can't protect her if I'm not here.

God, here I go again. I can't think of anything else but how to protect Mala. What I'll do if the fourth guy or a poltergeist tries to hurt her. I draw in a deep breath then lie, "I don't smell anything weird."

"It smells like baloney and cheese." She runs into the kitchen.

I'm careful not to rush, but I follow at a quick pace. There aren't any tracks on the floor, but she's right. Someone's been in here. I feel a strange, hair-raising sensation, like someone's hiding in a closet waiting to jump out with a chain saw to cut me into bite-size chunks.

Mala points to the greasy skillet on the stove. "I washed that this morning."

Dad. Damn it! If he doesn't learn how to clean up after himself, he's gonna get busted. "Are you sure? We were rushing to get out of the house this morning."

Her nostrils flare. "Are you calling me crazy?"

"Are you saying we're in the middle of another Goldilocks situation?" I force a laugh. "Who's sleeping in your bed, eating your food? A ghost?"

"Why would a ghost eat a baloney and egg sandwich?" Her voice rises several octaves. She shakes the skillet in my direction, splashing hot grease on her hand, and cries out. She slams it back onto a burner. "Earn your keep and catch the blond bitch living in our house or get out!"

I'm so screwed. "Do you hear yourself, Mala?"

After several deep breaths and hard sucks on her burnt fingers, she wipes her eyes.

"Are you crying over a dirty skillet?" I ask. "I'll clean it if it makes you feel better."

"It's not the skillet, Landry. It's that I never thought to hear you call me crazy. I guess I just expected you to trust me." She shakes her head. "Why am I wasting my time? Dena's as delusional as Clarice."

"What?"

"Forget it. I have to prepare for my magic act."

I'm more than happy to change the subject. "So what are you

gonna do? Wave a magic wand over Clarice's head and chant po-etry or something?"

"Something like that. If I don't, she'll never believe the curse is lifted. She'll end up spending her life as a stunt double for Humpty Dumpty. I'll find a spell on the Internet. There has to be one that's not too hard to copy. If I do it up real spiffy, I know I can pull it off."

"Maybe you can, but do you want to? Won't you feel guilty?"

"Nah, Clarice is my archnemesis."

"Well, go ahead. But be careful. If one of those ghosts possesses you again, it might blow your brain out for good this time."

She grimaces, then shrugs. I hear her mumble Dena's name again and "full of shit." She wipes leftover grease out of the skillet with a paper towel then proceeds to scrub it as if getting a pig spruced up for the fair.

I lean my hip against the counter. "What did you and Dena talk about that's got you so pissed off?"

Mala leaps back with a squeak, not having heard me walk up behind her. It startles me almost as much, since I wasn't aware of how close I'd gotten. "Sorry."

She waves off my apology. "Dena told me how she brought you over here that night."

I swallow hard. "Did she…" *Say anything else?* I back up until my back hits the edge of the refrigerator.

She gives me a long, steady look then shakes her head. "She didn't know the name of the fourth guy. Her father won't tell me what he knows until I get his body buried. I promised to take Dena to where he died. She'll be over later."

"Oh." I open the refrigerator and pull out a can of soda. When she doesn't say anything else, I ask, "You understand why I didn't tell you about her?"

"Yeah." She slams the skillet in the drying rack.

Prickles of unease run down my spine. *What aren't you telling me, Mala?*

I venture forth with another question. "With George hanging around after Acker's attack, I couldn't ask but…what happened to him?" I hop up onto the counter, but she shoos me off with a snap of a wet dishtowel. I barely dodge it.

"Mala?"

She lets out a heavy sigh. "Acker chased me into the Black Hole. He had me cornered by a tree. That's when he shot me again, point blank. No remorse. And while I lay on the ground bleeding, he taunted me with how excited he was to kill me. How he couldn't wait to watch me die. Lainey shoved him into quicksand before he could shoot me in the head."

Her breaths come in ragged gasps. I'm standing right in front of her, but she doesn't see me. It's Acker's face that fills her vision.

"Mala, stop," I whisper.

She blinks, glancing in my direction. "I could've pulled him out, but I didn't. Then he was gone."

I reach for her.

Her eyes flick to my hands, then she vanishes into my blind spot.

"You don't have to feel guilty. Evil begets evil," I say to her retreating back.

She pauses in the doorway. Her hand clutches the door frame. "Don't you get it, Landry? What I did or, rather, didn't do. That's evil."

* * *

Why am I doing this?

Mala sits at the kitchen table hunched in front of a laptop only a decade younger than she is, gnawing on the tip of her braid like a squirrel. She shouts the occasional order in my direction but doesn't stop researching spells to see if I'm following through. Maybe she knows I don't have a choice any more than she does.

A bald Clarice bothers me. We lived across the street from one another our whole lives. She was my best friend until middle school drove us apart. Our moms held the crazy idea their offspring would marry someday—though it seemed more likely Red and Lainey would get hitched. Our moms weren't subtle about their desire either. If I'd been born a couple hundred years earlier, I would've been betrothed to Clarice at birth.

I'd never been too keen on the idea of having my life planned out. Clarice didn't feel the same. She saw me as hers, and made sure the girls in town knew it. Most were too scared to go against her. The only person Clarice didn't scare was Mala.

I glance at her again. "You know, inviting Clarice over to perform a fake spell seems the epitome of hypocrisy. Remember how you felt about fake Madame Ruby?"

She sighs and stretches. "We're not discussing this again."

"The woman died after letting Lainey possess her."

"The difference between me and Ruby is I really can speak to the dead, and I don't need to be possessed to do it." She slaps the laptop closed. "Remind me if I forget to ask Clarice for my payment."

"You're really making her pay?"

"If I don't, she won't appreciate my efforts as much. Plus I need the money," she mutters. Her eyebrows droop. "Did you finish inventorying the spice rack?"

"Thyme?" I raise the bottle and shake it.

"I'm supposed to use sage, but I'm allergic. I don't feel like spending the next few hours sneezing. Plus it keeps spirits away."

I line up bottles of spices in front of her. She starts mixing them up in a bowl, referring off and on to a print-out of the instructions—*for the magic spell, which won't do shit!*

This has got to be the worst idea.

"What do you want me to do now?" I ask, sitting across from her.

She hands me a rolling pin and a cardboard container of Morton's Salt. "Grind this up."

I scowl, and she sighs. "Salt protects against evil spirits. It's why Acker couldn't pass the boundary of the house."

"And the thyme?"

"The thyme—far as I know, it makes super-delicious chicken soup."

I push the salt back across the table. "I hear a car pulling down the driveway."

"That'll be Clarice. Dena will be coming through the woods." She runs her hands down the sides of Ms. Jasmine's shimmery blue dress. It hugs her curves in all the right places. "Do I look okay?"

Fear flickers in her brown eyes. I wish I could talk her out of this. It seems wrong, but maybe she's right. Seeing Clarice earlier shocked me. She looked like she had lost a girl fight and got clumps of hair yanked out of her head. If the cause of her hair loss really is due to her mind playing tricks on her—a psychological response to the "curse" Mala put on her—then the only way to break the curse is for Mala do something supernaturally impressive.

Mala clears her throat. "Well, do I?"

I shrug. "Yeah, you look beautiful."

Her cheeks flush. She spins in a circle, giggling, as the bottom of her dress bells out, flashing sleek calves. My mouth goes dry…I mentally slap myself on the forehead. Why can't I keep my opinions to myself? I never thought I'd actually wish for George to show up to provide a buffer between us. I take a step back. "Let's go meet your guest."

She grabs my arm. "Why do you keep doing that—pulling away from me?" She bites her plump bottom lip, and my own starts to tingle at the memory of the kiss we shared earlier. She looks up at me with bitter-chocolate eyes melting in sadness. "Are you upset because you overheard Mama talking about me kissing Georgie?"

Whoa, unexpected. A rush of anger flows through me at being blindsided. I'm a guy. Doesn't she know guys don't talk about their "feelings"? Not that I want to discuss this now. Or yeah, ever.

I craft a mask of indifference on my face, praying it won't crack. "Your love life's none of my business. We're roommates, Mala. You don't owe me an explanation."

Her mouth opens, but I brush past her. I get to the door first in case it's not Clarice outside. Mala comes up to stand on my good side without arguing for once, smoothing down the front of her dress and then the curl that escaped from her braid, unable to stop her nervous fidgeting. A quick peek through the window makes me laugh. "Clarice brought Amanda for moral support."

"Hmm, not sure I want a witness if things go bad with Clarice."

"Mandy's kind of timid. If I go out onto the porch, I'll freak her out so bad she'll wait in the car." I reach for the doorknob, but Mala grabs my hand. Warmth flows into my chilled skin and travels upward.

She's too close. I can't breathe when she gets so close. Not without inhaling her scent. Why does she smell so good? I lift her fingers from mine and step aside.

Mala steps closer, forcing my back against the door. "You're pulling away from me again. Why?"

I hold back my sigh.

"George and I aren't—"

"Fine, we'll talk after your magic act."

"Promise you'll explain why you're acting so weird around me?"

I run a finger across my eye patch. The doorbell rings. I turn, forcing her to stumble back, and throw open the door. I step onto the porch with a wide grin. "Clarice..." I drawl, using my best Hannibal Lecter imitation.

We watched *The Silence of the Lambs* last night, and Mala laughs in reference to the serial killer. For a roommate, she's not too bad. We like the same movies and music. If I move away whenever she tries to sit beside me on the couch, even for the most innocent of reasons, she's diplomatic enough not to bring it up. At least until today.

Mala steps into the hallway. Clarice keeps her head down and the scarf pulled over her eyebrows. A strong wind wouldn't be able to blow it off. She edges around me without speaking.

Tension tightens my shoulders. I don't say another word but go outside. Amanda sees me and lets out a squeak. She dashes back to the car. My lips clench, but I keep the words locked in. I leave the door open and go sit in the rocking chair. With my chair tilted, I can see and hear everything going on in the house.

Clarice doesn't notice my absence. The girl looks around the small room, and her nose wrinkles. I felt the same way the first time I entered. Yeah, it's a run-down old farmhouse. The living room is the size of my old bedroom, but over the last week, it's become home, and I feel unusually protective of it. And of Mala, whose back stiffens when she notices the slight.

I glance at the painting of Velvet Elvis, and he winks.

"Have a seat," Mala says, pointing to the card table set up in the middle of the living room. I'd covered it with a tablecloth and lit the leftover candles that Mala's Aunt Magnolia had given her to cleanse the house. They add to the ambiance we're going for. This is a matter of psychological warfare.

"What are you planning?" Clarice asks. She runs her fingers through the thinning ends of hair hanging from beneath the scarf. Strands cling to her fingers. She shakes them onto the floor with a low moan.

Mala's eyes soften in sympathy. "You said I fixed a curse on you."

Clarice nods.

Mala wanted me to hide in the bedroom during the performance, but I refused. I want to be close if something goes wrong. And with Mala playing around with magic she knows nothing about, even if it probably is fake, chances are good something might go wrong.

The chair beside me rocks, and the hairs on my arms rise. "Ms. Jasmine? Is that you? Gaston?"

"BOO!" Mala's mom yells right in my ear and lets out a cackling laugh as she materializes. She slaps her leg and her white nightgown flutters. "Thought I could sneak up on you."

I rub my ringing ear. "You got me." My attention returns to what's going on inside.

Ms. Jasmine leans around me. "What's my girl up to?"

"She took a page out of your book and is performing a magic act."

"Oh? She gettin' paid?"

"Of course." My voice lowers. "She researched online and found a fake spell. Shush, she's about to start. This should be interesting."

Mala nods toward a metal folding chair, and Clarice follows her lead and sits down. "Things have been so chaotic I kind of forgot the exact details of our fight," Mala says in a fake, buttery voice.

"I didn't." Clarice's voice quivers. "I can't stop thinking about it. I'm sorry for slapping you."

Ms. Jasmine rises out of her seat with a cry. "That skinny bitch slapped my baby?"

"No, stop," I hiss. I forget I can't physically restrain her. My hand passes right through her chest, and her eyes widen.

"Did you just try to touch my breasts?"

A scarlet heat rushes through my body. "No, Ms. Jasmine. I'd never touch your—do that, I swear." I glance inside the house.

Mala's lips quiver. *Did she hear?*

"Please forgive me," Clarice cries, grabbing on to Mala's hands.

The smile drops from Mala's lips. She squeezes Clarice's hands. "I forgive you."

"You said you didn't want Landry."

Mala's gaze flickers in my direction. "I did."

My stomach tightens, and I sink lower in the rocking chair.

Ms. Jasmine shakes her head. "Mala's lyin'. She's got a powerful lust for you. A mama knows her child."

"If this is supposed to make me feel better, Ms. Jasmine, it's not."

"Course not. You're too busy denyin' yourself. Gaston told me you feel guilty and don't think you deserve my daughter. Does being a martyr make you feel like more of a man?"

"Neither of you would've been hurt if it wasn't for my family."

I choke on a bitter laugh. "I'm okay with it. I just want her to be safe—happy. She's got George."

"Ha, that boy's too conflicted to make her happy. Do you really think his mama, hell, even her own father, will ever accept their relationship? She's a livin' reminder of his infidelity." She waves me off when I glance at Mala again. "She's not listenin' to us, but it might save her a lot of heartache if she did. Never mind. I'm wastin' my breath, ain't I? Maybe someday you'll remember my words and take them to heart."

I expect her to disappear, but she doesn't. Guess she's bored enough being dead that this seems entertaining.

Ms. Jasmine shakes her head. "That poor girl looks tore up from the ground up. What happened to her anyway?"

"She says Mala cursed her into losing her hair."

"Heh, my girl's learned to throw curses. Knew she had power, but not how to use it. Sounds like they got into a fight over you, huh?"

Are they still talking about me? Time for me to pay more attention to the conversation going on inside. Mala leans over the table, listening to Clarice. I find both of their eyes on me, and I look back at Ms. Jasmine. The woman wiggles her eyebrows at me, and I laugh.

"I've loved Landry since we were in kindergarten," Clarice says. "He's never seen me as anything but a friend. Guess I dodged a bullet with him. He's gone crazy, hasn't he?"

I jerk in surprise. "What's she talking about?"

Ms. Jasmine rolls her index finger around her ear. "She can't see me, remember. Looks to her like you're sittin' out here conversin' with an invisible person."

Mala laughs. "He's no crazier than you begging me to un-curse you."

Tears fill Clarice's eyes. "I'm desperate."

"Well, take off your scarf." Clarice does, and Mala picks up the spices I mixed together—cayenne pepper, thyme, and oregano. She sprinkles the mixture onto Clarice's head. "Rub it in good."

She does. "It burns."

"Good. That means it's working." Mala covers her mouth and sneezes. "You're done. Go on outside and make sure you rub that in good. Don't wash your hair for a week. Don't run your fingers through it or scratch your scalp. After seven days, wash your hair with peppermint tea. On the full moon, burn a strand of hair and throw the ashes in running water, like a stream or creek."

Clarice's eyes narrow.

"What? Do you think I'm making this up?" Mala snaps.

"N-no, I trust you." Clarice pulls out an envelope. "Here's your money. Thank you."

Mala flips through it, lips moving as she counts the bills stuffed inside. "Good. Now go on and get out of here. Make sure you speak nicely to Landry on the way out."

CHAPTER 18

MALA

Pit Viper

I watch Clarice leave, then sink onto the sofa. Why did I ask her over? Part of me feels like I did a good deed. The other part feels dirty. Landry and Mama come inside with Cheshire Cat grins stretching their cheeks, and I sigh. "What now?"

"When did you learn how to throw a curse?" Mama asks.

I glance at Landry. "What is she talking about?"

Landry plops down on the edge of the sofa. He runs his fingers through his black hair then rolls his wide shoulders in circles. He looks as mentally drained as I feel. "Ms. Jasmine saw Clarice pay you and started complaining about how, if you can throw curses, you should get more than fifty," he says.

Of course, why did I bother to ask? I roll my eyes. "Are you kidding me?"

"She has a point." Landry shares a look with Mama, and I feel excluded. They've bonded during their time on the porch. Jealousy makes my stomach burn. I'm not sure who I'm jealous of, only that I envy the ease of their relationship. "I paid Madame Ruby a hundred dollars to contact Lainey's spirit," Landry says, and I blink at him. He leans in my direction. "Don't you get it?"

Mama settles in her favorite armchair with one leg propped over the arm. Her foot bops up and down. Luckily she wore her long white cotton nightgown the night she died; otherwise she would've spent eternity in a muscle skirt and thong. A shudder-worthy thought, since Landry can see her.

Fingers snap in front of my eyes. "Are you listening?"

I wave Landry's hand away and lean my head against the back of the sofa.

"With your ability to speak to the dead, you're more powerful than she was," he says. "Plus, if you can work magic…"

Nothing happened when I tried to take down Reverend Prince yesterday, but what if I really *can* work magic?

"You're talking about black magic," I snap, crossing my arms. "Curses are evil. If I really cursed Clarice to have her hair fall out, then that was wrong."

Mama and Landry share a confused grimace. They don't get it. *Two peas in a pod.*

My chest clenches. "That's the kind of magic Auntie Magnolia does."

"Exactly," Mama cries. "That's why you got to take yourself to New Orleans to apprentice with her."

I die a little death every time I think about visiting that woman.

Landry stiffens. "Hold on. What do you mean? New Orleans?"

"Mama made me promise to go to Magnolia so she can teach me how to use my powers." I feel like an idiot for saying the word. *Powers.* What a load of bullshit. I don't feel very power-ful—confused bordering on schizoid, yes.

"When did you plan on telling me that you're leaving?"

I pat Landry on the knee. It's a testament to how badly I've an-noyed him when he doesn't shift away from my hand. "Sorry. It's not a promise I can get out of, but I can choose when I go. Don't worry. I'll stay here until you heal up some more."

Landry's quiet for a long, thoughtful moment. "Getting out of Paradise Pointe isn't such a bad idea. It'll be less stressful…safer living with your aunt. Plus if you can learn how to use your gifts to make some money—"

"Then you go if you want to learn how to swindle the gullible bereaved out of their hard-earned cash. Not like I'm the only one in this room who can speak to the dead."

"Don't you need money to pay your bills?"

"I need to earn money by performing fake séances like I need a hole in my head." I meet his concerned eyes. I don't buy his excuse…money, hah. He's trying to get rid of me. My stomach burns at the thought. Man, I hope I'm reading too much into his sudden enthusiasm. "Look, I didn't tell you, since we weren't on speaking terms this morning, but Bill Aldridge called. He's Mama's attorney, been on retainer for years due to her repeated brushes with the law…" I shake my head. "Long story short, Mama had a life insurance policy, and I'm the beneficiary."

"Why do you sound so shocked, Mala Jean?" Mama says. "I told you I put my affairs in order after I got my death vision. Do you think I'm such a bad mother that I wouldn't set aside money for when I died? You also get your inheritance, which has been passed down through the generations."

"Yay…" I drawl, lazily punching the air with my fists. "See, Landry? I am officially the owner of a hunk of swamp."

Landry snorts. "Don't hold in your excitement. You might bust a gut."

"I'll try to contain it." I yawn, patting my mouth with a hand.

"Well, I can't lie. I'm sort of relieved you don't have to pull a fake madame routine to keep your house."

"Me too." I curl my legs beneath me, wishing I could take a nap, but I still have to head out once Dena shows up. My eyes get stuck at half-mast. The numbers on the digital clock tick forward with soul-numbing slowness.

Landry nods off in the opposite corner, head tilted against the back of the sofa and arms crossed. His mouth hangs open slightly, showing straight white teeth. His hair has fallen back, revealing the sharp angles of his high cheekbones. Long black eyelashes and eyebrows stand out in sharp relief against his skin. He looks vulnerable. And sinful as a Devil Creme cake.

I lick my lips, mouth dry. Heat radiates upward to burn in my cheeks. I inch closer, until his heat warms the coldness in my hands. His pouty lower lip taunts me, begging to be licked.

"How much longer are you planning on staring at me?" Landry asks. "If you haven't memorized my face by now, you won't." His gray eye opens. Today it warms me.

I sigh, sitting back before my shaky arms give out and I fall on top of him. He'd probably just dump me on the floor again. I glance over at the armchair, but Mama's vanished. Probably back in the bedroom watching never-ending repeats of *Y&R* on the Soap Opera channel.

"It's not my fault you're so pretty," I mutter.

"Yeah, blame my parents for good DNA." His laughter trails off.

I glance at the clock again, trying to ignore the minnows-swimming-in-my-tummy feeling I get when I think of my cousin. "Dena should be here by now."

"Maybe she changed her mind."

"It's her father. She can't move forward until she has his body." I grab Landry by the arm. He shrugs away with a slight dip of his shoulder. "I'm going to go look for her. Do you want to come?"

"No." His eye shuts again.

More avoidance. "Fine. I'll be back before dark."

I throw the door open so hard it slams against the wall and don't go back to close it behind me. *Landry's an ass!* To think I worried about living with him. I thought he'd be like before—flirty—a slightly dangerous threat to my virginity. That Landry I understand. I can shield myself from caving to his charm. This guy, yeah, not so safe. The more he pushes me away, the more I'm drawn to him like a freaking meteorite that will shatter when it crashes into the moon.

How did I become the one trying to edge into his life? He obviously doesn't want anything to do with me. If I keep chasing him, he'll run. Maybe he'll go to Clarice. And why shouldn't he? She loves him.

"Wait!" Footsteps run down the stairs, then I hear a crash and a grunt. I spin. Landry's on his knees at the foot of the staircase. He grabs on to the railing and pulls himself upright with a wince.

I step toward him and stop. He won't appreciate my concern. I turn back around and start walking again.

"Hey, I'm coming with you." His hand latches on to my arm. "It's not safe for you to be wandering around the woods alone."

"I've wandered my whole life. What makes today different?" I shrug off his hand the same way he did mine earlier. "Look, just go back inside and take a nap. Maybe you won't be cranky when you wake up. I'm stressing about Dena, and I don't need any distractions."

His lips tighten, and his gray eye turns stormy. "I'm worried about her too. Do you have a gun?"

This throws me. "Why?"

He scans the surrounding woods. "It's gonna get dark soon. I'd rather have protection."

The woods go silent as if waiting for my response. Even the slight wind ceases to blow. A moment ago I couldn't wait to escape into the thick brush. Now its shadows look menacing. I scowl at Landry. Way to freak me out.

"I have no idea where Mama put the shotgun." I rub my arms. "She never liked having Grandma Cora's gun in the house. The thing was so old, she worried it would backfire and blow off her face if she tried to use it."

I glance at him from the corner of my eye. "'Sides, if I had a gun, I would've shot your father's friends when they broke into my house!"

He raises his hands. "Sorry, I—"

"No." I wave off his apology. He has a right to be worried. If I had an ounce of self-preservation, I'd act more like him. "I get it. The fourth guy."

Somewhere the unidentified fourth guy waits for a chance to get us in his sights. I've lulled myself into a false sense of security by having Landry living with me. Truth is, he's in as much or more danger than I am. "You're right. That guy's still out there. Bet he's hiding out with Rathbone and your father, planning their revenge on us."

Landry's mouth opens like he's about to say something profound, like maybe confessing the truth about Rathbone's death. Wishful thinking.

He shakes his head. "I'd feel better if we had a weapon."

Fine. Rather than heading into the woods, I walk around the side of the house to the screened-in back porch. When Mama lived, I slept out here in the hammock during the summer. The heat made it difficult to get a good night's rest. The box I store my gear inside sits in the corner. I haven't used it since Landry and I went fishing. I dig out the utility belt that holds my sheathed fillet knife and wrap it around my waist. A stick from the woods makes a handy club. I left it in the umbrella stand instead of throwing it into the yard for this reason. I dart inside to get it and hand it to Landry.

Anxiety doesn't sit well on him.

"Don't worry," I say. "We'll just walk to Dena's house. We'll be fine if we stay on the path."

He breathes out a puff of air. "Okay, let's go."

I check overhead. White fluffy clouds and clear blue sky share space with the setting sun. We still have about three hours of daylight. More than enough to get to the Ackers' farm and back. Muggy heat drenches me with perspiration. The temperature drops several degrees once we get beneath the thick canopy of trees, but the stagnant pools of water increase the moisture in the air.

Mosquitoes buzz, and I swat a little sucker on my arm. The tension flows from my body. Nature relaxes me. The song of birds, the chirp of frogs, the buzz of insects, and the feel of dirt beneath my feet. The only thing chipping at my increasingly good mood? Landry.

I feel guilty about dragging him out. My panic about Dena is premature. She's probably fine. I should've ignored the tingling sense of unease turning my stomach into a knot. Being out here only shifts my nervousness off my cousin's safety onto Landry.

After the rebuff he gave earlier, I don't want to bring up the topic of our relationship, or lack thereof, again. It's pretty obvious that Dena's wrong about Landry having a crush on me. Or if he did, I've scared him off.

I shouldn't be surprised. Who'd want to date me after getting to know me? I have a bad temper. I'm too sarcastic. I see ghosts. My mama's undead or…whatever you call ancestral spirits who never give you any privacy even after they've supposedly crossed over to the spirit realm.

That's the scary thing. How in tune I've become to the spirit realm. At first, I felt overwhelmed by all of the ghosts flittering in and out of my hospital room, talking to me, asking me for help. I couldn't tell the difference between a real person and a spirit unless they displayed the gruesomeness of their death: A decapitated man roaming around the hospital searching for his head pretty much screamed GHOST.

I haven't told Landry, but I stopped taking my psych meds. Part of me regrets it because my PTSD symptoms have increased, but the medication blocked my ability. It kept me from learning how to tell the difference between the real world and the fake, because even while drugged, I still saw ghosts. Meds just reduced my anxiety level enough to keep me from freaking out as much upon seeing them. I also didn't care about George being my brother or Ms. March keeping that secret from me for years.

Now…now I'm pissed. And disgusted by the overwhelming hurt and betrayal I feel. I'm being crushed beneath the weight of all the emotions George must've felt in the psych ward when Ms. March revealed the truth. Now I understand why he ran from me.

I sigh, kicking a rock into the bushes. "Where the hell is she?"

Landry glances in my direction. "Something probably

came up at home, and she couldn't make it tonight. Why didn't you call her...or drive over?" He swats at a mosquito with a grimace.

"It takes longer to drive than to walk. It's the twisty way the bayou flows. 'Sides, maybe she's on the way and we'll meet up with her."

"And the phone?"

I bite my lip. "Honestly I forgot I could call. Her dad never let her use the phone unless it was for business or emergencies."

"So you'd just show up on her property?" He scowls. "That doesn't seem very smart either. I seem to recall Acker pulling a gun on you. Did that happen so often you got immune to it?"

"Who gets immune to having the barrel of a gun shoved in their face?" I scowl. "I never thought he'd really shoot me. Shows how much I know about human nature, huh?"

"Seriously?"

"No, we usually met at the pond." My lip curls at his expression. There's a break in the leaves ahead, and I see the sparkle of water. I grin up at Landry. "Race you to Daisy."

"Hey, I'm injured, remember? Stabbed...skinned knees from falling down stairs, one eye..." He grabs my arm and yanks me behind his back as he breaks into a limping run.

"Cheater!" I yell, sprinting after him.

"I'm handicapped. I get a head start." *Like he needs one.* His long legs eat up ground. Maybe he's not in prime condition, but he still moves faster than my stubby legs can keep up with. His hand slaps down on the bow of my rowboat about twenty seconds before mine. "I won," he crows, dancing around while giving the air high-fives. He looks like an idiot.

I tell him so.

Landry's lip pokes out. "You're jealous of my skills."

"You have an unfair advantage since you're unnaturally tall and fit."

"Unnaturally?"

"In comparison to me." I wade into the pond to rinse the sweat from my face. Crystal clear water shows my reflection, and I stick my tongue out. My curls have broken free of my braid and are in revolt again.

Landry slaps a hand on Daisy's hull. "We should've brought some water."

My head tilts. "Check inside the boat. We left so fast the last time I don't think we took the supplies back." I follow him and point to a storage compartment built beneath one of the benches. "Could be some bottled water in there."

Landry climbs into Daisy and rummages through the storage compartment. My eyes linger on the strip of bare flesh between the bottom of his T-shirt and his baggy jeans. He looks over, and my face flushes. "Two waters and three cans of soda. I'm surprised the carbonation didn't explode in this heat."

"It's below the waterline." I fan myself with a hand, feeling like I'm about to self-combust from the surge of desire flooding though me. I shove my hands into the water and duck my head beneath the surface. Cold water douses the flames burning inside of me.

"Uh, feel better?" He passes me a bottle of water.

"Fine…overheated." The words come out in a gargling, shrill tone that gives away my attraction even more than if I had run my fingers up the indentation of his spine peeking from beneath his shirt.

"How far to Dena's?" Landry asks.

"Remember where we saw her father? Their place is about a half mile from there." I jump up to sit on the edge of the boat.

"So here's the thing I'm worried about. Acker was one of those survivalists who thought either the federal government was out to steal his land or that a zombie horde would attack. I'm pretty sure he booby-trapped his property."

"You shitting me?"

"I wish…the man was psycho."

"You don't seriously mean for us to dodge booby traps to get to the house."

I give him a sideways grimace, annoyed by his fake ignorance. If Dena hadn't spilled about his visits to her place and his proclivity for stalking, I'd believe his false expression of shock. "Nah, if we make enough noise, one of the kids will meet us at the fence. They'll either lead us to the house or bring Dena to us."

After a five-minute break, we resume our hike. Landry occasionally presses his hand against his wound, and I slow my pace, until we're ambling more than walking. "It's a beautiful day," I say, smiling up at him.

Landry quirks a raven's-wing eyebrow. "What's with the small talk? I thought you wanted to have a deep, meaningful conversation about our relationship."

A bug flies into my open mouth, and I cough. Mother Mary, please don't let it be a poisonous species.

"Y-you *want* to talk? Now?" What's wrong with him? His mood swings faster than the Chair-O-Planes ride at the carnival.

Landry grunts, holding a low-lying branch aside until I pass. The muscles in my back bunch from the tension of having him behind me, but I keep walking, ignoring the increasing need to look at him over my shoulder.

"You asked why I keep pulling away." His voice sounds harsh, strained from effort.

"Uh, yeah…it's pretty obvious my touch disgusts you now." My lips twist.

"Dramatic much?"

I spin, throwing my hands in the air. "Okay, fine. But you know what I mean."

"Your mom's dead 'cause of my family." His head tilts as he studies me through an eye as distant and cold as the Arctic.

I shiver, rubbing the goose bumps on my arms.

His gaze follows the movement of my hands, and the gray softens. How can gray have so much depth? Hot, warm, cold—light or dark, all depending on his swiftly changing mood. I can't get a read on him.

"Why doesn't it bother you?" He strips a leaf from a branch, shreds it into three strips, then tosses the pieces to the ground. "I can't stop thinking about it. Every time you look at me, I'm reminded of what happened to Ms. Jasmine."

"You saved me."

"George saved you." His voice hardens. "I let you get shot. You ended up fighting Acker alone, and the only reason you survived is 'cause you were resilient enough to crawl to the road where George found you. He said you almost bled to death."

"Georgie thought you participated in the attack, so don't put too much stock in anything he said before finding out the truth." I lace my fingers through Landry's, and I tighten my grip so he can't let go. If I could telepathically link to him, he'd drown in the emotional mess inside me. Words seem so ineffectual. I can't seem to find the ones to break through the wall of guilt he's built up inside.

"Landry, the person who saved me is you. I would've charged in and tried to rescue Mama. I wasn't thinking rationally when you grabbed me. But even before that…you helped me survive

Lainey. You believed me when I said her ghost was haunting me. You *really* don't understand how important your belief in me is, do you?"

He brushes a wispy curl behind my ear. The gentle touch of his fingers makes the lobe of my ear tingle. His hand drops to my shoulder. "I do. Really. But, Mala, I'm not the guy for you. I don't deserve you. I never did…and"—he takes a deep breath and blows it out— "I won't let you throw away a relationship with George just 'cause I'm *way* hotter and sexier than he is."

My mouth drops. "What?"

His eye widens innocently. "I was born this way. Don't hate me."

"Are you kidding?"

"Who's kidding? Check out these muscles." He flexes a bicep.

My tongue sticks to the roof of my mouth. "Uh…yeah."

"See, totally unfair advantage."

I want to beat my head in with a rock. I even look around for one of good size. My brain has ceased functioning. It really has. What part of our conversation was legit and what part was him deflecting…or is he deflecting? Does he really believe I'm in a relationship with George? Would he even believe me if I tell him, again, that I'm not?

He has a teasing sparkle in his eye, a light-heartedness that I haven't seen in forever, and I'm afraid to ruin the moment. But this discussion isn't over. And I'm not giving up on him.

"I concede the fact that you're God's gift to the planet, Frog Prince, but even you have to admit that Georgie's kind of pretty for a guy. You have seen how my *brother's* hair sparkles in the sunlight, and his eyes are a lovely shade of green—"

"Plus he has two of them."

I growl. "Give me your stick."

"Why?"

"I planned on hitting myself but it's best if I beat you upside your thick skull until it finally sinks in. I don't want George."

Landry laughs and tosses me the stick. I snatch it out of the air and give it a test swing. Landry dodges out of its path. "Come on, stay still. Let me whack you a bit."

"Oh, I'll let you whack me all you want…"

It takes a minute before I get it. My cheeks heat.

The bushes beside the path rustle, and I turn. The gun pointed at my face looks huge. I can see straight down the barrel. Everything dims around me. The sky turns pitch dark—only the silvery shimmer of moonlight peeks through the branches overhead—and my heart tries to fly out of my chest.

Mr. Acker steps from behind the tree. A rolled-up black ski mask covers his crimson hair. Only seconds before, it shielded his face. "I found you…"

"No!" *Not again.*

The warmth of blood trickles down my forehead and drips into my eyes. They burn and blur. I stumble forward, trying to run. *I can't see!* My arms rise to cover my head as I duck. The gun barrel bucks as if fired. My shoulder burns and goes numb. I can't move my arm. He shot me.

I bounce off of a hard object. I push forward…moving away from the footsteps chasing me. I'm running through quicksand. Each step I take sinks me deeper until I'm dragging each leg forward. My chest feels tight. I can't breathe.

Where's my knife? A heavy weight wraps around my waist, dragging me deeper beneath the sand. *My belt. The knife.* I draw it and slash at Acker. He dances backward across the quicksand with a laugh. *Why isn't he sinking?*

Acker darts forward, grabs the hand holding the knife, and

bangs it on the ground. Pain radiates up my arm. The hilt slips from my fingers and drops into quicksand, which now reaches my armpits. I reach for Acker's pant leg, but he grabs my arm and pushes it beneath the sticky sand.

"I begged for your help," he says, palming the top of my head like a basketball. "Now you'll see how it feels to die."

"Mr. Acker, don't..." I try to shake off his hand, but his grip tightens. "Don't kill me, please."

No mercy, no empathy, only hatred blazes from him—a bone-numbing chill that burns through my scalp down to my toes. Cold burns more painfully than heat. The weight pressing down on my head increases. Quicksand tries to pry open my pinched lips. It reaches my nostrils and slithers up my nasal passages. Invasive as a weed, it enters every open orifice. My ears clog. I sink deeper. The sand reaches my eyes. I squeeze them shut. My chest burns for air. I try to thrash, but the suffocating weight of the quicksand keeps me immobile.

Red light flashes behind my eyelids, then everything stops.

CHAPTER 19

LANDRY

Martyr's Path Denied

*G*un! My brain stutters and freezes, leaving me standing with my mouth hanging open. Mala's high-pitched screams, like nails scratching the back of my neck, crack the cement holding me hostage. She ducks, spins, and crashes into my chest face-first, then bounces off with another bloodcurdling wail. I grab for her, but she slithers through my fingers. Boneless, she drops to the ground, curling into a ball with her arms covering her head.

Seeing her so helpless kick-starts a burst of adrenaline through my body that makes my heart stutter in my chest. My vision narrows. I grab the barrel of the shotgun and shove it skyward, then punch the guy holding it in the jaw. He cries out, falling to his knees. His grip on the shotgun loosens enough for me to snatch it from his grasp and turn it on him.

"Don't shoot me!" the kid screams, doubling over in imitation of Mala's position. Sobs shake him so hard his limbs look like they're about to rip from his body. If they don't tear off on their own, I might pull them off like I'd pull the wings off a fly.

My finger twitches on the trigger. I can barely see straight I'm so keyed up. "Which one are you?" I yell. The kid peeks through his fingers, and I recognize him—the skinnier, asshole-ish Acker twin. "Damn it, Carl." My arms tremble as I lower the barrel to point at the ground. "I almost shot you."

"I'm sorry, Landry. I didn't know it was you." He scrubs a forearm across his face, leaving a gooey trail of snot and tears on his bare skin, then points a shaky finger at Mala. "What's wrong with her? Did I break her?"

I'm afraid he did.

Mala's curled up in a fetal position with her head buried in her hands and her eyes squeezed shut. She shakes her head back and forth. I crouch beside her and touch her back. She reacts, lunging forward with a guttural wail. The tip of the knife in her hand slices my cheek, inches from my good eye. I rear back, bumping into Carl, who hides behind me. She swipes at me again. I grab her arm and throw myself on top of her, using my weight to pin her to the ground.

"Mala, stop!" I yell.

It's pretty obvious by the glassiness of her stare that she can't see me. The nightmarish vision playing in her head has taken over completely. "Wake up!" She strains toward me with the knife again. I bang her wrist on the ground, and the knife falls from her fingers. Her free hand slaps at my chest, and I hiss at the sting. God, don't let her tear what's left of my stitches.

I glance at Carl, who watches us with wide eyes. "Help me."

He takes a creeping step forward.

Mala takes advantage of my distraction. She bucks upward, slamming her forehead against my chin and, like in a cartoon, sparkling stars steal my sight for a few seconds. My grip on Mala tightens. When I can see again, I find Carl huddled behind a tree. "Don't just stand there."

"I can't," he cries. "Mala's scary even when she's not freaking out. She'll kill me."

"I've got her. Hurry."

He shakes his head.

"I swear, if she breaks free, Carl, I'll let her have you," I growl. "This is your fault."

Carl pauses, then grabs her legs. She kicks him in the stomach, but even though he *woofs* as air escapes his lungs, he doesn't let her go. High-pitched screams erupt from her throat over and over until my ears feel like they're bleeding.

"I can't hold on much longer," Carl yells. "Slap her!"

Fury rushes through me, and I snarl, "Hurt her, and I'll beat you bloody."

He utters a choked sob in response. I meet his sky blue eyes. Worry creases his forehead beneath thick blond bangs. He's breathing hard, about two seconds from either losing it himself or passing out. His cheek's red and slightly swollen where I punched him.

Mala strains upward. "Mr. Acker…don't…" she begs, "…don't kill me, please."

Carl's eyes widen. He drops her legs and crawls backward. "What did she say?"

I lift up her torso, pin her arms against my chest like she's wrapped in a straitjacket, and press her face into my shoulder. Unable to move, she strains against me one more time then wilts. Her head lolls on her neck. *Did she pass out?*

I shift her sideways until she lies in the cradle of my arm. I search for a pulse with shaking fingers. My racing heart beats so loudly I can't tell whether the rapid pulse beneath my fingers comes from her or is an echoes of my own. I lower my face above her open mouth. A puff of breath warms my cheek.

"What did she say about my dad?" Carl asks again. Maybe he's asked a few times but I hadn't heard. I pretend not to hear now.

"Where's Dena?" I don't know what he reads on my face, but he cringes back, eyes wild.

"Answer me first!"

"You want the truth or a lie?" My jaw clenches. I'm prepared to answer with both. Too bad for Carl, since the kid's only fourteen, but my patience flew away the moment I saw the gun.

He shakes his head. "No, don't tell me. I don't want to know." He starts to scramble off, but I grab his ankle.

"My turn. Where's Dena?"

He blinks. "She said she has to work late tonight. That's why I took perimeter duty, so I didn't have to babysit the kids. Did you come to see her?"

"Yeah." My lips tighten.

"How are you gonna get Mala home?"

I sigh. It's a long way to carry her.

Carl grins shakily. He pulls a set of keys out of his pocket. "Swear you won't tell Dena…I taught myself how to drive."

He offers to help me carry Mala to his house, but I can't let her go. *I'm done walking the martyr's path.* I thought that I had ruined Mala's life, and I encouraged her relationship with George, but she's not cooperating. The idea of his hands on her skin, of him holding her in his arms, and kissing her velvet-soft lips…My gut clenches, and I shake the image. Nope, I tried to be the hero, but it's too damn hard to not be selfish. I won't push her away anymore. *Sorry, George, but you're SOL.*

I barely register Mala's weight during the short walk through the woods, and she fits comfortably in my arms. Her face presses into the curve of my throat. Warm breath blows across my skin, letting me know she's still alive. I press my face against the top of her head and inhale the sweetness of her floral shampoo. Her scent surrounds me, relaxing the tension in my body. She's the perfect blend of soft and hard—squishy in the middle like the caramel center of a Lindor chocolate truffle.

Carl gives me a wild-eyed glance when I chuckle.

We enter the Ackers' cluttered yard. Junked cars and machinery litter a corner by the dilapidated two-story, plantation-style farmhouse. Mom has a thing for architecture. She foamed at the mouth every time she visited this "culturally historic landmark" and railed about how it's fallen apart due to Acker's neglect. She tried to get Dad to buy it from Acker, but he refused to sell. Looking at the broken shutters on the windows and missing railings on the wide porch, I agree the place has seen better days. It won't see better now unless Acker bought a good life insurance policy like Ms. Jasmine did.

In the other corner of the yard, rows of vegetables in various stages of growth lift green heads to the sky. A painted, wooden sign reading DENA'S GARDEN hangs on the gate. After her mother ran off, Dena took her place as homemaker. Her youngest brother, Axle, had just turned six. Now, four years later, he says he barely remembers her.

Carl runs ahead and bursts into the house, yelling for his brothers. They explode out of the front door.

"It's Landry! Landry's here…" Axle shouts, skipping in a circle around me.

Daryl, Carl's twin, grabs my arm. "What's going on? What happened to Mala?" He glances at his twin. "If Dad catches her here…"

Carl glances at Mala then meets my gaze. "He won't."

"If he comes home…"

"I said he won't!" He grabs Daryl by the arm and drags him away from me.

"Did Dena make it home from work?" I ask Jonjovi, who holds Axle by the hand so he won't poke at me. I shift Mala higher in my arms. No offense to Carl, but I'm not too thrilled with the idea of him driving. I'm even less enthused about my own ability. I haven't been behind the wheel since I lost half of my vision. Hell, I can barely climb down the stairs without tripping 'cause I can't see the last step. How am I supposed to navigate a road?

The twins huddle together, whispering.

Jonjovi bites his lip, looking at his older brothers. "Not yet. What's wrong? Did something happen to Dee?"

"No," I snap, voice harsh with impatience. The boy's face crumples, and I force a smile. "Sorry, Dee's fine. She was supposed to stop by Mala's place this afternoon, but she didn't show."

Carl breaks away from Daryl, who stares at me with reddened eyes and hands me the truck keys. "She's been working a lot of night shifts at Munchies. I'll tell her you stopped by. Leave the truck at Mala's, and I'll come get it later."

"I'm staying at her place now." My cheeks heat when the twins share another eyebrow-raised glance. I bark, "Do you have something to say?"

Daryl takes the lead this time. "Papa disappeared about a month ago. It happened the night of the fire at Mala's house. Carl said he hurt Mala's mom. Is that true? Did he? Is that why he hasn't come back…'cause he's on the run from the law?"

"Yeah…" Why tell them the truth? Until his body's found, the kids will sleep easier thinking he's on the run. Especially if

Dena doesn't…no, she wouldn't take off and leave them. My gaze touches the twins' faces. They're terrified, but hiding it from their younger brothers. Jonjovi's brow bunches in confusion as he picks up on the tension in the air.

Axle grins. "Cool…he's like *The Fugitive.* Think they'll give me a reward if I find him?"

Carl slaps his baby brother across the back of his white-blond head. "Not cool, dummy."

I carry Mala to the Ford F150. Axle opens the door for me, and I squeeze past him to set her inside. His blue-green eyes widen when I reach over to belt her in.

"You just touched Mala's boobs," he says with a gasp. Awe fills his voice. "What do they feel like? Are they soft?" His tiny, quivering hand inches toward her.

I smack him on the back of the hand. "Show your cousin some respect, kid!"

"Ow, no fair," he howls. The look he gives me is unrepentant. I guess at ten I had a healthy fascination with women's chests too. But this is Mala he's ogling. Not cool.

The windy dirt road almost kills me. Literally. I drive off of the fucking road four times. It takes an hour to get back to Mala's house, 'cause I'm terrified of going faster than five miles an hour. By the time I pull down the driveway, I'm shaking so badly it takes two tries to get the car into park. My stomach somersaults with nausea. I close my strained eye and rest my head on the steering wheel.

Mala's breathing changes.

I roll my head in her direction. She sits in the same position, but coffee-black slits crack her puffy eyelids. Tears stain her cheeks. I twist sideways to face her. She stares at me silently. My hand trembles as I reach out to cup a cheek as soft as a baby's bottom and brush her tears away with my thumb. "You're not okay, are you?"

"I will be," she whispers with a grimace. Her hand grips her throat as she mouths "Ouch."

"Don't talk yet." I unhook our seat belts then shift toward her. My arm goes around her shoulders, and she snuggles into the hug without protesting. I rub her back in slow circles. After a while, I ask, "What happened, aside from the obvious...kid points a shotgun at your face?"

Her head tips back. "Kid?" she croaks.

"Carl trying to act like the man of the family."

"Oh, I..." She lowers her head back onto my shoulder and sighs. "Flashback...I think, or Acker used the opportunity to get a little revenge."

"Acker attacked you? Why didn't I see him?"

Mala laces her fingers through mine. "I don't k-know...it felt so real. I went back to that night, only instead of him sinking into the quicksand, I did. He laughed at me..._again_."

I hug her hard enough that I expect her to struggle to get free. Instead, she nestles against my chest. She's still trembling. I lose track of time as I rock her back and forth. When she's ready, she sits up and looks at me with dry eyes.

"Whose truck is this?"

"Acker's. The kids let me borrow it to bring you home."

"Dena?" Her voice rises in hope.

"Carl said she's working the night shift. The twins will have her call us when she gets home. Maybe she'll decide to go look for his body by herself. You told her where he fell in, right?"

"Do you think she'll run away? She's doesn't have to stay now that her dad's dead."

I feed her the same line of bullshit I used to soothe myself during the drive. "She won't leave those kids, no matter how much they get on her last nerve. She loves them."

"Yeah, you're right." She rubs her shoulder as if it aches. "I can't believe I passed out. I wasn't even shot." Her laugh is forced. Lines still furrow her brow, and her eyes scan the woods.

I go around and help Mala climb out of the truck. She leans hard on my shoulder. I swing her up in my arms and carry her toward the porch. I hear the pop of gravel down the driveway and turn. The black Cadillac covered in road dust looks out of place. It also brings a tingling sense of foreboding.

I climb the stairs and sit Mala in the rocking chair. "Ms. Jasmine," I yell. "We need you."

The chair beside Mala tips. "What? I was watching my stories. By the by, thanks for leavin' the television on." She grins at her daughter then frowns when she notices how out of it Mala is. "What happened to you? Psychic attack?"

"PTSD," Mala says with a sigh.

Ms. Jasmine snorts. Her attention transfers to the Cadi, and she stands up. "Oh, you in for it now, Mala."

"Huh?"

"Told you to get your sassy ass to Auntie Magnolia, but you didn't listen. Now it's too late. She's come to collect you."

Mala sits up with a hiss. "Well, I'm not going."

"*Cher*, you got no choice. You made a promise at the crossroads."

The Cadi pulls to a stop in front of the house. A man unfolds his lanky frame from within, and he makes the hairs on the back of my neck stand on end. The top of his head brushes seven feet, but he's so thin the bones in his stooped back poke through the black suit jacket he's wearing. He moves with ponderous, jerky steps to the back passenger door and helps an elderly woman from the car. Something about her scares the spit out of me.

I lean toward Mala as if she can protect me. "I've seen that woman before."

"You couldn't have. I've never introduced you."

A cane flew at the window. Dad swerved, and the truck ran off the road. "No. I've seen her…" I shake my head, trying to recall the exact memory, but it's hazy. So much of the accident is blurry. The more I think about it, the more unclear it gets. Does the when or how really matter? Maybe.

It seems to matter to Mala 'cause she says softly, "Mama's right, Landry. I remember swearing at the crossroads. Aunt Magnolia said demons are raised at the crossroads. All I needed was a sacrifice, and Mr. Acker died that night. You died…If something came back…" Her eyes meet mine, and I feel like I'm staring into a dark, bottomless pit. "It's my fault. I'm so sorry."

Demons. Crossroads and sacrifices. I frown, not sure what the hell she's rambling on about or why she's apologizing to me. I glance at Ms. Jasmine, who looks terrified, and my heart plummets.

"Hey there. You gonna greet your auntie or sit there like bumps on a pickle?" the woman calls, and our attention fixes on her. Magnolia's the epitome of a Louisiana Creole lady. She has an ancient but terrible beauty. Silver hair with a yellowed cast hangs down her back in a long braid reminiscent of the way Mala wears her own hair. Skin like parchment, in color and density, stretches over high cheekbones. Brown eyes with a yellow tint stare in our direction. No smile lights them.

When they land on me, I shiver.

"Hello," I say, not moving down the steps to meet her. I learned my lesson when Acker attacked. The house has been warded, so it's safer to remain where I am. "May I help you?"

She dismisses my words with a toss of her head. "Mala, Jasmine, it's good to see you both looking well…considering." Her smile is smug. "I thought you might not still be in one piece. I felt Mala throwing magic all the way in New Orleans. Thought I'd better come down and see what she's about before she blows up the town."

CHAPTER 20

MALA

Hoodoo Queen

The crackle of energy flowing from Auntie Magnolia's direction raises the hair on my arms. The faint light of the setting sun gives her eyes an ocher glint when they meet mine. She stays by the car like a queen waiting for her subjects to approach.

Saints, I wish I could stay on the porch. At least up here I'd be safe from her, since Gaston has the house warded against evil, but that would be rude. Wouldn't it? Mama didn't raise me to be a coward or disrespect my elders, and with Mama sitting right across from me, I'm kind of obligated to use good manners.

Landry isn't constrained by the same instinctive parental control. When I try to rise from the chair, he presses on my arm. "You shouldn't be walking around." He glances at Magnolia. "Mala's injured, Ms. LaCroix. Why don't the two of you sit here on the porch? I'll bring you a glass of iced tea or water. Whichever you prefer, ma'am."

Magnolia gives him a toothless smile. "Why, thank you kindly." She snaps her fingers at the gaunt driver. I'm watching his eyes…It takes what seems like ages for the order to process. The big guy's not the sharpest tool in the shed. He creeps—yeah, he really does—like a daddy longlegs spider over to Magnolia's side. She places a hand on his bony arm and leans on him for support. When they reach the protective boundary, she pauses, reaching into her skirt pocket. Her hand is closed in a fist when she pulls it out. Fine white powder sprinkles across the line of salt I have laid.

"You're messing with my warding, Auntie Magnolia," I protest, straining against the hand that once again lands on my shoulder. Landry shakes his head at me and puts his finger to his lips. "What? She's the one who taught me how to shield against ghosts. Now she's messing it up. What if Acker attacks?"

Magnolia glances my way, overhearing my argument. "Nothing dead can pass your boundary. I'll fix it when I leave."

I frown. "Do you mean nothing dead can pass it now or before you messed with it?"

She ignores me.

The porch shrinks when Magnolia and the tall guy reach it. Landry stands at my back, leaving room for her to sit in the rocking chair between me and Mama.

"Who is your young man?" Magnolia asks, smacking her lips in Landry's direction.

My stomach twists. I don't want her paying attention to him. Why doesn't he go into the house? I twist around and stare hard at him, hoping he picks up on my urgency. "Can you go get our guests that glass of tea now, p-please?"

"I'm not thirsty." Magnolia studies him, and my breath catches. Her eyes flick in my direction, and she smiles. "Introduce us, *cher*."

Damn! What is she gonna do? I don't trust her. She's unpredictable, and I think she collects people with gifts like magic trinkets to play with for her own amusement. Like this creepy guy skulking over her. My nose twitches when he leans between us to help Magnolia into her seat. He smells musty. Like his clothing got left overnight in the washer and mildewed. But what makes me sneeze is the powerful scent of spices. I don't know what kind, but they set off my allergies something fierce.

I sniff, wishing for a tissue. "You don't need to know."

"Still a smart-ass girl, I see," Magnolia says.

"Don't think I've forgiven you for what you did to me." I stare at her hard. Elder or not, I won't let her bully me. Us.

Magnolia's eyes twinkle, but a shadow shifts beneath the surface. I tense so she can't see the shiver making its way down my spine. I want to confront her about what she did to me the night of the attack. Scream it out so Mama and Landry know how she shoved her tongue into my bullet wound and sucked out my blood like a stinking vampire, but it's so unbelievable. And I'm not positive whether the memory is real or a hallucination brought on by blood loss.

"I'll take your sacrifices," she said to me that night, and in return, I swore I'd come to her—to be a slave at her beck and call. A good little hoodoo apprentice. So stupid now, but then, I didn't have a choice. *Demons rise at the crossroads. Mother Mary, what have I done?*

I slip my hand into Landry's.

Magnolia's silver eyebrows rise. "Is this gonna be my new great-nephew-in-law, Mala Jean? You found yourself a white boy like your mama did." Her head tilts birdlike as she studies him. "He looks a bit fragile. Not sure he'll survive the LaCroix curse any more than any other man who enters our family."

My hand drops into my lap.

Landry lifts it, twining his fingers through mine. "I'm not as weak as my injuries make me seem, Ms. LaCroix. And I'll protect Mala with my life."

"Sure, you right." Magnolia dismisses him and turns to Mama. "How's being dead treating you, *cher*? Still craving the drink?"

"Every day," Mama says with a longing sigh.

"You lonely? You know you don't have to stay stuck in this house. I'm family. Tie yourself to me, and I'll take you to New Orleans. Might even find you a living body to inhabit if Mala asks nicely." Magnolia gums at me again. "How does that sound to you, girl? Would you like a flesh-and-blood mama?" She pats the buttock of the man standing next to her. "I'm pretty good at stitching in a soul."

Landry's squeezes my hand. "Oh God, he's undead."

Magnolia's eyes narrow on him. "The boy's pretty quick."

"What are you two talking about?" I ask, all confused. My brain must be stuck on stupid again. I look at the musty man.

"Don't you see it, Mala?" Landry says, voice trembling. "The same shimmer that's around Ms. Jasmine shines around this guy. He's a zombie."

No way! "There's no such thing."

Magnolia laughs. "I seem to recall us having a similar conversation a couple of months ago about ghosts." Her assessing eyes turn on Landry. "You a surprise though. You can see Etienne's shimmer. What are you?"

What are you? No… Magnolia looks at him like he's a dish of caviar. *Why do people even like fish eggs…oh, God.* What do I say? I have to distract her from him, but how? My mouth won't form words. I've forgotten how to speak. I know what I want to scream "Leave him alone!" but I can't get it out.

Magnolia smirks when her eyes meet mine. As if she sees the thoughts flashing like brilliant neon warning signs through my mind: *Stop. Danger. Cliff ahead.* The terror and confusion I feel, the old bat gets off on it. This is her bread and butter. Power. It's what she craves.

She stretches her hand toward Landry. He looks at me with a raised eyebrow, asking for permission. I can't even shake my head in denial. He sets his palm flat on hers. Magnolia hisses. Her snakelike tongue flickers out of her mouth, revealing tobacco-blackened gums. She rocks back and forth, and her eyes roll back into her head.

Energy jumps between her and Landry. It arcs over my head. Offshoots spill over into me. My body tingles and jumps. My heart races, and the hair on my arms and the back of my neck rise. The exhaustion that dragged me down after Acker's attack vanishes to be replaced with a zing, like I've downed a triple shot of espresso.

"Do you feel that, Mama?"

Mama's eyes widen. "I've never felt anything like it, Mala Jean."

My hand moves without making a conscious decision. One minute it's in my lap, the next, I lay it on top of theirs. The jolt of electricity locks my jaw and knocks me back into my chair so hard that it flips backward. I topple out and roll across the porch with a cry. The backlash hits Landry. He drops to his knees, panting like he's run a marathon.

"What just happened?" I yell, crawling over to wrap my arms around his neck.

Magnolia slaps her leg. "Power. Pure, unadulterated power. My, my, my, Mala Jean. You found yourself an equal. You'll make the tastiest babies."

My stomach clenches with nausea. "Why does it sound like

you plan on cannibalizing my children?" *Who says I'm marrying Landry?*

"This much energy can't go without training." Magnolia wipes her hands on her lap. "You're both coming with me. Go pack your bags."

"Like hell," I snap.

Landry holds up a hand. "If we go, you'll teach us how to control this power?"

"I'll teach control and how to use it to your advantage." Her head cocks to the side. She studies him, maybe even reads his mind. What's going on behind his emotionless expression? It unnerves me that he's contemplating going with Magnolia. Can't he sense how evil she is? She doesn't want to help out of the graciousness of a pure heart. She wants to eat my future children.

Yeah, I totally believe she's capable of doing something that heinous.

The longer I'm with her, the more I think the memory of her at the crossroads is real. She *did* come that night. She hurt me as bad as Acker's bullet.

"I healed you, girl," Magnolia says, interrupting my train of thought. It takes me a second to understand her. She's answering my thoughts. Oh Lordy, she really can read minds.

Magnolia pinches her thumb and forefinger together an inch. "You was this shy of being a ghost yourself. I healed you...so you owe me your life. And you, boy, I didn't kill you when I could've. It would've been so easy to snuff your life as you stumbled down the road, blind and confused as a newborn pup. Payment is due."

A full-body shiver runs through Landry.

Swear at the crossroads... Magnolia whispered while I lay dying. And I did.

Doesn't mean if she says "froggy" I have to jump. "I can't go right now. I've got to work at Munchies. Save up money for bills. Isn't that right, Mama?"

"You got a hundred thousand in life insurance coming your way. You ain't got to worry about bills for a while," Mama says.

"She's right," Landry says.

I want to throw a rocking chair at them. "Why are you taking her side? Mama I can understand, but not you." Tears burn in my eyes, but I won't let them fall. The smug expression on Magnolia's face makes me twitchy enough. *Damn it!* I won't give her the satisfaction of seeing me break.

Landry folds my hands within his larger ones. "Magnolia knows more about this supernatural stuff than we do. We can learn from her."

"I don't want to." I glare at the woman. "She does black magic. It's evil. Can't you feel it?"

"Well, ain't you the pot calling the magic black," Magnolia says with a cackle fit for the Wicked Witch of the West. "You got some nerve calling me evil when you throw curses willy-nilly. Or did you forget about that poor girl's hair falling out?"

How does she know... I shake my head, halting that thought. I don't want to know. I don't. *Did I really curse Clarice?*

Magnolia keeps blathering...blah, blah, blah demon spawn, blah. Why won't she shut up? Landry's falling deeper and deeper into her sticky web of lies. I can tell. He's so freaking gullible.

"...magic ain't black or white. It's the person who wields it that determines whether it's used for good or evil." Lecture over, Magnolia raises a silver eyebrow.

My mouth opens to tell her to get the fuck off my property, but Landry squeezes my hand. The corner of his eye tilts downward like a sad basset hound, and my heart stutters in my chest. I want to wrap my arms around him and feed him lies about how everything will be okay.

He knows better. "Mala, I can't protect you like I am. The attack by Acker, I couldn't stop it. If I learn control, I'll be able to keep you safe. More important, if I'm not around, you'll be able to keep yourself safe."

I run a hand up Landry's cheek and trace a finger across a scabbed-over cut beneath his left eye. "Where did this come from? It wasn't here this morning."

He tips his head back. The black patch stands out against his creamy skin. "You cut me with your knife thinking I was Acker."

I hiss. I almost blinded him...*again*. Acker had me so lost in the reality he created that I don't even remember hurting Landry.

"Okay," I say. "I'll go. We'll go, but if anything *weird* happens we're coming home."

"Deal."

* * *

Landry packs our bags while I call Munchies. The manager says Dena left an hour ago. When I call the Ackers, Jonjovi tells me that she's still not home. It feels weird leaving without talking to her. And I feel guilty about putting off finding her father, but I can't stay. Not when I'm throwing black curses like Mardi Gras beads. I need to learn control before someone gets hurt. Again.

I expected Gaston to show up while we were speaking with Magnolia. He hates his aunt with a passion. She was his mother's twin, so he knows what she's capable of better than anyone living or dead. He almost brought down the house with his displeasure the first time she visited, but this time he doesn't make an appearance. Does this mean he approves of me going to New Orleans?

Etienne takes our bags and places them in the car. My nose wrinkles and goose bumps rise on my arms when his hand touches mine while transferring the bags. His skin feels like ice, like he just stepped out of a refrigerator. He doesn't speak. Maybe he can't. Is he a spirit in the body of a man? Lainey thrust my soul out of my body and wore me like a coat. I drifted, unfettered, unable to interact with the people around me. With everyone but Landry, who could sense spirits even before his death.

I squint at the man, trying to make out the mysterious shimmer Landry spoke about. He says it's like a silver aura surrounding the body, like the glare of a passing car's headlights. Is this body's spirit chasing after him? I don't sense a disturbance in the Force.

The giggle sets my head to spinning. I'm not sure why I find it funny.

Landry massages my shoulder. "I feel like I'm pressuring you to do this."

"You are." He frowns, and I shake my head, saying "No, don't get your panties in a bunch. I almost put out your other eye when Acker attacked. I need to learn how to control these powers."

A cold shiver runs down my spine. "Do you feel that?"

"Is it—"

A gust of wind kicks up. My arms go over my head. "No! Not now."

A disturbance ripples at the edge of the woods. One minute it's empty, and the next, Acker appears within a mini-tornado of leaves and dirt. It swirls around him like a giant blender and he's the smoothie filling. "You've done it now, girl!" he yells, and I scream. I dart toward the house, but Landry grabs my arms.

"Let go! We have to get behind the protective boundary," I shout. My words float into the vortex and vanish.

"Magnolia destroyed it. Get in the car." Landry shoves me toward the open back passenger door then opens the front. "Ms. LaCroix, get in. Hurry!"

Magnolia arches an eyebrow. "I don't run from spirits." Her words pulse like a gong. The deep, chest-throbbing vibrations radiate outward from my center, through my arms, and down into my fingertips as she says, "Spirits run from *me*."

My knees quiver. Then I realize my whole is body trembling. I'm incapable of walking. Hell, I can barely stand. It's like I'm sinking in quicksand again. I stare at my aunt, unable to tear my eyes away from her. Even the threat of Acker doesn't scare me as much as what happens to her.

Magnolia shimmers. I blink…but the image doesn't drift away. I see her—my aunt—the spooky but human old woman who sat in the rocking chair and taunted me with her gifts, but superimposed over her physical body is a shadow that slowly goes from dark to light, then Technicolor. I see the creature that came to me at the crossroads writhing beneath her skin, sucking at the marrow of her soul, while leaving dark holes of emptiness within.

A top hat sits jauntily on Magnolia's head. A trio of cigarettes hangs from her lips. Power turns her eyes golden. The color swirls and shifts, spilling out in a river of molten gold as if mere irises can't contain the raw energy contained inside her body.

The whirlwind in the form of a man stalks closer. Acker rips up clumps of grass and flings them in our direction. The car vibrates as debris smashes on top of the hood. His fury makes the hair on my head rise. Strands wave back and forth in the static-charged wind. The air crackles with the immense amount of electricity. I think if Acker touches me, the reaction will be ten times worse than the zing of power that shot through me when I touched Landry and Magnolia. Worse than biting into a power cord or getting struck by lightning, but just as Krispy Kremed D.E.A.D.

The ghost plans to kill me. Worse, I'm scared Magnolia plans to do the same. Only, hopefully, not right now. Landry and I are trapped between them. Two mortals on a supernatural battle-field, and we don't know the rules of engagement.

"You can't hide from me, girl. I see you," Acker yells. "You and your meddlesome ways done ruined everythin'. I should've kilt you when I had the chance."

Magnolia lifts a lazy hand and flicks the tips of her fingers. "Be gone."

Acker screams. He clutches his chest and collapses. His body flickers like a dying computer screen, and I squint. Landry presses my face against his chest and covers my head with his arms.

"What's happening to him?" Landry asks, his gaze following Magnolia, who walks to the front seat without a single glance in Acker's direction. Etienne helps her inside the car.

Acker screams one final time then silence descends upon us.

I suck a breath into strained lungs. "How did you do that?"

"Come with me and I'll teach you all my tricks." Magnolia meets my gaze. The vision of her I saw earlier has vanished. "You, the last LaCroix."

CHAPTER 21

LANDRY

Glitter Bomb

The drive to New Orleans passes swiftly 'cause I'm out cold before we exit Paradise Pointe. The bright lights of the French Quarter now pierce the darkness but I don't want to open my eye. I sit wedged in the backseat with my head propped against the glass and my legs kicked out sideways. The seat belt strap digs painfully into the groove between my collarbone and neck. I suffer in silence, not willing to disturb Mala who, like a snuggly bunny, lies with her upper body draped across my chest and her legs curled up in her seat, perfectly secure in the protective circle of my arms.

A hissing laugh comes from the front seat.

My shoulders tense. The woman better not be reading my mind. I'm freaked out enough over the whole magic thing. I hope that's not a skill Mala plans to add to her arsenal. I have too many secrets rolling around in my addled brain. I don't want her having an all-access pass to my filthy thoughts. Still, the Acker-go-poof thing would be a handy thing to learn.

Mala yawns and does a full-body stretch. This means a wriggling Mala on top of me, and I'm gritting my teeth while thinking pure thoughts like...*an icy Slushee shoved down the front of my pants*...anything to distract me from how her body feels rubbing across mine.

"Are we in New Orleans yet, Auntie Magnolia?" Mala asks, sitting up. When she looks out the window, she ogles. Yep. No other word describes how her mouth drops and her eyes widen at the sights flashing past the tinted windows. I'm having a hard time not getting all goo-goo-eyed myself, and I've visited New Orleans a few times. I bet Lafayette's the biggest city Mala's ever been to. It's nothing compared to what she sees now.

"Oh. My. Gosh. It's so cool." She presses her nose against the window. "Do you see, Landry?"

I grunt.

She pinches my arm. "Are you asleep?"

I straighten, stretching my arms in front of me to undo the kinks in my back and shoulders. A cold spot replaces the warmth of her missing body. "How am I supposed to sleep with you manhandling me, woman?"

She giggles.

"I take it you've never been to New Orleans before?" I ask.

"Nope, first time."

I poke a finger into her side. "Maybe we'll have time to take a tour of the place in between learning how to be Ghostbusters. What do you say? Beignets at Café Du Monde? We'll shop at the French Market. Maybe take a swamp tour."

A passing streetlight illuminates her wrinkling nose. "Why in the world would I want to take a swamp tour? I want to see something new." She glances with hesitation at the woman in the front seat. "Will we have time, Auntie Magnolia?"

"There's always time for beignets, Mala Jean." Magnolia pats Etienne on the arm. "You'll take them around."

He gives a ponderous grunt, and I stifle my groan. Should've kept my mouth shut and just snuck out without asking permission. Like I want a zombie for a tour guide? Not. The fool doesn't seem capable of speech, and he gives Mala the shivers with a single glance through the rearview mirror. She scrunches closer, and I wrap my arm around her waist.

The car parks in front of an ornate, five-story hotel.

"Wow," Mala breathes.

I nudge her in the side. "Enough gawking. You look like a tourist. Come on."

Etienne comes around to open the door for us. I step out and edge aside the "dead one" with a quick sidestep. Mala blinks up at me in the bright lights and takes my hand as I help her out of the car. I stare at the big guy, but my rudeness doesn't register on his face. If the situation had been reversed, I'd be pissed. But he's either in total control of his emotions or he doesn't care. He shambles two steps, opens Magnolia's door, and helps her climb out of the Cadillac.

A uniformed valet runs from inside. He bobs his head toward Magnolia. "Madame LaCroix, welcome home."

Mala's jaw about drops onto the pavement. I'm pretty sure I have to lift mine up too. My parents and I stayed in this hotel the last time we came to New Orleans. Dad bitched and moaned about the price—six hundred dollars per night—way more than he wanted to spend, but Mom coerced him into it. The four of us shared a room the size of our living room. I still remember how cool it was though. Expensive, but freaking awesome.

I eye Magnolia with some awe.

Mala is still reeling in shock. "You live here?" she asks with an encompassing wave of her hand. "Really? We're staying here?"

Magnolia sweeps forward like the queen we *now* know she is. We mere subjects trail behind. The awe increases as the doorman holds the door open with a bow. The marble floor is shot through with golden flecks and shimmers beneath the light from the gold and crystal four-tier chandelier hanging from the vaulted ceiling. Double mahogany staircases grace each side of the room. To the left is the check-in counter, and Mala turns toward it.

Magnolia waves for us to follow her. I catch Mala by the arm and steer her in the right direction.

A man tries to remove Mala's suitcase from her grasp, and she slaps his hand. "Hey, that's mine."

I chuckle at the fury in her eyes. The guy's lucky she didn't have her knife. She might've gutted him for trying to "steal" her bag. "Don't get the bellhop in trouble for not doing his job," I say, handing him my own duffel bag.

"What are you talking about? Oh…" she breathes upon seeing the guy put my bag on the rolling luggage cart parked behind him. Her caramel cheeks turn cotton candy pink. I lick my lips. Damn, I'm hungry.

"Oh, I see." Mala hands him her suitcase with a muttered "Sorry."

Magnolia and Etienne have already entered the elevator and wait for us to join them. Mala can barely walk in a straight line. Her gaze travels through the lobby, touching on the potted palms and the paintings on the wall.

I drag Mala toward the elevator holding Magnolia, Etienne, and our bored-out-of-his-skull-looking bellhop. The door slides shut as soon as we board. I wrap my arm around

Mala's shoulders. She blinks up at me, and the dazed look in her eyes clears. I know how she feels. Having her in my arms grounds me in the midst of chaos. All this beauty is window dressing. Mala's the real deal. Her touch, her smell, her warmth radiates into my side.

"How do you like your new home?" Magnolia asks her.

Mala's eyebrows draw together. "What do you mean, 'new home'?"

The bell dings. The elevator door slides open to reveal a large apartment rather than a hallway. "Excuse me," the bellhop says.

Mala and I step inside. Our feet sink into the plush carpet. I scan the room, waiting for the owners to come out and greet us or for Ms. LaCroix to join us, but neither happens. The bellhop removes our bags from the cart and sets them on the floor. Then he gets back onto the elevator.

"Do you live here, Aunt Magnolia?" Mala asks.

"No, I don't stay here."

"Well, who does? I'd rather not be with strangers even if it's in a place as pretty as this."

Magnolia laughs. "Child, you don't listen very well. What do you think I meant when I said you're the last LaCroix?" Her hand waves to encompass the entire penthouse suite. "You're my heir, *cher*. Everything you see belongs to you once I pass on. Just don't count your millions before you're sure I'm staying in my crypt. Might be I hang around for twenty more years."

My arm tightens. "This hotel belongs to you?" I ask.

"This hotel, my shops, four or five houses in the Ninth Ward, but they still need some work. Got myself a seven-bedroom house in Gentilly, south of Lake Pontchartrain. The area flooded under eight feet of water during Katrina. I got the place for thirty-five thousand. The owners were real motivated to get rid of it once the mold started to grow. Other property you don't really want to hear about right now, I'm guessing."

"I never…" Mala spins in a slow circle, taking in the scope of the room. "You're a real estate magnate."

"Well, I'm no spring chicken, Mala. I've been around a long time. I've made a lot of deals. People owe me a lot of favors." Her voice sounds bleak as night. "You learn to take advantage of others' vulnerabilities. Why don't you and Landry settle in for the night? Be ready by noon so we can get started on your training."

With that, the elevator door slides closed, leaving me and Mala alone in a penthouse suite twice the size of either of our houses.

"Did she really say this belongs to me?" Mala stares at the spacious room. "You heard her say it, right? This place belongs to me and not just for the weekend while I stay here. This entire hotel belongs…to me?"

Yeah, I can't believe it either. This whole setup feels too convenient. What does the old lady want from us? Is she buttering us up 'cause our combined power is worth a multimillion-dollar hotel to her?

I focus on Mala, grinning to hide my unease so she won't worry. "Well, I'm kind of disappointed. I was hoping we could try out a vibrating heart bed, like the one at the Super Delight, but I guess this will do."

Mala's eyes narrow. "How did you hear about the Heart Suite? I only know about it because Mama bitched about the cost of bribing the owner into bumping the other prostitutes' reservations for a high-dollar customer. It has a month-long wait, if you can believe that."

"There's a girl I once planned on taking there. Then I got to know her and decided that she deserves better than the Super

Delight." I stare at her hard, hoping she reads beneath the surface to the emotions behind my words.

Mala's eyes drop to the carpet. At first I think she'll ignore the comment, but then she smiles. "As long as you're with the right person then it will be special," she says, meeting my gaze. "Don't you think?"

"Yeah, I do." Is that an invitation in her eyes? Does she want me to scoop her up and carry her into one of the bedrooms? I want her now. My hands itch to caress her body, like an addict searching for a fix. I'd abstained from touching her until today. Now it's all I can think about.

"Yeah, but how do you know if that person's the one, Landry? Especially when he keeps rejecting you. How do protect yourself from getting your heart broken?" Her eyes drop again.

God, I fucked up. Why did I keep pushing her away? And how do I tell her I've come to my senses without frightening her off?

She turns and bends over to slip off her shoes. Her heart-shape bottom shimmies back and forth. My hands tingle with the need to cup her firm cheeks. She glances up, and I turn away.

"I think we should take off our shoes."

"Uh, sure." I pull off my boots, and my feet sink into the plush cream carpet.

She wiggles her toes. "So soft."

We separate to explore the room. Mala runs her hand along the black leather sofa with a sigh, heading toward the kitchen. I turn like a guided missile toward the TV. "It's an eighty-two-inch plasma," I say, voice thick. "Isn't it beautiful?"

Love at first sight.

"I'm jealous," Mala teases.

My eyebrow rises. "Let's check out the rest of the place."

The kitchen has an electric range and marble countertops and

island. I pluck an apple from a bowl and take a bite. "Ow, it's plastic."

Mala laughs.

I wink at her. "Kidding."

"You are so not funny."

"Yeah, what kind of *girlfriend* are you? Laughing at me."

Silence.

The thuds from my chest sound like someone banging on the
front door. I almost expect Mala to mention it, but she acts like
she's engrossed in checking out the china in the cabinets. Did she
hear me? Should I say it again? No. Maybe pretending like she
didn't hear is her way of shutting me down. God, I must be delusional. Why did I spring that on her out of nowhere? I should've
waited for a more romantic moment.

Dazed, I walk down the hallway. I open the first door and
peek inside. A queen-size bed with an ivory coverlet is against
the west wall. A 60-inch television hangs from the east. An open
door reveals a bathroom straight ahead. I shut the door and continue down the hallway, listening to Mala's gasps and giggles as
she follows. I open the door to the master of all master bedrooms.
It's a total chick's dream bedroom. Something Lainey would've
squealed about like she'd turned into a Disney princess.

Much like what Mala does when she enters the room.

I'm kind of awestruck myself by the four-poster canopy bed
with breezy, sheer white curtains. A large potted palm sits in a
corner. French doors lead onto a balcony with an iron railing and
two lounge chairs looking out onto the street. More palm trees. I
don't know what kind. I'm not into trees or what kind of flowers
are growing in the flowerpots hanging from the railings.

And the bathroom drives Mala into a tizzy. "It's a whirlpool
tub."

She runs back into the bedroom. I'm lying on the bed with my arms folded behind my head. Her eyes linger on my midriff. A quick glance down shows the bottom of my T-shirt has ridden up, exposing the line of hair running into my jeans.

"Uh, yum," Mala says, staring.

I hide my grin 'cause, yeah, sit-ups do a body good. "Come here," I say, beckoning with a hand.

She backs up. "What are you doing?"

"Testing out my bed." I roll onto my side and pat the mattress. "Soft."

My words slowly sink in. "Oh, no. I see what you're doing." She launches forward, bouncing onto the mattress beside me. "This is mine. You can have the other room."

"I'm bigger. I should get the big bed."

"It's obviously a girly room. It's mine." Mala stretches out her arms. I roll over, and my hand flops onto her stomach, accidentally on purpose. Taut muscles tighten beneath the soft, fleshy layer of her stomach. Did she deliberately tighten them? I poke her again to be sure.

Air rushes out of her in a huff of annoyance, and I use her distraction to twist around until I can use her belly as a pillow. Her hands push at my head with a cry, but she doesn't put much effort into it. She sighs again and trails her fingers through my hair. Her fingers massage my scalp, and the headache that always lingers behind my eyes starts to fade.

"How about if we share?" I ask drowsily.

"I'd like to sleep by myself."

"I didn't say anything about sleeping."

"Oh, Lordy." Mala's off the bed in point five seconds and halfway across the room in two.

I follow her to the second bedroom and peer inside. It's not as cool as the master, but hell, it's still awesome. Mala lies in the middle of the bed—fuming. I can almost see smoke spiraling out of her ears. I make a running leap onto the bed. The other room was more visually stunning, but the mattress on this bed conforms to the shape of my body. I sink into it. I don't think I'll be able to get out without help. I close my eyes. My body rocks sideways.

"This bed is nice too," I say.

"What are you doing?" she hisses.

"Haven't you figured it out yet? Where you go, I go. I'll deal with it if you've changed your mind and want to be platonic again, but I won't leave you alone. Not after what Acker did to you this afternoon."

"That's a big change of heart, Landry."

I trace a finger down her cheek. "I'm new to this whole relationship thing. I'm learning, but I'll probably make a few more mistakes along the way."

"So what you said in the woods about me being with Georgie—"

"I thought I meant it at the time, but I changed my mind. How can he protect you when he doesn't even know what he has to keep you safe from? You've never told him about your connection to the dead, have you?"

"I'd be crazy to. Hell, he already thinks I lost my grip on reality after Mama died." Her mouth turns down at the corners. "I can't handle seeing it verified in his eyes."

"Plus there's the fact he's your brother."

"Ugh, don't remind me. It kind of grosses me out whenever I think about it. But he's not blood. George Sr. adopted him." Mala lightly runs her fingertips down my arm. "Why do you think I still like George?"

I stare up into her eyes. "He was your first love. That's hard to get past, but I want you to know how I feel. I won't leave you hanging anymore. The decision is yours. If you decide you want a normal life with Deputy George, be my guest. Doesn't mean I'll vanish. I still plan to protect you."

CHAPTER 22

MALA

Kiss Interrupted

The refrigerator yields an interesting mix of stuff. Yogurt, eggs, Canadian bacon—my nose wrinkles at the sight of the round pieces of meat. They look like mini pieces of ham. I like bacon. Real bacon. Ham…not so much.

Landry places his hands on my hips and steers me out of the kitchen. "Why don't you find a movie and rest? You've had a hard day. I'll cook for you."

I snicker. "Call me when you're in over your head."

"I have many skills…" He waggles his eyebrows. "Prepare to bow down to the master chef as I rock your world with my culinary abilities."

Heat floods into my cheeks, and I rush from the room, afraid he'll see. He's got me all befuddled. His earlier declaration of intent keeps running through my mind. He called me his "girlfriend." Says he wants to be with me. I believe he's telling the truth, and I'm terrified now that it looks like I'll finally get what I've wanted.

Stop overanalyzing and go with the flow.

I wrap myself in the thick blanket thrown over the back of the sofa and sink onto the leather. It's cold, but once I tuck the blanket around me, I snuggle in. It takes several tries to figure out how to use the universal remote. Apparently it works the overhead lights, the radio, which is set on the jazz station, and the widescreen television. I wonder where Mama has gotten herself off to—not that I'm complaining, since her absence gives me some alone time with Landry—but she and Gaston are supposed to be tied to me. I'm surprise she hasn't popped in yet. She'll freak the first time she watches her soap operas on the huge screen.

The smell from the kitchen makes my mouth water. I want to go see what Landry's cooking up, but I'm too comfortable. The effort of rising has gone way beyond my skill level. It involves too many coordinating skills, like walking. Not crashing into a wall because I'm sleepwalking.

Next thing I know, I'm waking up to the sun shining in through the open balcony door. Landry must've carried me to bed. Blankets pulled up to my neck make it difficult to turn. I lie there, taking in the breath-stealing vision of the large bedroom in the daylight. It's even more magnificent than the night before, and I pinch myself to be sure I'm not still dreaming. The heat warming my backside shifts, and I freeze. I slide a hand beneath the blanket and feel behind me. A hip conforms to the cup of my palm, as does the smooth skin of a bare, muscular back. I trace a finger up the knobs of a spine.

Landry moans.

My heart races like I've just outrun the gaping maw of a gator. I roll onto my side so we're face to face. I can barely calm my breath—all because of the assault on my senses. I inhale the crisp scent of Irish Spring soap and a musky scent that makes me clench my knees together. I wiggle closer and let out a heavy sigh just so I can fill my lungs again.

Landry lies flat on his stomach with his arms folded beneath his pillow to prop up his head. Black hair with a slight blue tint in the morning sunlight falls over the white pillowcase. He looks younger, more innocent asleep. His lips are slightly parted. My gaze lingers on his plump bottom lip then moves upward.

I rub my aching chest. My eyes burn, but I don't let my tears fall. He removed the eye patch before bed. A scar bisects his eyebrow, the eyelid, and part of his cheek. I did that to him. I'd sacrifice myself a thousand times if I could undo what I've done. If I could give him back his sight.

But I can't. What's been done can't be undone. I have to live with the regret. And it burns…an unquenchable fire, radiating outward to burn me from the inside out. I bet this is how it feels to spontaneously combust. Excitement races through me with each breath. Landry's a freaking pheromone factory, and I'm the spiraling bee.

My finger trembles as I reach out to trace the raised edges of the scar. My heart twists. Mama always kissed my owies "to make them better" whenever I got hurt as a child, and I swear, she had some potent smooches. Course she was usually feeling guilty for being the one who gave me those bruises. Logically I know the pain didn't really vanish. What made me feel better was she wiped away the hurt by reminding me of her love with those kisses.

What if my kisses have the ability to heal Landry?

Maybe not the external pain, but the internal. God, I hope so. 'Cause if they do, maybe his have the ability to heal me too.

I brush a soft kiss across his eye. The light touch only whets my appetite. I lick my tingling lips. Landry brings a craving up from deep inside of me. He tastes like the sweetest chocolate…the kind you savor in tiny bites that melt on your tongue so the ecstasy lingers. No matter how much you eat, you want more. Like an Easter egg junkie, I press another kiss against the arch of his high cheekbone.

Landry's breathing quickens. His back arches as he lifts his head to stare at me with an eye of pure silver; no thunderclouds darken his gaze. He rolls onto his side as a hand slides from beneath the pillow. The tips of his fingers trail down the side of my cheek, then wrap around to cup my face. I slowly lean forward, and his breath catches. A slight smile reveals his dimple, but it's hidden as our lips touch. His grip on my face tightens when I try to pull back, and his other arm wraps around my waist. With a quick roll, he pulls me flush against his bare chest. I gasp, and his tongue steals into my mouth.

Oh God, he tastes so good.

The kiss deepens as his heat soaks into me. I slide my leg over him, and he groans, pulling my body even closer. I can feel each breath, each frantic beat of his heart, and I know he can feel mine because we're connected in a way I never imagined possible. Never had any idea sensations like this existed, like our souls blended.

How sappy…the thought drifts through my mind, but swiftly disappears.

Cold prickles race across my back, and I shiver.

"What?" Landry whispers huskily against my mouth.

I kiss him hard in answer. His chest heaves as he chuckles but we don't stop kissing. His palm warms the indentation in the small of my back, which contrasts starkly with the ice seeping into the rest of my flesh. I stiffen, pulling away. My jaw quivers as I try to keep my teeth from chattering.

He stares at me with a concerned frown. "Seriously, what's wrong?"

"I don't—" Instinct flares, and I twist. *Crap!* "Mama?"

Landry rears up, and my forehead cracks against the bridge of his nose. Pain rocks me backward. I reach for Landry, but he's too busy holding his bleeding nose to catch me before I fall out of the bed in a tangle of blankets.

I stare up at Mama from the floor. She sits in the chair across from the bed with her legs drawn up beneath her nightgown and her chin propped on her knees, like she's lounging in front of the television watching a romantic comedy.

"Don't stop on my account," she says with a wicked smile.

Landry grimaces. "M-Ms. Jasmine, it's not what you think," he stutters, crawling from the bed. He has his nose pinched shut with two fingers. A trickle of blood spills across his lips and drips onto the sheets. I peek beneath the blanket and sigh. Thank God, I'm not naked. Nor do I have to do the walk of shame. I didn't do anything wrong.

"Oh God, I'm so embarrassed." I bury my face in the blanket.

"Don't look at me," Mama says. "I'd be a hypocrite if I said you ought to be ashamed of yourselves."

My lip pokes out. "You just said it, Mama."

"Wouldn't be my place to warn you about catchin' sexually transmitted diseases and unwanted pregnancies from havin' unprotected sex."

"Mama!"

"Whatever? I didn't say anythin'. I'm respectin' your right to do what you want. 'Sides, I'm dead. Not like I can stop you from making a huge—"

"AAHH!" I scream, covering my ears. "Tell her nothing happened, Landry."

Silence fills the room. I glance at the bed, but it's empty. The bathroom door slams shut, and Mama laughs. "See, it's like a man to leave a woman high and dry in this sort of situation."

"I'm not abandoning her," Landry yells from the bathroom. "I'm fixing my nose so I don't bleed to death. And nothing happened. We slept…and shared a few kisses, but that's it. Not that I wouldn't"—his voice rises in a strangled squawk—"Ms. Jasmine, get out of here."

Mama's voice comes from inside the bathroom. "You ain't got nothin' I haven't seen before, boy, so stop actin' all modest. Look me in the eye and swear nothin' happened. I can tell if you're lyin'."

I back away from the door so they don't hear me laughing. I grab my toiletry bag and a change of clothing and hustle off to the second bathroom. By the time I finish showering and dressing, I've recovered my composure. In the living room, Landry sits in a slump on the leather couch engrossed in a movie—a Syfy original involving a creature that looks like they genetically spliced a piranha with a crocodile—*Croconha*. Extremely cringe-worthy.

Landry doesn't bother to glance away from the screen, but the back of his neck and ears turn red when I cozy up next to him. I wrap his arm around my shoulders then stare up at his face in fawnlike adoration. A quick glance down at me and the blush spreads to include his entire face.

"Hi, sexy," I croon huskily, blowing in his ear. *This will teach you never to abandon me again.*

His Adam's apple bobs as he swallows. "Uh…"

I run my hand down his thigh and squeeze.

Landry throws a wild look over his shoulder and grabs my hand. "Don't…Ms. Jasmine said if I touch you, she'll—"

A deep rush of warmth fills my chest. How does he expect me to keep my hands to myself after he says something so sweet? "Thank you. You've no idea how much it means to me, knowing that you respect Mama. People looked down on her for the choices she made her entire life. I know she's trying to do right by me." I lay my head on his shoulder. "But I'm not a child anymore. She doesn't get to dictate how I live my life."

Landry snorts. "Big words from someone who fell off the bed trying to get away from me."

"I panicked. Old habits die hard." I stare at his mouth, willing it to move toward mine. A corner of his lip rises in a half smile, and I lift my chin. His mouth brushes across mine, and I groan, pressing against him. "Kiss me, please."

The ding from the elevator brings us both off the couch with darting looks.

"What time did Magnolia say she'd be coming for us?" Landry asks, running his hands through his tangled ebony locks. He's wearing his eye patch again, plus a pair of dark denim jeans and a T-shirt that matches his storm-cloud eye. He looks so hot.

I fan myself. Overheated. It's my own fault. If you don't play with fire, you won't get burned, right? *Silly girl.*

"Mala, are you okay?"

"Fine, I'm cool." *Not.*

What had he asked? Oh, yeah, Magnolia. I have no idea what time she said she'd come. My memories of the night before are hazy. I spent most of it in a daze. Overwhelmed by everything that happened. Today I'm reminded that there is a price for the luxury I'm enjoying. I just hope it's one I'm willing to pay. Auntie Magnolia seems more mafia boss than philanthropist. If I don't fulfill my obligations, I wouldn't put it past her to start cutting off body parts to use in her spells.

But I put myself in this situation. Granted I didn't have much choice—death or slavery—and dying hurt, so I agreed to her terms. Landry didn't. He's in this mess because of me, so I'm responsible for whatever happens.

The opening door interrupts my frantic thoughts. I'm not expecting to see the man standing in the elevator. Hell, I wouldn't expect to see him anywhere but on a movie set. He looks so much like Taye Diggs that I almost squeal like a fangirl, but subtle differences exert themselves as I study his chiseled face. None of the differences detracts from this guy's beauty and commanding sense of presence. My mouth waters as I drink in the muscular frame standing in front of me. Midnight velvet skin shines beneath the overhead lights. *Whoa, so yummy*.

Guilt curdles my stomach as I remember Landry. I glance over to see if he's noticed my short, minuscule bout of infatuation. He's staring openmouthed into space, like a dehydrated spaniel. Surely he's not mesmerized by the guy's hotness. Then I realize the Taye clone isn't alone in the elevator, and my gaze moves to the woman standing next to him.

She has skin the color of rich mahogany, silky smooth and without blemish. The kind of skin I wish I could have but never will because I've never used moisturizer in my life. I glance down at my callused palms and broken nails. With a grimace, I shove my hands into my pockets.

The woman studies me with greenish gray eyes emphasized by thick black eyelashes and wavy hair that hangs past her shoulder blades. "Malaise LaCroix" —she arches an eyebrow, then nods— "and Landry Prince."

"Who are you?" I ask, breathless.

They step together out of the elevator, and Landry and I are forced to shuffle back. A crackle of energy radiates from these two. It raises the hairs on my arms and sets off every alarm within my body. It's a force I've come to recognize. Power. These two are full of spiritual energy.

Landry tips his head down and whispers, "They're not ghosts. No shine."

The woman laughs. "No, we are very much alive." She gestures toward the man. "This is Ferdinand, and I am Sophia. We are servants of Queen LaCroix. Which means for today, we obey your commands."

Servants? "Why do I feel like I've been sucked into the Middle Ages? Did I fall through a time rift or something while sleeping?"

"I wondered why you were playing with the flux capacitor," Landry mutters. I elbow him in the side. I'm totally serious.

Sophia's perfectly arched eyebrow lifts. "Time rift. *Back to the Future.* I see. How quaint."

Oh hell, no, she didn't. "Are you insulting us now?" I step forward, not caring how powerful she is. I'm not a cockroach for her to squash. I didn't take Auntie Magnolia's insults, and I'm not taking this witch's either.

Landry takes my hand and squeezes. "We thank you for your hospitality."

Sofia smiles, and Landry's hand drops from mine.

I let out a huff of air, narrowing my eyes. He doesn't notice my glare. She's bespelled him again. What will it take to knock some sense into him? Thrusting my boobs into his face again? Stupid boy. Only thinking with his other brain.

Ferdinand chuckles. The contrast between his dark skin and his white, toothpaste-ad smile makes me forget to breathe. *I'm doomed!*

Ferdinand and Sophia steer us onto the elevator and out the doors of the hotel like they're herding their sheep. A smile here, a light touch there, and we follow along without having to get bitten. Although…um, biting. That might actually be pleasurable. Ferdinand smiles at me again, and I shiver.

Ugh, snap out of it! I shake my head, trying to banish the fuzziness so I can think clearly. Sunlight beats down on my body, and I draw in a gulp of muggy air. Perspiration dots my forehead. New Orleans in the summer, the perfect weather to clear my mind. I flap the front of my T-shirt, trying to cool down. It's soaked with sweat, and we've barely walked a block.

"Where exactly are we going?" I ask after walking for about ten minutes. Yeah, I'm now totally lost.

"Your aunt mentioned you wanted to go to Café Du Monde," Sophia says with a nod toward the café across the street. Coffee with a pungent hint of chicory and hot milk and the aroma of fried dough and sweet powdered sugar fills my nose when I inhale. I take in the crowd of people sitting at tables on a patio beneath a green-and-white-striped awning.

Landry rubs his hands together. "My mouth is already watering."

I bounce up and down on my toes. "Mine too. Let's go."

Landry and Ferdinand check out the inside while Sophia and I find a table beside the wrought iron fence surrounding the patio area, directly below a ceiling fan because it's damn hot. I lean back in my chair with a sigh, letting the cool breeze blow down the top of my T-shirt. I've never seen so many different types of people gathered in one place. Every ethnicity flows around us. I wish I could talk to them, find out what their lives are like, where they came from.

Sophia sits across from me with her legs crossed. Her tan slacks taper to reveal tan and cream heels. They look expensive.

"Do you like them?" Sophia twists her foot to the side.

I shrug. "They look like they pinch your toes."

"Actually they're very comfortable."

"Don't you have a hard time walking in them?"

"You'll get used to it."

What does she mean?

I shrug. "So what are we doing after we eat?"

Sophia doesn't answer. She's too busy staring a hole into my already holey sneakers, then her gaze travels upward to take in my faded jeans and sweat-stained blue T-shirt. "Do all of your clothes look like this?"

I stiffen. "What's wrong with my clothing?"

"If you must ask…" Sophia's attention shifts to the white-clothed, bow-tied waitress who appears as if out of thin air, and I want to slap the jaunty pill-box cap off the waitress's head for interrupting.

I breathe through my irritation as Sophia orders beignets and coffee for all of us. When the waitress leaves, I lean toward Sophia and hiss, "Look, I'm not rich. Maybe my aunt is a gazillionaire, but I'm a swamp girl, and proud of it. I get my clothes from the thrift shop on Grant Boulevard." *Why am I making excuses to her?*

Sophia lays a hand on my arm. Warmth spreads through my body, and the tension in my neck and shoulders drain. So does my anger. "I don't mean to disrespect your choice in fashion," she says. "Honestly, it works for you, but"—her voice lowers conspiratorially—"your aunt says I'm to dress you appropriately for the ceremony tonight. I've been told to take you shopping."

CHAPTER 23

LANDRY

Shop Until You Drop

The air conditioning is the main reason I haven't bailed out of the sitting room in the upscale woman's boutique. I lean forward in my chair so the full blast blows over my body. Women and shopping. I should've known better than to rush my own wardrobe selection to get back.

I glance at the dressing room door and sigh. I can't stop thinking about the kiss I got this morning. I'm still in shock. The memory of Mala's lips keep me grounded whenever Sophia's green eyes turn on me. The woman's beautiful. Like a work of art…the kind you stare at but don't dare touch 'cause you'll get your hand cut off. Bad things will happen if I give in to my lustful urges.

Then there's ol' Ferdinand. The guy's huge and more intimidating than an MMA fighter. Not that I'll ever admit this aloud. I *really* don't like the smoldering glances Mala keeps throwing in his direction.

The dressing room door opens, and Sophia walks out with a sultry smile. I pinch my arm. The pain helps me tear my gaze from her to focus on the woman who steps out behind her. The world rocks on its axis. My vision tunnels and wavers. I'm on my feet, not sure when I jumped up.

"Mala…" I breathe out the last bit of air in my lungs, too stunned to remember how to inhale. I blink, dizzy. Shaking my head, I take a step toward her.

Mala's bitter-chocolate eyes meet mine, and she smiles. "Do I look pretty?" She spins in a circle. The silky white dress clings to her curves, leaving nothing to the imagination. Hell, even in my wildest fantasy—and I've had plenty about Mala—I've never pictured her so stunningly beautiful.

Her traditional braid has been transformed into shiny spiral curls that frame her face in a layered cut that tumbles to her waist. The overhead lights bring out auburn highlights in her brown hair. She looks like she tumbled out of bed after having amazing sex.

I swallow hard, studying her face. She glows. "You have on makeup," I accuse.

Mala blinks, then smiles with red lips.

Would her kiss taste like strawberries? How would her lips feel on my body? I fall back. Luckily I hadn't moved too far from the chair. I sit down hard, clutching the armrests. *Oh, God, why can't I stop thinking about sex?*

Ferdinand strides across the room to lift Mala's hand. He brushes a kiss across her knuckles like some aristocratic dude from *Downton Abbey*. And she giggles. Giggles! What the hell? Why didn't I think to do that?

Makeup. That's the best I could come up with. Pathetic. I deserve to have her stolen from me. Except I can handle losing her to Georgie Porgie, but not to this guy. Never.

The heat of jealousy flows through my body. I cross the room and insert myself between Mala and Ferdinand, taking her hand from his and wrapping it around my arm. Mala's eyes widen, but she doesn't complain or make a joke at my expense. Instead she gifts me with a smile of my very own.

"You look handsome," she says.

I glance down at the white flowing cotton trousers and button-up shirt. "Can't go to a party looking like the help."

She brushes back my bangs, and I flinch. Her mouth tightens, but she doesn't ask why I didn't cut my hair. Maybe someday I'll feel comfortable enough not to try to hide my eye, but not today.

Sophia claps her hands. "You both look stunning."

I snort. "We'd better, after spending the entire day primping."

Mala steps on my toe.

"Oh, sorry," she drawls, covering her mouth with her hand. *Faker.* She bats insanely long eyelashes at me. "I'm not used to wearing high heels yet." She glances at Sophia. "You're right. They don't pinch."

Ferdinand waves us forward. "We should go. Queen Magnolia's waiting," he says, and again, I'm surprised by his thick French Creole accent. It's different from the one I'm used to. He sounds more like he's from Haiti than Louisiana.

I try not to roll my eyes over the queen business. It sounds ridiculous. Mala doesn't even try to be tactful. She hides a smirk behind her hand, and I prod her forward. Ferdinand and Sophia head for the front door. The tiny employee behind the cash register watches us leave with wide eyes.

"Hey, Ferdie," I call to his back. "What about paying—"

"Magnolia owns this boutique," Sophia says with a smile. "Come."

Night has settled, but it's not dark. Not with the neon lights.

A zydeco band plays one of my favorite songs, "La Vielle Chanson de Mardi Gras," on the corner before a packed sidewalk of drunken tourists. The stench of ripe bodies, booze, and spices fill the heated air. Energy crackles, filling me with anticipation.

Mala stares around with shining eyes. "I love this song!" she yells up at me.

I nod, wrapping my arm around her waist, afraid she'll get lost in the crowd. She sways in my arms, her hips rubbing and dipping against me in time with the high-octane accordion and fiddle playing. She's totally pumped up. I've never seen her so happy. If anyone deserves it, she does. I'm just glad to be able share this with her.

Ferdinand stands curbside with his hand in the air. A white stretch limousine pulls up in front of us. It feels like I'm going to prom. The chauffeur gets out and runs over to open the door with a wide grin. Mala and I follow Ferdinand and Sophia inside. They sit in the seats stretching down the left side of the limo, while Mala and I sit in the seats by the open door. Along the right side of the limo is a full bar with a bottle of champagne on ice, wineglasses, and a tray of cheese and crackers.

Mala scrunches closer. She crosses her leg, and I suck in a breath when it rubs against mine. The sweet floral scent of her perfume fills my nose as she lays her head against my shoulder with a sigh.

"As fantastic as it feels to be dressed up and heading to a party in a limo, I kind of wish we could go back to the hotel," she whispers. "My feet hurt."

"I thought they didn't pinch?"

"My shopping-induced endorphins have run out."

I lift her foot off the ground and slide off her shoe. I rub my thumbs along the indentation on the sole of her foot. She wiggles her toes and lets out a little moan that sounds an awful lot like a purr. "That feels so good."

"We don't need to go to a party. I could entertain you for the night." *Damn, did that sound cheesy?*

"Tempting." Mala slides her hand up my thigh. "Magnolia might not approve."

Our eyes clash. I don't know what she sees in mine, but the heat filling her gaze transfers like I've set my hand on a hot skillet. It's probably for the best that we don't go back to the hotel. I love the dress, but I can't stop thinking about slowly stripping her one layer at a time. I can only imagine what lacy, frilly lingerie she's wearing beneath the dress. Or…what if she's going commando?

Would it be awkward if I kiss her?

Sophia leans forward, breaking the mood before I make a fool out of myself. "Would you like some champagne?" She nods to Ferdinand who holds up a sweating bottle.

"Why not?" I glance at Mala and shrug. "You?"

"Sure, we're celebrating tonight." She leans forward, reaching for the glass. The front of her dress gapes, and her breasts spill forward in rounded mounds that would fit in my tingling palms, if not for the bra holding them hostage.

My hand trembles with the need to liberate them, and champagne sloshes over the rim of the glass to run down my fingers. I lick it off before it drips onto my white slacks and catch Mala staring at my mouth.

The tip of her tongue flicks her bottom lip, and my throat tightens. Heat rushes down to settle deep inside me. I've never been so turned on in my life.

Thank God the trousers I'm wearing are loose fit or I'd be totally exposed. I shift and cross my leg to block Mala's view, only to find another pair of eyes focused on the bulge in my pants.

Sophia stares with glazed eyes. A slight smile lifts the corners of her lips. Her gaze travels upward slowly. When our eyes meet, she doesn't look away. I read the invitation in the slight tilt of her eyes, the knowing smile, and the way she runs her hands down her thighs as if imagining my hands on her body.

The predatory desire in her gaze makes my stomach twist with a flood of revulsion as the beautiful mask she wore all day slides off.

I down the champagne in one gulp, then reach for the bottle again.

Mala intercepts my hand and presses her glass into it. "Take mine. I don't really like it."

"Not your thing?"

She shakes her head and leans forward to whisper in my ear, "It tastes like cat piss."

Sophia pours another glass and holds it out to her. "It'll grow on you. Like the shoes."

Mala waves the glass away with a flick of her manicured fingers. "I'm not cultured enough to enjoy it, and I'm too stubborn to fake it. Guess Magnolia's going to be disappointed. The hotel, fancy boutiques—I'm not fit to be an heiress. Hell, I'm not even sure if I want it." Her fingers wrap around my hand. "I like my life the way it is."

"Unfortunately, you don't have a choice. You have a responsibility to the people who will depend upon you when Queen Magnolia passes," Sophia says. "You'll meet her followers tonight. When you look into their eyes, you'll see their need. You'll feel their desire. They will welcome you into their hearts."

Mala stiffens. "Your sales pitch sucks. The last thing I want is to feel some strangers' desires or be in their hearts. That's fucking creepy."

"I didn't mean to frighten you."

"I'm not frightened, Sophia. I'm fed up with the cryptic bull-shit. Where are you taking us? Why are we going?" Mala asks the questions so fast that Sophia doesn't have a chance to answer. "And why is it so damn far away? You know what's going to happen. Why won't you tell us…"

Her words echo in my ears. I close my eyes. The words float in the air, hanging before my eyes in vivid neon. I squeeze her hand to get her to stop. The words are blinding me. "Calm down. Magnolia probably told them to keep quiet."

"But why?"

"Your aunt seems the sort who likes surprises. We'll find out soon. Whatever happens, I'll be by your side."

"You'd better be."

"I swear. You couldn't ditch me if you tried."

The motion of the car changes as the road becomes bumpier. Each time the car lurches, my head aches. I press my fingers to my temple, rubbing the throbbing vein that feels like it's about to explode. Why did I down those glasses of champagne? I haven't had a sip of alcohol since my arrest—not even pruno, the fermented concoction my cellmate hid in the toilet tank. Obviously, my tolerance has lowered in the last months.

The tinted windows coupled with the glare from the inside lights makes it hard to see outside, but we've left New Orleans behind. Thick trees line the dirt road. It's secluded—the perfect place for a serial killer to dismember and hide his or her prey.

Mala's paranoia's beginning to rub off on me.

I glance at Sophia again, then focus on Ferdinand, who sits in the back corner playing with his cell phone. He seems completely at ease. And bored out of his skull.

"Does this property belong to Magnolia?" I ask.

Sophia sighs. "You'll see soon enough."

Mala and I share a grimace. I hate not knowing what's going on. The vibe in the car gets even funkier. But maybe it's me. The tension ratchets up a level, but my body doesn't respond the way it should. My muscles loosen instead of tighten. I want to say something to Mala about it, but she's calmed down. I don't want to worry her again just 'cause I can't hold my liquor.

The car comes to a halt. The door opens, and the chauffeur is a bulky shadow in the doorway. I scoot out and reach inside for Mala. Her moist hand slips into mine and turns into a death grip that makes me wince. Sophia and Ferdinand follow us out while we try to get our bearings. The car's parked in a clearing with a bunch of other vehicles, but nobody's around but us. In the distance, the faint sound of drumming and singing echoes through the woods. The thick, humid air wraps around my body like a warm shower.

A flick of a lighter and the area lights up from the flame of a torch. Why don't they just carry a flashlight? It's not the 1800s, and I'm not impressed by the sideshow.

"This way," Ferdinand says, leading us into the woods. The dirt trail almost disappears in front of us due to the fading light.

Paranoia replaces the lethargy sapping my energy. I feel eyes watching, an evil presence thick with malevolence. Each step leads us deeper into its grip. Soon we won't be able to escape. We'll be trapped, overwhelmed, and devoured. My breath comes hard and quick. I wipe sweaty palms on my trousers, trying to pull myself together.

A warm hand touches my arm, and I stagger.

Mala squeezes my bicep. "Are you okay?"

I don't know how to tell her I'm losing it without sounding like an idiot. If I could clear the fuzz out of my head, I'd be all right, but it's only getting harder to tell the difference between reality and delusion. I never should've drunk those two glasses of champagne. It's more potent than a bottle of Jack. I'm totally spun.

I take Mala's hand and slide her arm through mine. "I can't see. Everything's blurry."

"Don't worry, I won't let you fall," she mutters. "It'd be better to ditch the torch and go without. It totally ruins our night vision. The full moon's enough for us to see by."

"For you, maybe. You're used to running through the bayou by the light of the moon." My increasingly mushy thoughts make speaking the words a battlefield of effort, but I get them out without slurring. "Normal city folk would get lost in two seconds. Or start thinking about all the things out here that could eat us."

"Like a rougarou? Vampires out to suck your blood, muwahahaa…" Her lilting voice shows she's not taking my fear seriously. But yeah, I could totally imagine something jumping out of the bushes to eat us.

My flesh ripples as the creature beneath my skin stretches, and I grit my teeth against the pain. With each step, my mind gets foggier. My thoughts come slower, and my fear grows deeper. The voices and drumming grow louder. Soon each beat pulses inside my body.

We leave the woods and step onto an open field dotted with ancient tombstones and decaying wooden crosses. In the middle of this cemetery, a large bonfire casts light on men and women dressed in white, swaying to the music of drums. Some kneel before a large stone covered in food, bottles, and candles. Ferdinand leads us through the dancers. The heat of the fire warms my skin. Thick smoke, pungent with herbs, curls through my nostrils to fill my lungs with each breath.

My muscles ripple as the snake stretches in its sleep, then awakens to the drums. I fall to my knees. Pain rolls my eye back. I try to fight, but I'm too weak or it's too strong. The alien awareness smashes through the mental walls I have built to hold it back until, with a hard thrust, I'm displaced—shoved deep into a corner of my mind to watch in horror.

CHAPTER 24

MALA

Zombie Rising

I lose track of Landry in the crowd.

People swarm around us when we enter the clearing. The noise of the drums, the singing and laughing, it overwhelms my senses. I'm not comfortable in large social situations. If Landry were with me, I could bear it, but not alone. If I could find a quiet corner to hide in, I'd be huddled there right now. Instead I have Ferdinand holding onto my arm as he drags me toward the altar and Magnolia. My aunt sees me and grins. Her face looks like carved oak, hard and wrinkled. She exudes power, every inch the queen with her high white turban and long cotton skirt.

Her aura ripples, visible in the firelight.

I want out of here. As if the crowd reads my thoughts, they press closer, totally invading my personal space, and I cringe away from their groping hands, almost dancing in a circle to avoid their touch. My skin tingles, and goose bumps rise. I try to shove away my unease, but it only grows worse. Shimmers radiate like halos above their skin. Landry said ghosts shine. Half of the dancers are dressed in silver light.

Speaking of...where did Landry go?

Ferdinand grabs my arm when I turn back to find Landry.

"Let go!" I twist my arm, breaking free of Ferdinand's grip. Just because he's bigger, stronger, and has a penis doesn't mean he can force me to do what he wants.

He lifts his hands into the air, placating me with a smile. My breath catches. Damn, he's fine. Where in the world did Magnolia find him and Sophia? The perfect minions. Her sacrifices would willingly follow them to her altar without a second thought, magnetized by their beauty.

Oh crap, bad thought. I'm at her altar.

"Mala Jean Marie, you don't look like you're having fun yet." Magnolia cackles. *Crazy old bat.* She hands me a wooden cup filled with thick red liquid. My nose scrunches at the coppery tang beneath the spice. "Drink."

"I don't think so."

"It's not poison. It'll help you relax."

"I don't want to relax. If everyone else is relaxing, who'll drive us home? I'll be the designated driver tonight. I don't mind." I push the drink away and step back. Hands keep me from running. I shrug away from Ferdinand. "Don't touch me."

"I need your help tonight, *cher*. And you need mine. Don't you feel the spirits calling out to you?"

"Is that why my skin feels like it's creeping off my bones?" I glance around the area. In the middle of the circle, I see dark hair. Landry's surrounded by spirits, their hands trace over his body. He's oblivious to them, in his own world as he turns in a circle with his arms outstretched. Each step takes him closer and closer to the fire.

"Shit!" I step toward him, but I'm yanked back by my arm. "Damn it, Ferdinand. Let go."

Magnolia snaps her fingers in front of my face, capturing my attention. "Landry's fine. Sophia will watch over him. She won't let the spirits suck him dry, though they want to. Oh my, yes. He's a tasty soul for those who have the palate for such things." She waves to Ferdinand. In a quick motion, he lifts me over his shoulder.

I scream, slapping at his back. "Put me down! Magnolia, what's going on?"

Magnolia leans on her cane as she hobbles, leading us from the party. "Landry has his own curse to bear. I don't want what's inside him interfering with what we need to do tonight."

I twist my head up so I can see her. "Do what? I promised I'd cooperate so you could teach me how to control my powers. You don't have to toss me around like a bag of bones. Landry understands. He won't interfere."

"He will if he thinks you're in danger."

My heart skips a beat. "Oh, hell…"

Magnolia's footsteps stop. I try to wriggle to the side to see around Ferdinand, but he's too damn wide. He grabs my waist and heaves. One minute I'm dangling over his shoulder and the next, flying through the air. I land on my feet but stumble over a rock. I topple backward, falling on top of a pile of loose dirt. All the air shoots out of my lungs. I roll off the dirt pile, whimpering.

Oh crap! Falling again.

This time I land on something soft and squishy, but the back of my head bounces off something hard. A gaseous smell of decay puffs upward, and I gag. Darkness covers my vision. Pain flares, rolling outward to fill every inch of my body. When I open my eyes, I see walls of earth on either side, opening up to a star-filled sky. Magnolia and Ferdinand stare down at me.

"Get out of the grave, Mala Jean." Mama whispers the plaintive warning in my ear. "This is bad juju. You've got to get out of here."

I jerk upright, spinning around, but I don't see her. Only the corpse I landed on. The wet, black, viscous stuff on my arms and coating my dress came from inside the body—rotting, decomposing flesh sticks to my skin and won't brush off. I stagger back, falling against the dirt wall. My throat burns from my screams. Hands grab me beneath the arms and lift. When my feet touch the ground, I fall away from Ferdinand, scrambling as far from the grave as I can on shaking legs.

Cold fingers press into my skin. "Mala, run." Mama's fear kicks mine up to officially freaking-out level.

Magnolia kneels by the grave. "Well, that's not good. You done broke the girl's head. How am I supposed to raise this child when you done smashed her up so bad?"

I'm frantically wiping the girl's stinking, gooey insides off on the thick grass. It takes a few seconds to realize Magnolia asked me a question. Another few to remember how to answer her. Fury shoots through me, and I quiver with the desire to punch someone.

I ball up my fists so I don't do something stupid.

"You're crazy! Raise her up? Raise…she's dead. For a long time. Oh God…I feel sick." This is so much worse than touching Lainey Prince, at least she wasn't rotting. Or covered with maggots. *Are maggots eating me too?* I roll onto my knees as my stomach launches itself up my throat. The lobster etouffee I ate for lunch covers the ground in a mushy pile and sticks in my throat as

I gag. The smell of the body mingles with the smell of my lunch, and I vomit again.

Magnolia goes to her satchel and pulls out a small leather bag. "I took this girl's parents' money and made them promises. Said I'd give them their child back. Didn't guarantee what condition she'd be in." She shrugs her narrow shoulders but doesn't stop riffling through the satchel during her instruction. "Magic can work miracles. You've seen my Etienne. He was dead almost half a year before I brought him back. This girl's not gone so long. The trick is stitching her soul back inside. Some want to return to the land of the living. Others prefer to stay on the other side. Together we can draw her from wherever she's hiding and stuff her back in her body where she belongs."

Magnolia believes what she's saying. That's the scary part. Before I would've doubted stitching souls were even possible. Now? Not so much. Nor is my belief, or lack of, what matters.

No, what's important is I swore not to dabble in dark magic. Raising the dead has to be the darkest.

"Hell, no. This is wrong. Etienne is wrong, Magnolia." I crawl backward, but Ferdinand steps into my path. His long legs stretch higher than the walls of the grave. He grabs the back of my dress and lifts me to my feet. Pain from my bruises makes me whimper in protest. My legs wobble, not ready to hold my weight, but I stiffen my knees. "I won't help you."

"You've already helped, *cher*."

Magnolia points her finger. A flicker of silvery light shines over the grave. It's hard to make out what it is. I focus on it. Is this the girl in the casket? Why isn't she corporeal like the other ghosts that haunt me?

"Because the other spirits haven't passed over to the other side," Magnolia says.

Witch read my mind again.

"Look hard, Mala. Do you see her now?"

I squint, trying to pick out individual features. Her head comes into focus first. Thick, tight curls twist around her ears. Eyes, sorrowful pits in her skull, sit above flaring nostrils. Her mouth stretches wide in a silent scream that sends an echoing shiver down my spine. She claws at her face with long fingernails, writhing in the air, a twisting, shimmering flicker.

It hurts to watch. Her pain transmits itself into me, and I crumble. Only Ferdinand's hands keep me from toppling head-first back into the grave. But from this bent-over position, I can see inside the casket. Wooden torches have been stuck into the earthen walls. Candles flare to life, casting light over the body.

The spirit hovers over the body.

"It hurts her to be so close but not inside, Mala." Magnolia sprinkles a handful of powder over the body, then takes my hand. Her skin feels oily to the touch. No matter how hard I pull, she won't let me go. "Stop fighting me."

"Never."

"How long are you gonna act the child and let this girl suffer? She didn't deserve to die so young. The man who killed her should've known better than to drink and drive. He didn't even apologize to the family or go to the memorial service. He sat in a bar and drank until he passed out the day this girl was buried."

"He should be in jail."

"Yes, but he's not. Hit and run. He's getting away with murder."

"That's not right." The girl stands in the air over her body. She's fully corporeal now. I can see her like I can any live person. She's a lot younger than I am. Maybe twelve. Too young to die. I frown at Magnolia. "If it was a hit and run, how do you know all of this?"

Magnolia shrugs. "Same way you'd know if you'd stop fighting your gifts. This girl's death was an imbalance. A black stain on the universe. She deserves to grow up and have babies. She won't now unless we give her a second chance. You want her to have that chance, don't you?"

This isn't right, but I'm not sure why. Magnolia's words twist and weave their way into my head. I try to follow the course they're taking. The girl stretches out her hand, and I reach for it. Her life flashes between us. In an instant, I see her birth, her life, and…the horror of her…of Lily's death.

The car sped toward her. Lily froze, knowing she didn't have time to get out of its path. Her eyes closed. The sudden shock of pain opened them when her head smashed against the windshield. She rolled across the hood and crashed onto the asphalt. I clutch my chest against the double agony of betrayal that Lily felt while lying in the road, bleeding and begging for help, only to have the man drive over her one last time to make sure she was dead.

Darkness consumed her spirit…like it took Landry.

So much fear.

"Oh my God, the bastard murdered her. It wasn't an accident. He could've called for help, but he didn't. He ran her over again."

"He did, didn't he? A man like that deserves to die. Not this girl."

"Yes."

"Put her back into her body, Mala."

I shake my head. *Why can't I think?* "I don't know how."

Magnolia squeezes my hand. "Focus on the hate you feel for the man. Pull on it and use the energy to push Lily back into her body."

My hate feels tangible. Like I could suck on it like a lollipop.

It rolls around in my mouth, leaving a bitter aftertaste. This girl deserves to live. I can give her another chance. My hand in Magnolia's grip tingles. The air crackles with lightning strikes. The sparks bring the sharp scent of ozone. Magnolia shifts the hate-funneled energy from herself to me, and I push it back. Back and forth. We draw it out, spinning it like a yarn ball. Only I won't be knitting a sweater. I'm stitching a soul.

The pit of my stomach clenches as I shove Lily toward her body. She screams, confused, but it's for the best. She'll get another chance to go to prom, to learn how to drive, to get a boyfriend and have kids of her own someday. She'll be alive.

She'll thank me.

I'm not sure when I blacked out, but I wake up in Ferdinand's arms. He has me cradled against his chest like I'm an infant. The warmth of the fire and the beats of the drums almost lull me back into unconsciousness. My body feels heavy. I can barely hold my head upright. "Did it work?"

The chuckle rumbles deep in Ferdinand's chest. It tickles. "The girl will be reunited with her parents after she recovers. Justice has been served. Her murderer has taken her place in the afterlife."

The hiss hurts my bruised ribs. "What?"

"Everything is balanced. For life to be restored, it must also be taken."

I shove forward. Ferdinand drops my legs, holding on to my arms so I don't do a complete face-plant. I yank free of his grasp, breathing hard. My mind turns his words over. Did he say what I think he said?

Ferdinand moves toward me, and I take a quick step out of reach. "Is there a problem?" he asks in his honey-gold accent.

I shiver, rubbing my arms. "Hell, yes! What do you mean by

balance? Are you telling me the guy who ran over that girl's dead now? As in, by raising her from the dead, I killed him?"

"He exchanged places with her."

I swallow hard. "How?"

"I don't know. The universe decides."

"So this could be complete bullshit. You have no idea." I scrub my face. *No, no. Ridiculous. I'm getting played.* "Where's Magnolia?"

"She and Etienne have taken the girl to recuperate where prying eyes won't see."

Convenient. I don't want to think about this anymore. I did not kill that guy. No way, I'm not a murderer. Or a pawn of the universe used to right an injustice with…magic.

I can barely hold myself upright. My muscles ache, like I've been working out too long. Ferdinand reaches for me again, but I shove him away. As hot as he is, the idea of his touch makes my stomach churn. "I don't believe you."

"I shouldn't have told you." His heavy eyebrows lower over his beautiful eyes. Eyes I want to scratch out. Coming here was a huge mistake. I knew it when I made the promise to apprentice with Magnolia. The woman is evil, no matter how pretty a bow she wraps around the use of our gifts. How did I let myself get sucked into her world?

"I want to go home."

Ferdinand crosses his muscular arms. "The queen said I could take you back to the hotel."

"No! I want to go home." I search the dancers for Landry. He promised to stay at my side. Why hasn't he come to find me? I take a deep breath, focusing on Landry. The tip of my nose tingles as his scent—faint and acrid, like battery acid's eating away at his insides—filters into my nostrils. While still a little freaked out over becoming a human bloodhound, this new ability to hone in on Landry's scent comes in handy.

It's not how he normally smells. It's the smell of fear.

"Landry's in trouble." I shuffle forward. "Ferdinand, help me find him."

I shove through the crowd. The ghosts surround me, whispering in my ears. I ignore them, but they fight for my attention. The live people have no idea about the spirits. They dance and sing, unaware of the hidden realm among them.

"Where's Sophia?"

Ferdinand shrugs.

I stop and stare at him. A shiver raises goose bumps on my arms. "You're lying. She's with Landry, isn't she?"

I saw how she looked at him. How Landry couldn't tear his eyes away from her. His fear grows stronger. The stench fills the air. He needs my help.

A woman with a boa constrictor wrapped around her neck steps from the crowd and wraps her arm around Ferdinand's waist. He smiles down at her then leans forward to kiss the snake on its head.

Not needing to see how much further he plans to take his snake love, I slip away, following Landry's scent from the cemetery into the woods. Beneath the trees, I see conjoined shadows. Sophia straddles Landry prone body. He writhes beneath her. She has his hand pinned to the ground over his head and kisses him as if she's diving for his tonsils.

A sharp burst of pain settles in my chest, and I release the breath in an inarticulate yell.

Sophia doesn't even remove her mouth, but her eyes flick up to meet mine. A smug smile curves the sides of her lips. Her smile goads me into a shambling run. I bury my fingers in her long, silky hair and try to rip it out of her scalp. She falls back with a scream. Her arms flail as she tries to smack me. I hold her hair with both hands and drag her backward. The strands are long enough that I don't get within arm's reach of her fists…at first. Once she's away from Landry, I release her.

"You bitch," she screams, scrambling across the ground.

My kick hits her in the ribs, and she falls onto her side. I don't wait to see if she recovers but run to fall beside Landry. I lift his head onto my lap, trying to protect him as he convulses.

I shake him, begging "Wake up, please. Landry!" Only the white of his eye shows, and his mouth hangs open as he sucks in huge gulps of air. He looks like he's dying. I hold him tighter. "What did you do to him, Sophia?"

Sophia rises. She runs a thumb across her lips then sucks on the tip. "I love the taste of power. He has so much built up inside. He must not have found a satisfying release in a long time. No wonder he came to me so easily."

"Don't flatter yourself. Think I'm too stupid to tell that he's been drugged? He would never, ever, give this up"—I wave my hand down my body—"for an old hag. I see your hidden face, Sophia." *And I do.*

Whatever magical spell she cast over herself no longer works on me. She now looks like a middle-age woman with crow's feet and slightly sagging skin. I sense her frustration and anger at the loss of her youth. I can understand her wanting to be with a younger man. I even get why she would hate me for taking her place as Magnolia's heir. Sophia's probably been kissing my aunt's wrinkled ass for years in the hope of getting into the will. Logically, I understand.

Maybe if I were a better person, I could forgive her deception, if it hadn't involved attempted rape.

But I'm not, and it did.

I curl my fingers, imagining them digging through her skin. Her scream sounds like it's ripped from deep inside her. She doubles over, clenching her stomach, and I grin.

I'm gonna carve her open like a pumpkin and tear out her guts.

CHAPTER 25

LANDRY

My Favorite Word

I fight free.

It's the hardest thing I've ever done. The demon inside doesn't want to let me go. I sense it has its own agenda. It needs my body to accomplish its goal, but it doesn't need *me*. I'm in its way. The worst part's not having control. Now I know how Mala felt when my sister possessed her body. Except Lainey shoved her out completely.

My head starts to clear, but it's still hard to focus. My limbs shake like I've got low blood sugar. Cold sweat rolls down my forehead to sting my eye. It's hard to breathe. A tongue dives down my throat, and I gag, biting down. Blood fills my mouth.

Mala yells my name.

It only takes a second for the shock to kick me in the head.

The demon has trapped me inside my own mind. I watch as it

uses Sophia, while she thinks it's the other way around and that she's violating me. I almost feel sorry for her.

But not quite.

She drugged me. I understand now that it's too late. She spiked the champagne, and Mala gave me hers. Maybe both drinks were drugged or only one. Whatever. It worked. I'm out of the way, and Mala's on her own.

I promised I'd protect her.

Instead, she's trying to protect me.

Some hero I turned out to be. This never would've happened to George. Deputy Dawg would've sniffed out the drug with his superpower cop senses. Not downed it like an alcoholic fiending for his first sip of the day.

Nausea twists my stomach. Sour champagne mixed with stomach acid burns my throat. I twist, trying to lift my arms. They're like two heavy weights attached to my shoulders. The woman sitting on my chest shifts onto my diaphragm, shoving the air from my lungs. I try to answer Mala, but multitasking is beyond my skills. I can only do one thing at a time. *Breathe.*

The weight lifts from my chest. I drink in great gulps of air.

My eye cracks open. Mala stands above me. Moonlight peeks through the branches above our heads, shining across her face. She glows like an angel sent down from heaven. A force of energy crackles in the air, blowing her curls back from her face. Determination juts out her jaw as she stretches out her hand. Her fingers clench into fists. The building energy bursts forth. I can't see it, but it crackles like lightning through my whole body. I grit my teeth from the tingle in my mouth.

A woman's scream tears through the air. I push up onto my elbows and prop my back against the tree so I can see. I still can't convince my lower body to work. My legs feel numb from the hips down.

"I'm gonna kill you!" Mala yells.

Sophia screams again and falls to her knees. Her arms wrap around her stomach, and her head falls forward so her hair hangs over her face. I grab Mala's ankle. She looks down at me with wide, horrified eyes, snapping out of her killing frenzy. Her hand wavers, lowering slightly.

"Landry," she whispers.

A chuckle comes from Sophia.

Mala's head turns toward her in slow motion.

The woman's laughter grows louder, rolling from deep inside her gut. She runs her fingers through her hair, flipping it out of her face. A smile stretches her mouth.

A cold chill runs down my spine, clearing the last bit of fog from my mind. Now I know how the hero feels in a scary movie.

Mala steps back, placing herself between me and Sophia, as if she plans to shield me from the witch woman. "Oh, crap!" she mutters.

Yep, it feels exactly like that.

"Did you really think that would work on me?" Sophia stands and brushes off her slacks. Where the hell did the woman's shirt go? Oh, there.

Sophia picks her blouse off the ground. A quick snap knocks loose the dirt and leaves clinging to the fabric. Rather than dress, she lays the shirt over her arm and stands before us, naked from the waist up. As if proud to show off her body.

A foul taste covers my tongue. I flip through the memories of when the demon was in control. "Did she kiss me?" I ask.

Mala doesn't answer. My fingers tighten around her ankle. Her leg trembles.

Ferdinand stalks into the clearing. Neither woman acknowledges his arrival, but I sigh, relieved. If anyone can stop this battle, he can. He comes to stand between the two women. "The party is over. It's time to go."

Mala doesn't remove her gaze from Sophia. "I'm not going anywhere with her."

"The queen has summoned Sophia." Amusement fills his voice, making his French accent thicker. "She is not pleased."

The woman draws in a deep breath. "No…"

Ferdinand doesn't look in her direction. "Come."

Mala wavers, biting her lip. She glances down at me. Whatever she sees makes up her mind. "Help me with Landry. She hurt him."

I don't feel hurt. Stoned, but no pain. Maybe after the drug wears off, I'll feel like crap. Between the two, they lift me off the ground. I'm still shaky and stumble like a drunken fool until Mala wraps her arms around my waist. The height difference makes it awkward. Finally she gives up and lets Ferdinand hoist me over his shoulder in a fireman carry. My head dangles between his shoulder blades, and I twist up to stare at Mala. A grim tension makes her steps heavy.

Silence has its own weight.

Blood rushes to my head, and I close my eye. My head bobs. I try to stay conscious, but it's a losing battle.

* * *

Warmth surrounds me. *I'm floating.*

Water laps at my chin. A bare chest presses against my back. I know those breasts. I obsess over them. My head rests on Mala's shoulder, and she has her arms wrapped around my waist. The sleek length of her legs wrap around mine. She shakes as she sobs.

"Mala…" My voice cracks.

Water sloshes over the side of the tub as she shifts.

I tip back my head, and my lips brush against her jaw. "Are you okay?"

Her arms tighten. She's scaring me. It's not like her to be so quiet. I grab on to the side of the tub and pull up into a sitting position, then twist around until I face her. She keeps her head down. Her hair hangs across her face, hiding her eyes. I cup her cheeks with my hand, rubbing away the tears with my thumbs, and lift her chin.

"What happened?"

She brushes my hands aside. "Don't…"

"Stop pushing me away."

Her scowl makes a smile flicker on my lips. So do her words. "We're naked in a tub, Landry. How exactly is that pushing you away?"

Point taken. My eyes drop from her face to her breasts bobbing in the foamy water. For the second time tonight, my head goes foggy. I swallow the lump in my throat. My voice sounds harsh from a surge of lust as I ask, "How exactly did we get into the tub?"

You'd think I'd remember. Getting Mala naked has been a goal of mine for a very long time. Many hours of fantasizing have been devoted to this very moment. Yet I have no idea what awesome, smooth lines talked her into this.

I glance around the room. We're in the Jacuzzi tub in the master bathroom of the hotel suite. It's huge. Big enough to hold two comfortably, but we're only taking up a tiny corner. "How did we get here?"

"You don't remember?" Her swollen eyes study my face.

Not a damn thing! My last memories…"We were all dressed up and in the limo heading to Magnolia's fancy party. I drank some champagne—" My head throbs, and I rub at the aching spot between my eyes. "Why can't I remember? Did we go? Did I get drunk?" I slide toward her through the bubbles. "I embarrassed you, didn't I? That's why you're mad?"

"I'm not mad, s-stupid." She grabs my shoulders and yanks me back into her arms. Her breasts mash against my chest. "I-I'm…happy."

"You don't seem happy."

"Well, I am."

"Prove it."

"I will…" She breathes out the words, chest heaving. Her fingers slide up my neck to thread through my hair, and she tugs my head down. Lips tasting of ripe strawberries touch mine. How she managed to keep lip gloss on the whole night, I'll never know. She starts out with slow kisses, exploring my mouth. I let her take the lead, excited, but also unsure of how far she's willing to go. Her being naked's a good sign.

My hand slides across her bare back. Her skin feels slick and smooth from the bubbles and oil in the tub. Her rounded hip fits in my palm. I caress the dimple above her plump ass before sliding my hands down to squeeze rounded cheeks. Her breath catches, then releases in a moan against my mouth. Her tongue traces my bottom lip, then slides between my teeth.

She slides her leg over mine and twists. I roll with her until my back rests against the tub and she straddles my waist. With one last thrust of her tongue, she pulls back. We're both breathing hard. I take a second to stare at the woman above me, trying to brand this image into my mind. I never want to forget seeing her like this.

Bubbles slide down the crease between her breasts. I press my face between them and lick the foam away. Her nipples harden. I roll my tongue across them, grazing the areolas with my teeth. God, she tastes so good.

Mala's back arches as she shudders. Tiny moans fall from her parted lips. She rubs the soft patch between her thighs against me, and I stir. Her wide eyes shine with desire...*for me*. Heat scorches my skin wherever her gaze touches. She sets me on fire. Her hand dips beneath the water to wrap around my shaft. It grows firm in her hand. She starts with a slow caress, hand sliding down my thickening length. My hips buck, and she gives a smug smile.

I groan, fingers gripping the side of the tub so I don't go under.

Her caresses quicken, responding like she can read my mind. The sensation builds. "Mala..." I gasp, grabbing on to her hand.

A tiny frown creases her forehead. "Doesn't that feel okay?"

"*Yes*. God, yes." The pressure builds inside me, filling me until it feels like I'll explode. If I let her keep going, I'll lose it.

I've planned this...I won't let it end with me shooting my wad into the tub and leaving her unsatisfied. "Wait..."

"No! Not this time." Mala wraps her arms around my neck and thrusts her tongue into my mouth. The kiss almost makes me lose control. I hold on to her waist, lifting her as I climb out of the tub. Our mouths never separate. Her hands caress my chest...my back, run up my neck, and grab onto my hair as she makes low, moaning sounds. My goal is to get her onto the bed, but she won't stop kissing me long enough for me to tell her. The easiest way is to pick her up.

Her muscular legs tighten around my waist.

Damn! She's hot and moist pressed against my stomach. I want to slide my fingers inside her until she cries my name. I grab a towel off the rack and stumble toward the bed. The back of my thighs hit the edge of the mattress, and I sit down. Mala wriggles on my lap, skin slick from the bath. She stops kissing me in favor of taking deep breaths.

"Tell me what you want," I whisper, needing permission. I've messed up too many times to take her for granted.

The bathroom light shines across her face and reveals the confusion in her eyes. "I don't know. Whatever you want?"

I stifle a groan. "This is your first time, isn't it? Are you sure—"

"Oh, that's what you…yes, damn it! Of course I want to make love to you." Mala brushes her fingers across my scar. "Don't you want me?"

Yeah. I do.

Only the first time should be special. Something she'll always compare with other partners. Not that she'll have other guys if I get my way. I'm gonna be her first and last. And I'll be damned if I'll let her wake up tomorrow full of regret about her choice.

It's my turn to pleasure her.

CHAPTER 26

MALA

Pleasure

Landry rolls me onto the bed. He gives my butt a quick kiss, grabs the towel, and runs out of the room, saying "Stay here. I'll be right back" before I have a chance to protest. I prop myself up on my elbows and stare at his retreating bare backside.

Thumps of drawers being slammed and Landry's curses come from the other bedroom. I throw myself back onto the mattress with a frustrated groan. *What the hell is he looking for, and why is it taking so damn long?* Warm air blows in through the balcony door, cooling my wet skin.

Okay, don't stress. This is good.

I need time to prepare for tonight anyway. Losing my virginity in this gorgeous hotel room is a hundred ways more romantic than doing it under a tree after almost drowning in the pond. A smile flickers over my lips as I sigh. Butterflies beat their wings in my chest as I shove the bedspread down to the bottom of the bed and drape the white sheet over my waist.

Should I cover my breasts or leave them exposed? I experiment with the blanket, studying the various poses in the mirror. I'm going for sexy and mysterious. With a sultry smile, I settle on covering only the tips of my breasts and leaving my legs bare. I fluff out my hair and spread it across the pillow.

I look hot! Fingers crossed…

Noises come from the kitchen now. The refrigerator door slams.

I trace my fingers over my lips then run them down my neck, touching each place Landry kissed or nibbled.

"Thinking about me?" Landry stands over the bed. The tray he holds carries a lit candle, a bottle of chocolate syrup, and a box of condoms.

The towel rides low on his hips. His muscled abs clench as he bends over to place the tray on the bedside table.

My heart races. "Did you bring this stuff from home?"

He ducks his head. "Only the condoms. Everything else is from here. You don't like it?"

"It seems like you've put a lot of thought into this seduction." Anticipation flutters my tummy.

"I figured, since you're giving me a second chance, I'll do it right." He crawls onto the bed, moving like a stalking tiger. The intensity in his eye makes my breath catch. I crawl backward. Not fast. I'm not really trying to escape, but his expression scares me. In a good way.

He grabs my ankle. My heart races as he drags me slowly across the silk sheets. His teeth nip the inside of my thigh, and I squeal. "You said yes to this, right?" he asks.

"God, yes." As if I could say no. Not with him on his hands and knees over me. I run my hands across his hard chest. Muscles flex in my palms as he lowers his head. The tip of his tongue traces a spiral on my neck, slowly swirling up to my ear. He kisses the lobe and grazes the skin with his teeth. His hot breath blows into my ear, and I gasp.

"I love you," he whispers.

I freeze. *Did I hear him right?*

His lips move across my neck to my other ear. I squirm, unable to remain still as he slowly presses soft kisses down the front of my body, teasing me. He flips me over onto my stomach and drizzles chocolate down my spine. It's cold from the refrigerator, and my back arches.

"God, you're so beautiful," he murmurs before his tongue sears a hot path up my spine. He takes his time, licking, nibbling, and kissing my skin, inch by *slow* inch. The intensity of need building inside of me grows hotter, and I grow wilder with each nibble.

I bite down on my lip, trying to hold the moans inside. Whimpers come from deep in my throat. My skin feels seared—sensitive to the slightest flick of his tongue or bite of his teeth. I'm gonna combust. It's too much. I'm on fire.

His teeth nip at my side, and I lose my fucking mind. I burst…and fly apart! Shivers rack my body. I roll onto my back with a groan.

His skin shines with a silver tint in the moonlight. I need to touch him. To taste the saltiness of his sweat on my tongue. He grabs my hands when I reach for him, stretching them over my head. His weight pins me to the bed.

"It's still my turn." He grins at my growl. "No touching. Promise, and I'll let you go."

I'm panting from the force of the desire flooding my senses. Unable to speak, I give a shaky nod.

He holds up the bottle and shakes it.

"What are you doing?" Why do I sound like a phone sex operator?

"Eating my sundae while the chocolate's hot," he says, and drizzles syrup between my legs. I raise up on my elbows. Landry grasps the back of my legs and, with a quick tug, lays them over his shoulders. My eyes close when his head moves between my legs, and I rear away with a choked cry. My fingers clench, jerking at his hair as I try to pull him up, but he ignores me. His tongue enters me, thrusting and pulsing against my most sensitive spot. My breath quickens, and I whimper. Landry's tongue doesn't pause but quickens in response to my moans. His fingers grip my legs, not letting go when I squirm, unable to stay still as a wave of pleasure curls my toes.

When my eyes open, I stare up at Landry. He's braced on his hands above me. What does my expression look like to bring out his self-satisfied smile? He dips his head down for a deep, chocolate-flavored kiss that leaves us both gasping for air.

His body gives a rippling shudder as he groans. "I can't hold back much longer, Mala."

My breath catches with the tiny spurt of fear, but I shove it back. "Yes…"

I reach for him, needing a semblance of control over the unknown to ease my anxiety. He looks like he'll split me apart, but the skin of his shaft is so soft. I caress him, loving the contrast of hard and velvety. He groans, head falling forward, as I guide him to my opening, then freeze. "The condom?"

"Shit, almost forgot." Landry passes it to me.

My fingers fumble like they belong to someone else. I should turn on the light, but that would break the mood. *Oh God…it's on.* "O-okay, I'm ready."

"Mala, I've heard the first time hurts." He flicks hair out of his eyes. Even now, he's worried about me. If I change my mind, he'll be okay with it. I don't have to do this. But I want to. I do.

Landry's tip presses against me. I take a deep breath and wrap my legs around him. I shove up as he thrusts. A burst of white-hot pain makes me groan. Landry tries to pull out, but I clench my thighs to hold on to him. "I'm okay. Just give me a second."

Okay, more than a second.

He pulses inside me—tiny, minute vibrations that kind of tickle at first. My muscles flex around him. Squeezing him. His breath catches, and I smile, loving his reaction. Pain fades as my body stretches to accommodate him.

I rock my hips upward.

Landry groans. He moves hesitantly at first, then his pace quickens. I give a roll of my abdominal muscles with each thrust. Soon our rhythm matches. Pleasure builds…building, building deep inside. It radiates outward in a crescendo of sensation. Spirals, swirls of light flash behind my eyelids.

It hits. A mix of pleasure and pain. Landry grabs on to the headboard and gives a final thrust. His shout matches my scream.

I think I pass out.

It takes a bit to come to my senses. Landry lays spent inside me, while our sweaty bodies cling together. I run my hand up his back. I don't even care that his weight makes it tough to catch my breath, but my heavy wheezes gives it away.

"Are you okay?" He rolls over onto his side, slipping out of me, but I'm still cradled in his arms.

I nod my head. Unable to speak. Who knew? Multiple orgasms.

No wonder Mama got hooked on sex.

Landry chuckles as I lay my head on his chest, totally spent.

His heart thumps in my ear. He rubs my back in slow circles. "You doing okay?" he whispers.

I press a kiss to his chest, too exhausted to form words. My eyes drift shut as I'm lulled by the warmth and security he brings.

A sharp tug on my soul pinches as I am released from my body. I haven't slipped my skin since I left the hospital. I don't know why I must now. I'd rather stay with Landry, but I'm being drawn out. If I fight, it'll be painful. I learned that the first few times it happened.

With a deep exhale, I give in. My soul slips from my body to float over the bed. I stare down at the two bodies. Landry and I lay with our limbs entwined as if fused together. We look so peaceful in our sleep. None of the worries and cares of the night remain. We washed them away.

Another jerk on my soul—

The shift in location brings me to my knees. Darkness covers the strange room. I stretch out my senses, such as they are while incorporeal. In some ways, they're sharper, more intense while I travel through the veil between the walls of reality, my fancy way of describing where I travel to when I astral project. It's a hell of a lot prettier than the other side.

A faint light shines from beneath a door. Drawn-out whimpers come from a slumped shadow huddling against the wall. My skin itches from a prickle of familiarity, and the harder I stare, the clearer the person becomes. The identity of the captive hits me like a ton of bricks.

I lurch forward, crying "Dena!"

My feet make no sound on the ground. My cousin shivers when I frantically run my hands through her, forgetting that I can't touch her or remove the duct tape wrapped around her hands and feet. And I can't ease her fear.

She can't even hear my words…"It'll be okay. I'll save you. I swear…"

The sound of a lock clicking comes from above. I glance up right when the door flies open to slam against the wall. The light blinds me for a second, then I focus on the shiny glint of metal from a gun.

"No, leave her alone!" I lunge forward to place myself between Dena and the gun. I'm sobbing because I want to shield her, but a bullet will go right through me. "Don't hurt her. Please…"

I'm trembling so hard I think I'll explode into a million molecules. If he hurts her while I watch, unable to help, my soul will be torn. Broken.

The man moves into the room. He's dressed from head to toe in black. If he's trying to hide his face by wearing a ski mask, it must mean he doesn't want Dena to be able to identify him. That's a good sign. She has a chance to get out of this alive. She just has to stop fighting and hang on until I rescue her.

But going down quietly isn't my cousin's style any more than it's mine. She kicks at him when he gets close enough to touch her.

"Let me go!" she demands more than begs, holding her bound hands toward him.

He grunts and throws the bag he's carrying onto the floor. His foot lashes out. Dena screams when it connects, doubling over and clutching her stomach. Blood flies from her lips to land in a pool of light.

"Mala…" Landry's echoing voice cuts through my panic. He reminds me I'm not trapped with Dena. Or helpless.

I shift fast, sitting up in the bed with a sharp inhale. The heavy weight of my body makes my lungs clench and burn as I suck in huge gulps of air. Blinking rapidly, I see a blurry Landry crouching on the bed in front of me. His wide eye and flushed cheeks shows his concern, which almost equals mine. His fingers dig into my shoulders.

"Mala, I couldn't—"

"Dena's in trouble—" Our words jumble as we shout over the other. Whatever he's got to say isn't as important as Dena. I lean forward, covering his mouth with my hand.

"Call the Sheriff's Office." I shake my head. "Not the ones here…George or Bessie. Dena's been kidnapped. I saw her."

Landry yanks my hand down. "We've got problems of our own."

Unbelievable! He's not even listening.

A cackle raises the hairs on the back of my neck. I lurch to my knees, shoving Landry aside. "What the hell is she doing here?"

Magnolia sits in the same chair Mama sat in yesterday. Today she wears a silver dress with rows of tiny buttons. Her silver hair sits in a bun on the back of her head. Ferdinand leans against the bathroom door with his muscled arms crossed. He stares at the ceiling. Thank God for small favors since I'm still bare-assed naked.

Sophia's on her knees beside the bed. I instinctively lunge toward her, my fingers itching to wrap around her throat, but Landry stops me. He pulls me against his chest with one arm and winds the sheet around my body with the other. As soon as I'm covered, I scramble off the bed. Landry yanks the tail end of the sheet, stopping me in mid-jump.

"Let me go!" I spring forward again, but Landry winds the sheet around his fist, dragging me back until he can wrap his arms around me.

"Stop fighting!" He squeezes just enough to make it difficult to breathe. "Calm down."

"You wouldn't order me around if you knew what she did."

But he doesn't. And…I don't want him to remember how she violated him.

I strain against him once more, but I can't break his hold. Sophia tips her chin with an expression of haughty disdain. I want to smack the lip-curling smirk right off. I wish I could suck out her soul and stuff it into a lab rat.

Still, I'm not too stubborn to know when I'm beat. For now.

Landry lowers his guard once I stop struggling. He doesn't release me, but doesn't hold on to me so tightly that I feel like I'm suffocating. My anger shifts from Sophia to Magnolia. After what happened to Landry and me in the cemetery, this motley crew is the last group of people I want to see after waking up from a night of hot sex. Then there's Dena being kidnapped. I'm too far away to save her, even if I knew where she was being held.

My idiocy constantly astounds me. I should've shifted through the wall to see where she was while I had the chance, instead of panicking like a nitwit. If he hurts her, it's my fault.

"You done fighting?" Magnolia asks with one of her toothless smiles. It sends an icy chill through my body.

I give a jerky nod. "How did you get in here?"

"I own this building." Her head tilts, and she sniffs. "Smells like sex and woman's blood in here."

A blush heats my face. A quick glance at the bed shows dried spots of blood on the sheet, and I groan.

I spin to face Magnolia and point toward Sophia. "Ferdinand told you what she did, didn't he? You've got some nerve bringing her here."

Magnolia snaps her fingers.

Sophia's shoulders jerk. She crawls over to Magnolia and lays her head in my aunt's lap. Magnolia pets her hair, and if Sophia had a tail, she'd be wagging it.

"Sophia's a good girl. She knows her place, follows orders, and doesn't question me all of the time unlike a certain hard-headed niece."

It takes a second to work out what she means aside from the insult. That I got loud and clear.

Landry tugs on the sheet. "What did Sophia do to piss you off?"

"Not now, Landry." Right now I've got to get to the heart of the matter. My anger's misplaced. Sophia's assault on Landry was at the request of the wicked Hoodoo Queen of New Orleans. "Why, Magnolia?"

Magnolia slaps her hand down onto the back of Sophia's head. "Why you always got to question me? You *begged* for my help in getting rid of the demon riding your boy-toy."

I stiffen at the word. *Don't recall no begging involved.*

"Landry's natural defenses had to drop for the demon to climb out of its hidey-hole and take control of his body." Magnolia puckers her liver-lips. "Sophia says it's strong. It's angry. Hates being powerless, but it's biding its time till it finishes eating Landry's soul. Soon it'll be plenty full and strong enough to use the boy's shell for its own purposes. What that purpose is, I don't know. 'Cause of your interference, Sophia didn't get a chance to find out."

Feeding on Landry's soul. *Damn.*

Cold sweat runs down my spine. I smell my fear. *Crap, I fucked up.* "Fine, fine, I misunderstood her motivations." *Still doesn't make her right.* My chin juts out. "If you'd told us your plan…" I shake my head, so confused. Would I have gone along with it if I'd known? No. I wouldn't have believed her. Not before seeing the girl rise from the dead. I didn't understand how powerful magic could be. *A demon's eating Landry's soul.*

"Hold on!" Landry spins me around. "What happened after I got drunk? 'Cause what I'm getting from this cryptic conversation is that the demon came out to play last night."

"You didn't get drunk. Sophia drugged you." I watch the shifting storm cloud gather in his eye as he processes my words. I lay my hand on his tense bicep. "Magnolia's saying it was to draw out the demon."

His Adam's apple bobs as he swallows. "Why didn't you tell me? What did Sophia do?"

"Trust me, baby. It's better you don't remember."

His arm drops. He stares at Sophia for a long, hard moment. The color in his face slowly fades until he's as white as the sheets on the bed. He meets my gaze, and I see his dawning horror.

CHAPTER 27

LANDRY

Chaos Rising

Sophia meets my gaze and raises an eyebrow in my direction. Her tongue flicks out to trace her lips, and I shudder. Cold sweat drips in my eye, and my stomach clenches. My heart pounds in time with the assault from the returning memories. She…she took me beneath a tree while I screamed, trapped in my mind.

Helpless.

Nothing but a worthless puppet who got his strings pulled by the parasite burrowing beneath my skin, and, worse, I couldn't stop Sophia. Her hot breath blew in my face, and her tongue thrust between my clenched teeth as she ran her hands across my heated flesh. How far did it go?

The groan comes from deep inside. I fall back against the wall, closing my eye. The memories replay like I'm watching an actor on a movie screen, only they're disjointed and unorganized flashes of an unedited melodrama.

"Landry? Are you okay?" Mala touches my cheek, and I flinch. I've got to get out of here.

I shove off the wall, avoiding Mala's hands with a twist. My feet don't want to leave her, refusing to cooperate as if they have minds of their own—each step an agonizing struggle. Ferdinand tries to stop me. Hell, everyone's yelling at me. Their voices buzz in my ears. But he's the only fool who goes hands on, like he can shove through the anger burning inside me.

Ferdinand's hand on my shoulder ignites the fuse, and I explode.

My first jab lands in the middle of his rock-solid gut. Air *whoosh*es out of him, and he doubles over with a groan. My downward punch hits square beneath his eye. I barrel out of the room before he collapses. My rage has barely been tapped. It boils, steaming over in a torrent of destruction. It's only after my foot gets stuck in the hole I kicked in the living room wall that I return to myself.

Still, it takes another minute before I calm down enough to pick away the plaster holding my bare foot in place. Sweat-soaked hair hangs in my face. Blood runs from my knuckles to drip into the white carpet.

And...I'm naked. With an audience.

My vision blurs from the sting in my eye.

Mala huddles against the refrigerator with a frying pan in one hand. The other holds the sheet around her trembling body. Fear widens her eyes. Her lips move, but I can't hear her over the thumping in my ears.

My gaze moves from Mala to the room. It's trashed. The plasma TV lies on the ground, the coffee table's been tossed on its side, and broken pieces of glass cover the floor. Smears of blood dot the white carpet.

I drop to the ground and press my back against the wall. My fingers flex, curling into fists, and I wince at the pain from my bleeding knuckles. A hand tentatively touches my shoulder, and I flinch.

"Landry," Mala whispers, voice cracking. She sits next to me and lays her head on my shoulder. Her warm tears drip down my bare arm.

How can she bear to touch me after what happened with Sophia? She saw us together. She should be as disgusted as I am.

"It's not your fault." She hugs me tighter. "I knew what Magnolia was capable of, but I never thought...I'm so sorry."

Damn. How can she believe she's responsible? I guzzled down her champagne along with my own. I should've said no, but passing up free alcohol isn't in my skill set. Hell, the Top Five Fuck-Ups that have screwed up my life happened 'cause I was smashed.

You'd think I'd learn from my mistakes.

Now I've got a new #1: Almost Fucking the Hoodoo Queen's Sex Puppet.

Stupid.

My breaths come in rough gasps, and I twist around to drag Mala into my arms before she changes her mind about being with me. As her warm body molds itself against mine, the rush of desperation fueled by the thought of losing her subsides. Our roles switch as I comfort her. It kills me she feels so guilty. I should say something, but I can't talk yet.

Mala thinks she should've seen it coming. It's the other way around. It's my job to protect her, and I failed. Again.

Her curls smell of the herbs from the bath—lavender and mint. I bury my face in the thick mass and inhale. My arms tighten, pulling so hard her breasts flatten against my chest. Her hand rubs my back, and she begins to rock in my arms, like she's listening to an internal lullaby. I can almost hear it myself, a low hum beneath the questions popping into my mind, one after another.

Were both of the drinks drugged? If so, what was Magnolia's ultimate plan for Mala? Did she follow through with it? Did she hurt my girl while I was being handled? I never asked Mala where she disappeared to or what happened to her.

We need to talk.

"Where did everyone go?" My voice sounds gruff from yelling.

Mala gives a shaky chuckle, but her arms tighten. "They shot out like lightning bugs were sparking their butts."

"Smart move. If I'd gotten my hands on Sophia, I might've killed her. Hell, I was so out of it that I could've hurt you by mistake."

"You'd never hurt me."

I sigh at the stubborn set to her chin. "Maybe you believe that, but I don't. The demon's feeding off my soul. This"—I wave my hand to indicate the hole in the wall—"wasn't me. Yeah, I'm pissed. But that *thing* did this. I lost control, and it took advantage."

That's the truth of the matter.

Mala gives a jerky nod, then rises. "You're right, but we still have time to figure out a solution. We've got a more pressing problem to deal with."

"What's the matter now?"

"Dena." Her mouth opens then closes. "I think she's running out of time. Come on. Magnolia said Etienne will drive us home. I'll explain everything in the car."

"Wait. Did you call the kids? Is she home?" I chase after her.

She freezes in the doorway to our suite with a muffled cry. "Where's the sheet?"

Confused, I stare at the bed. Sure enough, the mattress has been stripped. Mala turns to face me with wide eyes. *Woman's blood and sex.* Magnolia used those words. I run over to the trash can where I tossed the condom. The *empty* trash. "Son of a—"

"Why would she take…" Mala holds up her hand. "You know what? I don't care. The crazy witch can have them. We can't do anything about whatever spell she's brewing up. What's important is getting back to Paradise Pointe and finding Dena before that guy murders her."

"What guy? Who has Dena?"

Mala grabs a T-shirt and shorts from the dresser while I watch, cold and confused. A tear leaks down her cheek. She slams the empty drawer shut so hard the mirror rattles. Her movements are jerky as she flops onto the bed and stuffs her legs into the shorts, inching them up over her hips with a wiggle that should turn me on but doesn't. Not right now. Not when worry creases Mala's forehead.

"I guess it's the fourth guy. I saw him when I traveled…you know, like how I used to visit you in jail." She shoves her head out of the top of her T-shirt in time to catch my nod. "The asshole's got her tied up in a dark room. I'm not sure where. I should've checked since I was invisible." She lets out a huge sigh. "We'll call George, report her as missing. Get him to search for—"

"—a dark room?"

Mala stiffens at the skepticism in my tone. "What else can I do? He'll kill her. I don't know why she's still alive."

"'Cause she's bait. For us."

DA Cready predicted the guy would make his move. Does he know Dena's a witness? Or is she a convenient hostage because she's our friend? I have to believe she's still alive 'cause he's waiting for us to return. He'll use her to draw us to him and take us all down. The only way to stop him is if we can turn the trap around on him.

While Mala does one last check of the room to make sure we haven't forgotten anything, I stop off in the bathroom to use the first aid kit I find in a cabinet and quickly get dressed. I'm sad we have to leave. Even with all the bad shit's that's happened, this place feels safe. For one magical night, Mala and I connected. Now chaos returns to toss our lives to the whims of fate.

When I finish, I join Mala in the elevator with our bags. She grabs my hand, punching the down button with the other. "Hey, it's not so bad. I think all we have to do is tell George about our power, the ghosts, everything."

"That's your master plan?"

"Okay, I made that sound easier than it really is. I may resort to a show-and-tell. Bring him proof." A wicked light enters her eyes. "Not like we've got a choice. If we don't, he won't believe us about Dena being held captive. I can't let anything happen to her because I'm too scared to admit the truth."

* * *

As soon as we get in the Cadillac, Mala calls George. She doesn't go into any details of her vision other than to say she has information about why Dena's missing. The rest of the drive home is as quiet as the drive to New Orleans. Mala and I soak in our own thoughts, trying to plan how we're going to handle George.

George paces on the porch when Etienne parks the Cadi in front of Mala's house. Dena's twin brothers, Daryl and Carl, are also waiting for us. The boys have grown up in the last couple of days. They look like men, rough and full of sadness. It's a damn shame. First they lost both of their parents. Now their sister.

No, we'll get Dena back. Somehow.

I grab the bags out of the trunk of the car and head for the porch. Mala lingers by the car, thanking Etienne. She's procrastinating. This will be the most difficult conversation she'll ever have. If not handled right, not only will George refuse to help, we'll get locked up in the mental hospital and Dena's SOL.

Maybe spilling our guts isn't such a good idea. Too many things can go wrong by bringing in Deputy Dawg. We should handle this solo. Or get Dad. He swore he'd help to protect Mala, but he can't do that if he's hiding out from the law.

George bounds down the stairs. "What's going on?" He glances over his shoulder at the twins. "The boys filled me in on Dena's disappearance. I take it she didn't just run off? What does Mala know that she can't say over the phone?"

"Yeah, it's complicated." I drop the bags to wait for my girl. Mala comes running up. I grab her arm before she can bypass me and go for George, like I'm invisible or some shit. She shouldn't act so happy to see another guy when she's with me or lift her arms like she's about to hug him.

No. Hugging and kissing, definitely not allowed.

"Hold on." I pull her against my side and wrap my arm around her waist.

She squirms in my arms, throwing looks from George to me. "What?"

"We need to talk."

Mala pokes my side with a finger. "We've talked. Don't get squirrely now."

George steps closer. "Look, don't waste my time. If ya'll know something about Dena, spit it out."

I answer with a hard glare.

"Fine! Sort it out." George throws his hands into the air and stomps back over to the staircase to talk to the twins.

Mala watches him go, blinking hard.

I state the obvious. *Again.* "He's not gonna believe us,"

"I know, but I've got to try. You go find our skillet-dirtying Goldilocks. Tell him we need help and it's time to keep his promise." She stares hard into my eye, forcing me to interpret the emotional chaos in her gaze. Frustration, betrayal…Goldilocks and baloney.

Oh shit! Excuses and apologies race through my mind only to be discarded one after the other. None of them will dig me out of this hole. I'm so busted.

"Is that guilt I see?" she asks with a wicked half smile—half grimace that contorts her face. It's terrifying, in an unpredictable I'm-gonna-get-punched kind of way. "Good! Yeah, you should be ashamed about lying to me."

I rub at the burning hole in my chest. "When did you find out?"

"The day you met your dad in the woods, I got worried and followed you." She rises on tiptoes and plants a kiss on my cheek, whispering "I overheard how he didn't help kill Mama."

"Why didn't you say anything?"

"I trust you, Landry." She stares hard at the ground for a long moment, as if unable to meet my gaze, and I want to die. When she looks up, tears shimmer in her eyes. "I just wish you'd trusted me enough to be honest about who was eating all of our food."

Gut punched. *Ouch.*

I swallow hard, throwing a glance in George's direction to see if he heard. I think his reaction would've been more heated than the glare he's giving. That I think has to do with her kiss. It might not help our situation, but I give in to my inner caveman by wrapping my arm around Mala's waist and pulling her against me. She gasps as my mouth finds hers, opening up to my tongue. The kiss lasts until a clearing throat pulls us apart.

Yeah, George. She's mine now.

I give Mala one last kiss on the forehead for luck before sprinting off.

I'm halfway to the back shed where Dad's been staying before I hear the twins running footsteps. I spin around. "Naw, not happening. Go back to the house."

Daryl, the chubby twin, doubles over with his hands on his knees, panting. His flushed face screws up. "We're going with you."

"Like hell."

Carl puffs his narrow chest. "You can't stop us. Dena's our sister."

"Besides," Daryl says with a grin, "we know how to find Reverend Prince."

My eyebrows rise.

"We know he's been staying here"—Daryl runs out of breath so Carl finishes—"to watch out for you and Mala. When we told him Deputy Dubois was coming out, he told us where he'll be waiting for you."

"And where is that?"

The twins share a smug look.

"Fine, you can come, but only as far as the meeting place. Then you're going home. I'm not answering to your sister if you get yourselves hurt."

We head down the path leading to the pond. Figures. It's the one place Dad knows how to find. Grizzly Adams he's not. It's halfway between the Ackers' and Mala's place.

Ever since Mala mentioned seeing the "dark room" in her dream, I haven't been able to get Ackers' hunting lodge out of my mind. No other place would be more suitable for holding a prisoner than the one that has already been used for the same purpose. It's secluded, but also close enough to carry Dena to if he snatched her while she was on her way to Mala's. Sure, the guy would be an idiot to keep her there for the very same reasons, but I'd be an even bigger fool not to check it out. If only to cross it off my nonexistent list.

The path ends at the edge of the clearing, and I pause before exiting the woods to scan the area for danger. Dad paces along the edge of the water. The worry on his face makes me have second thoughts about dragging him into this mess, but he's the only person besides the twins who know how to find the lodge.

Time to ditch the kiddies and call in the cavalry.

Carl and Daryl sprint across the wildflower-dotted field, shoving and kicking each other out of the way in an effort to be the first to reach Dad.

Dad pats the twins on the shoulder when they reach him. "Thanks for bringing my son," he says in his booming church voice. The kids practically melt beneath his praise. I'm almost sorry to dash it.

"Yeah, nice job. Now keep your promise. Go back to the house and tell Mala and George to meet us at your dad's hunting lodge."

"Why are you going there?"

"Why can't we go with you?"

It takes too much effort to figure out which twin asked what. I shake my head, shooing them off. "Look, I don't have time to argue. If I'm right, Dena's been kidnapped and she's being held there. I need backup. The deputy kind with a big-ass gun. George and Mala don't know where the lodge is or that we're going to check it out."

"Carl will go back, and I'll go with you," Daryl says.

"You'll both go, or I'll kick your asses."

A muffled voice turns us around. "I'm thinking ya'll best come with me."

My heart somersaults in my chest when I see a guy dressed in black pointing a handgun at the center of my chest. One of the twins shrieks and breaks for the trees. The gun jerks and goes off. Wood splinters fly out from Daisy's hull. The running twin falls to the ground, covering his head with his arms, wailing. The other twin cowers behind me. His voice echoes the prayer I'm repeating to myself.

CHAPTER 28

MALA

Hail Mary

Sweat rolls down my back.

I wipe my sweaty palms on my jeans shorts and lead George to a rocking chair. I'm tempted to bring him a glass of tea, anything to put off having this conversation. But the longer I wait, the more likely I'll talk myself out of spilling my deepest, craziest secret.

Dena doesn't have time for my doubts.

The memory of her fear drills into me. I lean back in the rocking chair and stare at the ceiling. How to start? From the beginning?

"Tell me what you know about Dena's disappearance, Mala."

"It's not that easy." I flick a glance in his direction. He hasn't stopped frowning since Landry kissed me. He can't be jealous. We've already established the whole incestuous ickiness that comes from knowing we're related. Not by blood, but still. Sharing a father. And for all intents and purposes, George Sr. has been George's dad his whole life.

I shake my head. *Focus.* "For months I've been dreading having this conversation with you. It's neither simple nor rational from most people's perspectives. Hell, I fought against believing it myself when I first learned what was happening to me." I sigh and meet his eyes. "Hopefully you trust me enough to take me at my word."

"Spit it out."

Crap, he doesn't sound very trusting. More like pissed and impatient. Not at all receptive to me saying "I see dead people." Maybe Landry's right. I need to come at this from another angle. "The fourth guy who helped kill Mama kidnapped Dena. He's holding her as a hostage to draw out Landry and me. She's bait, and we have to save her."

"Uh-huh." He's frowning at a spider spinning a web between the porch's wooden slats.

"He's got her duct-taped in a dark room somewhere." My newly manicured nails tap a tattered rhythm against the chair arm, drumming faster and faster as the silence stretches between us. Finally I blurt out, "Don't you want to know how I know?"

"You gonna get around to explaining that? Or should I just call out the SWAT team?"

I recognize the sarcasm, but I'm still compelled to ask, "Can't you just call them out without more info?" The hopeful tone of my voice doesn't go unnoticed.

"Mala, what's *really* going on?" He leans over and lays a warm hand on my thigh. "Why does it feel like you don't trust me? Like you're holding back."

"Why do you need to know? Can't you just roll with what I've told you, please?"

He jerks his hand off my leg and slams it down on the table. "This secret…Landry knows it, doesn't he?"

Uh-oh, this conversation isn't going in the right direction. He glares at me for a long moment then leaps to his feet. My forward lunge almost tips over the rocking chair. I grab George's arm before he can storm down the stairs. My fingers dig into his bicep, and he wrenches them free. He steps into my personal space, and I stumble back against the table, staring at his hands as they flex then clench into fists at his sides.

"Georgie." I choke on his name, feeling smothered.

He looms, only inches from my body. "Damn, do you know how long it's been since you called me that?" He scrubs his hand across his face and through his hair. Red-gold spikes stick up in every direction, and my heart melts. His hands fall onto my shoulders. He doesn't hold tightly, but I'm frozen in place just the same.

"I'm sorry, Mala," he says, fingers kneading the tight muscles in my shoulders. It should be soothing, but it's not. "It's my fault. Everything…I screwed up. I should've told you about Isabel. And I shouldn't have pushed you away because I was pissed at Dad for…having you…for making you my sister."

"We're not blood," I whisper.

"I know. So why did we let it come between us?"

A rush of panic floods through me. "What does it matter now? Even if we didn't find out, it wouldn't have worked between us. I tried to deny my feelings, but the truth is I'm in love with Landry."

"You love me too. I know it." His jaw flexes. "Think I can't feel you trembling beneath my hands?" He steps closer, and I breathe in his clean, mountain-fresh scent. My eyes close as my legs waver. *What the hell…this can't be happening. Not now.*

I love Landry. *Only Landry.*

"Stop confusing me!" I yank free of his hands. Once he's not touching me, I can think. I take another step back, dragging in huge gulps of muggy air. My hands shake as I fan my heated cheeks.

George shuts his green eyes for a long, drawn-out moment. When they open, all of the emotion darkening them has vanished. He rests his hands on his duty belt, all business again. "Tell me how you know about Dena. Don't leave anything out."

"I see ghosts." *Oh crap! What have I done?*

"Say what?"

I want to smack myself upside the head. Did I really resort to blurting out the one thing that could really and truly drive him away? Or did I say it because I selfishly hope he believes and accepts my reality?

Blame it on my confusion. Whatever. Doesn't matter now. I have to make him believe me or Dena's dead. "You wanted to know my secret. The one Landry knows and accepts." I swallow around the lump in my throat. "That's it. All those pesky rumors about my family being witches are true."

"Are you—"

"Spilling my guts. Yeah, I'm desperate. Dena's life depends on how much you trust me. On whether you believe me or think I'm having a psychotic break."

He rocks back on his heels, eyes rolling skyward. The breath he blows out ends in a laugh. "You've got to be shitting me."

"No, I'm serious."

His face flushes. "Bullshit! You don't seriously believe you see ghosts? Or expect me to believe you? Is this a test…some sort of crazy attempt to see if you can drive me away? Haven't you figured out I'm not going anywhere? I care about you, Mala."

"This confession isn't about us. It's about *me*. I know it's diffi-cult to accept. I didn't believe it either, and it was happening to me. I tried my best to rationalize what I was seeing. Told myself I had posttraumatic stress from finding Lainey's body. I told myself that's why I kept seeing her." I give a shaky laugh of my own. "My disbelief almost got me killed. It got you beat up when she pos-sessed me in the hospital. I didn't know how to protect myself so Lainey thrust me out of my own skin and used me to expose her mother."

He blinks.

"Did you hear me?" I shift my weight forward onto my toes. If he runs, I'll tackle him from behind. *He'd better not run.*

"Yeah."

"Well?"

George crosses his hands in front of his chest and shifts into a bladed stance. It's how cops stand when they think they'll go hands-on with a criminal.

"Oh, great!" I grumble. "You're wearing your gunslinger ex-pression. You think I'm crazy, and you're trying to figure out a way of saying so without setting me off."

"I didn't say that."

"Mother Mary, you don't have to. Think I don't know you well enough to be able to read your mind?"

"You can read minds too?" His copper eyebrows rise.

"Not yet. If I could, I would've known you were sleeping with Isabel." *Jerk.* I shove past him and storm down the stairs. "Landry warned me not to tell you, but I hoped you'd believe—never mind."

His footsteps follow me across the yard. At least he's still will-ing to listen. Or is he trying to sneak up to throw me to the ground so he can handcuff me? Once upon a time, I wouldn't have minded. I cast a quick glance over my shoulder.

Handcuffs still in their holder.

I slow until he walks beside me. "Sorry. I'm not being fair. I admit my confession's a lot to take in. Guess some secrets shouldn't be shared. I get that." *Now.* I breathe out a sigh. "How about this, Georgie? Why don't you just take my words on faith?"

"I can't call out the SWAT team on faith. I need evidence."

"Dena's missing. How much more evidence do you need? Tell them a witness saw the fourth guy kidnapping her. Because that's the truth." I bite my lip, knowing since I'm serving up a heaping dose of honesty stew, I'd better tell him everything. "You also should know that Reverend Prince has been living in my shed."

George stops with one foot raised. He lowers it slowly to the ground. "Tell me that's a joke."

I kick a clod of dirt and realize it's one of Gaston's spiritual land mines. Can't go destroying my protection or Acker might show. "He told Landry he didn't kill Mama."

"And you believe him? Landry's lying to protect his dad."

"I heard his story too. He said he feels guilty about falling for Rathbone's lies and blaming Mama for Lainey's death."

"An innocent man wouldn't be on the run."

I shake my head. "Rathbone and the missing nurse, Gloria-something, nut-job, drugged him while he was in the hospital. They sneaked him out while he was unconscious. The fourth guy killed them, but the rev managed to escape. He's been hanging around to protect me and Landry."

"Did he give any proof that what he said was the truth? Where did all of this go down?"

"The hunting lodge. The rev said when he went back Rathbone's and Gloria's bodies were missing."

"The lodge on Acker's property?" He frowns at my nod. "Dad

took me there a few times. He went through a hunting phase for a few years. Back before he and Acker fell out."

Oh, George Sr. used to hunt?" *How nice they shared so many bonding moments over the years.* Bitterness leaves a tang in my mouth. I can't help feeling resentful. Especially after seeing how much Reverend Prince loves Landry. He's living in a shed to protect his son...to protect me, and I'm not even his child. I've been out of the hospital for almost a week, and my sperm donor never even called to say hello.

My eyes squeeze shut on the uncharitable thoughts. My old man never wanted me. He'll never accept me. Wishing on stars is something Disney made up. And if I don't show George proof of my abilities, he'll think I'm farting rainbows.

"What if I can figure out where the guy dumped Rathbone's and Gloria's bodies? Seeing is believing, right?"

"You can do that? How?"

"Gloria's been haunting me since I was in the hospital. Back then, I didn't know who she was or what she wanted. But it's probably the same thing Acker wants: his body found."

"Acker's dead too."

Another confession. Damn. I've withheld a lot from him. "He died on the same night as Mama. He chased me into the swamp, and Lainey's ghost shoved him into quicksand. That day you came over...well, it wasn't a tornado. Acker threw a rock at your head."

"Yeah, guess that makes more sense than a tornado in the bayou."

"Aha! Glad to know the rock didn't scramble your brain too badly."

"No more than you have with your ghost talk."

If anyone had the incentive to find Dena, it would be her loving father. The question is, how do I get him to make a ghostly appearance? Gaston warded the yard against him, and Magnolia hurt him so bad during his last attack that he'd be a fool to show. Except the man wasn't a supergenius when alive. Just stuffed full of hate and rage.

"Hey, Georgie, what if the reason he attacked me last time was because he knew Dena had been kidnapped? Maybe he knows where she is."

"Acker…the not-so-friendly ghost?" He absently rubs the back of his head.

"Yeah! It's a long shot, but it's the only chance Dena's got." I run over to another land mine and kick it across the yard. George follows, watching me like I've lost my mind. Kind of feel like I have, I'm so excited. "So my dead uncle Gaston warded the yard. Ghosts blow up if they come onto the property. We'll have to destroy the protection. Even with it gone, I'm not positive if he'll show up on his own. And I never thought to ask Magnolia to teach me how to call ghosts. I've spent all my time trying to shove them away."

I glance at George. "You're being annoyingly quiet."

"What can I say that won't make me sound like I'm doubting you?"

"Your tactfulness is much appreciated."

He releases a long-suffering sigh. "It's a skill I practice daily."

"Soon you won't have to." A cold wind raises goose bumps on my arms. My hair blows into a halo around my face, and I open my arms wide. George stumbles back, lifting his arms up to protect his face from the debris flying through the air. He stares at me with wide, slightly panicked eyes, and I grin.

I throw my head back and yell, "Acker, come and get me!"

Power converges from all directions, like I'm standing in the epicenter of a magnetized circle. The intensity of the energy makes my skin tingle. The rush almost buckles my knees. My senses heighten until I can hear individual birdcalls and the *scritch* of grasshopper legs rubbing together. I grit my teeth, breathing in the rich, loamy scent of the earth.

Acker arrives in an angry whirlwind, crazier than bag lady Junebug hurling her empty soda cans at the heads of the kids who tease her. *What the hell was I thinking? I can't control him. I broke the wards.*

"Gaston, help!" I spin, shoving George toward the house. "Run, Georgie!"

A gust of icy air hits my back so hard that it flings me forward. My hands catch my fall before I face-plant in a mud puddle. George stops and turns around. He grabs my outstretched hand, yanking me to my feet, but before I can catch my balance, a rope of air wraps around my legs at the knees and tightens.

George tries to pull me forward while the rope jerks backward, slicing through my skin. Warm liquid runs down my legs. It's blood. It's going to amputate me at the knees.

It hurts… "Let me go," I cry, twisting my fingers.

"No!" George grabs on to both arms. My legs float in the air. The only things keeping me from flying away are his sweat-slick hands. He bends at the knees, bracing his feet sideways, straining to hold on to me. His face turns red, and his arms tremble from the strain. George versus Acker. And he's losing.

A quick yank on my legs.

My fingers spasm from the excruciating pain, and I scream as George's grip slips. I'm airborne. As I hit the ground, the air in my lungs explodes, but before I can inhale, I'm being dragged across the yard. I lift my arms, trying to protect my head from the rocks sticking out of the grass.

Rocks and twigs scratch my skin. I'm flailing and kicking, but I can't break free. George runs after me, but he can't keep up. I'm moving too fast, like a rider being dragged by a horse because their foot got caught in the stirrups.

I lose sight of George when I'm dragged between the bushes bordering the woods. Then it hits me. I'm going to die.

That bastard Acker's gonna kill me this time.

CHAPTER 29

LANDRY

Demon Cursed

Time stands still.

The egret flying overhead freezes in the sky with its wings outstretched for a long, heart-stopping beat, and then time resumes, flashing forward too fast to process. Fear numbs my brain and burns in my chest.

I press my fist against my chest, rubbing it hard. *Stay calm.*

Daryl balls up the hem of my T-shirt and presses his face into my spine. The neckline of my shirt tightens around my windpipe. I cough, reaching back to rip the cloth from Daryl's hands, and he stares up at me with wide, tearing blue eyes.

"Reach for the sky!" the guy yells.

My hands whip upward, and I focus on the shine of the gun. How the glint of metal shimmers in the sunlight, making it appear bigger and shinier than it is. The barrel looks Desert Eagle huge. Big enough to blow a hole the size of Texas through my chest and take out Daryl's narrow head with it.

The gun points between me and Dad. With the flick of the wrist, the guy could shoot either of us or both before we could blink. His wide strides eat up the ground. He reaches Carl, who huddles on the ground, grabbing the kid by his right ear and hauling him to his feet. Carl screams. The gunman twists on Carl's earlobe, yanking upward until the boy's forced to run on tiptoes with the bigger, stronger guy.

My heart races with each step the guy takes. The gun doesn't waver. Why hasn't he pulled the trigger? We're at a disadvantage. This would be the perfect opportunity to eliminate us. 'Cause if he doesn't, I'll find some way to overpower him. I won't let him hurt the twins or my dad without a fight.

The guy gets close enough to shove Carl in our direction. The kid falls to his knees, holding his hand over his ear. He pulls it back far enough to see blood on his palm, then screams again.

The guy aims a kick at Carl's head, but the boy flinches backward. The boot skims where his face used to be. "Shut it 'fore I put a bullet in your head."

"I can't hear you, you asshole," Carl yells, face flushed. The gun drops, and the color drains from the kid's cheeks.

My heart stutters when Dad steps between the boy and the gun. "Enough! You've made your point," Dad says, and I stare at him in awe. His voice didn't even tremble. He crouches beside Carl without fear of being shot. "You should be ashamed of yourself, picking on a bunch of kids."

"Don't blame me for having to clean up your mess." The ski mask over the guy's face muffles his voice. It looks like the same one he wore when he killed Ms. Jasmine. His voice sounded familiar that night, like I knew the person who carried me to Dad's truck, but I was so out of it from pain that I couldn't place it then. I still can't.

"Where's Dena?" Daryl yells from behind my back. He peeks over my shoulder then ducks back down. "What did you do to my sister?"

"You'll be with her soon enough. But first tell me, where's the bitch?"

I stiffen as I figure out he means Mala. "You think we'd come out here without getting backup? The SWAT team's on its way."

"Nice try."

"It's the truth," Daryl says. "Deputy Dubois's at the house. They'll come find us."

"Then I'd better take you someplace where they won't."

"The Ackers' hunting lodge?" I ask.

The guy stiffens, and his finger caresses the trigger. "Suppose the rev blabbed about Rathbone taking him there. Never should've let him leave alive."

"Why did you?" Dad asks, lifting Carl into a seated position. The boy's still crying. I feel bad for him...for us all. This guy's nuts.

"No reason not to at the time. You didn't know I was involved with Rathbone. If you'd minded your own business, you would've been fine."

"My son is my business," Dad barks, rising to his feet.

"He shouldn't have taken the witches' side. He should've stayed with his own kind and left her to die with her mama." He gestures with the gun again. "Line up and drop to your knees with your hands behind your backs."

Dad and I share a long look. His bearded jaw flexes, the only sign of his fear. Scenes from mob movies play in my head. The gangster always has the victim go down on his knees before he shoots him in the back of the head.

"They're just kids. Why don't you let them go?" Dad asks.

"Long as they don't try anything, they'll be fine. Landry and the girl are the only ones I want."

I assess the determination in the guy's watery brown eyes through the holes in the mask, and a chill goes down my spine. He's lying. Things have progressed too far. He'll have to kill us all to be safe. Dad and I know it, but hopefully the kids believe him.

"Carl, Daryl, do as he says," I say, flicking my fingertips at the twins, urging them forward. "Don't give him any reason to hurt you."

"Landry, you'll protect us, won't you?" Daryl whispers, and I give a tiny nod.

Truth is, I don't know how to stop him, but I play it cool. The right time to act will come my way…I hope. Possible scenarios play through my head. Do I risk a suicide charge when he gets close? If he shoots, he could miss, or even if I catch a bullet, I might not die right away. Plus my pitiful screams could distract the dude long enough to give the others a chance to break free.

Daryl goes down on his knees and crawls over to his brother. They're almost as big as I am now, but they look so young huddled against each other. I walk over to Dad and drop to my knees. He puts a hand on my shoulder and squeezes, then crosses his wrists behind his back.

"Move and you die." I hear the *squick* of duct tape being unrolled and heavy footsteps stop behind my back. Cold metal presses against my temple. Hot, garlicky breath blows against my neck as a hand grabs my wrists, wrenching my arms out painfully behind me. "Hold still."

My breath catches as the sticky edge of tape touches my

wrist. The guy grunts as he wraps the tape one-handed. It's loose, but tight enough that I can't pull it apart. He then lowers the gun and uses both hands to bind me tighter. I can't even fight him.

What the hell? So much for my bold plan.

I couldn't find an opening. Not with him holding a gun to my head. Can't survive a bullet to the brain. The only real chance we've got now is if we stay alive and don't force this fool's hand. I've got to believe my girl will use her uncanny ability to know when I'm buried hip deep in shit and show up with Deputy Dawg to rescue my sorry ass.

Once my hands are tied, the guy squats behind Dad. He leans forward, taking Dad's large hands in his. He's so fucking overconfident that he doesn't hold the gun to Dad's head but sets it on the ground.

Dad throws back his head, and the head butt catches the guy in the middle of his face. He falls onto his ass. Dad twists around and throws his upper body on top of the guy, using his beer gut to pin him to the ground. His other hand wraps around the wrist of the guy's gun hand. The twins take off, running toward the woods. They don't stop to look back when they break the edge of the field and vanish into the trees. I'm struggling to rise to my feet without falling on my face. With my hands taped behind my back, my balance sucks, and it takes two tries before I can get off my knees.

Dad and the guy wrestle for control of the gun. They roll across the ground, leaving a trail of smashed wildflowers. Neither lets go of the other when they enter the pond, but Dad lands on the bottom. He fights to hold his head out of the water. At some point during the fight, the guy lost his mask.

Dad stares up into the familiar face and grunts, "Redford…"

My stomach twists. I never expected to see Clarice's brother. Even though his voice was familiar, I couldn't have placed it. We grew up together. And while he probably still holds a grudge from our last fight, I never thought he'd go so far as to try to kill me. Or Ms. Jasmine and Mala.

I break into a low, shambling run toward them. With Red on top, I can get him without hitting Dad. Red's eyes widen when he sees me. He falls back, jerking the gun from Dad's hand, and pulls the trigger. The bullet hits, throwing Dad back into the water. Shock drops me to my knees.

Red crawls out of the water, keeping the gun trained on me. His hand trembles as he stares from me to Dad. "Damn it. Why'd you make me do that?"

My world stops again.

"Get him up!" Red screams. *He's lost it.*

"How? My hands—"

"Fuck." He turns in a circle. "Where are the Acker brats?"

Hopefully halfway back to Mala's place.

Dad rolls onto his knees. Blood spreads across the shoulder of his wet shirt. I run over, and he grabs onto my belt and pulls himself to his feet. He doesn't say a word, just clutches his shoulder and stares at Red with glazed eyes.

Panic infuses Red, oozing out of his pores like a seeping virus, spreading to infect me, waking the sleeping demon inside. The creature stretches out its tentacles, stabbing them into my brain to see if it can strip away my control. My limbs tingle. I fight to hold on to myself while, at the same time, steadying myself against the growing desire to rip Red into bloody pieces. It becomes harder and harder to think. Prickles of sweat run down my spine.

I glance over my shoulder to meet Red's gaze. His eye twitches.

"Start walking and keep your eyes straight ahead," he orders with a jerky flick of his wrist.

The muscles between my shoulder blades clench in the expectation of a heated bullet piercing between them. For the next ten minutes, we walk toward the Acker property in silence. It's slow going with Dad stumbling over each step. The bleeding from his shoulder wound has slowed down but hasn't stopped, and his face has turned as white as one of Mala's ghosts.

I should keep my mouth shut, but I've got to know. "Why, Red? How did this happen?"

Silence meets my question. Just when I think I won't get an answer, it comes in a hollow voice empty of emotion. "I don't know."

"You don't—" I want to choke him out. "Rathbone, Gloria Pearson, Jasmine LaCroix. Three people murdered by your hand. And you say you don't know?"

"I *know* every one of them deserved to die." His voice turns implacable. "They were all guilty."

I duck beneath an outstretched branch and use my back to push it out of the pathway until Dad passes. Sweat rolls down his face, and he pants from exertion. He's bleeding to death. *God! Help us.*

My lungs tighten. *Breathe. It'll be okay. The twins… they're going for George.*

I've got to distract Red. Keep him talking so he doesn't give in to his panic and take us out. *Hang on, Dad. Just a little longer. Hang on.*

What did he say? They *deserved* to die. "Why? I don't understand. Rathbone I get. I would've killed the bastard myself after what he did to my sister, but Gloria and Ms. Jasmine? I don't get them. And what did Mala and I do to deserve this?"

Dad stumbles over a rock and goes to his knee with a grunt.

My voice breaks on the words "What did my dad do? He treated you like f-family."

I crouch beside my father, putting my shoulder underneath his to help him rise. He leans into me for a long moment with his eyes closed and blows out a heavy breath. "I'm okay, son."

"No. You're not." I spin to face Red, not caring about the gun he shoves between my eyes. *Shoot me. Do it. Don't make me watch him die.* "He's dying, Red! Do something. Help him."

"Never meant for any of this to happen, Reverend Prince." Guilt lowers his eyes to the ground, but the gun never wavers. "I swear, I only wanted to avenge Lainey. You know how much I loved her. Even after she broke up with me in high school, I never got over her."

"I always hoped you and my girl would get back together," Dad says with a weary nod.

"Rathbone lied to me. He said Jasmine LaCroix killed Lainey. Then her daughter goes and curses Clarice so her hair falls out like she's a mangy dog." Red stares wide-eyed at Dad, like he expects praise. Or sympathy. He glances at me, and his jaw hardens. "What did you expect me to do, Landry? I went to talk to you about it, but you tried to kick in my teeth. Did you really think I'd roll over and not protect my family?"

Ah, so it's my fault for holding back. I should've gone ahead and shattered his leg when I had the chance. He couldn't have caused problems while laid up in the hospital.

The path ends at a small clearing. At one time, it held a gated pasture for the livestock, but now it's mostly overgrown except what has been converted into a small yard area. My footsteps slow. Once we enter the lodge, we're not leaving.

Red's boot slams above the small of my back, and I fall forward. Dad grabs my waist, but my weight almost takes us both to the ground.

"Damn it! Stop screwing around," Red yells.

I flinch at the rage in his voice. Dad holds me upright until I get my feet back beneath me. We stumble to the door. It looms, dark and weathered, before us. Red comes around from behind to throw it open. The crooked smile on his face blows a chill down my spine. "Get inside. Someone's waiting to see you."

Dena. I'd almost forgotten about her. "What's the point of killing us now, Red? You can't escape. The twins will have reached George by now. He'll bring in backup and storm this place. And there's no way in hell he'll bring Mala. Let us go. Hop a boat and sail to Mexico. Don't make this worse."

Red shakes his head. A crazy light brightens his eyes. "Those brats took off before the rev pulled off my mask. They never saw my face. If I take care of you now, I can get the girl later. Once she's dead, the curse she put on Clarice is broken."

The curse? "Mala already broke the curse on Friday. Clarice came out to the house, and Mala performed a ceremony. She's fine now."

"I don't believe you."

A door opens at the back of the room—one of the horse stalls converted into a bedroom. Light shines out of the room, and I catch sight of a hunched form lying on the ground. Dena's head lifts and turns in my direction. She looks bad. Bruises turn her face a sickly purple and yellow color.

Tears spill from her swollen eyes when her gaze falls on mine. She shakes her head as her lips form my name. "Landry, no..."

The door opens wider.

Clarice steps across the threshold. She sees us and screeches. Her fists clench as she runs to her brother. She throws a punch at

Red's head but he ducks. "Damn it, Bubba! How the hell did you manage to screw up the plan again?"

"I'm sorry. They showed up out of nowhere. What was I supposed to do? Let them go?"

Clarice's face blanches to the color of Dad's when she sees the blood staining the front of his shirt. His legs give out.

Clarice rushes forward as he slumps, and she wraps her arms around his waist. She eases him onto the ground. "Shit! We've got to stop the bleeding. Hurry and grab the first aid kit. It's under the kitchen cabinet."

Red stares at her like she's crazy. "They've seen your face, Clary."

"What?" She looks up to meet my eye and gasps. She rises from her knees and steps backward. "No! No, no, *no*, this can't be happening." Her eyes shut for a long beat. Minute ticks of expression cross her face as she works through what this means.

Soon tears leak from beneath her sealed eyelids. "I told you to bring Mala LaCroix." She scrubs her bloodstained fingers across her skirt. "She would've come on her own once she knew we had Dena."

"Landry said she broke the curse on you." Red waves the gun at her.

"So what? Not like she can't curse me again if I get in her way."

"Is this about me?" I ask.

She scowls. "Ha, dream on."

"Be honest." I give her a sad smile, and her shoulder's slump.

"Maybe it started out about you. After I found out what my idiot brother had done to that old, slut witch, I figured we could get rid of Mala too. She cursed me, after all. Like I'd let her get away with doing that. Or with butting in on our relationship." She gives me a sideways grimace. "Of course that was before I saw you talking to invisible people, but by then Red already had Dena."

"Yeah, sis. Your plan sucks." Red goes into the other room. I hear a cry, and he comes out of the room, dragging Dena behind him by her duct-taped hands. He throws her down beside Dad. "Let's just end this now."

"But Landry…"

"He's seen your face. So has everyone else. The law's on the way so let's just kill them and get the hell out of here before we get arrested. Nobody else knows that Rathbone's dead. We'll use his gun, toss it where it'll be found, and they'll blame him for the murders."

Reluctance slumps Clarice's shoulders further, but resolve hardens in her eyes. She's always been good about compartmentalizing her emotions. If it doesn't benefit her in the long run, she gets rid of it. Like with her favorite Barbie dolls. She only kept the valuable ones. The others she tossed in the trash. Boyfriends. She only dated those who could afford to splurge on her. The only reason she obsessed after me was 'cause she couldn't have me. She never loved me. She wanted to own me. And now that she can't, she's got no problem discarding me.

"You don't have to, Clarice," I whisper.

Clarice gives a short shrug. "Sorry about this, Landry. Wish things could've ended differently. You understand why I've got to do this, right? Say you'll forgive me?"

"When hell freezes over."

"Well, guess who's getting there first," she says spitefully.

Clarice nods at her brother, who pulls me up onto my knees. The hairs on the back of my neck rise. Sharp twinges crack my spine. The demon's not fucking happy about what's going down.

"Why fight?"

Is this my thought or the creature's?

The awful awareness of the demon expands, filling my brain. Images play out. Dena, Dad, they're dying. *"Help them."*

It will save them if I retreat. Hide. Find a sheltered corner in my mind and close my eye. It'll come out to play with Clarice and Red. All I have to do is let it have control of my body.

Why don't I stop fighting?

'Cause the image of what it wants to do to them sickens me. Nobody should die like that. At least a bullet to the brain is clean.

"Murder is always messy."

I grit my teeth and try to ignore the voice whispering in my thoughts, but with each second, it gets louder and mine grows softer. My heart speeds as my gaze flicks to the window by the front door. I thought a shadow crossed it. If anyone's out there, they'd better hurry. I can't hold out much longer. Neither can Red.

I watch Red's shadowed hand on the wall and the finger hovering by the trigger.

I close my eyes.

The crash of breaking glass jerks my eyes open.

The gunfire explodes in my ear, and I scream.

Blood runs down my face.

The demon waiting inside rushes to the surface.

CHAPTER 30

MALA

Apocalypse Rising

Branches whip past my face. I grab for one and hold on for a brief second before I'm ripped free. My palm's warm from the blood, making my grip slick. George yells from far behind.

It sounds like my name. "Mala..."

I'm going to die. My stomach crawls up my throat as Acker flings me into the air. I fly toward an elm. Jagged pieces of bark grow bigger. Individual stalks of moss are magnified. I can even see the march of ants across the trunk. It's like I'm moving in slow motion, but not. I'm moving fast.

I flash back to the girl I raised from the dead. I know how Lily felt—the fear, confusion, and, inevitably, the unfairness of knowing that when I fall, it's over. Will I hit hard enough to crack my skull like she did?

That's really gonna hurt. "Fucking Acker!" I yell.

My hands rise to cover my face right before I collide with the tree. Only I bounce, like I've smashed into a pad of cushioned air, flipping over backward in a somersault to crash to the earth. I lift my face and spit out a leaf. The air crackles, wavers, then solidifies into a grinning, pug-ugly face.

"Dena's been kidnapped," I blurt out before he has a chance to torture me some more. "Help me find her."

Acker crouches beside me. "So this is what it takes to finally get you to listen? Tried to tell you that days ago."

"Maybe if you'd used your words like a grown-up ghost instead of trying to scare me to death, I would've been more receptive."

"Still a smartass."

"Always." I sit up, rubbing my aching head.

Gloria Pearson steps from behind the tree. She flickers. Her haunted eyes glow with vacant rage, as if her battery cells have run down and can no longer keep her sane. "He killed me." Her wail echoes through the trees.

"I know, Gloria. I'm so sorry."

"Help me…"

The chill of her need settles over my skin and I shudder. Cold burrows deep, turning my core to ice. Goose bumps rise on my arms, and my teeth chatter. "Where's your body?"

"Fuck her body." Acker shoves Gloria. The ghost screams and dissipates. "Save my daughter or I'll make your life hell on earth."

Yeah, priorities. Dena comes first. "Where is she being held?"

"Same place Gloria died."

A gunshot rings out.

I lurch to my knees right when George barrels through a tangle of bushes. He doesn't see me crouched on the ground and trips. Our arms and legs tangle, each fighting to get free. George sits up, wild-eyed and panicked, until he sees me.

"Mala," he cries, arms wrapping around my battered ribs. "I

thought I lost you…" Blood drips from a scrape on his cheek.

"Stop squeezing me. It hurts." I crawl out of his embrace.

"I'm sorry."

"Did you hear—"

"Where else are you hurt?" He runs his hands down my arms. "Can you move your legs? How many fingers am I holding up?"

I cover his mouth with my hand. "Shush, I heard a gunshot."

"What?" His head whips around. "Where?"

"In the direction of the pond. Landry…"

Screams come from the distance, too far away to pick out individual voices, but it sound like the twins. I lunge upward, steadying myself on the trunk of a tree. "Hurry, George."

I hobble more than run so George catches up quickly. He grabs my hand, wrapping long fingers around mine. I stick to the path leading to the pond. Going off-road means fighting through the brush, and it'll take too long. I need to find Landry and the boys now. Even if it means I'm running into an ambush. Time's running out. It may already be too late.

"Acker said Dena's at the place where Gloria died," I tell George. "The Acker hunting lodge."

He sucks in a breath, nodding.

The path curves around a corner. I take it full speed and slam face-first into something hard. I ricochet off and fall to the ground. It's one of the twins, who grabs my arms, pulling me to my feet. George cups my face between his palms and stares into my eyes. *Why are there two of him?*

"Her nose is bleeding."

"Is she okay?" The twins pat my arms and back. One of them sticks a soggy tissue up my nostril. I try to focus on them, but…four knobby heads are two too many to focus on. My knees unlock, and I sink to the ground.

"She bumped her head earlier," George says. "I think she's got a concussion. Can you take her back to her house?"

"You've got to help Landry…"

"…and Reverend Prince."

"Must you finish each other's sentences?" I complain, shaking my head. The fog rolls off, and I blink. I must've missed part of the conversation. "What did you say happened to Landry?"

George stands on top of a downed log, talking into his radio. Reception must be sketchy here because he keeps stopping to move it. The twins huddle on either side of me with their shoulders pressed against mine—probably to keep me from tipping over again. My brain feels mushy.

"The bad guy caught Landry and his dad," Daryl says over his shoulder as he gets up to walk over to the log. He stands on tiptoes, whispering up at George, "Tell them he's taking them to our hunting lodge. Dena's there too."

I nudge Carl in the ribs with my elbow. "You're awfully quiet."

Carl drags his index finger through the dust. "I'm scared. That guy's evil. He dragged me by my ear until it bled. He didn't care about hurting me." He leans his head onto my shoulder and whispers, "Don't tell Daryl, but I still can't hear nothin' out of it."

I bite my lip.

Carl nods, saying "That guy's gonna kill them. It'll take too long for the cops to get up here."

I know.

George and Daryl return. "Backup's on the way. You guys get her home safely, okay?"

The twins grab my arms and help me stand. Once I'm upright, I brush their hands away, moving around to face George. "Where are you going?"

"I'm gonna go scout the area. The more information we have, the better to help the hostage negotiator."

Crap. It's come to this. What's to stop the guy from killing Landry? It'll take at least two hours, maybe more, for the SWAT team to get through the bayou. George knows this as well as I do. "Oh, hell no. You're not playing hero and getting yourself killed. I'm going."

"You'll just get in my way."

"I'm fine." I shove the twins toward the house. "Let's go."

"Mala," George groans, but doesn't put more effort in trying to change my mind. He knows me well enough to understand it's pointless.

My body feels like one massive bruise.

He shakes his head. "Won't you reconsider going back? It's not safe." He speaks without inflection, but there is a slight tremble in the hand that brushes aside a branch from the path.

"I can do this." I give him a sideways glance. "How are you holding up under the pressure? Bet you never expected a day like today."

He shrugs. "I'm a deputy with the Bertrand Parish Sheriff's Office. I'm trained to expect the unexpected."

"But a rogue ghost attack?"

"Well, that might be the most interesting story I'll ever get to tell."

"Good God, no! My reputation's bad enough with all of the pesky rumors."

George grins, but his alert eyes never stop scanning the surrounding woods. Even when teasing me, he's on duty. "Think of it as a good thing. Imagine all of the people you can help by using your abilities. How many murders can you solve by asking the victim who killed them?"

My eyes widen with each word. "Holy hell, you believe me."

"I saw for myself." He shakes his head.

I grab George's arm and pull him to a halt. Ahead of us stretches the barbwire fence bordering my property from Acker's. A NO TRESPASSING sign hangs on a tree overhead. Of the ghost himself, there's no sign. Maybe he went on ahead. "Acker was a freak survivalist. He booby-trapped his property. Dena taught me what to look for, so follow exactly in my footsteps. Okay?"

George nods. Tension holds his shoulders tight, and he keeps his hand by his gun belt.

I point out the traps as we make our way past—the colorless fishing lines attached to aluminum cans, which would alert anyone of our approach, and leaf-covered carpets with nails sticking out set in the earth at irregular intervals. I sabotage as many as I can without slowing our pace. They'd present a problem for the SWAT team when they arrive. All it takes is one person to set off a trap and their cover's blown.

"Over there…" I point to the converted barn sitting on a hill. Windows face in our direction, and the lawn area leaves virtually no cover for us to hide behind. It's too quiet. How do we know for sure that Landry's in there?

"Acker," I whisper.

The old man appears in a storm of swirling leaves. "Hurry. Help my daughter."

He looks terrified.

I sprint toward the lodge.

"Mala," George hisses, but he's running too. He shoves me aside before I crash straight through the front door. His hands press down on my shoulders, and we squat beneath the front window. I peek inside through a slit in the curtain. My breath sucks in at the sight of Landry and Dena on their knees side by side.

Red Delahoussaye is holding a gun to the back of Landry's head.

He's about to be executed.

Acker materializes beside me. "My girl!" he bellows. A flowerpot rises from the ground. It revolves in the air, spinning faster and faster, and then shoots forward like a cannonball. The speed and force will take out anyone in its path.

"No!" I grab for the stem of the bush, but the thorns slice my fingertips as Acker sends the flowerpot crashing through the window. A high-pitched scream blends with the sound of breaking glass. The pot sails for Red's head, and he flinches. The gunshot reverberates deep in my chest. I shove the blinds out of the way.

George grabs my waist and hauls me back before I can climb through the broken glass. "Stay down," he orders.

I'm shaking, so freaked I can barely think. I'm pissed until the throbbing pain of the cuts on my hands brings me back to reality. Yeah, climbing through broken glass is suicidal.

George waits until I give him a shaky nod, then runs for the front door. One good kick busts it in, but instead of running inside, he crouches beside the broken door. I crawl over until I can kneel beside him.

More gunshots ring out. Wood splinters break off the frame by George's face. He flinches back, his elbow bumping my chest. I crawl a little farther out of his way. "Sheriff's Office," he yells. "You're surrounded. Lower your weapons."

More screams come from inside.

George and I share a long look. He lifts a halting finger, and I nod. I'm brave but not stupid. Unlike him, I'm not wearing a bulletproof vest or carrying a weapon. He draws in a deep breath and swings his gun around the corner.

"Get on the ground! Get on the ground now!"

Unable to beat down my curiosity, I peek inside the room. The scene that greets me makes the spit dry in my mouth, and my heart stutters. Reverend Prince lies in a pool of blood beside Dena's prone body while her father stands above them, wailing. Acker tears at his hair, flickering in and out as if unable to materialize fully in his grief.

Landry has Red pinned against the wall with both hands. The bad guy's legs dangle a couple of feet off of the ground. Clarice is clinging to Landry's back with her elbow centered on his windpipe, and her other arm bracing it. The inability to breathe doesn't make him waver.

What's worse is the vacant look on Landry's face. He's checked out. Nobody's home but the evil demon. George freezes for a moment, unsure of who needs help. Obviously it's Red, since he's turning purple. I don't care if he dies. But he is distracting the demon from coming after us.

Shit! This is so bad.

George points toward Clarice, and I nod. We charge forward. I grab Clarice by the back of her stringy hair and yank. Strands rip from her skull, and she falls backward with a screech. I don't let her rise, but throw myself on top of her. She swings for my head, and I block her punch with my right forearm, wincing from the pain, then jab her twice in the face.

Her eyes roll up.

I glance at Dena, then hit Clarice a few more times until I'm sure she's unconscious.

George is having a rougher time of it. Somehow he's managed to get Red away from Landry—who doesn't look happy about being denied his revenge. Red's lying on the ground, but I can't tell if he's unconscious or...or worse. George sidesteps Landry's wild swings, dodging and weaving in a circle, always keeping Red as a buffer between them.

George holds the Taser in his hand but hesitates.

"Light him up, Georgie," I yell. "It's not Landry."

Landry turns at my voice. His eye meets mine. The gray has a yellowish cast. The alien presence flickers. No dumb beast there. It is calculating its odds for escape. At the same time, I know Landry's inside fighting to break free of its control. From the corner of my eye, I see George leap forward. The probes shoot from the Taser. Landry's back arches, and he falls with a guttural cry. His muscles lock, but as the charge dies, he lunges upward.

"Hit him again," I yell.

George barely dodges the swipe for his ankle. He stumbles over Red, arms waving, and the Taser drops so he draws his gun from his holster. Landry crawls toward George with murder in his gaze. I just witnessed the strength he displayed while holding Red and Clarice. If he punches George, it's TKO, and then he'll be coming after me.

Landry will never forgive himself if the demon hurts me. And George might be feeling threatened enough to justify putting a bullet into him. I can't let either of those scenarios play out.

I leap up and run toward Landry. The demon hears me coming and turns. Foam flecks his lips, and he growls. I lash out with my foot, kicking Landry squarely in the chin. The back of his head slams against the floor with a *crack* loud enough to almost stop my heart. *Did I kill him?*

I glance at George. He keeps his gun trained on Landry as I kneel beside him and check his pulse. Upon feeling the steady beat, I press a kiss to his forehead. "Sorry, baby." I give George a shaky smile. "I think he'll be okay once he wakes up."

He gives a jerky nod. "What the hell happened?"

"More hoodoo-possession kookiness. I'll explain later." I crawl over to Reverend Prince. He has Dena cradled in his arms, despite the fact that he's bleeding from a wound on his shoulder. She stares sightlessly at the ceiling. Lainey wore the same expression when I pulled her from the water. "How?"

"She threw herself in front of Landry. Took my son's bullet." He chokes on the words.

George has his radio out. "Dixie, the scene's secure. Send in medical. I've got multiple gunshot victims."

I place two fingers against Dena's neck, checking for a pulse. "She's dead."

Acker appears at my side. "My girl..." He whirls around and rises to stretch out his hand to his daughter. She doesn't appear corporeal. She's a ball of silvery blue flame hovering over her body, like the girl in the cemetery. "Is she the reason I didn't pass on right away?" he asks. "Was I supposed to wait so we can go together?"

"No, I'll bring her back. I can do it."

Acker shakes his head, and his eyes shift sideways. "Talk some sense into her, Jasmine."

Gaston and Mama stand over Dena's body. Sadness oozes from them. So does resolution. Mama crouches beside me and holds her hand out as if to caress my face, then lets it drop. "Baby girl, whatever you think to do, don't."

"Don't worry. This is meant to be. Otherwise Magnolia wouldn't have shown me how to bring back the dead. Dena's not supposed to die. And I can't let her." I meet Gaston's eyes. "Please...say it's okay."

I look toward Acker. He's already moving toward his daughter. If I don't act fast, it'll be too late. But what if I do it wrong? What if she turns out like Etienne? Would Dena want to live like that?

"All things die, Mala LaCroix. It's the natural order of the world," Gaston says. "Let her be at peace."

"No!" I glare at Red. He killed Dena. It's not fair. He can take her place.

I focus on my hate…

Red screams.

CHAPTER 31

LANDRY

Sipping Chardonnay

Déjà vu rushes over me when I open my eye and see the man standing above my bed. I even pinch myself to make sure I'm not dreaming—that all the horrible things I remember happening aren't just a product of a fucked-up nightmare.

If this is a dream, then I never got released from jail. District Attorney Mitchell Cready never asked me to protect Mala. Dena never got kidnapped and shot while protecting me. And I never lost control of the demon and allowed it to go on a rampage. Or got kicked in the face by Mala.

My jaw aches when I ask, "Why are you here?"

Cready flicks a piece of fluff off his shoulder, and the feeling of déjà vu increases. My hands begin to sweat. Is he sending me back to jail?

He studies my expression for a long, drawn-out moment then

says, "You did well, Mr. Prince. I didn't think you had it in you, but I'll eat my words."

"Are you shittin' me?"

He sits on the edge of the hospital bed. "Don't beat yourself up. The situation would've been much worse if you hadn't intervened. We had no idea about Redford and Clarice Delahoussaye being involved in Jasmine LaCroix's murder. We've been trying to interrogate Clarice, but that girl's insane."

Mala will blame herself. She'll say that if she hadn't cursed Clarice, none of this would have happened, but that girl hasn't been right in the head since she hit puberty. Nobody could've predicted she'd go so far.

"What about Red?"

"He is still unconscious. It's the strangest thing, him and Waydene Acker both being in a coma. We're keeping an eye on him so he doesn't pull a Houdini like your father did when he escaped."

A rush of relief fills me. "So Dena didn't die?"

"I'm sorry, but the prognosis isn't good. Technically the machines are the only things keeping her alive. Red will go to prison for murder if he wakes up." Cready leans over and pats my shoulder. "Thank you for your help. I'll let you go. I'm sure there's folk who want to visit now that you're conscious."

I watch him walk out the door, then close my eye. My skin ripples. I concentrate on pressing the demon back down and building up a wall between myself and the otherness. The problem is that the fragile wall is made of glass, and it's cracking.

The door opens then clicks shut. Footsteps cross the room, pausing beside the bed. Hot breath blows across my cheek. "I know you're awake."

My eye pops open, and I see Carl's downturned lips only inches from mine. "Hey, I know you're grateful, but no kissing."

The kid huffs and throws himself onto the bed. I barely move my legs in time. "It's only been one day, and I'm already sick of this place," he says, staring at the ceiling with red-rimmed, puffy eyes. "They told me you'll be released soon."

"Have they let you in to see Dena?" I ask softly.

"What's the point? I overheard the doctor telling Bessie Caine that my sister's brain dead. They want permission to pull the plug and donate her organs." He glares over at me. "I'm the oldest. It should be my decision."

He looks back at the ceiling. "Bessie took Daryl, Jonjovi, and Axle to her house." His lip quivers. "She can't keep us forever, but I'm grateful she didn't ship us off to a foster home. With Dad being dead and Dena here, Mala's our closet kin. She'll take us in, right?"

"Uh, yeah." *What the hell?*

The door opens again, and Nurse Oliver wheels Dad into the room. He sees us sitting on the bed and waves the hovering nurse aside. "Okay, I'll take it from here. You go on about your duties."

"Reverend Prince, you've lost a lot of blood. You should still be in bed."

"If I didn't die from being shot, I am not about to now."

Nurse Oliver scowls in my direction like she blames me. I shrug. She rolls her baby blues and, after checking his IV line, storms from the room.

Carl gives Dad a wide-eyed grimace. "Hey, Rev, Landry just said the kids and I can live with him and Mala. You gonna stay with us too?"

Dad rubs his bandaged shoulder. "Where my son goes, I go. Besides, the church took possession of our house. Between the bills for the lawyers and doctors, my savings are pretty much depleted."

I swallow hard. "You could stay at the Ackers' house. Mala's place is a little small for—"

"We'll stick together." It was his no-discussion voice.

Moving on. "Have you heard about Dena? Carl overheard her doctor saying she's brain dead. They want to pull the plug. Can they do that without permission?"

"I don't know the legalities." Dad rubs his shoulder and sighs. "I tried to see Mala, but she's been at Dena's bedside ever since they allowed visitors. George wouldn't let me in the room. He claims she asked to be alone with her cousin."

I crawl out of the bed. *Where's my robe? Stupid hospital gown flaps open to show off my assets to anyone who walks by.* My jaw flexes, sending shooting pain through my neck. I'm lucky not to be sucking my food through a straw. Mala didn't hold back with her kick. And while I'm grateful she did what she had to do to protect everyone, my head hurts.

I slam face-first into the wall so Dad donates his wheelchair to my cause. With my blurry vision and shitty depth perception, I'd be safer walking around the hospital with my eye closed.

"Tell Mala I said to find me if she needs counsel," Dad mumbles around a yawn. He then crawls into my hospital bed and proceeds to flip through the television stations. My mouth opens in protest when he reaches for my pudding cup, but if anyone deserves extra pudding, it's Dad.

Carl pushes the wheelchair with a vengeance bordering on recklessness. His pace slows once we reach the intensive care unit. He opens the doors and pushes me through, then backs off. "I can't go in. You can handle the chair on your own, right?"

I nod, pitying the kid. I've got an idea of how he feels. I saw Lainey on the autopsy table. The image of her lifeless body haunts my dreams. It's better that he doesn't see Dena lying in the bed, hooked up to machines, waiting to die. His last memories should be of her full of life and fire.

I leave Carl and wheel forward. The hall stretches before me and looks like a distorted tunnel. A sheriff's deputy stands guard in front of one of the doors, but I'm careful to keep my gaze locked on George, who's reading a newspaper in front of a room at the end of the hall. I don't want to see Red, 'cause I'm afraid I might feel sympathy for him. I choked him or, rather, the demon inside did, until he lost consciousness. It's a miracle I didn't get arrested for putting him into the coma, but George vouched for me, saying I attacked Red in self-defense.

George shakes the newspaper in front of his face as I wheel over, not bothering to acknowledge my presence. Rather than confront him, I tilt my head and squint so I can read the front page of the *Bertrand Tribune*. The headline reads "Murder and Mayhem in Paradise." *Catchy.* I study the wide view, black-and-white photo of the crime scene. Two deputies drag a handcuffed Clarice toward a patrol car. She has her half-bald head thrown back and one leg in the air. I can almost hear the curses coming from her open mouth. George and Bessie stand in front of an ambulance, speaking to a blanket-wrapped Mala.

"She was going into shock."

I lean back and focus on George. "Huh?"

He snaps the newspaper closed. "You asked why the blanket."

I didn't realize I'd spoken out loud.

"Mala handled the situation better than many trained law enforcement officers. She kept her head in the game and handled the crisis. It was only after the situation stabilized that she collapsed from shock."

"'Cause of Dena?"

"And you." His lips pucker as if he's sucking on a lemon. "Mala told me you were possessed by a demon when you died in prison."

My heart thuds. I suck in a breath and hold it.

George gives a sickly grimace. "Yeah, okay. So it really is true. Geesh! I guess I'd be a fool to deny such a thing is possible after witnessing Acker's ghost attacking Mala, but a demon? Like in *The Exorcist*?"

"Mala's Aunt Magnolia said a demon crawled out of the void and infected me. I don't know for sure what it is or care to have a deep bonding session with the thing. I just want to rip it out before it destroys me."

"And you can't control it?" He leans forward, studying my face like he's a human lie detector, searching for clues to my honesty by the direction my eye moves or my microexpressions. Even if I wanted to avoid the truth, I can't.

"I could in the beginning. I mean, it hurt—a lot." I swallow hard. "I think Lainey came to me while I was trapped on the other side. Technically, I was DOA so I'm not positive, but I remember her. She helped me build a wall between the creature and myself, blocking it from completely taking over my body. Only every day it gets harder to keep the wall from crumbling."

George leans back in his chair and stares at the ceiling. "I almost shot you."

I blink at him.

"You went after Mala. I pulled my gun and aimed it at your head. If she hadn't knocked you out…" He heaves a sigh. When his eyes find mine again, they're hard as bottle glass. "I don't want you around her."

Anger rises. "It's not your decision. It's Mala's."

"You're a danger—"

I know. I wrap my hands around the wheels so he can't see them tremble. I hate him for saying what I'm trying my damnedest to deny. Whenever the thought pops up, I shove it into the deep recesses of my mind. It's not so much denial as avoidance. The time when I'll lose the ability to control the demon rushes toward me. It's unavoidable. It's what I'll have to do then that I'm afraid to confront.

Someday I'll have to get far, far away from her. And it'll feel like I'm ripping my heart out. But that day isn't right now. After what happened to Dena, Mala needs me. And I need her.

"I won't hurt her, George. I swear." *I'll kill myself first.* I jerk my chin toward the closed door. "Is she inside with Dena? I need to speak with her."

George shakes his head. "She asked not to be disturbed."

"Bullshit. You listened to her? She acts tough, but she shouldn't be alone, especially now." I push up out of the wheelchair, placing a hand on the door to keep my balance. "Move."

"I said no." He squares his jaw, but doubt flickers in his green eyes.

"Mala, open up!" I yell, banging on the door with my fist while at the same time daring George to stop me. He doesn't make a scene, but I can tell his fingers itch to slap handcuffs on my wrists and drag me out. A nurse leaves the station down the hall and runs toward us. George intercepts her at the same time the door opens.

Mala stands in the doorway with her puffy eyes downcast. When she glances up and sees me, she throws herself into my arms, almost taking us both to the ground. I hug her tightly, feeling her trembling. She seems so fragile that I'm afraid she'll break.

Over her shoulder, I see Dena lying in the bed. She has a breathing tube forcing air into her lungs and a heart monitor showing the steady beats of her heart. A sickly green shine coats her skin, and I let out a thick, horrified breath. "No…"

Mala avoids my gaze by keeping her eyes focused on the wall. I maneuver her backward, then shut the door behind us. "Dena's shining," she says. Her hands grip my robe.

The lump in my throat makes it hard to speak, but I force out the words. "Tell me it wasn't you. That you didn't try to bring her back."

"I did bring her back. Sort of." Mala twists out of my arms. She walks jerkily toward the bed and falls into the chair. "I-I messed up, Landry." She chokes on a sob. "I couldn't kill Red. God knows, I tried. But his scream sent chills down my spine."

I crouch down next to her. She gathers up my hands and presses her wet cheeks against my palms. "Gaston and Mama told me to stop. That raising the dead was black magic, and I was abusing the natural order of the universe. Like I give a fuck about consequences. Dena didn't deserve to die. It's not right!"

The chill moves from my spine to settle deep in my bones. "No, it's not…"

"But stuffing her into this shell. Leaving her in limbo. That's not right either, Landry. And I don't know how to fix this."

"Yeah." *There has to be a way.*

Mala leans forward, staring deep into my eye. "What do I do? If I bring her all the way back, I kill Red. But if I-I bring that prick Red back, then Dena dies. If I do nothing, they both stay like…*this.*"

I pull her into a hug. "This isn't a decision we've got to make today. We need an expert. We need Magnolia."

"I already know what Magnolia will say. She's the one who showed me how to do this. It's her fault for even tempting me with this power."

"But you chose to use it, Mala."

"Are you blaming me for this?" She shoves free of my arms.

"Go, I don't need you. I'll figure this out on my own."

I block her path to the door. "I don't blame you for the choice you made. If I was in your position, I can't say I would've made a different one."

"But you said—"

"I never once said I didn't understand. Hell, I would've taken a bullet for Dena if I could've, but she saved me instead. She chose to die for me. It burns me up inside that she did that. But she made her choice. And so did you."

"Landry…"

I want to pull her into my arms, but I hold fast. "Mala, what happens next is too important. Your decision can't be based on guilt." I put my hand beneath her chin when she tries to drop her gaze. "I can't lose you, Mala. We've been through too much and fought too hard to be together. I love you."

Tears well up in her eyes, but she shakes her head. "How can you say that after what I've done?" She grabs onto the front of my robe, pulling me close. "Don't you get it? I'm evil, Landry."

"Baby, I've got a demon sipping at my soul like it's a bottle of chardonnay. If anyone's evil, it's me."

Mala sniffs, but she also loosens her grip on my robe. "That's not funny."

"I wasn't joking. I said it to put this situation into perspective. You may not have listened to Magnolia, but I did. Magic isn't evil or good, it's the intentions of the person using it. Your intentions weren't evil." *Only a little confused.* "You didn't kill Red. I'm not even upset about the demon trying to take him out. He deserves to suffer after all the people he's murdered. I'm just glad you weren't the one to kill him. Not 'cause he deserves to live, but 'cause you don't deserve to live with the guilt of his death."

"Oh, Mother Mary, I almost murdered Red."

"But you didn't. You stopped. Now we'll figure out a way to fix this mess. I promise." If there is a way to save Mala from the consequences of her actions, I'll find it before I die. Whether that's bringing Dena back or letting her go, I don't know. But whatever it is, we'll figure it out together.

She's shaking her head. "You really mean this, don't you? I don't have to deal with this alone."

"You're my girl. My heart, my incredible sexy body—everything I am or will be—is yours, Mala LaCroix. You'll never be alone again." *In more ways than one.* I take a deep breath before spilling the rest of the news. "I told the Acker boys that you'll apply for guardianship. They're moving in with us."

Mala blinks. "Say what?"

"Dad too. We're all going to be one big happy family. Isn't that great?"

Did you miss the beginning of Mala and Landry's love story?

See the next page for an excerpt from *Dark Paradise*.

CHAPTER 1

MALA

Floater

Black mud oozes between my toes as I shift my weight and jerk on the rope, sending up a cloud of midges and the rotten-egg stench of stagnant swamp water. The edge of the damn crawfish trap lifts out of the water—like it's sticking its mesh tongue out at me—and refuses to tear loose from the twisted roots of the cypress tree. It's the same fight each and every time, only now the frayed rope will snap if I pull on it any harder. I have to decide whether to abandon what amounts to two days' worth of suppers crawling along the bottom of that trap or wade deeper into the bayou and stick my hand in the dark, underwater crevice to pry it free.

Gators eat fingers. A cold chill runs down my spine at the thought, and I shiver, rubbing my arms. I search the algae-coated surface for ripples. The stagnant water appears calm. I didn't have a problem wading into the bayou to set the trap.

I've trapped and hunted in this bayou my entire life. Sure it's smart to pay attention to my instincts, doing so has saved my life more times than I can count, but this soul-sucking fear is ridiculous.

I take a deep breath and pat the sheathed fillet knife attached to my belt. My motto is: Eat or be eaten. I personally like the last part. A growling belly tends to make me take all kinds of stupid risks, but this isn't one. If I'm careful, a gator will find my bite cuts deeper than teeth if it tries to make me into a four-course meal. Grandmère Cora tried to teach her daughter that the way to a man's heart was through his stomach. Since Mama would rather fuck 'em than feed 'em, I inherited all the LaCroix family recipes, including a killer gator gumbo.

Sick of second-guessing myself, I slog deeper into the waist-high water. Halfway to the trap, warm mud wraps around my right ankle. My foot sticks deep, devoured. I can't catch my balance. *Crud, I'm sinking.*

Ripples undulate across the surface of the water, spreading in my direction. My breath catches, and I fumble for the knife. Those aren't natural waves. Something's beneath the surface. *Something big.* I jerk on my leg, panting. With each heave, I sink deeper, unable to break the suction holding me prisoner. Gator equals death…But I'm still alive. *So what is it? Why hasn't it attacked?*

A flash of white hits the corner of my eye—

Shit! I twist, waving the knife in front of me. My heart thuds. Sparkly lights fill my vision. Blinking rapidly, I shake my head. My mind shuts down. At first I can't process what I'm seeing. It's too awful. Too sickening. Then reality hits—hard. The scream explodes from my chest, and I fling myself backward. The mud releases my leg with a *slurp*. Brackish water smacks my face, pouring into my open mouth as I go under. Mud and decayed plants reduce visibility below the surface.

Wrinkled, outstretched fingers wave at me in the current. The tip of a ragged fingernail brushes across my cheek. It snags in my hair. I bat at the hand, but I can't free my hair from the girl's grip. She's holding me under. Trying to drown me. I can't lift my head above the surface. *She won't let me go!*

My legs flail, kicking the girl in the chest. She floats. I sit up, choking. I can't breathe and scream at the same time. I'm panting, but I concentrate. *Breathe in. Out. In.* The girl drifts within touching distance. Floating. Not swimming. Why doesn't she move? Is it stupid to pray for some sign of life—the rise of her chest, a kick from her leg—when I already know the truth?

Water laps at my chin. I wrap my arms around my legs. Shivers shake my body despite the warmth of the bayou, and my vision's fuzzy around the edges. I'm hyperventilating. If I try to stand I'll pass out. Or throw up. Probably both 'cause I'm queasy. I close my eyes, unable to look at the body anymore. Which is so wrong. I've studied what to do in this sort of situation. Didn't I spend a month memorizing the crime scene book I borrowed from Sheriff Keyes? *Come on, Mala. Pull it together.* A cop—even a future one—doesn't get squeamish over seeing a corpse. If I can't do something as simple as reporting the crime scene, well, then why not drop out of college, get hitched, and push out a dozen babies before I hit twenty-five, like everyone else in this damn town?

I lift my hands to scrub my face. Strands of algae lace my fingers. I pick them off. My legs tremble as I rise, which keeps me from running away. I have to describe the crime scene when I call the Sheriff's Office, and I imagine myself peering through the lens of a giant magnifying glass like Sherlock Holmes—searching her body for clues. Each detail becomes crystal clear.

Her lips are slightly parted, and a beetle crawls across her teeth, which are straight and pearly white, not a tooth missing. She's definitely a townie. A swamp girl her age would have a couple of missing teeth, given she appears to be a few years older than me. Her expensive-looking sundress has ridden up round her waist. Poor thing got all gussied up before she killed herself.

The deep vertical cuts still pinking the water on both of the girl's wrists makes my stomach flip inside out. I double over, trying not to vomit. It takes several deep breaths to settle my gut before I can force myself to continue studying the body.

Long hair fans out like black licorice around her head, and her glazed blue eyes stare sightlessly at the heavens. Faint sunlight glistens on the flecks of water dotting her porcelain skin. I've never seen such a serene expression on anyone's face, let alone someone dead, like she's seen the face of God and has found peace.

After seeing her up close and personal, I can't stomach leaving her floating in the foul water. Flies crawl in her wounds, and midges land on her eyes. Slimy strands of algae twine through her hair. Soon the fish will be nibbling at her. Unable to bring myself to touch her clammy-looking skin, I take a firm grip on her dress and drag her onto the bank—high enough above the waterline that she'll be safe from predators while I get help.

I'm halfway across the stretch of land between the bayou and my house when a shiver of foreboding races through my body, and I slow my pace. *Shit! I took the wrong path.* Usually I avoid traveling through the Black Hole. It's treacherous with pockets of quicksand. Cottonmouths like to hide in the thick grass, beneath lichen-smothered fallen trees. Those natural obstacles are pretty easy to navigate if you're alert. What makes the hairs on the back of my neck prickle is the miasma that permeates every rock and rotten tree in the clearing I cross to get home. A filmy layer of ick coats my skin and seeps in through my pores until it infects my whole body with each step. I feel…*unclean*. I'm not big on believing in the whole concept of evil, but if there's any place I'd consider to be tainted ground, I'm walking across it.

Instinct screams that I'm not alone. I'd be a fool to ignore the warning signs twice. If I listened to my instincts earlier, I never would've found the body. I stretch out my senses like tentacles waving in the wind. Nothing moves…chirps, or croaks. A strange, pungent odor floats on the light breeze, but I can't identify it. My darting gaze trips and reverses to focus on the *Bad Place*. I swallow hard and yank my gaze from the dark stain on the rock in the middle of the circle. Mama said our slave ancestors used this area for their hoodoo rituals because the veil between the living and dead is thinner here.

It's always sounded like a whole lot of bullshit to me until I stumbled across the bloodstained altar and shards of burnt bone scattered across earth devoid of grass or weeds—salted earth, where nothing grows. Mother Mary, it creeps me out.

'Cause what if I'm really not alone? What if something stands on the other side of the veil, close enough to touch, but invisible? Watching me.

Whatever's out here can go to the devil 'cause I'm not waiting to greet it.

By the time I burst out of the woods that border our yard, the sun has started its downward slope in the sky behind me. I double over, hands on my knees, to catch my breath after my half-mad run. Our squat wooden house perches on cinder-block stilts like an old buzzard on top of the hill. The peeling paint turns the rotting boards an icky gray in the waning light, but it's sure a welcome sight for sore eyes.

With a final glance over my shoulder to be sure I wasn't followed, I dash beneath the Spanish moss–draped branches of the large oak that shades our house, dodging the darn rooster running for me with tail feathers spread. I brush it aside with my foot, avoiding the beak pecking at my ankle.

"Mama!" My voice trembles. I really wish my mother had come home early. But the dark windows and empty driveway tell me otherwise. I track muddy footprints across the cracked linoleum in the kitchen to get to the phone.

Ms. Dixie Fontaine answers on the first ring. "Sheriff's Office, what's your emergency?" The 9-1-1 dispatcher's lazy drawl barely speeds up after I tell her about the dead girl. "All right, honey. I'll get George on over. You be waiting for him and don't go touching the body, you hear?" She pops her gum in my ear.

A flash of resentment fills me, but I'm careful to keep my tone even. "Don't worry, I know better, Ms. Dixie. I only touched her dress—to drag her from the water."

"That's fine, Malaise, quick thinking on your part. Bye now."

"Bye," I mutter, slamming the phone in the cradle. I breathe out a puff of air, trying to calm down. I'm antsy enough without having to deal with Ms. Dixie's inability to see me as anything but a naive kid. I'm not an idiot. How can she think I'd make a rookie mistake like contaminating the crime scene? I've been working with her now for what? Nine…no, ten months. Hell! What does it take to prove myself to her? To the rest of the veterans at the Sheriff's Office who remember every mistake I've ever made and throw them in my face every chance they get?

Disaster. That should've been my name. Instead, I've been saddled with Malaise. Well, whatever. I stomp into the bathroom, slip off my muddy T-shirt and cut-off jeans shorts, and take a scalding shower. I scrub hard to get the scummy, dead-girl film off my skin. It takes almost a whole bottle of orchid body soap to cleanse my battered soul and wash the tainted, dirty feeling down the drain with the muck.

The whole time, three words echo in my head. *Deputy George Dubois.* My heart hasn't stopped thudding since Ms. Dixie mentioned his name. The towel I wrap around my heaving chest constricts my rapid breaths like a tightened corset. Hopefully, I won't do an old-fashioned swoon like those heroines from historical novels when I see him.

It's a silly reaction, but George comes in third on my list of People I Want to Impress the Most. It's not that his six feet of muscled, uniformed hotness tempts me to turn to a life of crime just so he'll frisk me and throw me in the back of his patrol car. Nope, that pathetic one-sided schoolgirl crush passed after we graduated and started working together. I'd be as cold as the dead girl if I couldn't appreciate his yummy goodness, but the last thing either of us need is for a romantic entanglement to screw up our professional relationship.

George epitomizes everything I want to become when I "grow up." He graduated from Paradise High School my freshman year and went to the police academy at the junior college. Once he turned twenty, he got a job at the Bertrand Parish Sheriff's Office.

When news of a part-time clerical position floated around town, guess who stood first in line for the job assisting Ms. Dixie with the data entry of the old, hardcopy crime reports into the new computer system. It's not always what you know at BPSO, but *whose* ass you kiss to get hired as a deputy. The recession left few open positions, forcing rookies to compete against seasoned officers who were laid off at other agencies. I don't have family to pull strings for me, but I've made job connections with people in positions of authority while obtaining practical experience working for the Sheriff's Office. I refuse to leave my future to the fickle whims of fate.

My last year at Bertrand Junior College begins in two months. I'll graduate with an Associate of Arts degree in Criminal Justice. I haven't decided whether to transfer to a larger university for a BA, but if not, I will definitely enroll in the police academy next summer. One year. I just have to survive one more boring year, and I'll finally get to start living out my dream of becoming a detective.

Calm down, Mala. I fuss with my thick, russet curls for a few minutes in the bathroom mirror then give up and pull it back in a high ponytail. My hair's a lost cause with the darn humidity frizzing it up. I finish dressing in my best jeans and a lavender T-shirt. Rocks pop beneath tires traveling down the gravel driveway. Instead of remaining barefoot, I slip on my rain boots, not wanting to look like a complete heathen or worse, reminding the higher-ups at the crime scene of my true identity—the prostitute's bastard.

Rumors about Mama's choice of occupation have been whispered about since before my birth. You'd think being the daughter of the town whore would be humiliating enough to hang my head in shame. Then add in the fact that most folk also think she's a broom-riding witch. The kids in school were brutal, repeating as gospel the stupid rumors they overheard from their parents, who should've known better. It boggles the mind that people in this day and age can believe ignorant stuff like Mama can hex a man's privates into shriveling if he crosses her. The only good thing about being the witch's daughter is it keeps most boys from straying too close. I don't have to deal with a bunch of assholes who think I'll blow them for a couple of twenties and an open bar tab like Mama.

With one last rueful glance at my face in the mirror, I shrug. This is as good as it's gonna get. I run onto the front porch and freeze halfway down the steps. The patrol car I expect to see in the drive turns instead into a good view of Mama on hands and knees beside her truck with a flowerpot stuck under her chin as she pukes in the geraniums. *Crud! Georgie will be here any minute.* I've got to hide her in the house. She can spend the night heaving up what's left of her guts in the toilet without me babysitting her.

Mama senses me hovering. She rolls onto her backside and holds out her hands.

"Don't just stand there gawkin' like an idiot, help your mama up," she says.

With a heavy sigh, I trudge to her side. I grit my teeth and lift her to her feet while she flops like roadkill. Upright, she lists sideways. A strong wind would blow her over. The vomit-and-stale-beer stench of her breath makes my nose crinkle when she throws her skinny arm around my shoulders.

"What you been up to today?" She tries to trail her fingers through my ponytail, but they snag on a knot I missed. She jerks her hand free, uncaring that it causes me pain since she's purposely deadened her own feelings with booze. Mama can't cope with her life without a bottle of liquor in one hand. It's like the chicken-and-the-egg question. Which came first? Was her life shitty before she became an alcoholic, or had booze made it worse? I can't see how it could be better, but maybe I'm naive, or as stupid as she always calls me.

I rub at the sting on my scalp. "Why are you home so early?"

She sways. "Can't I miss my baby girl?"

"Missing me never slowed you down before. What makes tonight any different?"

"Why you so squirrely? You act like you don't want me here." She pulls back far enough to look me over. "Expectin' someone or you all dressed up with nowhere to go?" She cackles, slapping her leg like she's told the funniest joke ever.

"Georgie Dubois's coming out."

"Why? I know the deputy's not comin' to see you."

I grit my teeth on the snappy comment that hovers on the tip of my tongue. "Found a dead girl floating in the bayou."

Mama pulls her arm back and strikes cottonmouth quick.

I end up flat on my back with stars dancing before my eyes. My cheek burns. I blink several times, trying to clear my head, then focus in on the shadow hovering over me with clenched fists. "God damn it! Are you crazy?" I roll over and stagger to my feet. She steps forward again, fist raised.

"Don't you dare, Mama!"

"Don't take the Lord's name in vain. Or threaten me."

"I haven't threatened, *yet*. But I swear, you hit me again, I'm out of this rat hole you call a house. I've earned enough scholarship money to move into an apartment."

"Why you sayin' such things, Malaise?" Tears fill her eyes.

Money. The only thing that still touches Mama's fickle heart.

"You just backhanded me, Mama! What? Do you expect me to keep turning the other cheek until you break it? Or accidentally kill me like that girl I found…"

Mama's mocha skin drops a shade, and she sucks in a breath. I don't think it has to do with any feelings of regret. No, it has to do with the girl. She hit me after she heard about George coming out for the body.

"Why do you look so scared?" Suspicion makes my voice sharp. "What did you do?"

Mama staggers toward the house.

"Don't walk away from me," I yell. "What's going on? Georgie will be here any minute. If I've got to cover for you, then I need to know why or I might let something slip on accident."

Mama makes it to the stairs and collapses onto the bottom step. She buries her face in her palms. Shudders wrack her body. "I need a drink, Mala. There's a bottle in my bottom drawer. Bring it out to me."

"That's not a good idea…"

She lifts her head. Her dark brown eyes droop at the corners, and I see the faint trace of fine lines. Strangest of all, her eyes have lost the glazed, shiny appearance they held a few minutes earlier. *The news shocked her sober.*

"I'm not askin' again, Malaise. Get in there if you want to hear the story."

ABOUT THE AUTHOR

Angie Sandro was born at Whiteman Air Force Base in Missouri. Within six weeks, she began the first of eleven relocations throughout the United States, Spain, and Guam before the age of eighteen.

Friends were left behind. The only constants in her life were her family and the books she shipped wherever she went. Traveling the world inspired her imagination and allowed her to create her own imaginary friends. Visits to her father's family in Louisiana inspired this story.

Angie now lives in Northern California with her husband, two children, and an overweight Labrador.

www.ingramcontent.com/pod-product-compliance
Ingram Content Group UK Ltd.
Pitfield, Milton Keynes, MK11 3LW, UK
UKHW021150020325
455674UK00006B/100

9 781455 554867